'As long as you c[...]
cousin's exploits, as long as y[...]
him like a delinquent schoolboy, rather than
as a dangerous and predatory adult, he will
continue to think that women like me are
simply there for the taking. And now, if you
want to sack me, you can. I have enough
money saved for my passage back to New
York.'

'Of course we're not going to sack you, are
we, Paul?' Beatrice, like so many normally
biddable women, could, when she dug in her
toes, show a core of steel. Paul recognized the
tone of voice and smiled. It banished the grim
look from his face, softening it with a
tenderness he rarely displayed in public.

'He loves her,' Margaret thought desolately, as Beatrice carefully guided her down
the stairway and out into the chill night air. 'I
love her, too.'

And, to her own horror, she leaned against
the cold stone of the gatehouse and burst into
tears.

A ROSE IN MAY

Brenda Clarke

Hamlyn Paperbacks

A Hamlyn Paperback

Published by Arrow Books Limited
17-21 Conway Street, London W1P 6JD

A division of the Hutchinson Publishing Group

London Melbourne Sydney Auckland
Johannesburg and agencies throughout
the world

First published in Great Britain 1984
by Hutchinson & Co. (Publishers) Ltd
Hamlyn Paperbacks edition 1985

Printed and bound in Great Britain by
Anchor Brendon Limited, Tiptree, Essex

. ISBN 0 09 939550 9

And she was fair as is the rose in May
GEOFFREY CHAUCER 1340?–1400

Part One 1901–1902

Paradys stood formed in hir yën

One

The pony-trap went at a brisk pace along Argyle Street and into Laura Place. The broad vista of Great Pulteney Street stretched imposingly ahead. So this was Bath, thought the younger of the trap's passengers, looking curiously about her.

It seemed to Margaret Dunham as if she had barely stopped thinking: So this is England! The train journey had passed like a dream, and she was only just beginning to find her land-legs after the weeks at sea. She felt confused, the more so as she had expected to go straight to London. Instead, when her sister met her on Southampton dockside, Jessie had said: 'The Devereauxs are in Bath. We're to join them there.'

'For heaven's sake, Jess, how many places do they have?' Margaret asked. 'I seem to remember mention of a house in Cornwall.'

'Latchetts. That's the family estate. Then, of course, there's the house in Hill Street, when they're in London for the Season.'

'And this house in Bath?'

'That's for business purposes. Some of Paul Devereaux's money is tied up in the Somerset coalfields. The Longreach mine. And now for goodness' sake get a move on, Maggie, or we'll miss the train. And try to look a little less . . . less colonial!'

'Jessie Dunham!' Margaret had been horrified. 'I never thought to hear an American use that word!' She reflected that seven years in England had altered her elder sister, and not altogether for the better. Jess never used to be a snob. Margaret had no idea how long she herself was going to remain abroad, but she silently vowed that, even if it were a lifetime, she would never forget she was a citizen of the greatest country in the world.

The trap drew up before one of the tall, soot-blackened houses in Great Pulteney Street. Bladud House, said the legend on either side of the door.

'We're here,' Jessie said briskly, climbing out of the trap without waiting for the driver to assist her. 'Come along, Maggie! Don't fuss with your cases. Harper can see to them.'

The young groom, who had been instructed to meet the ladies at the station, grimaced behind Jessie's back. He thought her a fussy little body, who traded on her friendship with the mistress and her privileged position as confidante and companion. But he did not share in the general resentment of the servants' hall. Teddy Harper was a good-natured boy, and conceded that had he been forced to go thousands of miles from home to live, like Mrs Devereaux, he too would want people of his own around him.

'That's all very well,' Cook had said darkly, when he had dared to voice his opinion. 'I don't deny but what you might 'ave a point about Jessie Dunham. But bringing 'er sister over from America, as well, to be Miss India's governess, that's carrying things too far.' Mr Stapleton, the butler, had nodded in agreement, and, encouraged by such august approval, Cook continued: 'Why, even them rich Yankees don't employ *American* governesses to teach their children. They sends over 'ere for one of ours.'

Teddy had felt unqualified to argue the point, even if the protocol of the servants' hall had permitted such a thing. As junior groom, he had already overstepped the mark by speaking out of turn, and he held his tongue. Anyway, it was none of his business, and a new governess, whether English or American, was unlikely to affect him.

He had had little chance to take stock of the new arrival at the station, and experienced a shock as he reached up to help Margaret Dunham descend from the trap. She had the same determined chin as her sister, but there the resemblance ended. Whereas Jessie Dunham was small and round, like a self-important robin, her younger sister had the sort of figure that Teddy, in his seventeen years, had so far only dreamed about. Every curve of her filled the eye. The thick mane of hair, coiled on top of her head beneath the little hat, was a rich, dark auburn, and where it caught the thin April sunlight it sparked with hidden fire. And the eyes – eyes which, in Jessie, were a bright, sharp blue – were, in Margaret Dunham, almost green.

Something of what he felt must have shown in Teddy's face, because Margaret Dunham smiled at him as she stepped safely to the ground. Teddy chuckled to himself. She was going to set tongues clacking in the servants' hall, and no mistake!

Jessie led the way down the area steps and into the basement-kitchen, which was deserted except for a stocky young man with a round, merry face and shrewd, twinkling blue eyes. He was seated in a rocking-chair, near the range, but got to his feet as the two women entered. Jessie seemed disconcerted.

'Daniel? Why aren't you upstairs, attending to your duties?'

'Jess, dear,' the young man said, kissing her familiarly on the cheek, 'don't be so censorious. A valet can't be valeting twenty-four hours a day. Mr Devereaux is at present in conclave with Hugh Stafford. The manager of the Longreach mine,' he added, as Jessie looked bewildered. 'Besides, I was naturally curious to meet my future sister-in-law.' He turned to Margaret with a disarming smile. 'I'm Daniel Cooper, Mr Devereaux's man, and, as she's no doubt told you, Jessie's intended.'

'You mean . . . ? You and Jess . . . ? You're going to be married?' Margaret looked and felt bemused.

Daniel sighed in mock reproach. 'She hasn't told you! Jessie! Jessie! How little you think of your beloved.'

'Nonsense!' Jessie snapped, colouring defensively. 'I haven't had time, that's all. We haven't seen each other for nearly seven years, and there were more important things to talk about.'

Her beloved rolled his eyes heavenward and murmured: ' "Truth is the highest thing that man may keep." Or women, either, for the matter of that.'

Margaret laughed. 'I don't think I know that quotation,' she said. 'It's not Shakespeare.'

11

'Chaucer.' Daniel regarded her appreciatively. Nothing Jessie had ever told him about the sister who was four years her junior had prepared him for this beautiful creature. When he had asked for a description, Jessie had been evasive.

'I guess she's pretty enough. At least, the boys back home always thought so when she was younger. But she's no heart-breaker.'

Now he saw her, however, Daniel was not so sure. He quoted admiringly: ' "And she was fair as is the rose in May." That's Chaucer again. His description of Cleopatra.'

'Oh, you and Chaucer!' Jessie exclaimed impatiently. She sent him a look which was partly affection, partly exasperation. 'Where's Cook? I told her what time to expect us. I thought she'd be here to make us a cup of tea.' She pulled off her hat and threw it on the kitchen table. 'I suppose I'll have to do it. Daniel, make yourself useful. Sit down there and talk to Maggie. Afterwards, you can find someone to take those cases of hers up to her room.'

Daniel bowed meekly, then winked at Margaret as he moved a chair forward for her to sit on. Jessie whisked efficiently around the kitchen, rattling cups and filling the kettle with water.

Margaret, too, removed her hat with a sigh of relief, patting her hair into some semblance of order. She smiled at Daniel, too tired to make conversation. There were a hundred questions bubbling inside her head, but for the moment she was too exhausted to ask any except the most trivial.

'Why is this place called Bladud House? It's such a peculiar name.'

Daniel explained. 'Bladud was a Prince of Britain who lived about five hundred BC. He's supposed to have been the founder of Bath. He was also the father of King Lear.'

Margaret frowned. 'How odd. I mean, I've never thought of Lear as having had a father. He seems so . . . so monumental, somehow. Hewn from the living rock.'

Daniel's appreciation deepened. 'Jess,' he accused his fiancée, 'why did you never tell me you had such a remarkable sister?'

Jessie snorted, slapping the sugar bowl down beside the milk jug in the middle of the kitchen table. She poured a stream of golden-brown liquid into each of the three rose-patterned cups.

'Maggie was always bookish. That's why Pa insisted on her going to college.' Jessie stood back, teapot in hand, eyeing her sister up and down. 'I haven't seen her since she was fourteen years old. I guess you could say she hasn't turned out badly.'

'My dear girl—' Daniel began warmly, then broke off, shrugging. It was no good arguing with Jess. She never saw beyond the end of her nose.

When they had finished their tea, Jessie consulted the fob-watch pinned to the breast pocket of her jacket.

'Three o'clock. Beatrice will just about be waking up from her afternoon nap. I'd better take you up to see her.' She rose from the table. 'And remember, Maggie! It may be all right to call her Beatrice when we're alone, but in public she's Mrs Devereaux.'

Margaret squeezed her sister's shoulders affectionately.

'Jess, dear, I'm not such a fool as you think me.'

'Hmm. . . . Come along upstairs, then. Beatrice's suite of rooms is on the second floor, overlooking the garden at the back.'

'Maggie! After all these years! Oh my, isn't it good to see you? And how you've grown! Quite the grown-up young lady.'

Beatrice Devereaux, who had left her native New York at the age of seventeen to marry into one of England's wealthiest and most aristocratic families, was genuinely delighted to see her childhood companion again. She embraced Margaret in a flurry of primrose satin and lace, having thrown on a négligé over her petticoats. She had removed her stays for her afternoon rest, and had not yet resumed them. Her body, pressed close to Margaret's, was soft and yielding.

'It's wonderful to see you again, Beatrice. And thank you for offering me this post. I'm sure there must be dozens of English governesses who would be far more suitable.'

'I didn't want an English governess to teach my daughters. I wanted you. Now, sit beside me and tell me all your news. I was deeply shocked to hear of your father's death. Uncle Herbie! Do you remember that's what I used to call him?'

Margaret, seating herself beside Beatrice on the pink-

13

upholstered *chaise-longue*, could not answer for a moment. Tears welled up and threatened to choke her. Yet, coming to Bath in the train with Jessie, she had been able to talk about their father quite calmly, even giving details of the stroke which had carried him off in a matter of hours. But then, Jessie had never been really fond of Herbert Dunham, nor he of her. Jessie was more like the mother who had died ten years ago, and for whom she had genuinely grieved. It was Margaret who had always been close to their father.

'Fact is, Jess and I get on one another's nerves,' Herbert Dunham had once said, half-apologetically. It had been when his boss, Coleman Smith, had first mooted the idea that Jessie should accompany his daughter to England after Beatrice's marriage. Herbert had felt guilty for welcoming the suggestion.

'Pa, Jessie wants to go as much as you want her to,' Margaret had reassured him. 'She and Beatrice are the same age, and they've always been great friends.'

And there was no doubt that the house in down-town New York had been calmer after Jessie had left.

'Peace and quiet, girl,' Herbert Dunham had said, pulling on the old churchwarden pipe which his great-grandfather had brought with him from England. 'Peace and quiet, they're all that matter.'

There had been little of either in Herbert Dunham's life. The son of a miner from the Pennsylvania coalfields, he had known a childhood of grinding poverty. At fifteen he had escaped to New York, where he had found himself a job in one of Coleman Smith's factories, helping to assemble the justly famous Arctic refrigerators and Snow Mountain ice-chests. A sickly constitution had kept him out of the final phases of the war between north and south, and by dint of back-breaking work and solid integrity he had risen to become manager of the Brooklyn factory. So highly, indeed, had Coleman Smith thought of him, both as an employee and as a man, that the two had become firm friends, in spite of the difference in their social backgrounds. After Florence Dunham's death, Jessie and Margaret were frequently invited to the big house on Fifth Avenue to play with the lonely and also motherless little girl who was the multi-millionaire's only child.

Beatrice Smith became, in time, as attached to the two Dunham girls as her father was to theirs; so much so that when she married Paul Devereaux and went to live in England she begged Jessie to go with her as maid-companion. And when the elder of her two daughters was ready for the schoolroom, it had been Margaret Dunham she had wanted as governess. Paul Devereaux, deeply attached to his wife and uninterested in domestic affairs, had told her to do as she wished.

The offer had arrived two days after Christmas. Margaret had already written her refusal, explaining that she could not leave her father and was, in any case, very happy teaching at a school in the Bronx, when Herbert Dunham's sudden death changed everything. And so here she was, four months later, in an alien, European world, Beatrice Devereaux and Jessie her only two links with the past. She was confused, frightened and determined not to show it. Resolutely she blinked back her tears. The next half-hour passed in an orgy of reminiscence until Beatrice glanced at the clock and let out a squeal of dismay.

'Jessie! Just look at the time! Half after three, and I'm calling on Olga at four. Quickly, my stays! And I'll wear the blue dress with the white silk braiding. Maggie, honey' – she got up from the *chaise-longue*, dropping a hurried kiss on Margaret's forehead as she did so – 'I'll introduce you to the girls at tea-time. Meanwhile, one of the maids can show you to your room. I've put you next door to the nursery and Nanny Watkins. . . . No, not that hat, Jess. The one with the feathers. And my pearls, and diamond ear-drops. You know how the Russians love jewels.'

Margaret stood at the window of her room, looking out over the narrow gardens and crowding backs of the neighbouring houses. She had unpacked, washed and changed her dress. She had also, lying on the bed, tried to doze, but sleep refused to come. She was unused to resting in the afternoon, and her body had still not fully adjusted to the time difference between New York and England.

She ought, she told herself, to feel excited. This was Bath, about which she had read so often in *Northanger Abbey* and

15

Persuasion. Jane Austen had walked these streets. From somewhere nearby, Sheridan had eloped with Elizabeth Linley. There was an older Bath, too, hidden beneath the elegant terraces and crescents of Georgian houses: the Aquae Sulis of the Romans. And, going back even further, if the legend of Bladud were true, there was the prehistoric village of five hundred years BC. . . .

Margaret stirred restlessly. The weight of so much history oppressed her: it was like living in a museum. She came from a young country, where the passage of time was measured in decades, not centuries. She realized that for the past few minutes she had been humming 'Get on Board, Chilluns', one of the Jubilee Singers' tunes which her father had taught her. He had sung her so many when she was young: 'Swing Low', 'My Way's Cloudy', 'Steal Away', 'Roll Jordan'. But his favourite had always been the rousing 'Battle Hymn of the Republic'. She could hear him now, roaring out the chorus: 'Glory, glory, Hallelujah! Our God is marching on!' When she was small, she had loved him to tell how he had heard the Massachusetts regiments sing it as they marched down Broadway in the early days of the Civil War. And later, when New York's first Negro regiment had left for the front, people had cheered the soldiers on their way with the by now familiar air.

'Oh, God!' she thought desperately. 'I'm homesick. Why ever did I agree to come?'

The door opened and Jessie came in.

'Sorry I've been so long. I'd hoped to help you with your unpacking. Don't get too settled in, though. We'll be moving to London in a few weeks' time for the start of the Season – although things are bound to be a bit muted this year, with the court still in mourning for Queen Victoria. I've asked one of the maids to bring our tea up here. It'll be more private than going down to the kitchen.' Jessie was disgruntled. She disliked these visits to Bath, however brief and infrequent they might be, because the house was too small to accommodate in comfort all the servants whom the Devereauxs brought with them. Consequently, Jessie was unable to have the private sitting-room which her status required. 'Well, sit down,' she continued. 'We still have a lot to talk about.'

Margaret drew up a delicate, spindle-legged chair to the bamboo table which stood near the window. A fire had been kindled on the hearth, for which she was grateful. The April weather was damp and chilly.

'Who is it that Beatrice has gone to visit?'

'The Duchess. She's in Bath to take the waters. The Duchess of Leamington,' Jessie added impatiently in answer to Margaret's enquiring stare. Then, as her sister persisted in looking blank, she said: 'For heaven's sake, Maggie! Surely you remember that the Duke of Leamington is Paul Devereaux's cousin!'

Margaret shook her head. 'I don't think I was all that interested in the details when Beatrice got married. I was only fourteeen. At that age there are too many other things to think about.'

There was a knock on the bedroom door and a maid came in, carrying a tray which she set down on the bamboo table. As well as the fat-bellied teapot, with its attendant milk jug and sugar bowl, there were wedges of fruit cake on a blue china plate, slices of sponge oozing cream and jam, and muffins, dripping with butter, in a covered earthenware dish. It was the typical English tea of the stories, and Margaret's sense of unreality increased.

'The Duchess,' Jessie informed her sister when the maid had left the room, 'was a Russian Countess before her marriage to the Duke. They have been married six years. He met her when he was part of the official British delegation to St Petersburg for the wedding of the Tsar and Tsarina, but her father was against the match, on account of her being Russian Orthodox and the Duke being a member of the Church of England. Then the old Count died and Olga changed her religion. She's mad about the Duke, although he's years older than she is and has a reputation with the women.' Jessie crammed the remains of a muffin into her mouth and dabbed at the butter on her chin. 'Her younger sister, the Countess Anna Rastorguyeva, lives with them. A real streak of vinegar. Doesn't approve of the Duke at all. For goodness' sake eat up, Maggie! You've hardly touched a thing.'

'I'm not hungry.' Margaret pushed her plate aside. 'Jess, why are you marrying Daniel Cooper?'

Jessie paused in the act of biting into a piece of sponge and stared uncomprehendingly at her sister.

'Because he asked me and because he'll make a good husband. Isn't that the reason most women get married?'

'I rather thought love had something to do with it.'

Jessie snorted. 'This is real life we're talking about, Maggie. We're not living between the covers of a novel.'

'It seemed to me that Paul Devereaux was very much in love with Beatrice when he married her, just as she was with him. At least, they gave me that impression, I remember.'

'If you are rich and handsome,' Jessie snapped, 'you can afford the luxury of falling in love. But if you look like me, you're just thankful for a respectable offer.' She regarded her sister thoughtfully. 'I daresay, with your looks, you might aim to fly a bit higher.'

Margaret stirred her tea. 'Why is Daniel marrying you?' she asked.

For a moment, Jessie looked affronted; then she smiled and shrugged. 'For much the same reasons, I imagine. He isn't exactly Gerald du Maurier. He's twenty-six and wants to settle down. His mother owns a candy store here in Bath. She's not well and she wants Daniel to take over the business.'

'You mean to stay in England, then?' The realization came as a shock to Margaret.

'It's become my home,' her sister answered simply. 'I know such a sentiment probably sounds like heresy to you just at present, but you'll be surprised how quickly you become acclimatized.' Jessie glanced at the fob-watch, now pinned to her tailored white blouse. 'Time for another cup of tea, I think, before I take you downstairs. Nanny Watkins was told to bring the children to the drawing-room promptly at five o'clock.'

Two

Margaret's first impression of her pupil, sitting demurely beside her mother on the brocaded sofa, was of a doll-like little creature, almost too good to be true; a profusion of fair ringlets, a frilled white dress tied with a pink satin sash, and a pair of enormous china-blue eyes which limpidly returned her own curious gaze.

'She's pretty,' Margaret thought, 'but she knows it.'

Beatrice rose from behind the laden tea-table to greet her. It was more the act of a friend than of an employer and would cause much eyebrow-raising in the servants' quarters. Nevertheless, Margaret was conscious that the atmosphere was not the same as it had been upstairs, and was careful to address Beatrice as 'Mrs Devereaux'.

Beatrice drew her elder daughter forward. 'This is India. India, darling, this is Miss Dunham who is going to be your governess.'

India extended her hand and smiled prettily. 'How do you do, Miss Dunham?' The voice was extremely English, with no trace of her mother's New England accent.

Margaret took the small, dimpled hand in hers. 'How do you do, India? I hope we're going to be good friends.'

At that moment, there was a diversion. The younger child, Mareth, had taken advantage of the interest in the new governess to escape Nanny Watkins's vigilance, heading for the tea-table and a plate of chocolate biscuits. As her fat little hands scooped up as many as they could hold, trying to cram them all into her mouth at once, Nanny Watkins descended wrathfully on her charge. Mareth caught Margaret's eye and began to giggle.

Beatrice smiled indulgently. 'You'd better take her upstairs, Nanny, and wash her hands. We don't want chocolate all over the furniture.'

As Mareth was borne, protesting, from the room, Paul Devereaux entered, followed by a thickset, truculent-looking man in his middle forties, with close-cropped grey hair and deep-set eyes of an opaque, peculiarly light shade of blue. The eyes reminded Margaret of pebbles, and she was disconcerted to find that, after a few moments, they were fixed unblinkingly on her.

Paul Devereaux tickled his erring daughter under her chin. 'Hello, pickle. What have you been up to now? Why are you taking her away, Nanny? You know I like the children here at tea-time.'

'Her hands are covered in chocolate, Paul,' Beatrice explained, resuming her place behind the tea-table. 'She's been stealing the chocolate biscuits.'

Her husband laughed and dropped a kiss on Mareth's curly head, while Nanny Watkins pursed her lips in disapproval. In her opinion, Mr and Mrs Devereaux were far too lax as parents, which she put down to what she termed 'free and easy American ways'.

Paul turned to the man behind him and beckoned him forward. 'I've promised Mr Stafford some tea, my love, before he goes. We've had a long session of it, going over the Longreach accounts.'

'Of course.' Beatrice gave the colliery manager her friendliest smile. 'Please sit down, Mr Stafford. Paul, dear, here's Jessie's sister, Margaret. You recall she was arriving today.'

From the look on Paul Devereaux's face, it was obvious not only that he had forgotten the fact, but also that he had difficulty in recollecting why Margaret was there at all. She held out her hand.

'I'm going to be India's governess, Mr Devereaux. I shall do my best to ensure that your confidence in me isn't misplaced.'

Her memories of Paul Devereaux had been hazy; memories based on brief glimpses of him during the wedding ceremony and, later, the reception seven years ago in New York. But she had retained the impression of a tall, powerfully-built young man, with broad shoulders and a thatch of brown hair. She realized now, as he took her hand in his, that he also had a pair of very fine grey eyes, a craggy chin indicative of a determination to get his own way, and a grip which was almost crushing her fingers with its strength. He was definitely not the effete English aristocrat of novel and stage. He looked, Margaret thought, more like a farmer.

For his part, Paul Devereaux, when he had acquiesced in his wife's plan to bring Margaret Dunham over from America, had imagined a younger, more studious version of Jessie. He had certainly never envisaged a red-headed girl with sparkling green eyes and an infectious grin. Oddly enough, it was perhaps the grin, with its suggestion of overflowing vitality and ready humour, which made him more uneasy than Margaret's other, more obvious attributes. Out of the corner of his eye, he could see Hugh Stafford staring at her as though he had been pole-axed. Paul pulled himself together with an effort.

'Welcome to England, Miss Dunham,' he said courteously, releasing her hand. 'I hope you had a comfortable crossing?'

Margaret returned some polite answer, but had no idea, afterwards, what she had said. The one thought uppermost in her mind was that in the whole of her twenty-one years no man had made such an impact on her as had Paul Devereaux in that brief moment of introduction. If someone had asked her, half an hour ago, if she believed in love at first sight, she would have answered emphatically: 'No!' Now, suddenly, she was not so sure.

The following weeks, before the family returned to London, were a kaleidoscope of unfamiliar sounds, sights and emotions. There seemed so many things to do, so many names to remember, so many servants to get used to.

'For goodness' sake, Maggie!' Jessie exclaimed loftily. 'There are hardly any servants in Pulteney Street compared with Hill Street, and very few there compared with Latchetts. And if ever you visit Hawksworth, the Duke's place in Wiltshire, then you'll realize that Mr Devereaux and Beatrice live very modestly indeed.'

'It still seems like an awful lot of people just to wait on one or two,' Margaret objected. 'Particularly as most of those people can barely afford to make ends meet.'

Jessie clicked her tongue. 'I was hoping that those egalitarian notions of Pa's wouldn't have rubbed off on you, Maggie Dunham, but I can see that I was praying in vain. You just watch your tongue. This is England, where everyone knows his place.'

Margaret smiled. 'Don't worry, Jess. If Marx and Engels couldn't stir up revolution in this country, I'm darned sure Maggie Dunham can't.'

'Mark who?' Jessie was suspicious. 'If you've been keeping doubtful company already, Maggie. . . . And don't talk about revolution. You'll have folks thinking you're odd.'

Margaret forbore to remind her sister that it was revolution which had given birth to America. She knew that Jessie would never understand, and she had more to do with her time than to embark on fruitless arguments. Beatrice had made it plain that she intended India, and, later, Mareth, to be educated in the broadest sense of the word.

'That's why I wanted you, Margaret, honey, and not some starchy, formal English governess who would concentrate solely on deportment and good behaviour. I want the girls to learn the value of those things, of course. I certainly don't wish to raise a couple of hoydens. But I want them to have something else in their heads besides the necessity of catching a husband. Oh,' she had added, with her shy, glinting smile, 'I guess I'm a fine one to talk! Married at eighteen! But I was exceedingly lucky to have met such a wonderful man. I want India and Mareth to have book learning, as well as the social graces. It's always been a great grief to me that Papa thought educating females a waste of money and time. Maggie, you wouldn't credit how ignorant I am. But as well as book learning, I want the girls to see things; to be interested in what's going on around them, and also be aware of the past. In Bath and London and Cornwall there are so many things to see. I don't wish you to feel restricted to the schoolroom.'

'And Mr Devereaux? Does he think the same way as you do?' Margaret had asked.

'He leaves domestic decisions to me,' Beatrice had answered evasively; and with that Margaret had to be content.

She saw very little of Paul Devereaux during the remainder of her stay in Bath. It was as though he were deliberately avoiding her, so often did Beatrice present his excuses on those occasions when she visited the schoolroom or the nursery. And frequently, when Margaret and Nanny Watkins took the children to the drawing-room, in the leisurely hours between tea and dinner, Paul would again be absent.

'It will be different when we're back in London, sweetheart,' Beatrice reassured a disappointed Mareth. 'Papa's always very busy when he's in Bath.' Although she later confided to Jessie that she had never known him as busy as this. It crossed her mind that he disliked Margaret and was deliberately avoiding the new governess, but she dismissed the idea. They had barely met, but the once.

All the same, the notion persisted, and a week after Margaret's arrival, as they lay in bed, content and sleepy after making love, Beatrice murmured: 'Paul, honey, you don't object to Margaret Dunham, do you?'

She stretched luxuriously as she spoke, intertwining her legs with his. Greatly to her surprise, Beatrice had, from the beginning, enjoyed the sexual act, even though she never expected Paul to take off his nightclothes, nor dreamed of removing her own. There was something about total naked- ness which seemed to her both lewd and abandoned; yet she looked forward to the nights with increasing pleasure the longer she was married. Often, during the day, she would find herself anticipating that moment when they would at last be alone and in bed together. It gratified her sense of the fitness of things, that duty and pleasure should go hand in hand. Paul wanted a son and heir, and it was her duty to give him one if she could.

Paul did not turn to look at her, but stared into the stuffy, enveloping gloom.

'I can't say I've thought about Miss Dunham, except on the day of her arrival,' he lied. 'No, of course I don't object to her, although I consider her rather young.'

'She may be young, but she's clever. She was always smart, even when she was small.'

'That's all right, then.' Paul yawned and kissed her good- night, rolling on to his side.

23

But it was not all right. He was constantly aware of Margaret Dunham's presence in the house. Why, on such a brief acquaintance, did he find her so disturbing? He knew what his cousin Francis would say.

'The trouble with you, my boy, is that you married too young. Twenty's no age to settle down. You ought to have seen life a bit first. If you fancy this chit, get her into bed. A few presents'll keep her happy.'

Paul, however, knew that Margaret Dunham was not what the Duke referred to as 'an easy lay', nor, perversely, would he wish her to be. He had never been unfaithful to Beatrice in the seven years of their marriage, which, in a society which regarded adultery almost as a way of life, was a remarkable achievement. So he supposed it inevitable that, sooner or later, he would be snared by a pretty face; and Margaret Dunham was much more than that. She was like a breath of fresh air blowing through a warm, familiar room. . . .

He must not think of her. He was in love with his wife, and had been ever since he first saw Beatrice during his trip to New York nine years ago, just after his father's death. He rolled on to his other side and folded Beatrice in a loving embrace.

It was on the last day of April, the day before they left Bath for London, that Margaret encountered Hugh Stafford for the second time. It was also the day on which she met the Duchess of Leamington and her sister, the Countess Anna Rastorguyeva.

In the middle of the morning, Betty Lewisham, the nurserymaid, poked her head around the door of the second-floor study which Margaret was using as a school room.

'The missus says will you take Miss India down to the drawing-room at 'alf-past twelve. 'Er Grace and the Countess is comin' to lunch, an' Miss India an' Miss Maref's to pay their respecks. Aw right?'

'Yes, thank you, Betty. And Betty—!' The girl, who had withdrawn her head, obediently reappeared. 'Have you been crying again?'

Betty hastily wiped her nose on the back of her hand. 'No, of course I 'aven't, miss. What gives you that idea?'

The child could be no more than fifteen, sixteen at the most, thought Margaret. She was thin and pasty-faced, like someone who had been raised on poor food and too little light and fresh air. Betty was a Londoner, despised by the country-bred Nanny Watkins, who bullied her unmercifully whenever she got the chance.

'Has Nanny been getting at you again?' Margaret enquired, but the girl looked frightened and shook her head. It would never do to complain about Nanny: good places were hard to come by, as her mother had impressed upon her before she left home.

'You make sure you keeps this place, you bleedin', good-fer-nuthink little bugger! You girls can't all fancy yerselves as ladies, like yer bleedin' sister.'

Betty said now: 'No, miss. I'm aw right. Honest.'

'Very well, if you say so. . . . Tell Nanny Watkins I shall be ready with Miss India at half after twelve. We'll take the children down together.'

As the door closed behind Betty, India looked up from her alphabet book and nodded sagely. She was, Margaret had discovered, precocious for her age.

'Nanny does bully her, you know, Dunny. She bullies everybody.'

The nickname 'Dunny' had evolved quite naturally from the formal 'Miss Dunham' of the first few days. India had started to use it without any prompting, and Margaret had been delighted, indicating as it did her swift and total acceptance by her charge. She, in her turn, was growing daily more fond of India, detecting beneath the veneer of childish self-satisfaction a warm-hearted, essentially loving little girl.

'Does she bully you and Mareth?'

'I think she'd like to, but she's scared we might tell Mama. But she can be very unkind to Betty.' India closed her book and smiled. 'I'm glad you're going to meet Auntie Go-go. She's not truly our aunt, of course, because Uncle Francis is Papa's cousin, but Mareth and I call her "aunt" on account of it's polite when she's so much older than we are. We call her sister Aunt Anna, as well, but she's horrid; all bony and she looks like this.' India pulled a thin, sour face. 'Auntie Go-go's all fat and laughing. Papa says they remind him of Pharaoh's fat and lean kine.'

'That will do, India.' Margaret tried not to laugh. 'I'm sure your Papa didn't mean what he said to be repeated. Now, open that book again and let's get back to the alphabet. After that we'll do some addition sums.'

When, however, she later accompanied India to the first-floor drawing-room where Beatrice was entertaining the Duchess and Countess Anna Rastorguyeva, Margaret was struck by the aptness of Paul Devereaux's description.

The Duchess of Leamington was barely a year older than Beatrice, but could have been mistaken for a woman in her thirties. Sunk in the depths of a large armchair, she spread to fill its every corner; a comfortable cushion of a woman, with podgy, heavily beringed pink hands, a plump face spotted from eating too many sweetmeats, sleepy, white-lidded eyes and a soft, guttural flow of very good English, which she emphasized with sweeping, indolent gestures of her short, fat arms.

The Countess Anna Rastorguyeva was her sister's opposite. She was whiplash thin, with a small, intent face, like a bud which had withered before ever it became a flower. She sat upright on a hard, armless chair, her little back poker-straight, the carriage of her head still more rigid. Her dark hair was parted severely in the middle and coiled neatly over her ears. Her great brown eyes, her finest feature, showed not a spark of humour. Her plain grey coat and skirt and starched white blouse were in direct contrast to the Duchess's over-trimmed pink dress, with its profusion of tucks and frills, and its jabot of finest Honiton lace.

'Ah! Darlink!' the Duchess exclaimed, as soon as she caught sight of India. 'Come at once and kiss your Auntie Go-go. Naughty Uncle Francis, he is not here. I say: "Come and take the waters at Bath," because he has a little touch of the rheumatics. But no! He prefers to stay in London. He says he has business to attend to.'

The Countess made a derisory noise and her thin lips were compressed still further. Her sister roared with laughter.

'Ah, the little one thinks he is in the whore-houses with the

26

women,' she proclaimed with paralysing candour. 'And I think she is probably right.'

Beatrice said sharply: 'Olga, please! Remember the children!'

The Duchess chuckled and pinched Mareth's round chin. 'The children, they are too innocent, too young. They do not understand. And if they were old enough to understand, then I should be telling nothink they did not know already. So either way, where's the harm?'

Margaret was to learn that this devastating frankness was typical of the Duchess, and was chiefly responsible for first attracting, and then holding, her husband's affection.

'Olga calls a spade a spade,' the Duke was wont to say admiringly. 'Never could stand those mealy-mouthed women.'

But for now Margaret could only stare, fascinated, at the Duchess until it was time for her and the tight-lipped Nanny Watkins to take the children upstairs for nursery dinner.

'Foreigners!' Nanny muttered, as she jerked Mareth into her high chair and tied a bib around her neck. 'God made a mistake when he created foreigners.'

Margaret was unsure whether or not to take the insult personally. She had already learned that many Britishers regarded Americans as rogue Englishmen who had gone native, much as the aristocrats of the Middle Ages had regarded the Anglo-Irish who lived beyond the Pale. She judged it best to say nothing, even though she suspected that Nanny had meant to be spiteful.

Later that afternoon, she and India were walking down Gay Street from the Circus. In accordance with Beatrice's wishes, Margaret was making lessons for the child as varied and interesting as possible. Today, they had been looking at some of Bath's architecture: the Upper Assembly Rooms, Royal Crescent and the Circus. By the time they finally headed for home, both of them were extremely tired.

On the corner of George Street Margaret paused, glancing down at the child, who was beginning to flag. She did not want to give Nanny Watkins the chance to complain, for the umpteenth time, that no good would come of all this junketing about.

'Would you like to be carried for a little way?' she asked.

India nodded and held up her arms.

'Allow me, Miss . . . Miss Dunham, isn't it?' And the man who had come up so quietly behind them replaced his raised hat, stooped, and swung India into his arms as though she had been no more than a featherweight.

Margaret turned, startled. 'Oh. . . . Thank you. Yes, I'm Margaret Dunham. And you're . . . you're Mr Stafford, Mr Devereaux's overseer at the mine.'

'Manager, Miss Dunham. Colliery manager. I'm flattered that you should remember me. Are you returning to Great Pulteney Street?'

'Yes. . . . Mr Stafford, please don't trouble yourself. Here, let me take the child.'

'She's much too heavy for you, and I've had more practice. I have a son of my own.'

'You're married?' Margaret felt a surge of relief, as if this man with the extraordinarily light-coloured eyes had threatened her in some obscure way.

'I'm a widower. William, my son, is about the same age as yourself.'

They turned into Milsom Street and Margaret searched for something to say. Once again, the strange sense of foreboding engulfed her. She recalled the way he had looked at her, that first afternoon of her arrival: so intently; so . . . so what? So hungrily; yes, that was it. She had felt like Little Red Riding Hood in the presence of the wolf.

It was so unlike her to have these nervous fancies. She glanced up at India, held so effortlessly in the strong arms, her little ones clasped happily around Hugh Stafford's neck. She obviously felt no repulsion; and didn't they say that animals and children could always tell?

'You're in Bath on business, Mr Stafford?' The silence was in danger of growing too oppressive.

'Not today. A friend gave me the offer of a ride in his pony and trap. I've come to see an old friend of mine, Jane Cooper, Daniel Cooper's mother.' They swung into Green Street. 'We'll be passing her sweet shop in a moment.'

'You know Mrs Cooper?' Neither Daniel nor Jessie had mentioned the fact.

'We've been friends these twenty years and more. It was through me that Daniel got his post with Mr Devereaux. He's going to be your brother-in-law, isn't he? May I ask when is the wedding?'

'They haven't decided yet. . . . And here is Mrs Cooper's store. There's no need for you to come any further, Mr Stafford. India can walk from here. It's not very far.'

'I'll walk now,' India corroborated, struggling to be set on her feet. Remembering her manners, she added politely: 'Thank you very much, Mr Stafford.'

Hugh Stafford hesitated, as though reluctant to part company with them. 'I might as well come with you all the way.'

But India had already wriggled to the ground and Margaret was holding her hand. 'It's been very kind of you, Mr Stafford, but we've no need to trouble you any further.'

He had no choice but to accept defeat. He took her outstretched hand in one of his, raising his hat with the other. With another hastily murmured word of thanks, Margaret and India left him.

They were on Pulteney Bridge, the shops hemming them in on either side, when Margaret heard someone running. A moment later, her name was called. Hugh Stafford, red-faced from exertion, held out a box of chocolates, decorated with a picture of Ellen Terry and a bright blue bow of ribbon.

'For you,' he mumbled awkwardly, thrusting them at her, almost as if he were ashamed of what he was doing. 'Most expensive in the shop. Mrs Cooper assured me.'

'Mr Stafford! I can't. Please, no!'

He looked so hurt and bewildered by her refusal that Margaret began to feel sorry for him and angry with herself. What had she thought so menacing? He was just a big man, ill at ease in his shiny best suit, his hat sitting uncomfortably on top of his curly hair. As gracefully as she could, she took the chocolates.

'Thank you. It's very kind of you. And now we really must be going. It's nearly tea-time, and Nanny doesn't like it if we're late.'

Three

The move to London occupied all the next day, and Margaret had no time to think of her meeting with Hugh Stafford. For this she was grateful. In spite of her momentary spurt of pity, she did not like him. She could not explain her reasons; she only knew that he repelled her.

Together with Nanny Watkins, Betty Lewisham and the two children, she travelled to London by train. The girls slept for most of the way. Nanny Watkins also dozed, so Margaret took the opportunity to get to know Betty Lewisham better.

Betty's conversation was almost exclusively concerned with 'my sister, 'ilda,' and it became obvious that Hilda Lewisham, the eldest of five, was the mainstay of the family, upon whom all the other members relied. Hers was the steadying influence on the younger children during Mrs Lewisham's frequently recurring bouts of illness; an illness which Margaret quickly diagnosed as having more to do with her visits to the Duke's Head than to the undernourishment and anaemia which might well have been the causes.

Hilda was better educated than her brothers and sisters; a fact which was due to an old lady called Mrs Frensham, for whom she had worked as a maid soon after leaving school.

'Lived in Borough 'igh Street, she did, above one of the shops. 'Er 'usband was a pork butcher, but 'ilda always said Mrs Frensham was in a diff'rent class. Proper lady. Married beneaf 'er, she did, but she an' 'er 'usband were as 'appy as sandboys. She never cared tuppence that 'er fam'ly wouldn't 'ave nuffink to do wiv 'im.'

Mrs Frensham, it appeared, had owned books. 'Shelves full

of 'em, 'ilda told me.' Betty seemed amazed that Southwark had produced anyone who actually read for pleasure.

But Hilda, too, eager to extend the skimpy board-school education she had grudgingly been given, and encouraged by her employer, had worked her way steadily through Dickens and Fielding and Scott, revelling in a fantasy world she had never realized, until then, existed. The practical Mrs Frensham had arranged for her protégée to be taught book-keeping and the new-fangled typewriting, with the result that Hilda now had a job at Bloomfield's, the diamond merchants, in Hatton Garden. Her eldest sister was plainly Betty's chief source of pride.

Margaret suspected that there was precious little about either of Betty's parents to give her pleasure. She elicited the fact that Mr Lewisham was a journeyman plasterer, out of work more often than he was in it, and, like his wife, addicted to drowning his sorrows in the Duke's Head. Mrs Lewisham, when her health allowed, took such casual work as she could find.

'Sometimes, she goes up west. Cherry Bruvvers, in Covent Garden,' Betty confided, forgetting that London was as alien a landscape to Margaret as New York would be to herself. 'Shellin' peas an' scrapin' taters for the Savoy Hotel. Or sometimes she goes cleanin' up the Vic. That's where our sheets all come from.'

The 'Vic', it seemed, was short for the Old Victoria Music Hall in Waterloo Road, and Mrs Lewisham bought up the discarded sheets of scenery for a halfpenny or a farthing, depending on the state they were in. They were then soaked for a week in the family's tin bath, at the end of which they were pliable enough to be used, after bleaching, on the bug-infested beds of the Lewisham home. The narrow street of two-up two-down houses where Betty lived was due soon for demolition.

'Warders' cottages, they used ter be,' Betty explained cheerfully, as the train steamed into Paddington station, 'belongin' to the old Marshalsea Prison. They pulled that down ter make way fer the railway.' She began helping Margaret and Nanny gather together all the paraphernalia of the journey: hats, scarves, food-hampers, story-books and

31

pencils. ' 'Ere you are, Nanny, 'ere's yer gloves, fallen down under the seat. They only need dustin' off a bit.'

A carriage was waiting to convey the little party to Hill Street, but as she was about to step into it Margaret was detained by Nanny Watkins, who motioned Betty and the children in ahead. The nurse pursed her lips disagreeably.

'I appreciate you're an American, Miss Dunham, and still unused to our ways, but it isn't done to gossip with the under-servants. You may have thought I was asleep in the train, but I assure you I was merely resting my eyes. I heard most of what passed between you and Lewisham. That girl will be getting ideas above her station if you encourage her to chatter in that informal way. I advise you not to make a habit of it.'

Margaret made no reply for a moment or two; then she said, slowly and distinctly: 'Understand this, please, Miss Watkins.' Nanny hated to be addressed by anything except her proper title. 'I shall make friends with whomsoever I choose. If you have any complaint about me, please inform Mrs Devereaux. We'll see what she has to say, and I'll abide by her ruling.'

Paul, standing beside Beatrice at the door of the Hill Street ballroom, decided that it must be nearly midnight. The actors and actresses were beginning to arrive.

It was mid-July and the Season was in full swing. Tonight's ball was the Devereauxs' first major contribution to the calendar of social events which occupied Society from May until August. Derby Week and Ascot were behind them; ahead lay Cowes Week and then a trip to Scotland for the shooting.

Beatrice had been anxious that everything should go smoothly tonight, even though King Edward and Queen Alexandra would not be present. Because they were still officially in mourning for Queen Victoria, who had died in January, Their Majesties were limiting the number of their purely social engagements. They had dined the previous week in Mount Street with Francis and Olga, but had declined invitations to more public festivities. Nevertheless, the Devereaux ball was sufficiently distinguished; titled heads

32

outnumbered the politicians, and the cream of London's theatre-land added to the lustre of an already glittering throng. Beatrice, at last able to leave her post by the door and join her guests on the ballroom floor, had reason to congratulate herself on the success of her arrangements. She looked, and knew she looked, extremely beautiful tonight, her fair hair drawn back from the wide, calm brow, her creamy skin offset by the triple row of perfectly matched pearls which had been Coleman Smith's wedding present to his daughter. Her soft voice, with the added charm of its faint New England accent, was, at that moment, lulling into silence one of Parliament's most volatile and talkative MPs as she waltzed with him around the flower-decked ballroom, which covered almost the entire ground floor of the house.

The whole place was redolent with the scent of roses, red and white, flame and yellow, adorning stairs and hall and supper-room. The dinner for twenty which had preceded the ball had kept Cook and three kitchen-maids slaving for the best part of the day over the black-leaded Cambrian range in the basement kitchen, and had been praised by one of the capital's most noted gourmets. Everything had gone, and was going, extremely well, reflected Beatrice. She saw Paul in the distance and smiled at him across the intervening sea of faces. The orchestra struck up another waltz, and she saw him stoop over Anna Rastorguyeva, asking her to dance.

'May I have the honour, Countess?'

Anna was wearing a puce satin dress which did not suit her, and which revealed too much of her scrawny breasts. Going to bed with her would be a penance, Paul decided. How different she was from Beatrice or Margaret Dunham.

He frowned. He had not intended to couple Margaret's name with that of his wife; and he realized uncomfortably that it was not the first time he had done so. The girl's presence in the house continued to disturb him.

'I do not perform the waltz,' the Countess stated. 'I consider it most improper. But perhaps the next country dance?' And she produced her little tasselled pencil and gilt-edged programme. Paul could see that it was almost empty.

'Yes, of course. It will be my pleasure. Until then. . . .'

'Must you go? Please . . . sit and talk to me.' Anna indicated

33

the vacant, spindle-legged chair at her side, and coloured awkwardly, surprised by her own temerity.

It would have astounded and dismayed Paul had he known the extent of Anna's feelings for him; or, indeed, that she had any feelings for him at all. He had never thought of her except as someone who must be endured for the sake of his cousin, of whom he was very fond. It had always seemed to him the height of folly that Francis should have burdened himself with this unattractive young woman in order to marry her elder sister.

'Had to, old fruit. Absolutely no option,' Francis had said on the only occasion Paul had ever raised the subject with him. 'Olga and I get along like a house on fire. Knew we should from the first moment I saw her at Nicholas and Alexandra's wedding. My type. Swears like a trooper and don't give a fig for my indiscretions. Trouble was, when that old brute of a father died, he made Olga give him a death-bed promise to look after her sister. Mother was dead, no relatives to speak of – at least, none that wanted Anna – so what could the poor girl do? "Forced your hand," I told her. "Promise not binding." But Russians take these family obligations far more seriously than we do. And Anna's docile enough. Bound to be, with all that blasted religion. Most of the time it's possible to forget she's there. It's my opinion she prefers it that way.'

Remembering his cousin's words, Paul was just about to excuse himself when he was struck by the unhappy expression in the liquid brown eyes raised so beseechingly to his. Panic seized him. He wanted to run away, but compassion was stronger. He sat down by Anna and managed a smile.

'For a moment or two, then. My other guests mustn't think I'm neglecting them to talk to an attractive young woman.' Why on earth had he said that? His anxiety not to betray his dislike of her was making him insincere. He forced another smile and wrote his name on her programme for the next country dance.

On the other side of the room, Beatrice, waltzing now with one of the West End's most handsome leading actors, observed her husband and smiled. Dear Paul! He had taken pity on poor Anna and was talking to her. His essential kindness was one of the first things which had attracted her to him.

34

Francis, too, had noticed his cousin, but his reactions were different. Paul was a fool, burdening himself with Anna. The Duke knew her type: all ice and religion on top and, underneath, as randy as hell! He chuckled to himself. He had done his duty by his wife; stood up with her for a couple of dances. But Olga would amuse herself very well, now, without him. He paused by one of the long windows giving on to Hill Street, deserted at this time of night, except for a man standing under a lamp on the opposite pavement. The Duke watched him idly for a moment, then turned and made his way to the card-room.

Had the Duke obtained a closer view of the young man across the street, he might have recognized Sergei Zhirov, one of the three servants brought by Olga from St Petersburg. The other two had been her and Anna's personal maids, and young Sergei had escorted the ladies on their long overland journey. At least, that had been the reason advanced by Olga for the inclusion in her party of this handsome boy. If Francis had been sceptical, he had been too indolent, and far too certain of her affection, to raise any questions.

Sergei was, in fact, the son of Olga's former cook, who had begged her mistress to take her younger son to England before he became involved, like his elder brother Dmitri, in a revolutionary plot. Dmitri had been sent to Siberia on a charge of distributing seditious literature and uttering anti-Tsarist slogans, and he had died after only a year in those unending, snow-bound wastes.

Olga, who had been genuinely devoted to Katia Nicolaievna, had agreed; and in the summer of 1895 Sergei, then barely sixteen years of age, had been packed off to a strange country, thousands of miles from his home. What neither Katia nor Olga knew, however, was that Sergei had already joined a small cell of dissidents operating in St Petersburg and calling themselves the New Decembrists, after those early revolutionaries who had risen against Tsar Nicholas I on 14 December 1825.

Sergei's first thought, once he had known his mother's plan for him, had been to run away, perhaps to Moscow, where he could go to ground in the rabbit-warren of filthy back-alleyways, the home of the despairing and the poor. But the leader of his cell, Pavel Brodkin, had persuaded him otherwise.

'If you run away, comrade, your mother will persuade the Countess to call in the police, and before you know it your association with us will be discovered. And that will mean Siberia for us all. You carry on the cause for us in England, Sergei Alexandrovich. You can do a lot of good for us there.'

Sergei had been too young to realize that Pavel Brodkin saw in the handsome, dark-haired youth a future threat to his leadership. Sergei's courage and daring had made him popular with the other members of the group, and the older man had foreseen that there could come a day when his authority might be challenged.

So Sergei Zhirov had arrived in England and remained for several years in the Duke and Duchess's employ, helping in the gardens at Hawksworth, where he had shown an unexpected talent for making things grow. He had been a quiet, well-behaved boy, seemingly deferential and quick to learn. He had mastered the essentials of the English language within a twelvemonth, and by the end of a second year he could speak and read it fluently. He was, however, never able to write it proficiently, finding the spelling too wayward and difficult.

Eighteen months previously he had disappeared from Hawksworth, suddenly and without warning. The Duchess, who was in Cornwall at the time visiting Latchetts, had written instructing that enquiries should be made. But when, at the end of six months, no trace of Sergei's whereabouts had been discovered, she had called off the search.

'He is, after all, nineteen years of age, so what is one to do?' she had demanded of the Duke. 'He is a man now. How can I control him?'

'You can't m'dear,' Francis had agreed wholeheartedly. 'Shouldn't have been saddled with the brat in the first place. Not saying he hasn't been useful, mind. A wizard, from what old Abson tells me, in a greenhouse. But we'll soon replace him. Gardener's boys are ten a penny.'

Olga was even spared the disagreeable chore of having to write and explain Sergei's disappearance to Katia, by news of the latter's death. From then on, as far as the Duchess was concerned, the matter was closed.

Sergei had made his way to London, where he had survived with the help of various jobs, including his present one: drayman for a brewery in Blackfriars Road. He had lodgings in a cramped first-floor room in St Thomas Street, close to Guy's Hospital, and enough money, when the rent was paid and food and clothing allowed for, to enjoy an occasional evening in the West End. He had come up tonight to join the crowds milling around the theatres and brothels of the Haymarket; then, on impulse, had turned into the side streets of Mayfair, where the town houses of the wealthy stood in elegant, serried ranks, and where the policemen were able to patrol their beats alone, instead of in pairs, as elsewhere in the city. Having wandered around Berkeley Square, Sergei had found himself in Mount Street, with vague recollections of having been brought to a house there when he first arrived in England. He identified the house, but it was dark and shuttered, with only a dim light glowing in an upstairs room, as though some maid were waiting for her mistress's return. He made his way along South Audley Street, passing a policeman who twirled his truncheon and glanced at him suspiciously. Sergei turned into Hill Street. He had no wish to be accused of 'loitering with intent'.

Just beyond the junction with Chesterfield Hill stood a house where a party was in progress. The windows on the ground floor were ablaze with light and the front door was standing open. A roll of red carpet spilled out on to the pavement like a tongue from a gaping mouth. From inside came the sound of music and muted laughter. A carriage lumbered round from Hays Mews to collect an early departure. There was the flash of diamonds and the gleam of silk. Voices were raised in farewell. A woman, a green silk cape draped negligently over her shoulders, was followed by her top-hatted escort. Liveried footmen slammed the door of the carriage before returning to the house. The vehicle moved off slowly and disappeared into Waverton Street.

Sergei contrasted the life these people led with that endured in the vicinity of Borough High Street and Blackfriars Road. He thought of the squalor and the sheer grinding poverty of many of the inhabitants of Southwark. But he had long ago accepted that revolution was unlikely in Britain. The English, particularly, were lazy and argumentative, and would instantly be put to shame by any hard-working continental European. They chattered ceaselessly about their rights, and got through the minimum amount of work to keep body and soul together. They were in a constant state of flux. He had never known people split into so many dissenting factions, every man speaking and thinking for himself, and convinced of the rightness of his opinion. One had only to look at the English church to justify such a statement. The English, it was true, closed ranks to ward off any foreign interference, but once the danger was past it was every man for himself again, and the devil take the hindmost. Trying to push them all in one direction was a task to try the patience of Job.

Sergei quickened his steps. He had been forced, this week, to pawn his watch, and so had no means of telling the time, but he guessed it to be gone midnight. His landlady objected to his being out so late, even though he had his own key. He emerged once more into Piccadilly and negotiated the back streets around the Haymarket until he came to the Strand. As he crossed Waterloo Bridge he could see the river, iridescent with putrefying matter, spread out on either hand. By the time he reached Borough High Street he was beginning to feel very tired. As he turned the corner into St Thomas Street, he collided with a woman.

'Here! Look where you are going!' he exclaimed angrily, gripping her shoulders. He realized with surprise that she was quite young, and added austerely: 'It is not right that you should be out alone, so late at night.'

'Let me go!' The girl wrenched herself free of his detaining hands. 'I must get to the hospital. I need some medicine.'

'I am sorry. Someone is ill? I shall come with you, yes?'

'No, for God's sake! It's only a step and I've known these streets all my life. . . . Oh, very well. Come if you must, but it's nothing exciting, if that's what you're hoping. It's only Ma. She's drunk again. Sick as a dog. At the hospital they give me some white stuff which settles her stomach.'

'Where do you live?'

'Not far. . . . Near Pocock Street, if you really want to know.'

'I will wait and accompany you home,' he said.

The girl shrugged. 'Please yourself. Here we are. You can wait at the gate if you want to.'

He did so, watching a thin cat sniffing at the rubbish in the gutter. The girl puzzled him. She had the flat, nasal twang of the working-class Londoner, but she spoke correctly and rounded out her words, like the 'toffs'. After twenty minutes she rejoined him, a bottle of the white stuff clutched in one hand.

'I didn't expect you'd still be here,' she said, and he thought she sounded pleased. They began retracing their steps in the direction of Blackfriars Road. 'You're foreign, aren't you?' she asked, after a minute.

'Yes. I am Russian, but I have been living in this country for over six years. My accent, is it so bad?'

'We-ell, you certainly have one, but it isn't really that. It's more the pedantic way you have of speaking.'

'Please? Pedantic?'

'Careful. Precise. English people run their words together. My name's Hilda Lewisham, by the way. What's yours?'

'Sergei Zhirov. I am from St Petersburg.'

'I don't know many places west of Bermondsey, myself; but my sister Betty, who works as a nursery-maid to a Mr and Mrs Devereaux, says that Mr Devereaux's cousin, who's a duke, is married to a Russian wife.'

'The Duke of Leamington?'

'Now, 'ow the 'ell do you know that?' In her astonishment, the girl was betrayed, for the first time, into dropping her aitches. Sergei felt sure it did not often happen.

'It is a long story, but I will tell it to you if you promise to come out with me tomorrow evening.'

They had reached the girl's house and stopped outside. From within, a woman's voice could be heard moaning and swearing, with pauses to be violently sick.

'Well, I don't get off work until nearly seven, and then only if Mr Bloomfield has no extra work for me to do. . . . I tell you what. I'll ask him as a special favour, tomorrow night, if I can leave on time. He's very nice. He'll probably agree. But then I've got to get home and have my tea.'

'That is all right. These summer evenings are long. Where shall we meet? And what time?'

Hilda considered the problem. 'I know,' she said, after a moment or two's reflection. 'In the Borough High Street, outside Shuttleworth's. It's a tea-shop. We'll do the thing in style. Instead of me coming all the way home, we'll go out for a meal. Dutch treat, of course.'

Four

Two weeks later, Betty Lewisham was dismissed from her post.

Nanny Watkins's gold fob-watch, given to her by her last employers, was missing. The first, cursory search of the nursery and Nanny's own room yielded no trace of it. Further, and more thorough, investigation still revealed nothing, and Nanny became convinced that the watch had been stolen. She carried her suspicions to Beatrice.

At Beatrice's instigation, the whole house was searched, and the watch eventually came to light tucked under Betty Lewisham's mattress, in the attic which she shared with one of the upstairs maids.

'I knew it!' declared Nanny Watkins triumphantly. 'I always knew that girl was no good.'

A frightened Betty at first denied all knowledge of the watch; but later, persuaded that if she were guilty it was better to admit the theft before Paul Devereaux called in the police, she broke down and confessed.

'But why?' Paul demanded, baffled, when the tearful girl was brought before him. It was the sort of situation he loathed. 'We pay you good wages; twelve pounds a year, all found.'

Betty tried to say something, but choked on her tears. Margaret, who had found the watch, and was therefore one of the little group in Paul's study, stepped forward and put her arm about the child's thin shoulders.

'If you'll permit me, Mr Devereaux. . . . Betty, dear, why did you take Nanny's watch?'

'Because. . . .' sobbed Betty.

'Because what?'

'Because she's a no-good, thieving vagabond,' Nanny put in viciously, folding her hands on her starched white apron.

'Nanny, please. . . .' Beatrice looked beseechingly at the older woman, deeply upset by the whole unpleasant incident. She was sorry for little Betty Lewisham, but it would be unfair to the other servants to keep a self-confessed thief in the house. She only prayed that Nanny could be persuaded not to press charges. To someone of Beatrice's gentle nature, the thought of being instrumental in sending anyone to prison was most distressing.

Betty indulged in a fresh bout of tears which strained even Margaret's patience, but at last she managed to blurt out: 'Because me da's out of work and me ma's sick. I was goin' to pawn the watch, but I'd've got it back, some'ow, honest! It's jus' . . . jus'. . . .' She became incoherent again, crying into her apron and hiding her tear-swollen face.

Paul cleared his throat and glanced uncomfortably at his wife, then back once more at Betty.

'Yes . . . well . . . personal misfortune is no excuse for taking other people's property, I'm afraid. Thou shalt not steal. That's one of the ten commandments.' He was too young to enjoy playing the heavy-handed employer, and too honest not to admit, if only to himself, that there might be extenuating circumstances even for theft. He appealed to his wife. 'Do we know if what she says is true?'

Beatrice was at a loss. The private lives of her servants were no concern of hers unless they made them so. Unlike most employers, she would have been ashamed to be guilty of prying. She said: 'I have no idea, my love, but I'm sure we could find out. Lewisham, if things are difficult at home, you should have told me. You know that Mr Devereaux and I would have done what we could to help.'

Betty wiped her nose on her apron and sniffed. 'Me da won't take charity.'

'I don't suppose he'd be happy living off the proceeds of stolen goods, either,' Beatrice objected.

Betty stared. If the missus thought that, she must be a fool!

'I demand the law,' said Nanny Watkins, but Paul quelled her with a frown.

'The girl will be punished quite enough in the circumstances, Nanny, by losing her place. I am sure, Lewisham, you realize that we cannot keep you on after what has happened, as much for your own sake as for everyone else's. If anything ever went missing again, you would immediately be suspected. I'm afraid I can't give you a reference, either. That would be unfair to other employers. But I shall not call in the police and you will not go to prison. Now, dry your eyes and go upstairs and pack. I'll send someone home with you, to make sure you get there safely.'

Margaret stepped forward for the second time. Nanny regarded her malevolently.

'I should like to accompany Betty, if I might, Mr Devereaux,' Margaret said.

Paul glanced at her, surprised. 'You, Miss Dunham? Why?'

'She trusts me. And from the little she has told me of her parents, I think there might be trouble over her losing her job. Unpleasant trouble,' she added.

'In that case, surely, one of the men . . . ?'

'With respect, Mr Devereaux, I don't think that any of the men would be willing, or able, to speak in Betty's defence.'

A shade of reserve crept into his tone. 'You think that there is a defence to be offered?'

Her look challenged him. 'Yes. Don't you?'

'Miss Dunham, there can be no excuse for stealing.'

'Quite right,' sniffed Nanny angrily. Margaret ignored her.

'Mr Devereaux, I come from a country to which people were deported for taking a loaf of bread when they were starving. Many Americans are descendants of those people, and proud of it.'

'Margaret! Miss Dunham!' Beatrice interposed swiftly. She recalled Jessie's warning that Maggie had inherited many of Herbert Dunham's subversive views and opinions. She turned to her husband. 'I think it a very good idea, my love, that Miss Dunham should accompany Betty. One of the men can go with them. I'm sure it would be safer.'

'There is really no need for that, Mrs Devereaux.' Margaret smiled. 'I am quite capable of dealing with any situation which arises.'

Paul looked at her from the other side of the wide walnut

43

desk, and had no doubt that she was speaking the truth. There was an air of self-confidence about Margaret Dunham which he had rarely encountered in a woman. She was never flustered by moments of crisis and was totally uninhibited about stating her mind. Moreover, she had an inbred sense of dignity which impressed him. He would stake his last farthing that she never gossiped behind people's backs, and that she was completely trustworthy and reliable.

After that little exchange just now, however, his admiration suddenly knew some reservations. Was it possible that the girl was a radical? North American women were far more independent, far more self-reliant, than their English counterparts. Even sweet, gentle Beatrice tended, at times, to be outspoken on subjects normally regarded as male preserves. It was an intrinsic part of her charm for Paul, who, from the moment his father died, leaving him a very wealthy young man, had been a target for the most sycophantic female adulation. But Beatrice never overstepped the mark. She knew precisely the moment when playful defiance should give way to wifely deference. Paul doubted if the same would ever be said for Margaret Dunham.

He wished with all his heart that he did not have to be near her, to see her every day; that she did not lodge under his roof; even that she was married and beyond his reach. He loved Beatrice. He must hang on to that fact.

He rose to his feet and glanced coolly at the governess. 'I shall send Daniel with you, Miss Dunham. You cannot walk about the streets of . . . of wherever it is on your own. Your future brother-in-law will at least afford you some protection.'

'Lost yer place, you stupid bitch?' screamed Mrs Lewisham. 'Lost yer place? 'Ere, Joe!' She rounded on her husband as he pushed into the already overcrowded little room from the street. 'Yer bleedin' daughter's lost 'er job fer stealin'.' The lips were whiplash thin, and the woman's eyes glittered with a dangerous, drunken anger.

Margaret could feel Betty, standing beside her, grow rigid with the carefully controlled stillness of absolute terror, and she thought with gratitude of Daniel, waiting just outside the door. The younger brothers and sisters were huddled together

44

in a whimpering group in one corner. The youngest, a thin, gangling boy with eyes like a startled fawn's, was shivering uncontrollably.

Joe Lewisham, a hard-looking man with mottled hands and red-veined cheeks, started to unbuckle his trouser belt. 'Lost 'er job, 'as she? I'll 'ave the 'ide off the thievin' cow.'

The door opened again and a girl stood in the doorway, breathing hard as if she had been running, her hat awry on soft brown hair. A pair of large brown eyes stared fiercely at Joe Lewisham. Margaret heard Betty mutter thankfully: ' 'Ilda!' through stiff lips.

Hilda Lewisham took in the situation at a glance. 'Touch our Betty,' she threatened her father, 'and I walk out of this house tomorrow morning and I don't come back. And that's a promise!'

'What you doin' 'ome?' screeched Mrs Lewisham. 'Fer Gawd's sake, don' tell me you lost yer job, an' all!'

'Don't worry, Mother.' Hilda's face was a mask of contempt. 'Your beer money's safe. I was up west, on an errand for Mr Bloomfield, when I met one of the maids from Hill Street. She told me what had happened. I told Mr B. I had to have time off, urgent, for family matters. He said all right, as long as I make it up tonight, so I've run all the way. And arrived not a moment too soon,' she added grimly. 'I warn you, Da, I mean what I say. You leave Betty alone. Let's hear the story from her side.'

Mr Lewisham hesitated, but he knew that without Hilda's contribution to the family income they would be hard put to it to survive, and she was a girl who always meant what she said.

Seeing him hesitate, Margaret also rounded on the hapless man.

'What sort of parent are you, to threaten your own child with violence?' Her beauty, plus the additional glamour of her American accent, gave her words an extra weight.

Mr Lewisham lowered his upraised arm and scowled.

'That's right. You tell him,' Hilda said approvingly. 'Not fit to be bringing up kids, he isn't. Nor her, neither. Don't snivel, Bet. Haven't you got a hankie? Here, take mine.'

Mrs Lewisham subsided tearfully on the one chair in the

45

room. The only other seating accommodation was a stool and two boxes.

'She'll never get anuvver job like that,' she predicted ominously. 'Ain't I allus told you kids that fievin's wrong?'

Betty blew her nose vigorously on her sister's handkerchief. Now that the immediate danger was past, she had recovered a little of her courage.

'I thought the money'd 'elp. I was only goin' to 'ock the watch. I'd've saved up outa me wages and got it back. Honest I would.'

'It'd've bin sold afore you could 'ave saved up enuff money ter redeem a gold watch, you stupid bint! Don't you never use yer brains?'

'You shut up, too, Mother.' Hilda gave her sister a squeeze. 'She was only thinking of you two layabouts by the sound of it. All the same, Bet, it was a dangerous thing to do, as well as being wrong. You could've landed up in prison. Now, now! Don't take on so. Dry your eyes. I know someone who'll get you a job in Borough Market, and no references needed, either.' She glanced at Margaret. 'This Mr Devereaux. He won't change his mind and prosecute, I suppose?'

Margaret shook her head. 'No, I'm sure he won't. He would never admit it, but I think he does appreciate that there might be extenuating circumstances.'

Hilda grinned at her, her worried young face suddenly relaxing. 'You don't half talk posh. You're American, aren't you? I've always wanted to meet one.'

Margaret laughed. 'Just to make sure that we don't have horns and a tail?'

There was a tentative knock on the street door, and Daniel peered in, looking anxious. 'Everything all right?' he enquired.

Margaret suppressed a grin. Poor Daniel! No one could have been unhappier on this sort of mission than he was. Although she had known him only a few months, Margaret was well aware that when trouble loomed Daniel preferred to make himself scarce. He did not believe in seeking out events; not even in going halfway to meet them. Jessie frequently taunted him with being a coward, to which he replied shamelessly that that was the way God had made him, and who was he to interfere with the Almighty's handiwork? When he and

46

Margaret had arrived at the Lewishams' house, he had suggested that he stay outside, on watch. On watch for what, he did not specify, nor had Margaret pressed him.

She said now: 'Yes, everything's quite all right, thank you, Daniel. Your services won't be required.'

A little colour crept back into his plump cheeks and he heaved a sigh of relief. Mr Lewisham looked a nasty customer, and the possibility of having to take a swipe at him had stretched Daniel's courage to its limit. He managed a smile.

'Sorted it all out, then, have you?'

'Miss Lewisham here has sorted things out. My services weren't required, either.' Margaret turned to Hilda and held out her hand. 'Mr Cooper and I ought to be going.'

'Hold on a minute. I must get back to Hatton Garden. We could walk part of the way together. And mind, you two' – Hilda addressed her parents – 'if I find either of you's so much as laid a finger on our Betty when I get home tonight, out I go and take my wages with me. Understood? Right, then, Miss—?'

'Dunham. Margaret Dunham.'

'Right, then, Miss Dunham. I'm ready.'

They walked in silence for a while, Daniel politely bringing up the rear, two paces behind them. Now that she no longer had the hysterical Betty to comfort, Margaret was at liberty to look around her. In the few months she had been in London, she had never moved outside the West End. She had read Dickens's novels when she was younger, but, until today, had naïvely supposed that the extreme poverty he described was a thing of the past. Britain, after all, was the hub of the richest and largest empire the world had ever seen. It therefore came as a shock to discover that so many of its citizens lived in such abject poverty. There was poverty in New York, in America generally, but not so abysmal – surely? – as this. The Dunhams themselves had not been rich, but they had always had shoes for their feet.

Hilda's voice echoed her thoughts. 'Awful round here, isn't it? One day, I mean to get away.'

'Where would you go?' Margaret asked, genuinely interested. She had taken a liking to this pugnacious, freckle-nosed girl.

'Russia. That's where I fancy going.'

'Russia?' Margaret was surprised. 'Whatever makes you want to go there?'

'My young man's Russian. We've been walking out together for over a fortnight. He's ever so nice. Doesn't try to take advantage of a girl at all. He's told me a lot of things about St Petersburg. That's where he comes from. And he knows Mr Devereaux's cousin; the one who's the toff. Duke of something-or-other. It was the Duchess – Countess Olga, Sergei calls her – who brought him to England. You won't tell her, will you? He doesn't want her to know where he is.'

Margaret smiled. 'Hilda, honey, I'm just the governess. Jane Eyre is my role, not Blanche Ingram. I'm not allowed to chat with the drawing-room guests. Your young man's secret is safe with me.'

They had crossed Blackfriars Bridge and were approaching the Strand. Hilda paused regretfully.

'We'll have to part company here, Miss Dunham.'

'My name's Margaret. Do you think we could meet again sometime? I don't know many people in England, and it would be good to have a friend.'

'I'd like that, too.' Hilda grinned broadly and wrung Margaret's hand. 'And thank you for looking after Betty. Da's right, you know. She is a stupid little cow. If ever I get to Russia with Sergei, God knows how they'll all manage without me.'

'Be careful, Mareth! There's a wasp on your bread and jelly. Mind you don't get it in your mouth.'

Mareth shrieked, dropping her jam sandwich in the dirt. India sighed and looked superior.

'Wasps won't hurt you if you don't annoy them, will they, Dunny? There's no need to behave like a baby.'

Margaret laughed. 'I'm not so sure about that. Wasps can be very malevolent creatures. And Mareth is still a very little girl.' She retrieved the jam sandwich from the dust, tearing it into pieces and throwing it to the birds.

It was beautifully peaceful here, in the woods above Latchetts, with the glimmer of sunshine seen through the interlacing trees, the distant hush of the sea and the gentle, never-ceasing chatter of the birds. The family had moved to Cornwall at the end of August, after Paul and Beatrice had returned from Scotland, worn out by the exigencies of the Season.

'It will be lovely to get away by ourselves!' Beatrice had exclaimed during one of her visits to the nursery. 'You'll adore Cornwall, Maggie. It's every bit as romantic as they say it is.'

And Beatrice had been right, Margaret thought, looking about her. To someone who had been born and brought up in the Bronx, Cornwall, with its wild beaches, open moors and ruined castles, was something in a story-book. She had fallen in love with it at first sight.

She and the children and Nanny Watkins had travelled as far as Bodmin by train; and as they had rattled across the Tamar, across Brunel's famous bridge between Plymouth and Saltash, India had jumped up and down with excitement.

'You're in Cornwall now, Dunny! Come and look out of the window.'

At Bodmin, carriages had been waiting to convey them to Latchetts, built in a natural, wooded hollow between Wade-bridge and Port Isaac, within sight and sound of the sea.

Margaret's first glimpse had been of the gatehouse, a two-storeyed building with a proliferation of arches and columns, and a small cupola, a sugar-cake confection in pale grey granite. The dark tunnel of its archway gave access to the formal gardens surrounding the house, which lay at the end of the drive.

The house itself dated from the early part of the seventeenth century, and had originally been quadrangular in shape. Paul's great-great-grandfather, however, had removed the south wing to give Latchetts its present three-sided appearance. The rising, wooded ground all about it, the profusion of rhododendron and azalea bushes crowding it in, the mock towers and battlements, gave the impression of a fairy castle, guarded by an enchanted forest. The Sleeping Beauty, Margaret had thought, might easily lie within. . . .

'It's dark, damp and thoroughly insanitary,' Jessie had complained peevishly, when she and Daniel arrived the following day. They had travelled in advance of Beatrice and Paul, together with some of the other servants from Hill Street and vast quantities of trunks and portmanteaux. 'How people can like living here for five or six months of the year is beyond my comprehension.'

'Oh, Jess! It's beautiful,' Margaret had protested, laughing. 'It's straight out of Hans Andersen or the Brothers Grimm.'

'The plumbing is primitive and it's perishing cold. Well, thank goodness I've spent my last winter at Latchetts.' She paused in the act of unpacking her valise and glanced self-consciously at her sister. 'Daniel and I have decided to get married this autumn. Here, in the church on the estate.'

'Jess, that's wonderful.' Margaret had kissed her sister's cheek, fighting off the sense of shock and isolation. 'What . . . what will you and Daniel do then?'

'We're going to live in Bath, with his mother. There's room above the shop, and it's time Daniel learned the business. Mrs Cooper hasn't been well lately, and the doctor has hinted that it could be serious. I shall be able to look after her and the apartment, and give Daniel a hand behind the counter.'

'If you're sure that's what you want,' Margaret had said doubtfully.

'Pehaps it isn't exactly what I had in mind when Ma used to read us those fairy-stories. Remember?' Jessie had shaken out a brown alpaca skirt, which had been put away during the summer months. The little room was filled with the pungent aroma of moth-balls. 'But life isn't a fairy-story, and I want my own home; not to be constantly at someone else's beck and call.'

Margaret had thought of the ailing Mrs Cooper, but merely said: 'I thought you were happy with Beatrice?'

'I am.' Jessie had pushed the emptied valise under the bed and glanced around the pleasant corner room with its double view of the woods and formal gardens. 'She's my friend. She's been kind, and I've enjoyed working for her. But now I need a life of my own. I want children.'

Poor Jess, Margaret thought now, having cleared away the remains of the children's picnic. She leaned back against the trunk of a tree while the girls played hide-and-seek in the woods with Mary Palmer, the nursery-maid who had replaced Betty Lewisham. Poor Jess, what chance did she stand, with a sick mother-in-law and an indolent husband? For fond as Margaret was of Daniel, she could not ignore the fact that he hated anything which came between him and his beloved books.

Margaret wondered if Jessie knew that Daniel was a poet. She doubted it. She had only found out herself by chance. He had lent her a book of essays, Stevenson's *Virginibus Puerisque*, and when she opened it two thin sheets of paper had fallen out, covered in Daniel's small, precise writing. At first, she thought it was something he had been copying, and it was only after she had read the poems through twice that the suspicion crossed her mind that they were Daniel's own work. It was not that they were in any way amateurish; in fact, just the opposite. It was simply that she could not place the style. Herbert Dunham had imbued his younger daughter with his passion for the English-speaking poets, and there were few whom Margaret failed to recognize.

She had taxed Daniel with her suspicions, to his acute embarrassment.

'I didn't mean anyone to read them but myself,' he said. 'I write for my own pleasure, not to inflict my scribblings on others.'

'Daniel, they're good,' she had assured him.

He shook his head. 'Not good enough. For God's sake, don't breathe a word to Jessie.'

Margaret had promised to keep his secret, and had faithfully done so. But she could not help wondering if her sister really appreciated what sort of man she was marrying. They were an ill-assorted pair; too much common sense on one side, too much imagination on the other.

It was getting chilly. The September day was growing cold, with a thin wind fretting the branches and running like a silver thread amongst the leaves. Margaret got to her feet, calling to her charges.

'Oh, not yet, Dunny, please!' India was tearful. 'It's too early to go back to the house.'

'It's time,' Margaret said implacably. 'Besides,' she added, quite ruining the image of stern disciplinarian, 'if we don't go soon, we shan't be able to pay our evening visit to the gatehouse-room, now shall we?'

Five

Margaret had discovered the room above the gatehouse the
day after her arrival at Latchetts. She had taken India for a
walk to gather specimens of leaves and berries for their nature
scrap-book, and also to watch for the carriage bringing Jessie
and Daniel from the station. As they passed through the
tunnel of the gatehouse, on their way from the formal gardens
into the park, she noticed the gaping mouth of the staircase in
one corner.

'That must lead to the room above,' she said, and India
nodded. 'Have you ever been up there?'

'When Grandmother Devereaux was alive, she used to use
it in the summer,' the child answered, following Margaret's
example and peering upwards into the gloom at the top of the
winding stairway. 'But nobody goes up there now.'

'Is the door into the room locked, do you know?' India
shook her head. 'Shall we go up and see?'

Cautiously they mounted the narrow stone steps, whose
treads had been worn away by generations of Devereaux feet.
The staircase twisted once, then stopped before a wooden
door, studded with nails, standing half open. Margaret
pushed it wide and they went inside.

There was an old armchair of faded brocade, which had
once been green but was now almost white and blotched with
mould, a couple of wicker chairs, a table and, against one wall,
some rusting garden implements: a hoe, a rake, a scythe.
Everything was coated in dust. The four mullioned bay-
windows gave on to magnificent views of the gardens, the
house, the rising parkland and the woods. In one of the bays
stood an Albion paraffin heater, its dimpled, ruby-coloured

glass dome indistinguishable beneath the dirt and grime of years.

'Ooh, Dunny, this could be our secret room,' India said, her eyes wide and luminous with excitement.

'Not just as it stands,' Margaret protested, smiling. 'First, we need your mama and papa's permission for someone to clean it up.'

She had broached the subject soon after the Devereauxs' arrival, and Beatrice willingly gave her consent.

'I think it's a splendid idea,' she told Paul that evening, while they were dressing for dinner. 'A room the girls can regard as their very own.'

'I should have thought Latchetts big enough to provide any number of playrooms,' he answered drily, as Daniel helped him into his coat, 'without bothering to clean up the gatehouse.'

'Don't be grumpy,' Beatrice scolded. 'You know it isn't at all the same thing. It will be like having their own little house.'

'Nanny Watkins won't be pleased.'

'Then Nanny need not go there,' Beatrice retorted with spirit. 'Maggie is quite capable of looking after Mareth as well as India. I'll give orders to start the cleaning tomorrow.'

'You must do as you see fit, my love.'

She thought him unusually grudging, and was puzzled by his attitude. Normally, he was so anxious to promote the children's happiness. It crossed her mind yet again that he did not like Margaret Dunham, although she could not imagine why. She shrugged and went away to write to her father, in New York, for news about the continuing aftermath of President McKinley's assassination.

So the gatehouse-room was swept and scrubbed, not without some opposition from Mrs Hinkley, the housekeeper, who complained that there was enough to keep the maids occupied without burdening them with extra work. But, in the end, it was done, and by the middle of September had become playroom, nursery, schoolroom, rolled into one. Mareth and India loved it, but, as Paul had foreseen, Nanny Watkins did not.

'Then you must let Miss Dunham take charge of Mareth,' Beatrice informed her coldly. She had never, perversely, cared for Nanny Watkins after the affair of the stolen watch.

Nanny was furious, managing to convey her displeasure to Olga when the Duke and Duchess, together with Anna, visited Latchetts towards the end of October.

'You allow that Dunham woman too much freedom,' Olga said lazily, as she and Beatrice sat on the terrace one morning, sipping coffee and eating macaroons. At least, Olga was eating macaroons. Beatrice merely watched, marvelling at her cousin-in-law's capacity for sweet and sickly foods.

The weather had suddenly turned warm again, as it was so apt to do in October; autumn's last, brief, defiant fling. The leaves of the trees, already on the turn, were metallic in the fiery copper-brightness of the sun. What clouds there were, in the blue expanse of the sky, rode high and thin. A faint breeze bore inland the sharp salt tang of the sea.

Olga, undeterred by Beatrice's resolute silence, continued: 'A governess is only a servant, you know, and servants should understand their place. In Russia, we handle these things much better. In America, it is well known, you have no sense of position or rank.'

Her sister, seated at a little distance, on one of the hard, upright chairs which she preferred, nodded in agreement. Anna's only concession to the warmth of the morning had been to dispense with the navy-blue serge jacket of her walking costume, which she had folded and placed carefully on a nearby seat. Her severely tailored, unadorned white blouse was buttoned high to her throat, and her unfashionable, broad-brimmed hat was of plain grey felt.

'Olga is right,' she said. 'In America and, to some extent, in England, you treat your servants too much as friends. This wedding of your maid and Paul's manservant next week! There is no need for you to attend the ceremony. You need only put in an appearance at the celebrations, afterwards. Towards servants one must be paternalistic, but one must never treat them as equals.'

'Jessie and Margaret Dunham are my friends,' Beatrice retorted. Ignore them, she had told herself; arguing is just a waste of breath. But something about Olga's complacency, as she crammed one macaroon after another into her mouth, and Anna's patronizing attitude to all things American, had goaded her into speech. 'We grew up together. Our fathers were friends, even though Herbie Dunham worked for Papa.'

Anna looked down her nose and Olga said: 'America is, after all, a society based on wealth, not on land or its ancient families. . . . Ah! Here are our menfolk, returning from their ride.' She waved a languid hand at the Duke, who was mounting the terrace steps beside his cousin. 'How far did you go, my dear?'

The Duke flung himself into a vacant chair and accepted a cup of coffee from Beatrice. 'Too bloody far,' he answered, grinning at Paul. 'He forgets I'm not a youngster, like himself.'

Paul grimaced. 'Some youngster. I'm twenty-five.'

'And I'm over forty. What were you ladies arguing about? We could hear Beatrice at the other end of the drive.'

It was a stupid and pointless exaggeration, and Beatrice flushed with annoyance. 'We were discussing servants and the way to treat them,' she said. 'The differences between Russia and America.'

'We were talking about the Dunhams, and how Beatrice insists on treating them as friends.' Olga popped the last macaroon into her little pink mouth, and wiped her plump fingers on a lace-bordered handkerchief.

'Oh, the Dunhams.' Francis glanced slyly at Paul, who seemed mesmerized by the pattern on the fine Worcester coffee-set, and indifferent to their conversation. 'The younger one is a damned fine-looking filly. Very unusual hair. Not often you see just that particular shade of red.'

The Duke was not sure when the suspicion that Paul was attracted by the Dunham girl had entered his head. Probably the first time, with any certainty, had been the preceding evening, when she had brought the children to the drawing-room to say goodnight. Paul had been anxious not to notice her, barely glancing in her direction even when forced to address her, and studiously ignoring her the rest of the time. It was unlike Paul to treat his staff with anything but the utmost courtesy, and his unaccustomed brusqueness had caused Beatrice, later, to remonstrate with him.

'I cannot understand why you dislike Margaret Dunham so much,' she had said.

The woman's a fool, Francis thought now. Can't she see

that he really wants to go to bed with the girl? Not that he supposed Paul would. His cousin would have scruples, something which had never troubled Francis. Margaret Dunham was a beautiful woman: he had a good mind to cast out a lure himself. Should he do so, he had no doubt of his success. He had never met the woman yet who was not flattered by the attentions of a duke.

Jessie and Daniel were married towards the end of October in the little parish church of St Endymion on the Latchetts estate.

'I don't know what Pa would have thought,' Margaret observed, as she helped Jessie to get ready, 'one of his daughters being married in an Episcopalian church. You know how staunch a Methodist he was.'

'I know how staunch a Methodist he said he was,' Jessie snorted, looking with dissatisfaction at her reflection in the mirror. 'I remember he used to send us all the way from Lafayette Street to John Street chapel, because he insisted the preaching was superior there. But I don't recall his going with us very often.'

She should not have chosen this silk-braided suit in chrysanthemum-yellow. It was too fussy for her dumpy figure, and the colour was all wrong for her complexion. The white blouse, with its frothing jabot of lace, made her look as though she had no neck. The little tricorne straw hat, swathed in veiling and tulle, perched on top of her hair like a bird's nest. Oh, well! There was nothing she could do about it now, and she doubted if Daniel would even notice what she was wearing. Still, it wasn't everyone who had been born within shouting distance of the Bouwerie Lane Theatre who had a duke and duchess as guests at her wedding. She did not remark on this fact out loud. Somehow, she felt Maggie would disapprove of the sentiment.

The inside of St Endymion's church was dank and smelled of mould. Margaret stood beside her sister, holding a posy of late-flowering roses, pale cream to match her dress. It was the dress which Jessie should have chosen, and would have, if Margaret had had her way. But Jessie had set her heart on something grander. The light filtering through the leaded

56

windows was weak and pallid, waxing the faces of a congregation comprised, apart from the Devereauxs and the Duke and Duchess, of estate workers, domestic staff and one or two curious villagers. Mrs Cooper's health had not permitted her travelling from Bath, and Daniel's only other relation was a great-uncle who lived in Bradford, whom he had never seen. Jessie had no one but Margaret.

'We shan't be troubled much by in-laws on either side of the family,' she had once remarked, and Margaret had sensed the loneliness behind the jaunty little smile.

As they left the church for the wedding breakfast, provided at Latchetts, Margaret was conscious that the Duke was regarding her fixedly. Later, as she sat beside Jessie at the top of the long dining-room table, she could almost have sworn that he winked. She felt uncomfortable. She was used to men looking at her, but not in that openly lecherous way.

The little party was joined for the meal by the Countess Anna, whose strict Russian Orthodoxy had not permitted her to enter an Anglican church. She offered half-hearted congratulations to the bride and groom; but, as she took her place at the table, she commented *sotto voce* to the Duke on the folly of allowing servants, for whatever reason, to sit at the same table as their masters, particularly in the place of honour.

'The wedding feast should have been held in the servants' quarters.'

Jessie's face flamed with anger, but Daniel squeezed her hand, whispering: 'She wanted you to hear, so pretend you didn't. It's the only way to deal with that sort of person.'

Paul Devereaux, who had also heard the remark, did even better. When the champagne glasses were filled, he got to his feet and proposed a toast: 'My wife's very good friend, Jessica Dunham, now Mrs Daniel Cooper.'

It was a direct snub to the Countess, and made Jessie's colour rise again, but this time in a glow of pleasure. Margaret, meeting Paul's eyes across the table, sent him a look of gratitude. Ridiculously, her heart began to hammer in her chest. She thought she had managed to overcome those early, foolish sentiments she had cherished for Paul Devereaux. She had convinced herself that she thought him simply a nice man with easy manners, even though he was a little sharp sometimes towards herself. Now she knew that ever since their first meeting she had been aware of him, conscious of his presence whenever they had been together beneath the same roof. She recalled that she had thought him kind over the dismissal of Betty Lewisham, persuading Nanny Watkins not to lay a charge with the police. Yet, at the same time, she had been disappointed that he would not allow all the mitigating circumstances in Betty's favour. It was a disappointment not only unreasonable, but also indicative of a desire to change him; to force him into the heroic mould. She should have been warned. She had already set him on a pedestal, and been hurt when he fell short of her impossible ideal.

Margaret sat down, still sipping her champagne and listening with only half an ear to Daniel's stumbling speech. She felt desperately lonely, with the realization that from today she would see very little of Jessie. Why had her sister not warned her, before she left New York, that she was soon to be married? Jess should have told her, Margaret thought angrily. It could have affected her decision to come to England.

She was engulfed by a sudden and violent wave of homesickness for the familiar streets around the Bowery, which, for a short time, more than seventy years ago, had been the fashionable quarter of New York. There was almost nothing nowadays to show for that brief moment of glory – Colonnade Row and the Old Merchant's House – but there was grandeur of a sort in Louis Sullivan's new Bayard Building in Bleecker Street, and in the Italian façade of the last iron building at 807 Broadway. And whatever its shortcomings, whatever it lacked in the way of green fields, thatched cottages and Georgian terraces, the whole city was vibrant with life and bursting with ideas. It was representative of a young, forward-looking country, untrammelled by the past and the need to keep faith with tradition. . . .

The wedding breakfast was over and farewells were being said. Jessie and Daniel were to have three days' honeymoon at Newquay, before travelling north to Bath and their new home above the sweet shop in Green Street. There was nothing more for Margaret to do: Jessie had no separate going-away outfit. The short journey to Newquay would be accomplished in one of the Devereaux carriages, and Jessie had seen no need for the expense of a second costume. Margaret followed the newly-married couple out on to the steps of the house, where Jessie dutifully kissed her sister's cheek.

'The most prosaic girl in the world, is Jess,' Herbert Dunham had often complained about his elder daughter. 'She'd ask you if you had your sun-hat if she saw you disappearing into the jaws of hell.'

But at least Jessie's unsentimental attitude helped Margaret to preserve her dignity. She waved goodbye with a smile and turned calmly back into the house as the carriage vanished from sight.

'I'll go up to the schoolroom and see if India needs me,' she said to Beatrice.

The children were in bed at last, the October evening inky-black. Margaret stood at her bedroom window, staring out over the gardens which were slabbed with gold from the uncurtained rooms downstairs.

She could not settle to read or sew or write letters to her friends in New York. She felt restless; angry and unhappy. Her anger was partly directed at the absent Jessie, who, she considered, had treated her badly, and partly at herself for feeling that way. No one had made the decision to come to England for her.

Her unhappiness was harder to define. It was true that it was rooted in loneliness, but there were also elements of jealousy and longing. She was jealous of Beatrice, she wanted Paul, but the knowledge was too difficult to face. So she shied away from it, searching for other reasons.

As always, in moments of stress, she resorted to the novels of Jane Austen, whose gently sardonic humour usually had a calming effect. But tonight, not even her favourite *Emma* could quiet her jangled nerves. She put the book down, wrapped a thick knitted shawl about her shoulders, and went down the back stairs and through the kitchen out of the house.

Everything was silent and deserted. Dinner was over, and Mrs Hinkley had retired to the housekeeper's room. The scullery-maids had finished washing the dishes and also retired, thankfully, to bed, in preparation for their five o'clock start next morning. The clerestory windows under the high gabled roof showed as faint oblongs of grey. A single lamp, left burning on the well-scrubbed kitchen table, illumined the roasting-spits and the black-leaded range. Rows of copper pans glowed dully in its light.

There was no light at all in the dairy, but the great marble slab in the middle of the room gleamed sepulchrally white in the darkness. Against the tiled walls, the bowls and jugs above the slate runnels held milk and cream for the following day's breakfast. Next to the dairy was the dairy-scullery, where the soups and mousses and junkets were prepared, and the cream skimmed from the pans of rich Cornish milk, brought in churns every morning from a nearby farm. The milk was poured into vats, standing in baths of cold water.

The stone-flagged passage which lay beyond the scullery led Margaret past the meat-larder, where rows of metal hooks and sloping sinks allowed the meat to drain; past the fish-larder, with its ice-chest and cool slate slabs; past the dry-larder, where commodities such as rice and oats were stored; past the still-room and its well-stocked shelves of pickles, chutneys and jams; and, finally, past the bakehouse, with its oven, proving-oven and flour-chests.

The door at the end of the passageway remained open until midnight, when the butler went on his final rounds. Margaret lifted the latch and slipped into the fragrant darkness, heavy with the scents of the rain-dampened ground. She made her way around to the front of the house, where the white ribbon of driveway wound between shadowy lawns, the inverted-pear-shaped contours of the sculptured yews just discernible in the blackness.

Margaret pulled her shawl closer about her shoulders. Glancing backwards and upwards at Latchetts's imposing façade, she could not help contrasting it with the Lewishams' house in Southwark. There, seven people were crammed into four rooms, two upstairs, two down, with the lavatory built on at the back; an insanitary lean-to shed in the walled strip of concrete which passed as a yard. Hilda had told her that a sheet divided one of the upstairs rooms.

'Betty and I sleep in one half. The three younger kids share the other.'

'But Marjorie's thirteen,' Margaret had protested, horrified.

'And Billy's seven.' Hilda had shrugged. 'It's no wonder incest and poverty so often go hand in hand. I keep 'em on the straight and narrow as much as I can, but, as I said once before, I shan't always be there. One of these days, Sergei will want to go home, to Russia.'

Margaret had met Sergei when the three of them had gone, one evening, to the Old Victoria Music Hall. He had seemed a quiet, inoffensive enough young man, but appearances could be deceptive. From things Hilda had let drop, Margaret guessed him to be deeply involved with politics; mainly with the groups of dissident Russian exiles living in London and plotting to overthrow the Tsar. But he was also interested in British and American affairs, and was busy completing Hilda's education. Her opinions, Margaret had noticed, were becoming far more militant. She read avidly the works of George Bernard Shaw and Sidney and Beatrice Webb, and quoted from Oscar Wilde's *The Soul of Man Under Socialism*. In addition, Sergei had questioned Margaret closely about a part-Indian one-eyed American called 'Big' Bill Heywood, who was making his mark as the labour leader of the Western Federation of Miners, leading strikes at Teluride and Cripple Creek. Margaret had never heard of him, and, instead, told Sergei about her father, who had organized the workers of the Coleman Smith Corporation to get better wages. Sergei had been unable to understand how, in those circumstances, Herbert Dunham and his employer had remained friends.

'I think it is very difficult to comprehend the Americans,' he had said, in his precise English. 'They do not seem to think it wrong that some people have great wealth, while others live in abject poverty.'

Margaret had tried to explain to him that in America everyone wanted to be a millionaire. No one objected to wealth, only to the lack of it.

'To be rich,' she had told him, 'is the American dream.'

He had still not understood, and she had been baffled by his obtuseness. But sometimes, as now, walking through the beauty and serenity that was Latchetts, and contrasting it with the squalor of London's East End, she had a glimmering of how Sergei felt.

Margaret passed under the arch of the gatehouse and cautiously groped her way up the narrow, twisting stairs. She lit the oil lamp and the paraffin heater, then sat down near one of the windows, staring into the darkness and the reflected images of the little room. She smiled to herself. Her walk had undoubtedly done her good. For at least a quarter of an hour she had forgotten how miserable she was feeling.

It was still in the window reflection that she saw the door being pushed gently open. She slewed round in her chair, the hairs rising on the nape of her neck, then froze into immobility. The Duke of Leamington stood, smiling, in the doorway.

Six

Francis had seen Margaret from his vantage point at the drawing-room windows, and recognized her from the quick, graceful way she moved. Although the night was dark, the light from the uncurtained windows had illumined a section of the driveway. It was not warm enough for walking, and he guessed that her destination must be the room above the gatehouse. Francis's two young cousins had initiated him into its mysteries and pleasures soon after his arrival at Latchetts, and he had, on occasions, seen the light burning there when the children were asleep in bed.

'I believe Miss Dunham uses the room now and then,' Beatrice had replied in answer to his query. 'She seems to find it as congenial as do India and Mareth. Myself, I think it cold and spooky.'

The Duke had had his eye on Margaret for some time, but there had been no opportunity in London to find her alone. He had decided to bide his time until his visit to Latchetts, and fate had played neatly into his hands. The isolated gatehouse-room was a godsend.

He thought Margaret beautiful and spirited, a combination which, to him, added up to a woman of the world. He did not stop to analyse just how he reached this conclusion. It had simply been his experience that such women had, to use his own phrase, 'been around'. Shyness and plainness were the two qualities he equated with virginity. As far as his own attractions went, he relied, as ever, on the aphrodisiacs of power and fortune to counteract the thinning hair and thickening paunch.

Dinner was over, but it was still a while to supper-time. He was bored. Olga and her sister were playing bezique, squabbling as usual. At least, Anna was finding fault in an irritating, high-pitched whine; Olga was being slyly unpleasant. She was far too indolent to quarrel. Beatrice was reading a letter from her father giving belated details of Theodore Roosevelt's swearing-in, and Paul was writing letters of his own at the inlaid rosewood desk. Francis himself had been trying to get on with Conrad's *Lord Jim*, but found it tedious stuff. He had never been one for reading.

The sight of Margaret had sent his boredom flying. He glanced over his shoulder, but no one was interested in his movements.

'Think I'll just get a breath of fresh air,' he said, stepping through the windows on to the terrace. Five minutes later, he was mounting the gatehouse stairs.

He had seen the glow of the lamp from below, so it was no surprise to see Margaret sitting there, in one of the basket-weave armchairs. He smiled at the sight of her startled face.

'Good evening, my dear. I hope you don't object to my company. No, no! Please don't get up,' and he pressed his hand on her shoulder as she attempted to rise. He let it linger a moment, caressingly.

'I ... please ... won't you sit down, Your Grace?' Margaret indicated the other armchair.

Francis hesitated momentarily, then did as she suggested. There was no need to be in too much of a hurry.

' "Your Grace" is too formal,' he objected, still smiling. 'Call me Duke. It sounds more relaxed.'

Margaret did not feel relaxed. All her instincts were warning her of danger. Jessie had often spoken of the Duke's reputation with women. And Margaret remembered how he had looked at her in the church, and at the reception, that afternoon.

'Very well ... Duke.' She began to talk, hoping, with words, to hold him at a distance. 'I came up here because I felt so lonely, now that my sister has gone. I know that sounds foolish, but sometimes you can feel lonelier with people all around you than you can when you're on your own.'

'Indeed you can,' he interrupted her smoothly, getting up and moving his chair so that, instead of facing one another, they now sat side by side. He reached out and fondled her knee. 'But there's no need to feel lonely, you know. Your sister's not thinking of you tonight. She's enjoying herself.' The grip on her knee tightened. 'You could be doing the same.'

Margaret stared at him, unable to believe her ears. She had expected to be embarrassed by some mild flirtation – and had been wondering how best to discourage her employer's cousin without either sounding or being rude – but she had been unprepared for such a direct and unequivocal invitation.

'I . . . I beg your pardon?'

The Duke's hand slid from her knee up to her thigh. Never before had a man touched her with such familiarity. Margaret felt sick and her temper began to rise.

'Please take your hand off my leg.'

Francis laughed, but there was an edge to the sound. The stupid bitch was playing hard to get, and he could not afford to be absent from the drawing-room too long.

'You know you don't mean that,' he said. Leaning over, he kissed her, pushing her back against the chair, so that she felt the wicker-work biting into the flesh of her neck.

Frightened, outraged, she reacted instinctively. She struck him as hard as she could across the face. His eyes, so close to hers that she was able to see the specks of hazel in the blue of the iris, dilated, first with astonishment, then with fury.

'You cow! For that you're going to be taught a lesson!'

He released her, but only while he heaved himself out of his chair. Before she could escape, he had both her wrists in an agonizing grip and jerked her roughly to her feet. Next moment his arms closed about her, forcing her back against the wall. For a fleeting second, she caught sight of the two of them, locked together, in that ghost-room of reflected light and shadow beyond the windows. Then she was conscious of nothing but the stone of the old wall grazing her back and his hands fumbling at her skirts.

She opened her mouth and screamed.

Paul Devereaux laid down his pen and flexed his fingers. He would finish his correspondence tomorrow. He remembered that he had promised the Duke a game of billiards before supper, and glanced around the drawing-room for his cousin.

'Where's Francis?' he enquired of Olga.

The Duchess shrugged, and the myriad bugle-beads which adorned the breast and sleeves of her pink evening gown coruscated in the light thrown by the chandelier.

'I do not know. I have not been watching. He was here a moment or two ago.'

'He went into the garden,' Beatrice said, without looking up from her letter. She wished Papa's style was not quite so florid: it made him so difficult to read.

'I think I'll join him.' Paul took a cigar from the box on the desk, clipped the end and went outside to light it. 'Francis!' he called. 'Where are you?'

The cigar-tip winked and glowed, a burning eye of light in the gold-slabbed darkness. Paul strolled in the direction of the gatehouse. He was almost there when he heard a woman scream. He stood still, frightened in spite of himself. There was something petrifying about unseen terrors lurking in the night.

The sound came again, but muffled this time, as though a hand had been clamped across a mouth. He recognized the voice as Margaret Dunham's. He tossed away his cigar and took the gatehouse stairs three at a bound.

He was prepared, before he reached the top, for the scene which met his eyes, but not for the surge of anger which filled him. Paul was fond of the cousin, so much older than himself, who had been in many respects a surrogate father. He knew the Duke's way of life, and, without wishing it for himself, had always been indulgent towards it. But seeing Margaret Dunham's white face, her slender body arched against the stone, his cousin's furious attempts to force himself upon her, he was disgusted beyond all reason. He crossed the room, seized the collar of Francis's coat and hauled him off the trembling girl as unceremoniously as a policeman man-handling a criminal.

'For God's sake, Francis, what do you think you're doing? Keep your animal behaviour for the farmyard where it belongs. Don't abuse my hospitality by trying to seduce my children's governess.'

The Duke was shaking with rage and humiliation. God,

what a mess! And all because that silly bitch was so prudish! She had completely misled him with her free and easy, Yankee-American ways. Worse still, she had managed to set his cousin against him. The Duke had not realized until that moment how much Paul's opinion mattered to him. And how on earth were they going to explain the coolness which would inevitably result between them? About Olga, Francis had no worries. She would merely be indignant on his behalf, a governess, in her mind, ranking no better than a servant. Her late father had kept female serfs especially to copulate with his dinner guests, and Olga had been brought up to believe it was the duty of women servants to pleasure the men. Russians, he reflected bitterly, had the right ideas!

The Duke straightened his coat, ostentatiously smoothing out the creases which had resulted from Paul's rough handling. There was only one course open to him: to make as light of the situation as he could.

'Don't believe everything the girl tells you, will you?' he asked, with an attempt at jauntiness. 'Hysterical women are notoriously unreliable.'

Paul replied quietly: 'Miss Dunham is neither a liar nor hysterical. Besides, I saw for myself what was happening.'

'I shall go back to the house,' Francis said. God! How he needed a drink! 'Will you come with me?'

'I'll follow in a minute or two. When I'm sure that Miss Dunham is all right.'

'Very well.' There was an uncomfortable silence; then the Duke hunched his shoulders and turned for the door. Without looking at either of them, he let himself out. His footfalls died away on the stairs.

Margaret groped her way to a chair and sat down. 'I'm afraid,' she said, 'I'm going to be sick.'

She half-expected Paul to run, or at least to back away with that sheepish look men usually assumed in embarrassing situations. But he did neither. He merely glanced quickly about him.

On one of the window-seats was a collection of plates, cups and saucers which the children used when giving parties for their dolls, together with a water jug and large white enamel basin. Beatrice had insisted that the girls be made to wash up their own dirty crockery. Paul Devereaux picked up the bowl and handed it to Margaret. . . .

'Are you feeling better?' he asked later, looking down at her white face and half-closed eyes.

'Yes . . . yes. I'm sorry. I didn't mean to make all this fuss.'

'You have every right to make a fuss. You are a member of my household, and could have expected to rely on my protection. Instead of which—' He broke off, colouring, and murmured indistinctly: 'A member of my own family . . . I should have warned you.'

'Jessie warned me. It was simply that I didn't anticipate—' It was Margaret's turn to leave her sentence unfinished.

The nausea had passed and she opened her eyes a little wider. She could remember very few details of the past fifteen minutes, other than feeling, and being, revoltingly sick. She was astonished to discover that all traces of that nasty little interlude had been removed, although she could not recall that Paul Devereaux had left the room. She looked at him, and fell more deeply in love than ever.

'No, I didn't anticipate it, either,' he answered, after a second's hesitation. 'I expected my cousin to have more respect for me.'

Anger flooded through her. It was a sensation she was to know well for the rest of her life; this loving and hating within the same brief heart-beat. For the moment, she felt much as she would have done had someone she trusted suddenly robbed her.

'I should have expected your cousin to have more respect for me!' she retorted, getting unsteadily to her feet. She was aware that Paul was regarding her in amazement, quite unable to understand the reason for her anger; a fact which infuriated her even further.

'I must go.' Margaret took a step towards the door and was enveloped in a yellow mist. She sank down again into her chair.

The next thing she knew, he was pushing her head between her knees, his handkerchief, wrung out in cold water from the jug, held against her forehead. She heard the click of the lifting door-latch and jumped, every nerve in her body stretched to its limit. But it was Beatrice who spoke.

'Paul, what's going on? I've been searching everywhere for you. Francis has come back to the house looking like a whipped dog. He's gone to bed in a sulk, without any supper.'

'Very appropriate,' Paul said, 'for a delinquent schoolboy.'

'What do you mean?' Beatrice suddenly took in Margaret's presence and hurried forward. 'Paul, what's happened?'

'My dear cousin seems to have formed the idea that Miss Dunham was fair game for one of his amorous adventures. I discovered him up here, trying to seduce her.'

'Rape,' Margaret contradicted him, lifting her head and leaning back, exhausted, in her chair. 'He was trying to rape me.'

Beatrice exclaimed in horror, and her husband frowned.

'Don't you think that's rather an exaggeration, Miss Dunham?'

'No.' Margaret got to her feet once again, determined, this time, to stay on them. The feeling of faintness had at last receded. She regarded Paul Devereaux with hostility. 'And as long as you continue to be amused by your cousin's exploits, as long as you go on treating him like a delinquent schoolboy, rather than as a dangerous and predatory adult, he will continue to think that women like me are simply there for the taking. And now, if you want to sack me, you can. I have enough money saved for my passage back to New York.'

'Of course we're not going to sack you, are we, Paul?' Beatrice looked challengingly at her husband.

'No, of course not,' he answered tetchily. 'I realize you've been through an unpleasant experience tonight, Miss Dunham, but please stop being so melodramatic.' His tone was sharper than he had intended. Her remarks about his attitude towards Francis had touched him on the raw, finding, as they did, an echo in his own subconscious.

Beatrice put her arm about Margaret's waist and urged her in the direction of the door.

'I'll take you back to the house and put you to bed,' she said. 'Stay there all day tomorrow, if you want. I'll think up some excuse for the children.'

Margaret smiled at her gratefully. 'I shall be all right. But . . . the Duke . . . ?'

'I'll see that he leaves tomorrow morning.' Beatrice, like so

69

many normally biddable women, could, when she dug in her toes, show a core of steel. Paul recognized the tone of voice and smiled. It banished the grim look from his face, softening it with a tenderness he rarely displayed in public.

'He loves her,' Margaret thought desolately, as Beatrice carefully guided her down the stairway and out into the chill night air. 'I love her, too.'

And, to her own horror, she leaned against the cold stone of the gatehouse and burst into tears.

Paul never discovered, nor did he enquire, what Beatrice said to the Duke which persuaded him to leave Latchetts, together with Olga and her sister, at some ungodly hour the following morning. It was sufficient for him to know that they had gone, without any recriminations on the Duke's part.

'Sorry, old fellow. Must have drunk too much at dinner,' Francis had said at parting. It was the nearest thing to an apology Paul had ever heard his cousin make. He was duly grateful and prepared to let bygones be bygones.

Beatrice, however, was not. She had been too tired and too shaken to make any fuss the previous evening, but was determined now to have her say. When she came downstairs at ten o'clock she found Paul in the library, going through some of the estate papers and drinking coffee. He glanced reproachfully at her over the rim of his cup.

'You might at least have seen Olga and Francis off this morning. And Anna.' How easy it was to overlook the Countess.

'Why?' Beatrice demanded bluntly. 'I've never liked them. And now I like them even less. I'm sorry, because I know you're fond of Francis. But that's the trouble. If you'd found one of your estate workers, or miners, behaving as Francis did, you would have dismissed him on the spot.'

'Francis was my guest,' he retorted in exasperation, 'not my employee. And, socially, I'm his inferior.'

'Mmm.' Beatrice sat down on the opposite side of the library desk.

'What does that mean?' He was growing irritable. He had passed a broken night, angry with Francis, but, irrationally, even angrier with Margaret Dunham. He had spent sleepless hours trying to ignore, or explain away, the fury which had consumed him when he saw her struggling in the arms of his cousin. In that moment he could have murdered Francis without compunction. Surely he could not harbour the same lascivious feelings for her as did the Duke? But he had felt something, and if not lust, then what? He dismissed the answer to his question as ridiculous. He was in love with Beatrice. But he could not ignore the fact that Margaret Dunham was becoming an obsession.

Why had he really gone out, last night, looking for his cousin? Not because he had promised him a game of billiards and was reluctant to disappoint him: he knew Francis had no great affection for the game. Was it because he, too, had seen Margaret in the light from the window as he sat behind the rosewood desk, and guessed her destination? Had he really been searching for Francis, as he made his way towards the gatehouse . . . ? He became aware that Beatrice had been speaking.

'I'm sorry,' he apologized. 'I'm afraid my mind was wandering.'

'I said that the caste system in this country is nearly as rigid as that of India.'

'What do you know of India?' he snapped, unable to think of a better answer.

'I've read a lot. And as an outsider, a foreigner, I say that Britain is every bit as bad.'

'An exaggeration. You want to talk to Olga and learn about Russia.'

'I have talked to Olga, although I don't imagine I shall be doing so a great deal in the future; not now that I've offended her precious husband.'

'Well then!'

'Why do people always compare themselves to the worst they can be? Why don't they compare themselves with the best?'

'In this instance, you mean America, I suppose?' His voice was cold, but she saw the gleam of laughter in his eyes.

'Naturally! In the United States we're much more democratic, our social structure is far more fluid. Olga would tell you that it's because our caste system is based on money.'

'Not strictly true, but near enough,' he said, getting up and holding out his hand. 'Shall we cry quits? You know I can't bear quarrelling with you.'

'We're not quarrelling.' She rose, also, putting her hand in his. 'I just wanted you to understand how I feel about Francis.'

'That because he's who he is, he's allowed to get away with murder? Miss Dunham said the same sort of thing last night.'

'I know. I was there, remember?' She glanced at him, suddenly suspicious. But of what, she was not quite sure.

'Let's go riding,' Paul said. 'I could do with a breath of fresh air.'

'Oh, so could I!' Beatrice exclaimed happily, whatever shadow it was that had darkened her thoughts rapidly receding.

Margaret saw them leave from the schoolroom window, and experienced a pang of jealousy so strong that it frightened her. Beatrice Devereaux was the best friend she was ever likely to have, and she would have given everything she owned in the world not to have fallen in love with her husband.

Margaret had ignored Beatrice's advice to rest in bed. She felt tired and bruised, but did not wish to alarm the children or arouse Nanny Watkins's curiosity. Fortunately, India was a well-behaved child, and during school hours Mareth remained in the nursery. Margaret had set India some sums to puzzle over. Later, they would go for their walk.

Margaret thought back over the events of last night, but they were blurred, running together like the colours of a painting which had been left out in the rain. Only two things stood out clearly: her love for, and her anger with, Paul Devereaux. But why should she be angry that he was as he was? If she loved him, could she not accept him 'warts and all'?

'You expect too much of human nature, Maggie,' her father used to tell her. 'You have to learn to take people for what they are.'

She had been unable to accept that dictum then; she could not now. She wanted the people she loved to be perfect; and

72

she was sufficiently self-analytical to recognize this desire as a serious flaw in her own nature.

She tried to forget the previous evening; to think of Jessie and Daniel and wonder what sort of honeymoon they were having. Last night had been Jessie's wedding-night. She had slept for the first time with a man. Margaret was shaken by a little gust of silent laughter. Dear Jess! So prosaic, so unromantic. She would undoubtedly approach that part of her wifely duties as briskly and efficiently as she did all the rest. And, luckily, Daniel would see the humour of the situation.

'I've finished, Dunny.' India was carefully blotting her exercise book, with its neat little rows of figures. 'If I've done all my sums right, can we go into Port Isaac this afternoon? Auntie Go-go gave me half a crown to spend.' She raised a face of puzzlement as Margaret bent over her to collect the book. 'I thought Uncle Francis and Auntie Go-go were staying until Saturday. I wonder why they went away in such a hurry. They didn't even kiss Mareth and me goodbye. Wasn't that naughty of them?'

Seven

It was her first Christmas in England. This time last year, Margaret thought, as she looked from her bedroom window on Christmas morning, her father had been alive. Together they had gone to look at the lighted shops on Fifth Avenue and listen to the carol singers in Longacre Square. Everywhere there had been bustle and noise and laughter. Even the partially built Algonquin Hotel on West 44th Street had looked festive. And there had been so many people, smiling and wishing each other the compliments of the season. . . .

The gardens at Latchetts and the rising parkland beyond suddenly seemed oppressively quiet; lapped about by a strange, wild silence which spoke of deserted beaches and the lost, lonely crying of the gulls. The leafless trees spurted like fountains from the iron-hard ground, the wintry sun, low and red, netted in their branches. Margaret's homesickness grew. She longed for the stone canyons of New York.

This Christmas, she would have no one of her own. Beatrice had generously proposed a week's paid holiday if she wished to visit Jessie. But her sister had written to say that Daniel's mother was very ill, probably dying, so, after all, she had not gone.

'Then we must be your family,' Beatrice had said, and Margaret had responded with a smile she was far from feeling. She had hoped, by going to Bath, to escape from Paul Devereaux for a while. Daily proximity to him was tearing her apart.

Not that she saw much of him; even less than before. And when they did meet, he barely spoke to her. Earlier in the month, he had been privileged to visit the Poldhu Station and watch Guglielmo Marconi send the first wireless message across the Atlantic. On his return, he had been so excited that he had explained to everyone the marvellous invention of wireless telegraphy, herself included. Then, suddenly, in mid-sentence, he had stopped abruptly and turned away, addressing the rest of his remarks pointedly to Beatrice. Did he blame her for the rift between himself and his cousin?

As Christmas approached, Margaret's unhappiness had increased. The sense of being a stranger in a strange land grew. At least, she told herself that was the reason why she felt so miserable on this Christmas morning.

She looked at herself in the long pier glass which hung on the wall beside the wardrobe. She had made no concessions to the day's festivities, and had put on the plain grey skirt and white tucked blouse she normally wore for the schoolroom. There were no lessons today, nor for the coming week, but India had made her promise to visit the nursery as early as she could, in order to see what Father Christmas had brought.

As Margaret entered the bright, airy room, overlooking the sloping lawns and kitchen garden at the back of the house, India's face fell reproachfully.

'Oh, Dunny! This is Christmas. I thought you'd be wearing something pretty.'

'Sumfin' pitty,' echoed Mareth, but without much interest. She was busily unjointing a jointed wooden doll which she had found in her stocking that morning.

India's disappointment, however, was so real that Margaret felt mean-spirited. Because she was unhappy herself, was that any reason to mar the children's pleasure? She smiled down at India and gave the little girl a hug.

'I'm saving my party dress for later on,' she said. 'Your mama has invited me to have Christmas luncheon with you all.'

'I only wish it could have been for dinner, Maggie, dear,' Beatrice had said, when the invitation had been issued. 'But we have the Bastardos coming from Roscarrock in the evening.'

Margaret knew Henry and Charlotte Bastardo by sight; a rather decorous young couple, not long married, with a great air of self-consequence about them. They were deferential towards Paul because he was the cousin of a duke, but they regarded Beatrice with scarcely veiled suspicion. The daughter of a Yankee refrigerator manufacturer was, they felt, socially beneath them, but as Paul Devereaux had chosen Beatrice to be his wife they forced themselves to overcome their prejudice. It was hardly surprising, however, that Margaret's existence went entirely unremarked by either of them; a mere governess was beneath their notice.

'I'm glad you're having lunch with us, Dunny,' India said, putting up her face to be kissed. 'Come and see the baby-carriage Father Christmas has brought me.'

'Baby-cawidge,' came the inevitable echo from Mareth, who, having dismembered her doll, was now turning her attention to her sister's jack-in-the-box. Unobserved, she opened it and began tugging furiously at its spring.

Later in the morning, back in her own room after returning from the service at St Endymion's, Margaret remembered her promise to India to make herself pretty. She opened the mahogany wardrobe, in which her clothes hung sparsely. There really was no choice. She had only one pretty dress: the cream one she had worn at Jessie's wedding. It brought back memories of a day's shopping in Plymouth with her sister; a day of gossip and laughter and the delight of choosing new clothes. Afterwards, they had walked on the wind-swept Hoe, where Drake had played bowls before the Armada was sighted.

She slipped the dress over her head, smoothing the poplin across her hips and arranging the narrow jabot of Irish crochet – the poor woman's lace, she reflected wryly – at her throat. The high, boned collar concealed her neck, and the long sleeves ended in points which reached to the base of her fingers. Her hair was piled high on top of her head, its gleaming coils speared with a little pearl pin which had once belonged to her mother. Reluctantly, she picked up her carefully wrapped presents and went downstairs.

Margaret knew that the rest of the staff resented her presence at the family luncheon, and had demonstrated their displeasure by pointedly excluding her from the evening's entertainment belowstairs. She suspected Nanny Watkins to be the moving spirit behind this petty revenge. Nanny had never forgiven Margaret's friendship with young Betty Lewisham, nor the fact that, in the months since Jessie's marriage, mistress and governess had drawn closer together.

Margaret crossed the great hall, decorated with mistletoe and holly, the granite fireplace housing a blaze of sweet-smelling logs, and paused at the door of the music-room.

'We always give our presents in the music-room, before luncheon,' Beatrice had said.

Margaret knocked and went in.

It was a room which never failed to enchant her, with its high, intricately patterned plaster ceiling, its walls hung with William Morris's chrysanthemum wallpaper, a lovely old Broadwood piano across one corner, and a Kirkman Patent Improved Trichord in the middle. Two comfortable rubbed leather armchairs stood one on either side of the fireplace, and a deep, brocaded sofa ran almost the length of one wall. Over the fireplace hung a portrait of Beatrice, painted by Sargent. The long windows, which, on a sunny day, flooded the room with light, looked out across the gardens at the side of the east wing. Today, a Christmas tree, reaching from floor to ceiling, sparkled and shimmered in front of them.

India and Mareth were awaiting her arrival with impatience.

'Goody!' exclaimed the former, running to greet her. 'Now you're here, Dunny, we can begin.'

'You would think,' Beatrice said, laughing, 'that Father Christmas had overlooked the pair of them last night. You would never imagine that they'd been up since the crack of dawn opening all the things he left them.' She came forward and kissed Margaret's cheek. 'Happy Christmas, Maggie, dear. Your first in England.'

'You've already wished Dunny a merry Christmas, Mama,' India protested. 'This morning, before we went to church. Do, please, please, let's get on.'

Paul said nothing. He and Margaret had briefly exchanged the season's greetings earlier in the day. His whole attention now, seemed to be absorbed by Mareth.

'Pwesents,' declared that single-minded young lady, pointing to the pile beneath the tree. 'Maweth want her pwesents.'

'So you can destroy all those as well, I suppose, you monkey,' her father upbraided her. Everyone laughed.

The laughter seemed to ease the tension which had hung over the room like a pall; that and the uninhibited chatter of the girls, whose ears were not yet attuned to the constraints of their elders. Beatrice felt relief wash through her. She had been afraid that Paul was going to be difficult. Margaret must surely be aware of his dislike. She was never herself when he was around. She took a small package from beneath the tree and handed it to her friend.

'For you, Maggie, honey. From both of us.'

Margaret unwrapped the paper to reveal the jeweller's case inside. On a bed of velvet nestled a pair of earrings; silver filigree, each set with an emerald-green brilliant at its heart.

'I can't accept these,' she gasped.

'Don't be silly.' Beatrice slid an arm about her waist, and Margaret could smell her fragile, expensive perfume. 'They're nothing very much. Only brilliants.' Beatrice hesitated, conscious of sounding patronizing. She went on quickly: 'Paul chose them. He bought them months ago, in London. He said they were the colour of your eyes.'

Margaret looked up, startled, to meet Paul Devereaux's fleeting gaze. He turned away, stooping to hear something that India was saying.

'They're – they're lovely,' Margaret stammered.

'Yes.' Beatrice was staring at the earrings without seeing them, listening to the echoes of her own voice inside her head. How odd that the inconsistency of Paul's action, the even greater inconsistency of his words, had never occurred to her before. At the time, she had thought nothing of it. They always gave Christmas presents to all their staff, at Latchetts, Bladud House and Hill Street. There were so many to buy that Beatrice found it easier to accumulate them throughout the year, rather than make a last-minute dash to London in December. Paul occasionally contributed to her growing hoard by purchasing something for one of the men. But he had never bought a gift for one of the women before – and how peculiar that it should be for Margaret Dunham.

Beatrice looked from her husband to her friend and back again. Neither appeared to have the remotest interest in the

78

other. She was being foolish. Paul had never, in all the seven years of their marriage, given her the slightest reason to be jealous.

It was quiet in the room above the gatehouse. Margaret had not turned up the wick of the lamp, but the globe of the Albion paraffin heater made a soft red puddle of light. She leaned back in one of the wicker armchairs and tried not to remember that this was Christmas.

As she left the house, sounds of merriment had floated under the door of the warm and decorated kitchen. She had paid dearly for that meal with the family. The rest of the staff were uneasy with her now; afraid that any indiscretion would be reported back to Beatrice. No doubt Nanny Watkins had fostered this notion, even though she must know it to be untrue.

Margaret opened her eyes again and glanced at the watch which had been her bridesmaid's present from Daniel. She could just make out the time: ten o'clock. In the upstairs drawing-room, Christmas dinner over, Paul and Beatrice were entertaining their guests. In the nursery, under the nursery-maid's watchful eye, Mareth and India were asleep.

Margaret rose and fetched a rug from the cupboard where the toys were kept. It was used for dolls' picnics, on those days when the weather was too bad to venture out. She returned to her seat and spread it across her knees. She had changed from the cream dress into one of brown alpaca, but she was still cold, in spite of the warmth from the stove. She had not wanted to remain in her room, with the echoes of revelry from other parts of the house. She had not wanted to think of Paul and Beatrice together.

Yet she could not help but think of them, as she had done for months past; eating together, laughing and talking together, sleeping together. . . . Margaret moved restlessly, as though in pain. How cruel of life, to bring her thousands of miles from home to fall in love with another woman's husband.

The fault, dear Brutus . . . the words echoed mockingly inside her head, and she smiled wryly. Here was she, who had always believed in man's control over his own destiny, blaming fate like any adolescent schoolgirl. She sat up straighter

79

and reached for the lamp, intending to turn up the wick so that she could see to read her book – *A Christmas Carol* had seemed an appropriate choice for Christmas evening – but before she could do so, she heard someone ascending the gatehouse stairs.

So vivid was the memory of that night, two months ago, when the Duke had found her there alone that she sat petrified, her heart slamming against her ribs, her hands gripping the arms of her chair. Her eyes were fixed on the door, faintly outlined in the blackness of the wall. It opened and Paul Devereaux came in.

He blinked owlishly in the gloom. He had not been certain that she was there. He had looked in vain for the lamplight as he crossed the frost-bitten lawns, and it was only when he was close to the gatehouse that he had seen the faint, pinkish glow of the paraffin heater. He advanced slowly into the middle of the room and stopped on the other side of the table.

'Beatrice sent me to see if you were all right,' he said. 'We've only just realized that you're on your own. We had assumed you would be with the rest of the staff at the Christmas party.'

Her heart, which had stilled its frantic beating on first seeing him, now began to pound again. Margaret made a desperate attempt to sound normal.

'They didn't ask me.' She noted with satisfaction that her voice was quiet and steady. 'It's often the lot of governesses, I believe. They're neither upstairs nor down. Neither flesh nor fowl nor good red herring. In any case, I quite enjoy being on my own.'

'Do you?' He was clasping and unclasping his right hand as it hung at his side. He seemed more nervous than she was.

'I don't dislike it, at all events,' she answered.

He ignored this. 'Why are you being ostracized?' he asked bluntly. 'Is it because Beatrice treats you as a friend?'

'I suppose so. Jessie suffered in much the same way, but, of course, she had Daniel.'

'And you have no one.'

'I have the children. And, as I told you, I don't mind being alone.'

He had gradually moved closer to her chair, until now he stood over her. Like a man in a dream, he began pulling the pins from her piled-up hair, so that it tumbled about her shoulders in rich profusion, winking now bronze, now copper, in the light from the heater. He stooped and took hold of her hands, lifting her up into the circle of his arms. She went unresistingly. Her hands were cold with sweat and her legs were trembling. She felt as she did so often when she was dreaming; as though she were moving breast-high through water, wading through a running sea. . . .

He kissed her and her lips parted willingly under his. Somewhere in the park an owl hooted, the long, ululating cry dying away into the darkness, heralding a silence profounder than before.

'I love you,' he whispered against her cheek, and she answered with a low, sobbing moan.

The rug had fallen from her knees to the floor and he drew her down towards it. She had no strength to resist him, nor any desire to oppose his will. She felt mindless, floating on a wine-dark cloud of happiness. Here, in his arms, was the culmination of her twenty-one years; all the joys, the hopes, the longings. His hands were at her breasts, her thighs. No memory stirred of the repugnance she had felt when Francis Devereaux had done these things.

She felt him enter her, but even the pain did not seem to be hers; it was just the sweet agony of passion, the total merging of two minds and hearts. And when it was over, she could still feel him, as much a part of her flesh as the bones and sinews of her clinging arms. . . .

Margaret sat up abruptly, suddenly cold. She was shivering in every limb and her mouth felt dry. Guilt racked her from head to foot.

'Beatrice,' she said and stumbled to her feet, tugging any-how at her disarranged clothes.

He got up with her, imprisoning her hands once more in his.

'I love you,' he repeated. 'Beatrice need never know.'

Margaret laughed wildly. 'Of course she'd know. Under her own roof? Do you think I wouldn't know if you fell in love with some other woman?'

'We could arrange it so she need not suspect.' Margaret heard the rising note of panic in his voice. 'You must resign as the children's governess. Go away somewhere, where I can

81

visit you. These sorts of arrangements are made all the time.'

'By people like your cousin,' she answered bitterly. 'But such arrangements are not for us.'

'Don't you love me?' The cry was like a little boy's, begging for reassurance, and she blinked back the tears.

'Yes, I love you. I don't know why, but God help me, I do. But I won't become your mistress while Beatrice is alive. I won't betray her trust a second time. We both owe her far more than we can ever repay.'

He turned away from her, dressing in grim silence, then went to stand by one of the windows, looking out into the winter's night. She gazed helplessly at his tall figure, at the implacable set of his shoulders and the arrogant tilt of his head. Not for the first time, she recognized the haughtiness, as well as the sweetness, of his nature; an arrogance which stemmed from centuries of the Norman's domination over the base-born Saxon at his gate. She sat down, holding on to the sudden spurt of enmity between them as one of those Saxons might have clung, in battle, to his shield.

Paul swung round to face her again, and, with a movement of impatience, turned up the wick of the lamp. A golden radiance flooded the centre of the room. He leaned down and grasped her wrists.

'Are you asking me to forget you? Are you saying that you can forget me?'

'I'm demanding no promises from either of us,' she answered with a catch in her voice. 'I'm saying that I must go away as soon as possible, and that, in the meantime, we must see one another as little as we can.'

He released her wrists and straightened his back. 'Well, I do ask for a promise,' he said. 'Just one.' She raised her eyes questioningly to his. 'I'm asking you – begging you – not to return to New York. I must know that if ever I need you, I can reach you, at least within a matter of days.'

Looking into his eyes, she saw the bewilderment in them; the confusion of a man always used to getting his own way. Since he was eighteen years old, when his father died, it must have been rarely, if ever, that anyone had opposed his will. But that basic sweetness of disposition which made him a fond and doting father, an indulgent husband, rather than the tyrant of hearth and nursery which so many of his contemporaries had become, prevented him from being angry. He was hurt and resentful of her attitude, but that was all. One day, he might even be grateful. He had a deep affection for Beatrice, and Margaret's decision had spared him the unhappiness which deception would have brought in its train.

'I promise I won't go home to New York.'

She experienced a stab of self-reproach because the promise was so easy to give. She had no wish to return to America; no desire to put the wide, rolling Atlantic between herself and everyone she held most dear.

'Where will you go?' he asked. 'What reason will you give to Beatrice for quitting your post after such a short time?'

'I shall go to Jessie for a while, if she'll have me. I have a little money saved. I can pay my way until I manage to find fresh employment. As for Beatrice, I shall tell her that I have become too lonely since Jessie's marriage to remain. Besides, Jess is expecting a baby, and might be glad to have someone of her own near at hand.'

He felt a moment's surprise that she could already have thought things out so clearly. He was still too caught up in the turmoil of his emotions to be able to make any plans. He had no idea what he was going to say to Beatrice and the Bastardos when he finally returned to the house. What reason could he offer for the length of time he had been gone?

Margaret, braiding up her hair, said, as though she were able to read his thoughts: 'Tell Beatrice the truth; that I have decided, after Christmas, to quit my post as governess, and that you have been trying to make me change my mind.'

'And won't you?' he cried, crushing her against his breast and kissing her.

This time, however, she did not yield. Gently she freed herself.

'You know I can't,' she said. 'Think of Beatrice. Think of the children. Think of the son you might one day have.'

He made a strange, harsh noise, then swung on his heel. He went from the room without a backward glance, and Margaret was left staring at the door. Everything was misted with her tears.

Eight

The April day was cold. Now and then, sunshine broke
through the clouds to lend a ghostly radiance to the graveside
scene. Across the open grave, Margaret glanced at Jessie's
composed face and Daniel's strained one. Near the raw gash
of earth which marked old Mrs Cooper's final resting place
other graves stood, neglected and rotting. One cracked, grey
stone thrust through a smother of ivy, like a bone from a
broken skin. All around Bath, the flat-crested hills were
etched against a racing sky.

Margaret wore her grey alpaca coat and skirt, and had
retrimmed her hat with matching ribbon. A mourning band
encircled her left sleeve. The other members of the little party
were more funereal. Jessie and Daniel, Hugh Stafford and his
son William, an ugly, gravel-voiced young man, all wore scarcely
relieved black. Only the white shirts of the men and the cold,
pinched faces above them added some tonality to the group.

'So that's that,' Jessie said, fifteen minutes later, as they
walked briskly from the cemetery and out to where the funeral
carriage was waiting. 'A merciful relief, after all her suffering.'
She looked over her shoulder at Hugh Stafford and his son.
'You'll come back with us and have a bite to eat?' She did not
wait to hear their reply, knowing full well that they were
unlikely to refuse. She heaved herself into the carriage, spurn-
ing various offers of assistance, and settled her spreading
figure in one corner. Even though six months pregnant, Jessie
hated any sort of fuss. Margaret followed her and Daniel shut
the door.

'I'll walk with Hugh and William,' he said. 'I feel like a
breath of fresh air.'

Jessie called to the driver that they were ready, and the carriage pulled away from the kerb. The muffled clopping of the horses' hooves sounded loud in the silence. Through the window, Margaret could just catch a glimpse of the nodding black plumes.

'That went off very well,' Jessie remarked with satisfaction. She had done her duty. She had nursed her mother-in-law devotedly during the six months since her marriage, and could look forward with a clear conscience to a little peace and quiet. In her own mind, she had already redecorated the rooms above the shop and thrown out much of the dowdy, old-fashioned furniture. She eyed her sister sharply. 'Have you thought any more about Hugh Stafford's offer of marriage?'

'You won't let me forget it,' Margaret pointed out.

Jessie pursed her lips. 'You could do worse. A great deal worse. He's manager of the Longreach mine. Paul Devereaux thinks very highly of him, so you can be sure he pays him well. I know Hugh's twenty-five years your senior, but young men don't always bring happiness. A mature man has sown his wild oats and is more willing to settle down.'

'Jess, I'm the same age as his son. Don't you think William might resent me?'

'Why should he?' Jessie asked practically. 'A woman of any sort about the house is better than no woman at all. I don't know why Hugh Stafford didn't remarry long ago. Daniel says there has been no lack of women willing to have him.'

Margaret made no reply, leaning back in her own corner and watching the soot-grimed streets of Bath pass in slow procession. She had forgotten Hugh Stafford's friendship with old Mrs Cooper, and it had been something of a shock, when she first arrived to stay with Dan and Jessie, to find him such a frequent visitor in Green Street. Whenever he was in Bath, which was at least once a week, he made a point of calling at the shop. Daniel hinted that Hugh's visits had increased since Margaret's arrival.

If her sister and brother-in-law had suspected some hidden reason for Margaret's sudden departure from the Devereaux household, neither had probed beneath the surface of her explanation that she was lonely. Daniel's natural delicacy had prevented him asking any awkward questions: Jessie quite simply did not want to know.

'If she's made a fool of herself, I'd rather not be told,' she had said to Daniel, in the privacy of their bedroom. 'After all, I talked Beatrice into giving her the job in the first place.'

Daniel thought it improbable that either of the Devereauxs could be persuaded into anything contrary to their natural inclinations, but he had said nothing. He had his own ideas as to why Margaret had left their employ. He saw more than Jessie, and remembered that the leather-bound. copy of Elizabeth Barrett Browning's *Sonnets from the Portuguese*, which lay on Margaret's bedside table, had formerly belonged to the library at Latchetts. How she had come by it, he could only guess. He knew she would never steal it.

The carriage turned left at the Sydney Hotel and rumbled down the wide, tree-lined expanse of Great Pulteney Street. Margaret glanced at the prim Georgian exterior of Bladud House as they passed. It was a year ago – a whole year – since she had walked down the area steps and into the life of Paul Devereaux. She could not think of it without being near to tears.

She jutted her chin and refused to cry. She had made her choice, the only right and honourable choice, even though it would have been so easy to do otherwise. Beatrice had begged her not to go. India had sobbed: 'You can't leave me, Dunny, you can't!' Mareth, without really understanding what it was all about, had lifted her voice in sympathy with her sister.

'It's those goddamned servants,' Beatrice, who so rarely swore, had fumed at Paul. 'I'll sack the lot of them, rather than part with Maggie.'

'It wouldn't do any good,' Paul had answered with constraint. 'She wants to go. It's understandable. When she came to England she had no idea that Jessie would be leaving to get married.'

Beatrice had pleaded and argued, but to no avail. Margaret had left for Bath the following week.

Daniel had welcomed her with unfeigned pleasure, genuinely glad, Margaret had suspected, to have someone other than his wife and ailing mother to talk to; someone with interests more akin to his own. She recalled one evening when they had sat, one on either side of the fire, in the little sitting-room above the shop while Daniel propounded his theory on English class-consciousness.

'It goes back to the Norman Conquest, my dear girl. For three hundred years after that, until Chaucer came along in the fourteenth century and wrote the first popular novel in the English tongue, England was a country where peasants and nobles spoke different languages, wore different clothes, had different names. To this day, that feeling of "them" and "us" has never been eradicated.'

Jessie had come in just then, her plump face agitated, to say that his mother was asking why Daniel had not been in to see her.

'I didn't tell her that you prefer to waste your time in idle chatter,' she had scolded him sharply. 'And you, Maggie,' she had added, her back ramrod stiff with displeasure, 'can give me a hand by starting the ironing.'

Had Jessie been truly pleased to give her a home? Margaret wondered, as the carriage skirted the fountain in Laura Place. She had been shocked at her sister's throwing away what she considered to be the chance of a lifetime; although she could appreciate that between Beatrice's attitude on the one side, and that of the servants on the other, Margaret's position in the Devereaux household might well have become untenable. Jessie had consoled herself with the thought that Margaret would soon find another place. With the reference Paul Devereaux had given her, how could she possibly fail?

Jessie had not seen that Margaret was too young and too beautiful to be accepted by any household where there was a susceptible father, son or husband. Prospective employers took one look at the green eyes, the gently voluptuous figure, the skeins of auburn hair, and hurriedly declined her services. Now, in April, Margaret was growing desperate as her small store of money began to run out. She could not become a burden on Jessie and Daniel. The shop barely earned them a living, and they would soon have another mouth to feed.

There was one way of escape open to her which would ensure her a good home and a place in society: marriage with Hugh Stafford. He had proposed to her only the third time after meeting her again, and had been pressing her to accept his offer ever since. Jessie thought her mad to refuse.

He had called one Sunday afternoon at the end of March, and invited Margaret to go for a drive in his new pony and trap. While she hesitated, Jessie had accepted for her, and Hugh had taken her to the little mining village of Longreach, one of those collections of drab streets and houses, slag-heaps and tired, sad-eyed, grey-faced men, scattered so incongruously amidst the cow pastures and apple orchards of Somerset's rural green. Daniel had once told her that coal-mining was more hazardous and more arduous in north Somerset than anywhere else in Britain, because the underground seams were so narrow.

Hugh had proudly shown her round the grey stone house, standing in its own garden, at the end of the village street. It was badly neglected inside, but Hugh had promised her a clean sweep of everything she did not like, and the freedom to redecorate and refurnish as she chose, if only she would consent to be his wife. Margaret had stalled, asking for time to think it over, and had been glad to get home – until it occurred to her that Jessie's was not, and never could be, really home. She had no home. She should not have given her promise to Paul. She should have gone back to New York while she had the money to pay for her passage. Now that was nearly all gone.

The funeral carriage, its width almost blocking Green Street's medievally narrow thoroughfare, drew up before Cooper's – High Class Sweets and Confectionery. The two women alighted and thanked the driver, and Jessie unlocked the door. Margaret followed her through the shop and upstairs to the living-room. Jessie took off her black hat with a sigh of relief and sank into the nearest chair.

'Make a cup of tea, Maggie, would you?' she said. 'Then you could lay the table. The men shouldn't be long.'

Margaret went into the kitchen and filled the kettle with water, then put it on the range to boil. Jessie had become as avid a tea-drinker as any native-born Englishwoman, but it was not this fact which caused Margaret to grimace at her reflection in the mirror which hung beside the sink. She had suddenly realized that, for some weeks past, Jessie had been omitting the word 'please'. Margaret was ceasing to be a guest and was rapidly becoming someone whom her sister took for granted. A little longer, and she could easily turn into an unpaid drudge.

Margaret warmed the teapot as Jessie had taught her to do and spooned in the requisite amount of tea from the caddy. She poured on the boiling water and left it to brew. While she was in her bedroom, removing her hat and coat, she heard Daniel and the two Staffords come in.

'Find out where Maggie is with that tea,' her sister's voice called peevishly from the living-room.

Margaret sat down on the bed, her hands fiercely clasping its edge. What was she to do? She could not go on living on Daniel's charity and she was unable to find another post as governess. She could work in a factory, as her father had done, but that would seem like a betrayal of all the sacrifices Herbert Dunham had made, all the hardships he had endured, so that his clever younger daughter could be put through college. She shivered, suddenly cold, and thought of Paul. Her hand went out automatically to the book he had given her. She had found it in her room at Latchetts on the morning of her departure. There had been no note, only an inscription on the fly leaf – To M.D. from P.D., January, 1902 – and a piece of paper, marking a page. She had turned the leaves with trembling fingers and read the words he had underlined. *Go from me. Yet I feel that I shall stand Henceforward in thy shadow.*

She withdrew her hand now from the book without opening it, the hopeless tears rolling silently down her cheeks. It was foolish to torture herself: Paul was not for her. He was the husband of Beatrice, whom they both loved; and even if he were not, he would not marry her. Margaret knew enough of English society by this time to realize that it would be social ruin for him to marry his children's governess. He would be an outcast, ostracized by family and friends.

There was a tap on her bedroom door and Daniel called softly: 'May I come in?'

Margaret blew her nose and hurriedly dabbed at her eyes with her handkerchief. 'Yes, of course,' she answered, with tolerable composure.

Her brother-in-law opened the door and advanced a pace or two inside the room.

'Jessie's pouring the tea,' he said. 'I found it in the kitchen. Come and have a cup. You must be chilled from standing at the graveside.'

Margaret got up from the bed, averting her face so that he should not see that she had been crying.

'I was just coming,' she lied. 'Thank you for taking the tea in. I'd forgotten all about it.' She grimaced. 'I shall be taken to task by Jess for failing in my duty.'

He frowned. 'You're not a servant. Never mind Jess. Leave her to me.' He came across to her and forced her round towards the window, so that he could study her face. 'Have you been crying? Has Jessie upset you?'

'No, of course she hasn't. I'm used to her funny ways. It's just the day, the occasion. I hardly knew your mother, but funerals are always sad.'

'It's not really that, is it?' Daniel asked gently. When she did not reply, he added: 'You can tell me. You see, I understand. I've loved Beatrice Devereaux for years.'

Margaret was startled. 'Does . . . does she know?' she stammered.

Daniel laughed wryly. 'Good heavens, no! I've never told anyone but you. I've just worshipped from afar. It sounds silly, doesn't it? But she's been the inspiration for many of my poems.'

'Well, I've never thought for a moment it could have been Jessie. I assume that Jess doesn't suspect?'

'Such an idea would never cross her mind; and even if it did, she would dismiss it as romantic nonsense. If I admitted it, she'd tell me to "grow up" or "be my age". Unfortunately, as I know to my cost, love is no less painful, no less profound, because it's never expressed or requited.' He shrugged philosophically. 'One cannot control one's affections.'

Margaret gave him a quick hug. 'No,' she whispered.

'And you?' he asked shyly, nodding towards the green, leather-bound book. 'You're luckier than I am. At least he knows you love him, and loves you in return.'

Margaret looked out over the roof-tops of the neighbouring shops and houses.

'I suppose,' she said in a low voice, more to herself than to Daniel, 'I could have stayed and become his mistress. But

90

neither of us could bring ourselves to hurt her. We both love her too much for that.'

'I'm glad you couldn't,' Daniel said simply, and left it at that. 'Now, we'd better go and drink our tea, or Jess will be wondering what's happened to us.'

They smiled at each other, like conspirators. At the door, Margaret hesitated. 'You know that Hugh Stafford wants me to marry him?'

'Jess has mentioned it,' Daniel answered with his ironic, lop-sided grin.

Margaret laughed and kissed her brother-in-law's cheek. 'You're a very perceptive and very kind man. A gentleman in the truest sense of the word.'

He flushed with embarrassment, but he was pleased, nonetheless. She preceded him along the passageway into the living-room.

Hugh Stafford and his son were seated on the brown plush sofa in front of the fire. Jessie, a tray of tea-things placed before her on a low table, glanced up in annoyance as her husband and sister came in.

'Where have you two been? Looking at some book or other, I'll be bound.' She handed Hugh his tea. 'I don't hold with book-learning, except for the gentry. What good is it to the likes of us?'

Daniel sat on the other end of the sofa, next to his guests. 'You'd never think, would you,' he demanded of the room at large, 'that my wife is a native-born New Yorker?'

'I don't know what you mean,' Jessie countered, growing even more annoyed. She jerked her head at the empty arm-chair on the opposite side of the fireplace. 'That's your seat, over there. Why don't you use it? Then Maggie can sit next to Mr Stafford.'

The ploy was so blatant that even Hugh looked uncomfort-able. William Stafford sniggered.

'It's all right, Daniel, stay where you are.' Margaret pressed a hand on her brother-in-law's shoulder. 'I'll lay the table for the meal. Do you want the best plates and cutlery, Jessie?'

The meal – ham, pickles, cheese and another pot of hot, strong tea – was finished. Daniel leant back in his chair and unbuttoned his waistcoat.

'That was lovely, Jess. A real good blow-out.'

Jessie clicked her tongue disapprovingly. Why could Daniel never behave like a gentleman? Like Hugh Stafford, for instance? Jessie looked at her guest. A little rough in appearance, perhaps, but his table-manners were impeccable. Jessie had no patience with her sister, turning down a perfectly respectable offer of marriage. Good men did not grow on trees.

'Can I give you another slice of cake, Mr Stafford?' Jessie asked, cutting a thick wedge from the richly spiced fruit cake in front of her. 'It's made from a recipe of my grandmother Dunham's.'

Hugh shook his head, laying a hand on his distended paunch. 'I've done very well, thank you, Mrs Cooper,' he said. 'An excellent tea.' He looked across the table at Margaret and continued diffidently: 'I wonder, Miss Dunham, if you would consider taking a walk with me before it gets dark? That is, if Mr and Mrs Cooper don't object.'

'Of course not,' Jessie beamed, before Margaret had time to gather her wits. 'William can wait for you here. I'll show him my views of New York. A walk in the fresh air will do you both good.'

'Hold hard, Jessie,' Daniel remonstrated quietly. 'Perhaps you should allow Margaret to speak for herself. After all, it's her that Hugh is asking.'

Jessie was dumbfounded. It was rarely that Daniel reprimanded her, and never in public. She looked as though she were about to burst into tears.

'It's all right, Daniel,' Margaret said quickly, getting to her feet. 'I'll go for a walk with Mr Stafford.' She saw the query in his kind eyes, and, reaching out, touched the back of his hand. 'It really is all right,' she reassured him.

'If you're certain,' he muttered.

'Of course she's certain. She wouldn't say so if she weren't.' Jessie pushed back her chair and stood up too, her cheeks pink with misery.

Daniel sighed to himself. In her condition he had no right to upset her. He only hoped that Margaret knew what she was doing.

Margaret went to her bedroom and put on her coat. She picked up her hat and speared it with hatpins to the heavy coils of hair, watching her reflection in the mirror. Why had she decided to accept Hugh's invitation? He was going to propose again, and she had no idea what she was going to say in reply.

Her gloves were lying on the bedside table, where she had dropped them, next to the book of Elizabeth Barrett Browning's poems. Beatrice was a young woman, Margaret reflected; she had all her life ahead of her. And she herself was also young; younger than Beatrice. She, too, had to fashion a life for herself. She could not afford to have Paul Devereaux standing forever in her shadow. But was marriage to Hugh Stafford, who had always filled her with a kind of repugnance, the only alternative? She was slowly coming to the conclusion that it was.

Circumstances had trapped her. She had to remain in England; she had no money to escape, and she had given her promise to Paul. She had no job, nor, it seemed, any prospect of getting one, unless she went to work in one of the Bristol factories. Even marriage to Hugh Stafford was preferable, surely, to that. She resolutely tried to ignore the whisper of her conscience that by marrying Hugh she would be linking herself, however tenuously, to Paul. As if to prove this treacherous thought a lie, she picked up the book of poems and locked it away in her travelling trunk, which stood in a corner of the bedroom. Besides, she told herself defiantly, Hugh might have no intention of asking her a fourth time to marry him.

He did, of course, as she had known very well that he would. They walked down by the river, the weir and Pulteney Bridge behind them. The shops on the bridge hung in the evening air like mystical fairy palaces. Long saffron ribbons of light threaded the western sky, and a fragile crescent moon swam up from behind a tree. They paused, watching its pale radiance reflected in the softly rippling water.

Margaret's hands grasped the tortoiseshell clasp of her handbag as though it were a lifeline. She realized that the moment had come when she had to make up her mind. Some instinct warned her that if she refused him now, Hugh would not ask her again.

He had removed his hat and was twisting it awkwardly between his hands, his ugly, florid face creased with anxiety, his close-cropped hair, dusty as a fleece, springing in tight, grizzled curls all over his head. His eyes, with their light greyish-blue irises, were staring mutely into hers, his stocky, compact frame placed squarely in front of her, as though to prevent her running away.

He wondered why he wanted to marry this girl, who was young enough to be his daughter. Had he lived some centuries earlier, he would probably have accused her of witchcraft. As it was, he simply knew that she was the most beautiful woman he had ever seen, and the thought of possessing that body, of running his hands through that fiery hair, filled him with a torment of longing. He had thought of her constantly for a year now, ever since his first glimpse of her in the drawing-room at Bladud House, and this unslaked passion was driving him mad.

'Miss Dunham – Margaret,' he blurted, 'will you marry me?' She was aware of his circumstances, knew that he could support her. There was no point in covering old ground.

Margaret was cold. She wanted to return to the warmth of the flat above the shop. She wanted, suddenly, to bask in her sister's approval. She wanted to make Jess happy.

She took a deep breath and answered formally: 'Thank you, Mr Stafford. I should be honoured to become your wife.'

Part Two 1907

Love wol not be constreyned by maistrye

Nine

'I was glad you could come, if only for a day or two,' Hilda said, squeezing Margaret's arm affectionately. 'I was afraid Hugh wouldn't approve of your visit.'

Margaret laughed shortly. 'He didn't. I decided to come, just the same. The children are staying at Jessie's.'

Behind them, Sergei Zhirov closed and locked the door of the tiny house in Tabard Street where he and Hilda had lived since their marriage, three months earlier. They had two rooms above a greengrocer's shop, an all-purpose living-room and a bedroom. Last night, the night of her arrival, Margaret had slept fitfully on an old horsehair sofa, her nose assailed by the pungent smell of the bubble and squeak which had accompanied the bacon for supper. Apart from the discomfort of not being able to lie out straight, she had been worried about Lilian and Ralph: it was the first time they had been separated from their mother.

At least, she had worried about Lilian. Two-and-a-half-year-old Ralph was a sturdy, aggressive boy, just like his father. He had the same closely curling hair, which covered his scalp like a woolly mat, and the same very light blue-grey eyes. Lilian, who would be four next month, took after her mother, auburn-haired, green-eyed and fiercely independent. Only Margaret knew how warmly affectionate was her underlying nature. Lilian did not make friends easily, and reserved her love for the handful of people whom she trusted: her mother, her brother, her adored uncle Daniel and her cousin, Mark Cooper. Jessie's brusque ways intimidated the child, and she felt as uneasy in her aunt's company as she did in her father's, although with a lot less reason.

Lilian was more affected by the quarrels between her parents than either her step-brother or Ralph. The latter was too young, as yet, to accept the raised voices and bitter words as other than normal; while William ranged himself on the side of his father. He had never cared for his step-mother, and had been against the marriage from the beginning. The constant rows justified him in his opinion. But Lilian had been frightened of Hugh ever since one night, a year ago, when, waking from a bad dream, she had gone downstairs in search of her mother. She could hear her father shouting even before she opened the kitchen door, and had been just in time to see him deal her mother a vicious blow. Margaret, recoiling, had hit her head on a cupboard door and lost consciousness for several seconds. Hugh's frantic remorse and attempts to revive Margaret had in no way softened his daughter's feelings. From that day on, Lilian would never kiss her father, nor even speak to him unless she were forced to do so. Hugh became convinced that it was Margaret's fault; that she persistently influenced the child against him.

It was one of Hugh's most infuriating traits of character that he could never accept the blame for anything. But what had really soured their marriage, almost from the start, was Margaret's inability to pretend she loved him. She had been prepared, having married him, to do anything else; to be an exemplary wife; to make him a good home and minister to his and William's creature comforts. She had done everything he asked of her in bed; borne his two children; but she could not feign the love he demanded as a right. Two months after their wedding, he had blacked both her eyes, and she had realized for the first time that beneath the apparently stolid exterior was a man of violent temper. She had also realized that some sixth sense, warning her of this, had been the reason why he had always repelled her.

Common sense prompted her to leave him before she became pregnant, but guilt would not let her do it. She had made use of him when she agreed to marry him, and she owed him something. He must understand, however, that she could not love him on demand: he must give her time, and then her affection might grow.

Hugh refused to understand. He refused to countenance

her attitude, even though she had made it plain before their wedding that she was not in love with him. To Hugh, there was a simple answer to every problem: brute force. He would make Margaret love him, even if he had to put the fear of God into her to do it. It had worked with his first wife, who had been frightened enough to do and say anything he wished. His armour of self-confidence had not been pierced by any disturbing suspicion that Elsa's dutiful expressions of affection had all been lies.

Margaret, however, would not be browbeaten. Physical violence only made her more obstinate, and if she was afraid of him she kept her fear well hidden. Hugh could not tolerate defiance, and things went from bad to worse, the rows becoming more frequent and his outbreaks of rage more violent.

Margaret often wondered how much longer she could stand it, and had, in moments of despair, even contemplated taking the children and running away to Paul. Once she had even written him a letter, and had only stopped herself posting it at the very last minute, as she stood in front of the Longreach pillar-box. She had forced herself to think of Beatrice and Hugh, two people so utterly different, but to whom she owed loyalty and what she could muster of affection.

She saw Daniel and Jessie and their five-year-old son, Mark, every Saturday and Sunday, when the two families exchanged weekly visits. If her sister and brother-in-law suspected the state of affairs between herself and Hugh, they declined to comment. Daniel did not want to know, or he might have felt obliged to intervene in the situation, while Jessie blamed Margaret for any failures or problems of her marriage.

'You don't appreciate how fortunate you are,' she would say enviously, inspecting the rooms at Laurel Cottage; although the word 'cottage' was a euphemism as far as the ugly, square, grey stone building was concerned. 'A whole house, and a garden for the children to play in, instead of just a few rooms above a shop and trips to Sydney or Henrietta Gardens.'

'And slag-heaps instead of Georgian terraces to look at!' Margaret always tried to make light of the disparity between their circumstances. What she really wanted to say was: 'And

Hugh for a husband instead of Daniel,' but she doubted if her sister would appreciate that difference in quite the same way. Margaret could guess how her brother-in-law irritated Jessie with his total lack of interest in the business, and his unworldly attitude towards life. But the sisters had stopped confiding in one another.

Hilda's invitation to spend a few days with her in London had arrived unexpectedly a week ago. Their correspondence had flagged in recent years, and this was the first letter Margaret had received in more than six months. The news that Hilda and Sergei were married had come as a complete surprise.

'When Sergei asked me, I decided it was now or never,' Hilda had written, in her almost indecipherable scrawl, 'or I could see myself looking after Ma and Dad and the children for the rest of my life. Betty is old enough, and earning enough, to take on the responsibility for a while, and Marjorie is working as well, now. The old house near Pocock Street was pulled down, as I think you know, and the new place in Walworth Road is not nearly so bad. Cleaner and less bug-infested. Sergei and I have a couple of rooms over a green-grocer's shop in Tabard Street. Nothing fancy, and I can't offer you a bed, but we have a sofa plenty big enough for you to sleep on. Please say you'll come. I should so like to see you again.'

Margaret had not hesitated. The desire to get away from Longreach was so overpowering that neither the thought of the sofa nor the claims of her children could deter her. She had listened impassively to everything Hugh had to say on the subjects of her 'common friends' and 'low connections', and then announced calmly that she was going.

'Lilian and Ralph can stay with Jessie. I'll arrange it with her when I see her on Saturday. Mrs Bragg can come up and cook for you and William. She'll be glad of the extra money. And I warn you, Hugh, if you make any more fuss than you've done already, I might stay away for good.'

She was not sure quite how much of an empty threat that was. She only knew that, one day, she would be unable to endure her present existence any longer.

'It isn't just Hugh,' she had told Hilda last night, when

supper had been cleared away and, together with Sergei, they were sitting in front of the fire which sputtered cheerfully in the tiny grate, listening to the April rain as it pattered against the windows. There had been something about the claustrophobic atmosphere of the little room which inspired confidences. Margaret had talked more about her affairs to Hilda in half-an-hour than she had done to Jessie in the previous five years. 'It's the whole business of mining which upsets me. Hugh says it's none of my concern, but my father wouldn't have thought so. Do you know that when the coal is brought to the surface, it's sieved for dirt? And if it *is* dirty, then the men of that shift are each fined two and sixpence out of their wages? God knows, miners earn barely enough to keep body and soul together as it is. Another thing. It sometimes takes the men three quarters of an hour to get from the shaft-bottom to the coal-face, and they don't earn a penny until they actually start hewing coal.'

Sergei had become very animated at that juncture. 'You cannot blame your husband for these things,' he had shouted, waving his arms and knocking over the clothes horse on which all Hilda's clean washing was airing. She had been as indifferent to the mishap as Sergei, letting everything lie where it was, on the floor. 'He is only the . . . what do you call it? What do you call it? The manager. Yes! The colliery manager,' he repeated excitedly, in response to the prompting of his wife. 'It is the employers who are the villains! Their only concern is to make money out of the exploitation of human flesh. It is the owner of the mine who gets rich!' And he had plunged into a long, political dissertation, in which the words 'Marx' and '*Das Kapital*' were heard over and over again, and to which Margaret paid little heed, because she was thinking of Paul.

She had tried for a long time to persuade herself that Paul was not responsible for conditions at the Longreach mine; that he was, to a great extent, kept in the dark by Hugh. She still believed this to be true, in part, but it was some time since she had been able to exonerate him entirely. He must be aware, as all mine owners were, of the conditions necessary to make coal-mining a profitable concern. The trouble was that Paul had been brought up as a member of only one of those 'two nations' outlined by Disraeli, between whom there was

'no sympathy and no intercourse . . . the rich and the poor.'
As a foreigner, like Sergei, Margaret could recognize that lack
of communication and understanding better, perhaps, than
could Paul himself.

She must not think about him! She loved him too much;
hated him too much; never wanted to see him again; longed
for him every day of her life.

As they crossed London Bridge, she asked Hilda: 'Where
are we going? Where is Sergei taking us tonight?'

Hilda smiled guiltily. 'It's a political meeting in Southgate
Street. In Whitechapel. I hope you don't mind. I'm afraid you
won't understand much of what's going on. The people concerned are all Russian.'

'It is the third Russian Social Democratic Party Congress,'
Sergei said, catching Margaret up on her other side. 'It should
have been held in Copenhagen, but the Danish authorities
refused permission at the last moment. Also the Swedish,
when the delegates moved to Malmö. Then, fortunately, your
Mr George Lansbury invited them here.'

'Margaret's American,' his wife corrected him, but Sergei
only shrugged and muttered something about it being all the
same. 'In any case,' he added, as a kind of *non sequitur*, 'Lenin
and Krupskaya know London well. They lived here, in
Holford Square, three or four years ago. Many of the men you
will see tonight left Russia with only the clothes they stand up
in, so that they should not arouse the suspicion of the *Okhrana*.
That is the Tsar's secret police.' He spat on the pavement to
the indignation of a passer-by. 'After the revolution, when
Bloody Nicholas is swept away, also *Nemka* – the German
woman, his wife – there will be no more *Okhrana*. No more
secret police. These men have risked much to be here tonight.'

'But how are they managing, if they have no money and no
clothes?' Margaret wanted to know, and received the impression that Sergei was reluctant to answer.

Eventually, however, he said: 'Money has been provided by
Mr Joseph Fels, of Fels Naphtha Soap.'

'You mean capitalists have their uses, after all?' Margaret
queried, suppressing the tremor of amusement in her voice.

Sergei turned red and refused to comment. When they
arrived at the Reverend F. R. Swan's Brotherhood Church in

Southgate Street, he ushered Margaret and his wife inside, with instructions to sit at the back and wait for him while he spoke to some of the other people present.

Margaret glanced around the narrow, bare hall, with its high lancet windows, and reflected, not for the first time, on the bleakness of the extreme forms of Protestantism. How could love be expected to flow, either to God or to one's fellow men, in these arid and barren surroundings? Similar thoughts must have passed through Hilda's mind, because she turned her head and grimaced, indicating her dislike of the chapel.

Sergei returned and sat beside them on the hard wooden pew. He was grinning.

'Gorky tells me that Lenin is fussing like an old mother hen. He is staying at the Imperial Hotel in Russell Square, and Lenin arrived last night to inspect the sheets, to make sure that they were not damp.' Sergei chuckled and squeezed his wife's hand. 'He says he knows how lax the English are over such matters. And Krupskaya has invited us to go with them to the music-hall tomorrow night. Lenin adores clowns.'

Margaret nodded towards a young man who was standing in the aisle at the front of the hall, looking for an empty seat.

'Who is that?' she asked. 'The one with the fierce eyes and the moustache?'

Sergei followed her gaze. 'Oh, him! I don't know his name, but we call him Stalin. Vladimir Ilyich – Lenin, that is – does not like him. Neither does Trotsky.' And Sergei indicated a young Jew, sitting not far from Maxim Gorky.

Promptly at seven o'clock, a man in a morning-coat, high collar and silk tie – 'Plekhanov,' whispered Sergei in Margaret's ear – rose to declare the congress open. After him there were many speakers, all very excited and voluble in what Hilda described as typically Russian fashion; but only one, the small, balding, bearded man whom Sergei referred to as Lenin, dominated the proceedings. Although unable to understand what he was saying, Margaret found herself spellbound by the force of Lenin's personality. The deep, guttural voice rolled sonorously around the packed hall, condemning, so Sergei informed her afterwards, all those who were against the Bolsheviks: the Mensheviks, the Kadets, Trotsky and his clique of supporters, landowners both in

Russia and elsewhere, the Tsarist government and the loyal Russian peasants. He was plainly trying to sway his audience to his own way of thinking, but, in the end, when a resolution was voted upon, it was the Mensheviks, Sergei growled angrily, who carried the day.

'But Vladimir Ilyich will come again,' he added. 'He will not be denied.'

Margaret could well believe it. Although she knew little of Russian revolutionary politics, she could recognize a born leader when she saw one. And Vladimir Ilyich Ulyanov, otherwise called Lenin, was a man of potent charm. It was a charm, Margaret reflected, the more powerful because of its underlying streak of ruthlessness. This man, whose elder brother had been hanged for treasonable activities while Vladimir was still a boy, burned with a fanatical hatred for Tsar Nicholas and everything he stood for. But, unlike the young man who called himself Stalin, the fires were damped down. Only now and then did they flare into blazing life; flames glimpsed briefly through a camouflage of smoke.

But Margaret found that even Stalin could be amusing, with a quirky sense of humour and a lively interest in English literature. She was wedged between him and Lenin when, with Sergei and Hilda, she was invited to supper, after that first night's meeting, at the Anarchist Club in Jubilee Street.

The club was run mainly by, and for, Jews, but its organizers offered food and a welcome to all workers, whether British or foreign, Jew or Gentile. Its atmosphere was smoky and predominantly male, but women were not refused admission to the outer room.

It was Stalin, with the help of Sergei, who kept Margaret entertained for the first half of the meal. Lenin was still brooding over his defeat, and anticipating further failure to come. Suddenly, however, he seemed to throw off his ill-humour and started to amuse his guests with anecdotes of his London past, when, as Dr and Mrs Jacob Richter, he and Krupskaya had rented rooms, first in Sidmouth Street off Gray's Inn Road, and then at 30 Holford Square, Pentonville.

'I came,' he said, 'with maps of London showing all the roads leading to the British Museum. One of the first things I did was to obtain my reader's ticket. I had a personal recommendation from Isaac Mitchell, Secretary of the General Federation of Trades Unions. And so' – he spread his arms, smiling benignly – 'on April the twenty-ninth, 1902, Dr Jacob Richter of St Petersburg University became a member of the British Museum's reading-room.'

April the twenty-ninth, 1902, thought Margaret. That must have been about the time that she and India had met Hugh, as they walked home to Great Pulteney Street. Perhaps if she had never met him that day, never accepted his box of chocolates, he would not have thought of marrying her. She would never have been tempted to accept his offer. But her real mistake had been to give Paul her promise not to return to America. No promises, she had said to him that Christmas evening, in the gatehouse-room; and then had given him her word not to go home. She had been weak and foolish, and had compounded her error by marrying Hugh. . . .

Lenin, amidst laughter, was recalling an incident when he, Trotsky and Krupskaya had visited the London Socialist Church, where the singing of revolutionary hymns was interspersed by prayers that God would immediately transport His faithful congregation to His Socialist Paradise, away from this vale of tears and capitalism. The little man shrugged, and the flickering candlelight was reflected on his shiny, balding head.

'I said at the time, did I not, Leon?' – Trotsky nodded, wiping his pince-nez in a grimy handkerchief – 'that in this country revolution and socialism are so mixed up with religion and conservatism that they are never able to surface and become the property of all.'

Sergei translated rapidly from his place opposite Margaret. Suddenly, Lenin himself broke into English and, turning towards her, flung an arm about her shoulders.

'Sergei Alexandrovich tells me that you are American. We revolutionaries must stick together. You were the first, France was the second, and Russia must be the third to throw off the imperialist yoke.'

Margaret said: 'There is a lot of sympathy for the plight of the Russian people in the United States,' and Lenin nodded, looking, with his high Slav cheekbones and drooping moustache, like some wise Chinese mandarin.

'Of course. Of course. Your brave people showed us all the way, even without the benefit of Marx and Engel. You have read *Das Kapital*?'

'Not from cover to cover,' Margaret answered, laughing. 'Little pieces here and there, pointed out as of particular interest by my father.'

'A pity. A pity.' Lenin gave her shoulder a final squeeze, then, warmed and exhilarated by the rough red wine they had been drinking, flung out his arms again as though to embrace the whole table.

'We shall go to the theatre tomorrow night, after the meeting. We shall see clowns.'

And he was off once more, reminiscing about his life in London; his trips to Primrose Hill and Speakers' Corner, and to Westminster Abbey. *Their* famous Westminster Abbey, he called it, but precisely whose he did not pause to define. He was recounting now the suspicions of his Holford Square landlady that he and Krupskaya were not married, because of the latter's refusal to wear a wedding ring. It had taken all the persuasive powers of his fellow exiles, Martov and Vera Zazulich, to convince the old dragon that her lodgers were legally married according to Russian law.

Hilda nudged her husband. 'Sergei, we ought to be going. It's nearly midnight. You know how the neighbours pry, and we don't want to lose our rooms. Besides, this lot will be singing in a minute, and you know how I hate those morbid Russian songs.'

She had risen as she spoke, and, reluctantly, Sergei followed suit. Margaret got up, also, scraping back her chair. Sergei put some money on the table and asked Rosa Luxemburg to give it to the waiter for him. Rosa nodded, and said in her thick Polish accent: 'We see you again tomorrow?'

'You're not going? Not already?' Lenin was smiling up at Margaret, and she was forced to smile back, tired as she was, and to give him her hand.

'What personality,' she thought again. 'It's like a tidal wave. It swamps you.'

She glanced at Josef Stalin, neither happy, nor tired, nor tipsy; just sitting there, as solid and unemotional as a rock. There was something primitive and menacing about him, which his odd sense of humour and veneer of culture could not quite dispel. It would be too easy to dismiss these men and women as dreamers; as builders of castles in the air. Every one of them could convince her, if only temporarily, that their impossible goals were real.

A distant clock was chiming midnight as she, Hilda and Sergei emerged into the cold night air.

'Rabbits,' muttered Hilda. 'It's now May the first,' she explained to her mystified companions. 'We kids always used to say "rabbits" on the first of each month. It's supposed to bring good luck.'

'Superstitious bourgeois nonsense,' chided Sergei, and Margaret laughed.

A man passed them, going in the opposite direction. As he stepped off the pavement to allow them to proceed unhindered, he stared hard at Margaret. She returned his look, but without much interest. She was used to strangers' curiosity. Men, particularly, had looked at her ever since she was twelve years old.

She did not recognize the Duke of Leamington's manservant, nor would she have thought anything of it if she had. All she could think of at that moment was sleep. Even the horrors of the horsehair sofa would not be able to keep her awake tonight.

Ten

'Have they been good?'

Margaret stooped and hugged her children. Ralph was whooping around her legs like an excited young animal; Lilian clung to her mother's hand as if she would never let it go. Neither attitude was flattering to Jessie, who looked suitably annoyed.

She wiped her floury hands on her apron and moved her own son, none too gently, out of her way.

'Good enough,' she answered tartly. She was much thinner, Margaret noted, than she used to be. 'But it hasn't been easy with three of them under my feet all day long. I hope you're not going to make a habit of gallivanting off to London.'

'Oh, Jess!' Margaret did not know whether to be amused or vexed. 'It was only three days, and it's the first vacation I've had since I was married. You know I'd do the same for you.'

Jessie snorted as she drew water from the kitchen tap to mix the flour and fat into a dough.

'Chance would be a fine thing! I haven't had a vacation at all since my honeymoon. We can't leave the shop.' She slapped the pastry on to a floured board and took her rolling pin from the table drawer. 'And I certainly couldn't go alone. Daniel needs watching every minute of the day. Do you know, I found him *giving* sweets away to some schoolboys the other day? Why? Because they told him they'd spent their pocket-money, and he was sorry for them. Oh, yes! You can laugh, but you have no need to watch every single penny, as I do. Put the kettle on and make us both a cup of tea. I expect the train journey has made you thirsty. What time is your connection to Longreach?'

'I thought I'd catch the half after four. I didn't want to rush in here and then rush straight out again.'

'In that case,' said Daniel's voice behind her, 'I'll take you in the trap. It'll do Bluebell good to stretch her legs. She was looking very frisky in the stables this morning.'

'And who's going to serve behind the counter while you're gone?' demanded Jessie, regarding her husband angrily, hands on hips.

'I thought we could shut the shop early, my love.' He smiled guiltily. 'There's never much trade after four.'

'No, Dan,' Margaret said firmly. 'The children and I will go by train.'

But in his mild, inoffensive way, Daniel was adamant. Neither she nor Jessie could deflect him from his purpose. As the pony-trap bowled along the country lanes, the distant hills amber-gold in the afternoon light, the eggshell-blue dome of the sky tufted with fluffy white clouds, Margaret began to see, perhaps more clearly than before, that Daniel was not an easy man to live with. Outsiders would see him as a gently humorous being with a shrewish wife. It rarely occurred to people that nagging women were not born, but created by circumstances.

He was genuinely unconcerned with any trade he might have lost, and was full of a new book he was reading, John Galsworthy's *The Man of Property*.

'There are too many novels written about the so-called middle classes,' he said, flicking his whip inexpertly, an action rightly ignored by the placid Bluebell. 'What is needed is a book about the working class.'

'Then you must write it, Daniel,' Margaret suggested with a smile. It was impossible to be cross with her brother-in-law for long. He was very lovable, in spite of his faults. And that, thought Margaret with a sigh, was the chief difference between him and Jessie.

'Maybe I shall, one day,' he said. 'Maybe I've already started. But don't tell your sister.'

He sent her a twinkling glance, like an errant schoolboy; one of those to whom he gave free sweets in his shop. On occasions he seemed no older than his four-year-old son.

Margaret looked about her, feeling rested after her holiday.

A swathe of wine-dark trees slashed the horizon, and the slumbering hedgerows were starred with cuckoo-pint and campion.

Daniel said suddenly: 'Mrs Devereaux called at the shop yesterday afternoon. Did Jess tell you?'

'Beatrice? Is she in Bath? No, Jess said nothing. Mr Devereaux. . . . Is he in Bath, as well?'

'Of course. He's here because of the accident at the mine. A couple of men killed, I think Mrs Devereaux said. Mr Devereaux wanted to find out what had happened for himself.'

'An accident at Longreach? But why didn't you or Jess tell me right away?' Margaret was incredulous. 'Didn't you think it might concern me?'

'I'd forgotten it, and I suppose Jess didn't want to worry you. After all, there's nothing you can do. It isn't the first accident at Longreach, and it won't be the last. Pit deaths and injuries are hazards of any mining community.'

'They needn't be. Not all of them. Not if the pit is properly run.'

Daniel pretended not to hear. He had no wish to be involved in any crusades but his own.

'Mrs Devereaux should not have come to Bath,' he murmured. 'Did you know that she is expecting another child?'

'What? Oh. . . . Yes . . . I think Jess mentioned it some time ago.'

'She is very near her time. In fact, I believe the child may already be overdue. Mr Devereaux had no right to let her accompany him.'

'He'd have a hard time dissuading her,' Margaret retorted drily, 'once Beatrice had made up her mind.'

She could see the slag-heaps now, as the first straggling cottages of Longreach came into view. In the back of the trap, Ralph and Lilian broke into excited whispers as they recognized the familiar village street.

The trap bowled down the hill and stopped at the crossroads, where two narrow country lanes joined the main road leading to the mine. The mine itself was out of sight, over the hump of Longreach Rise, decently concealed in a neighbouring hollow. An unnatural silence hung over the houses. Curtains were drawn across windows, and the knocker of one front door was tied up with black crape.

Daniel assisted Margaret and the children to alight from the trap and lifted down their luggage, but refused an invitation to enter Laurel Cottage.

'I ought to get home.' He had the grace to look shamefaced. 'I ought to make my peace with Jess.'

Margaret smiled and kissed his cheek. She and the children watched him go, waving until he and Bluebell were out of sight. Mrs Bragg was at the gate, having been on the look-out for Margaret's return.

She began without preamble: 'Oh, Mrs Stafford, Mr—'

Margaret interrupted her. 'What's happened, Mrs Bragg? I hear there's been an accident at the pit.'

'That's right, ma'am. Mr Dev—'

'Someone was killed. Who was it?'

'Young Tom Barlow and Simon Wakely.' As she mentioned the first name, Mrs Bragg nodded towards a cottage at the near end of the street. 'But—'

'Take the children indoors, please, Mrs Bragg,' Margaret instructed. 'Leave the cases. I'll attend to them later. I must see poor Mrs Barlow immediately.'

She moved away, ignoring the older woman's repeated attempts to finish her sentence. Gently, Margaret rapped on the Barlows' front door.

It was Mrs Barlow herself who opened it, her eyes puffy and red from weeping. A thin, almost skeletal woman, with grey hair which wisped untidily from a bun at the nape of her neck, she looked nearer sixty than forty. She was, in fact, only thirty-nine. She had lost her husband ten years ago, in another disaster at the Longreach mine, when a pin in the winding engine had broken, precipitating the cage to the bottom of the shaft, which was six feet deep in mud and water. Frederick Barlow and two other men on the lower deck were suffocated under the slime.

'Mrs Barlow!' Margaret reached out, in the uninhibited American way which commended her to so many of the villagers, and took the woman's hands in both her own. 'I've been away for a day or two. I've only just heard about Tom. I'm so *very* sorry.'

111

'So you bloody well should be,' said a voice from behind Mrs Barlow. Margaret recognized the sharp features of the older brother, Arthur, who also worked at the mine.

'Hush, Arthur, hush!' begged his mother, but Arthur Barlow had no intention of being silenced.

'Why should I hush, Mother? When it was her husband's negligence that caused the accident.'

'That's nothing to do with Mrs Stafford. Come in a minute, ma'am, and sit yourself down.'

Margaret stepped into a dark, narrow passage and was ushered into the tiny front parlour, equally dark because of the drawn blinds, and musty from lack of regular airing. This was the room, with its antimacassars and potted fern, which was used only on high days and holidays, or for important guests, like the colliery manager's wife. Margaret would have much preferred the cluttered, but friendlier, kitchen.

Mrs Barlow shut the door behind them, pointedly excluding her son, and invited Margaret to sit on the lozenge-patterned sofa, upholstered in red and green moquette. She herself perched uneasily on the very edge of one of the two matching armchairs.

'It's kind of you to call, Mrs Stafford. Tom's death has been a bitter blow, coming only ten years after his dad's.'

'What did your son mean when he said that the accident was caused by my husband's negligence?' Margaret asked directly.

'Take no notice of Arthur, ma'am. He's upset. He doesn't know what he's saying.' There was fear in Mrs Barlow's careworn face. Arthur was now her sole means of support. She could not risk his losing his job.

Margaret leaned forward. 'I think I have a right to be told, Mrs Barlow. I give you my word that nothing you say will go beyond the four walls of this room.'

The other woman hesitated, then lifted her thin shoulders in a helpless gesture.

'I daresay you'll hear it, anyway. Everyone'll hear it,' she added bitterly, 'if I can't persuade Arthur to keep a still tongue in his head.' She twisted her hands together nervously. Could she really trust Mrs Stafford? On reflection, she thought she could. It was generally agreed among the women of Longreach that the manager's wife was a lady, and far too good for him. It was also generally agreed that the Staffords did not 'get on', and the sympathy lay all with Margaret. Hugh Stafford was a bully and universally disliked by his workers. Mrs Barlow continued: 'A few days back Arthur reported that some of the pit-props were rotten. The timbers were badly broken, he said, and he asked Mr Stafford to get them repaired at once, before there was an accident. Mr Stafford said Mr Stafford junior hadn't thought the damage sufficiently serious to report – Mr William being the mine surveyor, as you know, ma'am – and that he was only allowed so much money for working expenses every quarter. He said he'd already spent his allowance for the past three months and the pit-props would have to wait. And he said Arthur was an agitator, always trying to stir up trouble.'

'So he did nothing?' Margaret asked tautly.

'No, ma'am. Nothing.'

'And then?'

Mrs Barlow started to cry, her thin body shaking so much that Margaret got up from her seat and went to her, kneeling by the chair and folding the woman in her arms. After a moment or two, however, Mrs Barlow gave a defiant sniff and sat upright, feeling in her apron pocket for her handkerchief. She blew her nose.

'Two days later,' she said, 'two of the posts gave way, and the roof collapsed. My Tom and Sim Wakely were . . . were buried alive. By the time they dug them out . . . they were dead.' Unable to prevent herself, she burst once again into racking sobs.

Arthur Barlow was banging on the door. 'Are you all right, Ma?' he shouted.

His mother fought back her tears. 'Dratted boy,' she sniffed. 'Why must he carry on like that? Doesn't he realize this is a house of mourning? Whatever will the neighbours think?'

Margaret got up and opened the parlour door. 'Your mother is very upset,' she said quietly. 'Please don't make it worse for her than it already is.'

Arthur Barlow glowered resentfully, and held up for her inspection a noose of rough hempen rope, to which was attached a chain and a metal hook, similar in size and shape to the hooks used in the meat-larder at Latchetts.

'Know what this is?' he demanded. 'It's a guss and crook, lady. A guss and crook. The rope goes round a lad's waist, the chain between his legs, and the crook is hooked to the putts of coal. A carting-boy, all but naked, crawls along the seams on his hands and knees, and drags the putts, filled with coal, behind him. Day after day, week after week, year after year, until he's too old to be a carting-boy any longer. What do you think that does to a growing lad's body, eh, lady? Like me to show you?'

'That'll do, Arthur!' Mrs Barlow had left her chair and was standing beside Margaret in the open doorway. 'Good God, boy, remember who you're talking to! Do you want to find yourself out of work?'

'It's all right, Mrs Barlow,' Margaret soothed her gently. 'I promise I shan't say anything to my husband.' She turned back to Arthur and held out her hand for the guss and crook. 'It's like a medieval instrument of torture,' she said, horrified. 'Isn't there any other way of carting coal?'

She was beginning to realize how very little, during her five years at Longreach, she had learned about the actual process of mining. She had been too wrapped up in her children and her own unhappiness to have taken the interest she might have done, even supposing Hugh would have allowed it. He had not encouraged what she had done; giving aid to the sick and needy, urging the village children to play in the garden of Laurel Cottage with Ralph and Lilian, making friends amongst the women. With the men, however, she had had almost no contact, except to see them in the Methodist chapel on Sundays, shiny-faced and shiny-suited, looking as if their collars and ties would choke them.

'Oh, there's other ways of carting coal, all right,' Arthur Barlow informed her. He tried to sneer, but Margaret's genuine indignation disarmed him. 'Tubs on rails, instead of putts.'

'Then why haven't they been installed at Longreach?'

Arthur Barlow laughed at the naïvety of the question, and even his mother gave a watery smile.

'Because it would cost time and money, that's why not,' he

said. 'A lot of time and a lot of money to broaden seams which, in this part of the world, are thin and narrow. Here! Look at this!' And before a scandalized Mrs Barlow could prevent him, Arthur had rolled up his trouser legs to reveal his knees. They were both acutely inflamed. 'That's beat-knee,' he said. 'Nearly every carting-boy in Somerset is crippled with it. And it's nothing to see lads with blood running down their sides, day after day, from wearing that thing.' He jerked his head at the guss and crook, which Margaret was still holding. She handed it back. Arthur Barlow went on: 'Do you know that in the rest of this country, and in Wales and Scotland, the highest figure for beat-knee is just over four per cent? In Somerset and Gloucestershire – the Forest of Dean – the incidence is well over fifteen per cent!'

'Well, that's not the almost hundred per cent you were claiming just now,' Margaret argued fair-mindedly. 'All the same, it seems extremely high, if what you say about the rest of the country is true. You seem to know a lot about it.'

'I do. And I mean to know a great deal more before I'm finished. One day,' he added cryptically, 'it'll be our turn.'

'Oh, give over, do, Arthur,' Mrs Barlow scolded. 'All this revolutionary talk! It's senseless! There'll never be anything like that in this country, and a good thing too.' She apologized once again to Margaret. 'He doesn't know what he's saying, ma'am.'

Before Arthur could contradict his mother, Margaret said quietly: 'I think he does, Mrs Barlow, and I admire him for it. My grandfather was a miner in the Pennsylvania coalfields, back home. I'm glad Mr Barlow has told me the truth. Everyone should understand the price that is paid for all the lumps of coal that they burn.'

'You won't make trouble?' Mrs Barlow urged, sensing a new danger from Margaret's unexpected sympathy. 'You promised you won't say anything to Mr Stafford.'

'And I won't. You needn't worry.' She held out her hand, first to Mrs Barlow, then to Arthur, who took it reluctantly, loth to concede that anyone connected with the management could be worthy of respect. 'If there is anything I can do for you, please let me know.'

Margaret realized miserably how patronizing and hollow

the conventional phrases sounded. After all, what was there that she or anyone could do for a woman who had just lost a son? It would have been wiser to have said nothing. She could tell from the expression on his face that she had forfeited Arthur Barlow's grudging regard, and for some reason she would have liked to have kept it.

The door closed behind her, and she was alone in the deserted street, normally so busy at this time of day. The sky had turned white as milk, with here and there the first, faint, purple stains of evening. In the distance, beyond the menacing hump of the slag-heaps, the rising Somerset pasture was rinsed by shadows, and a flock of chattering starlings was flying home to roost.

Margaret dug her hands into the pockets of her jacket and turned in the direction of Laurel Cottage.

'I've put the children to bed,' Mrs Bragg announced, as soon as Margaret got inside. 'Poor little mites, they were both tired out. I gave them some bread and milk. That was what they wanted.'

'Thank you, Mrs Bragg.' Margaret dumped the cases on the floor of the hall and took off her hat and coat. 'Where's Mr Stafford? Will he be home to supper?'

'He's down at the pit still, working in the office. Young Mr Stafford as well. I daresay things are all at sixes and sevens after the accident. But they'll both be home for supper, and bringing Mr Devereaux with them.'

'Mr Devereaux?' Margaret felt the blood drain from her face, and she turned hurriedly to look in the hall mirror, under the pretence of arranging her hair. Her hands were shaking.

'That's right. I tried to warn you before you went over to Mrs Barlow's, but you wouldn't stop to listen.' Mrs Bragg was smugly reproachful. 'But don't worry. There's a cold ham, and some cider if the gentlemen fancy a drink.'

Margaret was now in command of herself. She gave her hair a final pat and moved away from the mirror.

'I knew Mr Devereaux was in Bath. My brother-in-law told me. But I had no idea he was at the mine.'

'He was here all day yesterday, and all day today. Making enquiries, I suppose, into what happened.'

116

Margaret asked: 'Has he, by any chance, talked to Arthur Barlow?'

'Him!' The word, as delivered by Mrs Bragg, was almost an expletive. 'That troublemaker! He's always trying to stir up the men. I said to Bragg, "Don't you listen to the likes of Arthur Barlow," I said. "Remember you have a wife and children to support." ' Mrs Bragg pulled on her coat. 'I must be getting along. The night shift'll be on soon, and Bragg'll be wanting his evening meal. I've left everything ready for you in the kitchen. You only have to lay the table.'

Margaret thanked her automatically, half of her mind elsewhere.

'Did Mr Stafford say when they were likely to be back?'

Mrs Bragg glanced at the grandfather clock, whose hands registered a quarter to seven.

'Not long, I shouldn't think. I expect they'll be hungry. They only had a sandwich for their dinners.'

The front door slammed behind her, and Margaret suddenly felt inexpressibly weary. It had been a long day; first, the train journey from Paddington to Bath, then the ride with Daniel, the news about the accident and the subsequent visit to Mrs Barlow and her son. And now, on top of all that, her first meeting with Paul since she left Latchetts. It was more than four years since she had seen him.

Suddenly, she was running upstairs to the room she shared with Hugh, lighting the lamp with unsteady fingers, and holding it up to her face as she peered into the looking-glass. She was twenty-six! Were those wrinkles she could see around her eyes? How sallow she looked. She pinched her cheeks to give them colour. . . .

She put down the lamp on the washstand and threw a shawl over the dressing-table mirror. What on earth was she doing, prinking and preening, like a girl getting ready for her lover? Slowly, she went downstairs and fetched up the cases one by one. She looked in on Ralph and Lilian, to assure herself that they were both asleep. She kissed them and tucked them in before returning to her own room to do the unpacking. Only then did she permit herself to wash and tidy her hair, and to change her travel-stained blouse.

She went downstairs again and began to set the dining-room table. Laurel Cottage, she reflected, was the only house in the village to boast a dining-room as well as a parlour and a kitchen.

She heard them come in at last; the front door opening and shutting, Hugh's gruff voice, trying to sound at ease, William's nervous spurt of laughter. Paul spoke: he also sounded uncomfortable. Margaret had often observed how difficult the English found it to blend into one another's domestic backgrounds. There was none of the easy friendliness of North Americans. She had no doubt that at the pithead Hugh and Paul Devereaux spoke as man to man; but in Laurel Cottage, they were unmistakably master and servant.

The door opened and William appeared. 'Mr Devereaux's gone upstairs with Pa, to wash his hands. You're back, then,' he added unnecessarily. He did not ask her if she had enjoyed herself in London, or enquire after his half-brother and sister. He glanced towards the table and said: 'Ham! Good. I'm so hungry I could eat a horse.'

He began picking at the cheese, an uncompromisingly yellow slab lying on an ugly green glass dish in the centre of the table. Hugh's promise that Margaret should have a clean sweep of everything she disliked had never been fulfilled. Furniture, wallpaper, china, cutlery were all exactly as they had been during the lifetime of the first Mrs Stafford.

Hugh followed his son into the dining-room. He, too, made no enquiry about her trip to London, nor did he attempt to kiss her. But Margaret recognized the old, predatory look in his eyes as he stared at her, taking in every curve of her body. Her heart sank, but she had no time to feel panic. Behind him stood Paul Devereaux, watching her across Hugh's shoulder.

Their eyes met, and Margaret knew at once that nothing had changed between them.

Eleven

'You're upset,' Beatrice said. 'More so than yesterday. Is it anything you want to talk about?'

It was past eleven o'clock at night, and she was already in bed. Paul suspected that she had been there all evening. She had probably dined in bed, a thing she rarely did at Bladud House, even when alone, because she liked the intimacy of the smaller rooms. This latest pregnancy was proving more difficult than the previous two. At the outset, Beatrice had been plagued by almost continuous sickness, and then, in the past few months, by lethargy and backache. He had not wanted her to accompany him on this trip to Bath, but she had proved inordinately stubborn. It was as if she needed to be close to him; as though she had some premonition of disaster. The child was due to be born within the next two weeks, but even that prospect had not deterred her.

'I went over my time with both of the girls,' she had argued. 'We shall be back at Latchetts with time to spare.'

He supposed, looking at her wan face against the lace-edged pillows, that he should have taken a firmer tone with her and refused to let her come. But the thought of having to visit the Longreach mine, the possibility of encountering Margaret, had weakened his resolution. Somehow, he had felt that if Beatrice were with him, awaiting his return at Bladud House, he would be better able to resist the temptation to make love to Margaret; the woman whose image had haunted him for the past five years; whose absence had been like a gaping wound.

Make love to Margaret! He could have laughed out loud; that is, if he had been in the mood for laughing.

He had been relieved yesterday when he had discovered her

absent from Longreach. Hugh Stafford had muttered something, in his surly way, about her visiting friends in London. He had not disclosed that she would be back today. The shock of seeing her, standing by the supper-table, had thrown Paul off balance. He had floundered idiotically, unable to string two sentences together; first ignoring her outstretched hand, then clutching at it like a drowning man clutching at a straw. Hugh Stafford's suspicions must surely have been aroused had not Margaret, with enviable presence of mind, covered for him. She had seated him at the oval table between her step-son and her husband, thwarting the latter's embarrassing apologies for the plainness of the meal with an easy flow of chatter. At that moment, Paul had been as helplessly, as hopelessly, in love as ever. . . .

'Do you want to talk about it?' Beatrice persisted, patting the edge of the bed and inviting him to sit down. 'Something has disturbed you.'

'Not disturbed me. Angered me.' He sat beside her, taking her hand in his. Dear, dear Beatrice! Not always predictable, but always gentle and womanly and safe!

'What has made you angry?' Beatrice prompted, when he remained silent. She had recognized the pinched, white look of temper the moment her husband had entered the bedroom. Paul never blazed with anger: it smouldered inside him, like a banked-down fire.

'It would be more to the point to ask *who* has made me angry,' he answered. 'And the reply would be your friend, Margaret Stafford.'

'Oh dear!' Beatrice's look of concern changed to one of comical dismay. 'What has poor Maggie been doing?'

Her tone of amused indulgence irritated Paul even further. He dropped her hand and got up, prowling around the bedroom to calm himself. He straightened the silver-backed hair-brushes on his wife's dressing-table, rearranged the battery of cut-glass gold-topped bottles containing perfumes and lotions from the most expensive shops in London and New York, all without having the slightest idea of what he was doing. Beatrice realized he was more upset than she had supposed, and remembered that Margaret had always been able to ruffle his feelings.

'What did she say or do to annoy you?' Beatrice asked, her voice composed and serious. She could guess what was coming. Herbie Dunham, she thought fiercely, had a lot to answer for!

'She as good as accused Hugh Stafford and myself of being responsible for the accident; her husband because of negligence, me because of parsimony and greed. She practically told me that Hugh is a rotten manager who should be dismissed, and that I am a bungling fool for having employed him all these years. She implied that Hugh is disliked in the village.'

'And is he?'

'God knows! He wouldn't be a good manager if he didn't make an enemy or two. It would mean he was far too soft, or putting my employees' interests above my own.'

'But is it just that?' Beatrice enquired as tactfully as she could. 'Honey, Margaret lives in the village, and you haven't been near it for years. Mr Stafford always comes here to discuss any business details with you.' She felt like Brutus stabbing Caesar, but her sense of fair play was something which Beatrice had inherited from Coleman Smith long before the millions which had become hers when her father had died the previous year.

Paul swung round angrily. 'That argument speaks for itself,' he said. 'It shows that Stafford is efficient; that he runs Longreach well enough to make my constant presence there unnecessary. That woman' – it salved his lacerated pride a little to refer to Margaret in such a contemptuous fashion – 'has been talking to someone, but she won't say to whom. She insists it's all from her own observations.' He added, with an odd glow of pride: 'But she's too truthful to make a good liar.'

Beatrice made no comment, judging it wiser while she was still uncertain where her sympathies lay. She wanted to side with Paul, to assure him of her unstinted support, but she had never fully understood the British attitude to commerce and money. The whole concept of absentee landlords, absentee employers, was alien to her American mind. Her father would have scorned the idea of allowing other people to run his business for him while he led a life of pleasure and ease; would have scoffed at the notion that it was ungentlemanly to concern himself with trade. How, he would have asked, can a man know what his workers are thinking and feeling if he sets himself apart? The money he derived from commerce had made Coleman Smith richer than, but not superior to, his employees.

The silence lengthened, while Paul still fidgeted about the bedroom, picking up a book, putting it down, sitting in the armchair near the fireplace, getting up again. Beatrice frowned. She had never known him so agitated. He was usually impervious to other people's opinions when he believed himself to be in the right. Why should it worry him what Maggie Dunham – Maggie Stafford – thought? Surely, she was a woman totally unimportant to him?

Paul saw the frown, and came to sit on the bed again. 'I'm sorry,' he said, kissing her gently. 'I shouldn't be burdening you with my troubles, not at the moment. It's just that "poor Maggie" always did have an uncanny knack of getting under my skin.' He watched the frown lift, and kissed her once more. 'As soon as this little chap's born' – he laid a hand on her swollen stomach, and was rewarded by a vigorous kick from the baby – 'we'll go away for a holiday. Anywhere you like. London will have to do without you for the Season.'

Beatrice laughed. 'I'm sure London will survive. You're very certain that this child is going to be a boy.'

'If it isn't,' he responded lightly, 'she's going to be the first female rugby player this country has produced. Now, you must get some rest. You shouldn't have stayed awake, waiting for me to come home.'

'I like to see you before I go to sleep.' Beatrice traced the outline of his cheek with one of her fingers, and he was racked with guilt. In that moment, he hated Margaret and himself with equal intensity. He kissed the palm of Beatrice's hand.

'I love you,' he said, and meant it. There were so many different kinds of love.

'I love you, too. Must you go to Hawksworth tomorrow?'

'It's only for one night. Francis particularly asked me to visit him as soon as I had an opportunity. It's only business. It won't take long.'

'What sort of business?' Beatrice asked. But she was tired: she did not really care.

'Goldfields, in Russia. Somewhere near the Arctic Lena

122

river. One of Francis's acquaintances wants to sell his stake in the British holding. Francis thought we might form a partnership. I'll put up a third of the money.'

'Only a third? That doesn't sound like Francis.' Beatrice's voice was gradually growing fainter as she drifted on the borderlines of sleep.

'Countess Anna wants to invest, as well.'

'Oh. . . . Love you,' she murmured again.

She did not hear him leave the room.

'What the bloody hell do you think you're playing at?' Hugh Stafford glared at his wife across the old-fashioned four-poster bed.

Margaret was afraid. She had never seen Hugh so angry, so dangerous. He was like a cornered animal, at bay.

After Paul had left in the carriage which had been sent to fetch him – a carriage which had been driven by the newly promoted Teddy Harper, who had grinned at Margaret in appreciative recognition – Hugh had been unusually quiet. He had sat in his armchair, smoking his pipe, while Margaret cleared the table and washed up the dirty dishes. She had been thankful for his silence, thinking back over the evening and trying desperately to recall if she had said anything which might implicate Arthur Barlow.

She had had no intention of saying anything at all about the accident: her thoughts had been centred entirely on Paul. She had not realized, until his entrance, that he had not expected to see her, and she had been concerned to gloss over his obvious surprise. William, far more than Hugh, would have noticed any irregularity in their conduct. He had a nose for other people's secrets.

It was only later, when the ham and pickles had been replaced by a bread and butter pudding which Mrs Bragg had left warming in the oven, that the matter of the disaster at the pit had been raised.

'There will have to be an inquest, of course,' Hugh had said, 'but you can safely leave that to me, sir. No need for you to be present, Mr Devereaux.'

'And the verdict?' Paul had asked, not without some apprehension. 'Was the timber rotten, do you suppose?'

123

'The verdict's a foregone conclusion.' Hugh had been reassuring. 'Death by misadventure. The man who inspected that seam will have to be sacked, of course. Inevitable in the circumstances, I'm afraid. He should have spotted that the support was cracking.'

Margaret had almost blurted out: 'But you knew! Arthur Barlow told you!' She had recollected herself just in time.

'Could the coroner make trouble?' Paul had wanted to know, but Hugh had again been encouraging.

'Not if it's old Gatesby, sir, as it very likely will be. A friend of your late father's, sir, if you recall. I shall make it plain that we're getting rid of the man responsible.'

It had been with a kind of detached astonishment that Margaret had heard her own voice.

'*You're* responsible. The pair of you. Miners are no more than slaves in this country. They might as well be living in ancient Greece or Rome.'

She had proceeded from there. The sight of Paul's face, looking as though she had dealt him a physical blow, had only spurred her on to say more, perhaps, than she meant. Like most red-headed people, her temper, once roused, was difficult to control, and in this case she had the added incentive of being morally in the right. But her anger had been chiefly aroused by the fact that someone like Paul Devereaux, a man of deep affections, humour, tolerance and understanding, should have this blind spot where the working conditions of his own employees was concerned.

Hugh, white-faced, had ordered her to hold her tongue. Paul, she recalled now, had made no defence, pushing his food around his plate and avoiding her eyes. To begin with, he had reacted to her outburst with all the instinctive good manners of his class, making light of her remarks, with an attempt at humour. But once he realized that she was in earnest, and had no intention of being silenced, he had withdrawn behind a barrier of exquisitely British politeness. When he left, he had thanked her, still without meeting her gaze, for an entertaining and memorable evening.

Margaret had been expecting trouble from Hugh as soon as Paul had gone, and the longer he remained quiet the uneasier she became. Now that her temper had cooled, she was miserable because she had hurt Paul, and ashamed because she recognized that the motive for her attack had been mixed. Genuine indignation at the carting-boys' plight had mingled with the desire to force Paul into a mould of her own choosing. To make him, she thought sardonically, worthier of her love. God! What hubris! And *she* had accused Paul Devereaux of pride!

She finished the dishes and went quickly and quietly up to bed, hoping to be undressed before Hugh followed her. But she was still unlacing her stays when the bedroom door was flung open and Hugh was shouting at her from the other side of the room.

'What do you mean,' she countered, ' "playing at"? I was never more serious in my life.' The stay-laces were knotted, and her fingers had suddenly become all thumbs. Margaret took a deep breath, trying to steady the beating of her heart.

Hugh came round the bed. His face was oddly pale, but his neck was beetroot-red. The veins in his tightly clenched jaw were plainly visible. Margaret was cornered, the four-poster between her and the safety of the door.

She said as levelly as she could: 'All right. Calm down, Hugh. I'll admit that I said more than I should—'

'More than you should?' His voice was almost a screech. His right hand caught her a stinging blow across one cheek. A finger-nail tore at the edge of her mouth, breaking open the soft flesh and making it bleed. 'You were trying to lose me my job, with all your insinuations about my incompetence!'

'You are incompetent!' The blow had made her angry again. 'The welfare of the miners is your concern. You're the one who should be telling Paul Devereaux that if he put back some of his profits into the mine Tom Barlow and Simon Wakely might still be alive.'

'How long do you think I'd last as manager if I told him that, you stupid cow? The miners have an agent. That's his job, if he dares.' Hugh swung his other hand, this time with the fist clenched, and hit her high on the left cheek-bone. When her ear had stopped ringing, Margaret thought vaguely that tomorrow she would probably have a black eye. A portion of her mind wondered how she would explain it to the children.

Hugh went on: 'That's why I'm called the manager; because I manage Mr Devereaux's colliery for him.'

Again he swung his fist, but this time Margaret saw it coming and ducked, butting Hugh in the stomach with her head. He staggered backwards into the washstand and fell. While he was momentarily dazed, Margaret snatched up her nightdress and made for the door and the safety of the children's bedroom. If she could just lock herself in with Lilian and Ralph for the night, Hugh might have calmed down by morning; sufficiently, at least, for her to decide on the future. Common sense told her that after her outburst this evening nothing could ever be the same again. Had that been yet another subconscious motive? To bring things to a head between herself and her husband?

She was on the landing, at the head of the staircase, when Hugh caught her, swinging her around to face him in a frenzy of frustration and rage. The desire for her burned in him as fiercely as ever. No matter how many times he forced himself on her in an orgy of love-making, he was never satisfied. He possessed her body, but not her mind. That was always elsewhere, eluding him; mocking him by its absence. Without her mind, he could not subdue her; hold her in subjection, as he had Elsa. No way but that could he be sure that she loved him. He knew from the example of his own dear mother that only total submission denoted a truly devoted wife.

'Let me go, Hugh,' Margaret pleaded, then screamed as his hands encircled her throat. She was unable to breathe. The blood was drumming in her ears; her eyes were starting from their sockets. . . .

Suddenly William was there, prising his father's hands loose, his face grey and terrified in the dim glow from the night-lamp on the table. He pushed Hugh roughly against the wall, and looked vindictively at Margaret.

'She isn't worth swinging for,' he said. 'You should never have married her. She's trash. You should have listened to me.'

Hugh, like a man awakening from a nightmare, shook off his son's embrace and, still dazed, went back into the bedroom, shutting the door behind him. Margaret stumbled into

126

the children's room and spent the rest of the night sharing Lilian's bed.

'I'm sorry, Daniel. I wouldn't have come if I'd known Jessie was ill. I didn't intend staying, in any case. I just wanted somewhere I could think rationally for an hour or two. But you have your hands full, I can see that, so I'll be on my way.'

'You'll do no such thing.' Daniel pushed his sister-in-law into an armchair. The warm sunlight of the May afternoon filtered through the lace curtains of the little sitting-room above the shop, irrigating the worn carpet with rivulets of gold. Although past three o'clock, the remains of the midday meal stood on the table, a sure sign that Jessie was indisposed. 'Did Hugh do that to you?' Daniel asked, after a moment's careful scrutiny.

Margaret gingerly touched her swollen eye. The bruises on her throat were concealed by the high collar of her blouse.

'I daresay I deserved it.'

'Violence is not the answer to anything,' Daniel said disgustedly.

'Perhaps not. But there is such a thing as committing violence with the tongue, and I'm afraid I was guilty of that.' Daniel raised his eyebrows and the story came tumbling out. 'So you see,' Margaret finished, 'Hugh's not altogether to blame. But there's going to be trouble at that mine, Dan. It doesn't really need the agitators like Arthur Barlow to stir things up.'

'Where are the children?'

'At home. Oh, they're safe enough. Hugh's very fond of them in his own way.' She had expected her story to provoke more reaction from her brother-in-law, and when none came she asked: 'Well? Do you think me impossibly ill-mannered and boorish?'

'I think you very courageous,' he answered slowly. 'It's the sort of courage I've never had. I hate unpleasantness. Even when I know there are things which ought to be said or done, I let matters slide. You have moral fibre and I envy you.'

'Nonsense.' Margaret glanced up at him affectionately. 'I'm just one of those know-it-all Yankees, with no respect for British tradition.' She smiled wanly. 'We're well known for speaking our minds. I guess it's why Europeans find us so hard to get along with.'

'What are you going to do now?' Daniel asked.

'Go home. Try to make my peace with Hugh, for the children's sake, if not for my own. Make the best of things. Try to keep control of my tongue and my temper. And pray that I haven't lost Hugh his job.'

'That won't happen,' Daniel predicted with confidence. 'Paul Devereaux wouldn't punish Hugh for something he regarded as your fault. On the other hand, your words won't have fallen on entirely stony ground. The Devereauxs are a stubborn family, and hate to be put in the wrong, but Paul Devereaux is an honest man, according to his lights. If he begins to feel that there is some truth in your allegations, he might, I suppose, get rid of Hugh.'

'Oh dear.' Margaret sighed. 'Either way, I can't win. That mine is like a powder-keg, and this last accident has created very bad feeling. . . . Is that someone calling from the shop, downstairs?'

Daniel grimaced guiltily. He knew that Jessie would scold him if she realized he had left the shop unattended. The petty thieving which resulted from his laxity was a constant source of irritation to her, as well as a considerable reduction in their annual income.

Margaret whispered: 'I'll go in and see if the noise has disturbed her.'

Daniel nodded. 'If so, try to divert her attention.'

Jessie, however, was still asleep, lying on her back and breathing heavily through a nose made red and puffy by a virulent spring cold. Various patent medicines and cough mixtures and boxes of pills stood on the bedside table. Four-year-old Mark, fully dressed, was curled up on top of the bedclothes at his mother's side. He, too, was fast asleep, his ruddy curls tumbled over the pillow, one thumb stuck firmly in his mouth. There was a look of Ralph about him, which suggested to Margaret that she and Jessie were more alike than was generally supposed. She bent and kissed her nephew lightly on the forehead. The child stirred and muttered, but did not wake up.

She heard Daniel on the stairs and tiptoed out to meet him.

He arrived at the top breathless, and plainly in great distress.

'It's all right,' Margaret reassured him. 'Jessie's still asleep.'

Her brother-in-law shook his head. 'It's not that,' he said. 'That was one of the maids from Bladud House. Mr Devereaux is away from home. Gone to Hawksworth to see the Duke. Mrs Devereaux started her labour just after he'd left this morning. She gave birth to a son half an hour ago, and now she wants Jess.' Daniel closed his eyes, like a man who had been dealt a mortal blow. 'The labour was very difficult. The child is doing well, but Mrs Devereaux is extremely ill. So ill that the doctor says she's dying.'

Twelve

Margaret took charge, quietly and competently, as though she had never been away. Nanny Watkins was in Cornwall with the girls, so there was no opposition from the stunned and grieving staff of Bladud House. Most remembered Margaret from her days in Hill Street, but even the newcomers succumbed to her air of calm authority.

It had been hurriedly agreed between Daniel and herself that Jessie was in no fit state to be moved, and that Margaret would go to Beatrice in her sister's place. She could not really believe that the summons was genuine, and half-expected to be informed, on reaching Bladud House, that it had all been a terrible mistake. But from the moment the door was opened by one of the upstairs maids, instead of the butler, she knew that something was very wrong. She gave the weeping girl a message of explanation for Mr Stapleton, and went upstairs to Beatrice's room. As she entered, Margaret heard the laboured, stertorous breathing of the dying.

Ranged about the bed were two midwives and Dr Plumley, whom Margaret recalled from the brief time she had spent at Bladud House; a big, red-faced, bearded man, who lived in Edgar Buildings. He looked as stupefied as the little maid who had let Margaret in. She laid a hand on his arm and he turned to her in relief, even though he did not recognize her, as someone to whom he could unburden his despair.

'A sudden haemorrhage,' he said. 'There was nothing I could do to stop it. The child was too big for her. He tore her apart.'

'Has Mr Devereaux been sent for?'

'Hawksworth was informed by telephone as soon as the

130

labour started, but he had not then arrived. Another message was given an hour ago, but by that time Mr Devereaux had left.'

'He doesn't know, then, that Mrs Devereaux is dying?'

'No.' Dr Plumley consulted his pocket-watch. 'I'm afraid he won't be here yet awhile, even allowing for the excellence of his horses.'

'Is there nothing we can do?' Margaret knew the futility of her question before she asked it; and Dr Plumley had already given her the answer.

'No, nothing. It's a matter of perhaps half an hour, if that.'

Margaret went to the bedside and leaned over Beatrice; but this was not the woman she had known and loved. The flesh was already shrinking on the bones, the death-mask a mere parody of its living counterpart. The nose was prominent; 'sharp as a pen,' thought Margaret, through her grief.

She whispered: 'Beatrice,' not expecting any response, but the heavy lids flickered and lifted. For a moment, the eyes were blank; then recognition filled them and Beatrice smiled.

'Maggie.' The name was barely more than a flutter of breath, but one of the hands moved slightly, and Margaret took it between her own.

'Jess couldn't come,' she explained gently. 'She has a bad cold.'

'Poor Jess. . . . Never liked being . . . unwell.' There was a long silence during which Beatrice's breathing grew shallower and the eyelids closed. The bedroom door opened softly to admit the vicar of the church which the Devereauxs attended when they were in Bath. He approached the bed, but Beatrice seemed unaware of his presence. Then her eyes opened again and she looked straight into his face. She nodded, as though satisfied on some point, and rolled her head on the pillow to smile at Margaret. 'Don't make . . . Paul . . . unhappy.' The feeble voice had almost tailed away, and Margaret had to bend lower to catch the words. 'He's in love . . . with you . . . you know.'

There was a rattle in Beatrice's throat. A second later, the only noise in the room was the squalling of the baby, as, red in the face with fury, he demanded to be fed.

*

131

'Thank you for being with her. Someone of her own from the past. A friend from her own country.'

They faced each other, as they had faced each other so often in the past in such different circumstances, across the width of the first-floor drawing-room. Paul looked dazed, still unable to take in the news which had greeted him on his arrival in Great Pulteney Street a quarter of an hour before. He had expected to find Beatrice sitting up in bed, happy and smiling, and had been prepared to swallow his disappointment if the new baby turned out to be another girl. Instead, he had found Margaret, very pale, so that her bruised eye looked vivid and faintly grotesque, as though she were wearing a mask over one half of her face.

No one else had undertaken to break the news of his wife's death to Paul Devereaux. Without saying a word, the doctor, servants, midwives, had all made it plain that they had delegated the job to Margaret.

She had waited for him on the first-floor landing, her heart sinking as she heard his excited voice in the hall below. Stapleton, sufficiently master of himself by now to resume his normal duties, had taken Paul's hat and cane.

'Don't keep me in suspense, Stapleton! Is it a boy or a girl?'

The butler had muttered: 'A boy, sir,' and Paul ran up the stairs two at a time, only to fetch up short, his face livid with outrage and astonishment, when he saw Margaret.

'Mrs Stafford! What are you doing here? Have you come to inform me of a few more of my shortcomings? After our last meeting, I wonder you have the effrontery to meet me.'

She had indicated the open door of the drawing-room behind her.

'Mr Devereaux, there is something I have to say to you. Please listen to me before you go up to Beatrice.'

He had made to push past her, but something in her attitude had stopped him. He hesitated; then silently, warily, he had followed her into the room and closed the door.

She could never remember how she broke the news to him, or what he said in reply. She had an idea that he thanked her and called her Beatrice's friend. She was locked inside her own private agony of grief; an agony which owed something to the realization that, had she been a free woman, she could now have

132

given herself to him freely, without fear of hurting that friend.

Beatrice's last words kept going round and round inside her head. Margaret would have sworn that Beatrice knew nothing of her and Paul. Had the nearness of death helped Beatrice to see things clearly? She would never know; but she could console herself that the knowledge had not made Beatrice's final moments unhappy.

Margaret turned towards the door.

'I must go,' she said. 'I have to get back to Longreach, and I must call at Green Street on my way.'

She suddenly realized how tired she felt; how much incident had been packed into the past twenty-four hours. The visit to Hilda and Sergei, the meetings with their Russian friends, seemed like events which had happened in another life, instead of only days ago. She had to leave Paul to his dead. There was nothing to be achieved by staying.

'Margaret!'

He had moved between her and the door. She saw the tears in his eyes and the hands outstretched towards her. She went to him and laid her head against his shoulder, his arms closing around her like two enfolding wings.

'I loved her,' he whispered hoarsely. 'I truly loved her. What I feel for you is different, that is all. She was a part of me, like Mareth and India. She was . . . she was just Beatrice.'

'I know. I know.' Margaret raised her head and brushed her lips against his cheek. 'That's her epitaph. She was always . . . just Beatrice.'

They remained, holding one another for a moment longer, then Margaret freed herself and opened the door. Neither had mentioned her disfigured face: it was not the time or place, but she knew he must have guessed the reason for it. She went downstairs, where Stapleton was waiting to help her on with her jacket.

Outside, Great Pulteney Street was bathed in the late afternoon sun. A man went by on horseback. On the opposite pavement, two girls were strolling and laughing together. One of the attendants from the Pump Room was pushing an old lady in a Bath chair. However many private tragedies there were, life went on as before.

*

133

'I've sacked him,' Hugh remarked with satisfaction. He helped himself to more rhubarb tart and custard. 'I've sacked him,' he repeated. 'Your friend. Arthur Barlow.'

Margaret replied as coolly as she could: 'He's not my friend. I've only spoken to him once. Why have you sacked him?'

'Because he's one of the ringleaders of this strike.' Hugh spoke viciously. 'Three months it's been going on now. It started just after Mrs Devereaux died.'

'Have you spoken to Mr Devereaux about raising the carting-boys' wage?' Margaret began stacking the dirty dishes from their tea-time meal. She nodded at Ralph and Lilian. 'All right, you two, you may leave the table as soon as your father has finished. Half an hour in the garden, as it's such a lovely evening, but no more. It's nearly time for bed.'

'Mr Devereaux's abroad,' Hugh said thickly, through the last mouthful of pastry. 'Gone to Monte Carlo with the Duke and Duchess. He won't thank me for worrying him just now about business. Besides, I can handle a few carting-boys, especially now that I've removed Arthur Barlow.'

As Lilian and Ralph slithered to the floor and vanished into the garden, Margaret said thoughtfully: 'I shouldn't imagine that an increase of a halfpenny would break a man as rich as Paul Devereaux. He has all Beatrice's money now, as well as his own.'

Hugh filled and lit his pipe before replying. When he spoke, his voice was dangerously quiet.

'You agreed to keep your nose out of matters which don't concern you. Your job is to be a wife and mother. Mine is to run the colliery at a profit.'

Margaret poured the tea. Hugh liked it strong; a thick, brown liquid in a big white china cup. Margaret could not stomach it, and contented herself with milk and hot water.

'I think this does concern me. As you say, this strike over the carting-boys' pay has lasted for more than three months. I hear things when I'm shopping in the village; not a lot, because the women won't say much in front of me, but enough to know that the men are in a very belligerent mood. There's great sympathy for the carting-boys; a feeling that their claim is a just one. You might find yourself with an all-out strike.'

134

Hugh sneered. 'The face-workers aren't going to risk their jobs for the sake of the carting-boys' dispute. Those boys get a penny a ton for the first fifty yards haulage, and a halfpenny a ton for each subsequent fifty yards. They're asking for a penny a ton for *every* fifty yards! Those illiterate peasants! Most of 'em can't even write their own names.'

'Is that relevant?' she flashed back at him, then bit her tongue. What was the use? They would only quarrel again, as bitterly as before.

During the past three months, she had genuinely tried to keep the peace. Hugh, too, had been more subdued. His attack on her had frightened them both. He was aware how near he had come to killing her; to laying himself open to a charge of murder. Had it not been for William, his body might even now be mouldering in a felon's grave in an obscure corner of some English prison. He made love to her at regular intervals, but no longer tried to force a response. He had come to realize that he did not care very much about her. Perhaps he never had. Maybe it had been the challenge to possess her; to prove to himself that plain, middle-aged Hugh Stafford could win such a beautiful young wife. It now seemed to him that he had acquired her in much the same spirit as he had acquired his house, his pony and trap, and his status as colliery manager. All these things represented an achievement; a rising above his despised slum upbringing in the back streets of Bristol. And marrying Margaret Dunham had been his crowning achievement. He felt now that as long as she stayed faithful to him, did her duty as a wife, and did not indulge her radical notions at his expense, he was quite happy to leave matters as they were.

Margaret, however, felt increasingly trapped by Hugh's more reasonable attitude. She would not have been human had she not seen, even in the moment of her greatest grief for Beatrice's death, the way clear, at last, to be with Paul. She felt sure that it was merely a matter of time before he asked her to go to him, and she knew that she would have to refuse. She had a duty to Hugh. She was under an obligation for having used him. She should never have married him, disliking him as she did, no matter how straitened her circumstances. Having done so, she had no option but to stay. Margaret knew

135

that her father would have endorsed that view. The only valid reason for leaving him would have been if he had continued to mistreat her. This he now seemed determined not to do.

'Where's William?' she asked, more to change the subject than from any real desire to know. William, as colliery surveyor, a job which took him all over the coalfield, was often late for meals. Warmed-up food, however, never appeared to spoil his digestion.

'Down at the pit-head.' Hugh wiped his mouth on the back of his hand. 'There's been trouble with some of the pickets. They've been preventing the carting-boys who are working getting through.'

Margaret recalled the vicious hiss of 'Blackleg!' which had greeted Jimmy Dando's wife in the village shop that morning. In a mining community, the women were closely identified with their men.

'What can William do?' she enquired.

Hugh grunted and leaned back in his chair, replete. 'That's up to him,' he said.

William had stationed himself at the entrance to the colliery, near the railway track which linked Longreach to the branch line between Camerton and Limpley Stoke. The mine building stood starkly against a thickly wooded backdrop of rising green; the Cornish pump-engine, the phallic chimney stacks, the winding-engine shed and the three-deck cage. The carting-boys' picket lines were also drawn up near the entrance, allowing the next shift through the gates, with the exception of their own kind. Any carting-boy who wished to work had to run the gauntlet of catcalls and whistles, shouts of 'Blackleg!' and 'Judas!' A number of them were roughly man-handled before managing to get inside.

It had not escaped William's notice that the rowdiest of the pickets was led by the dismissed Arthur Barlow, who, with nothing more to lose, was urging his companions to ever more strenuous efforts. The luckless Jimmy Dando and his mate, Pete Stavely, were immediately picked on, and Jimmy was eventually sent sprawling to the ground, blood dripping from his nose and a badly cut lip.

'I've 'ad enough of this,' he grunted to Pete Stavely, as he picked himself up. 'I'm goin' home.'

There was a cheer of triumph from the neighbouring pickets, and someone shouted: 'Well done, Arthur!'

William moved forward and took the arms of the two strike-breakers as they were about to retreat.

'You're not letting those hooligans frighten you away, are you?' he jeered. 'Not two great lads like you?'

'Well, if you're so keen to see someone get knocked about, why don't you get in amongst 'em?' Jimmy Dando spat at him, trying to staunch the blood from his nose.

'Yeah. You try gettin' kicked in the balls,' Pete Stavely added viciously.

'I'll commend your courage and loyalty to Mr Devereaux,' William offered, noticing, out of the corner of his eye, several more strike-breakers hesitating before the ferocity of the picket lines.

'What fuckin' use will that be, if every bone in our bodies's broken?' Jimmy Dando objected. He was in sympathy with the strikers' demands, and only withheld support because May, his wife, was expecting, and he could not afford to be idle. 'Come on,' he said to Pete Stavely, 'let's go.'

'Wait.' William raised his voice so that the rest of his audience could hear. 'Every carting-boy who works this evening's shift will receive double wages.'

He had no idea what his father would say to this unauthorized offer, but William's uppermost desire, at that moment, was to get the better of Arthur Barlow. He could only hope that Hugh would see it in the same light.

Jimmy Dando and Pete Stavely hesitated, half-turning back towards the gate. The other blacklegs, too, on the point of dispersing, had second thoughts and wavered.

'What d'you reckon, me old acker?' Pete Stavely said at last, and Jimmy Dando shrugged without answering. For him, the offer was too tempting to refuse. As the hooter blew again, signalling the end of one shift and the start of another, the renegade carting-boys made slowly for the gate.

'Bribery and corruption, brothers!' yelled Arthur Barlow. 'Without blackleg labour they'd've been forced to close the pit weeks ago. Without anyone to shift the coal, they wouldn't

137

have been able to carry on. And where would Mr bloody Devereaux have been then, eh? Link arms! Stop the scabs getting in!'

His last words, carried on the warm evening air, were the spark which ignited the tinder. Violence erupted. The pickets had armed themselves with shovels and pick-handles. These weapons, originally meant only to intimidate, were now being used in good earnest. One of the strike-breakers was already writhing on the ground, blood gushing from an ugly wound in the side of his head. Two more had been knocked unconscious; a fourth had been kicked in the groin and was retching into the hedge. The rest had taken to their heels.

'Get him!' Arthur Barlow shouted, pointing at William. 'Get Stafford!'

William did not wait. He saw the angry crowd surging towards him, and began to run. He must get to the village and send someone for the police, while he went to warn his father.

He staggered to the nearest house, panting for breath, one hand clamped to his side. With the other, he hammered on the door. As luck would have it, it was the Dandos' cottage, and no sooner had May Dando's white face appeared at a crack in the door than she slammed it shut again.

'Go away, Mr Stafford,' she called angrily. 'You'll only make things worse.'

William tried the next cottage, with the same result. Jimmy Dando and his friends had already spread news of the trouble, and were cowering upstairs, with their equally terrified mothers and wives. William knew that from the families of the militants he could also expect short shrift, if for a different reason. He would have to go for the police in the neighbouring village of Sawton himself. He would have to take his father's pony and trap.

The pickets, marching in a solid phalanx, had arrived at the first of the cottages. Arthur Barlow had managed to calm the strikers sufficiently to dragoon them into a semblance of order. Tempers were running too high for normal picketing to be resumed, and many of the out-going shift workers had gathered at the pit-gate to sympathize and cheer on the carting-boys.

'We'll make for Mr Stafford's house,' Arthur Barlow told them. 'We'll give him an ultimatum. Either our demands are met, or we'll close the whole pit.' He had forgotten, in the excitement of the moment, that he was no longer employed at Longreach.

The boys tramped along the dusty road in orderly fashion, but the sight of May Dando's scared face peeping from an upstairs window reawakened their worst instincts. Someone in the front rank picked up a stone and flung it at William Stafford's retreating figure. More by luck than judgement, it hit him on the back of his head. There was a roar of approval. Someone else found half a brick in the gutter and heaved it through the nearest window, indifferent to whose house it was. In the heat and fury of the moment, the property of friend and foe was equally at risk.

'Calm down, lads! Calm down,' Arthur Barlow implored them, but he was talking to himself. The carting-boys were beyond reason.

All the frustration of the three-month strike, the struggle to make ends meet, the hand-outs, the charity, the so-far vain attempts to involve the colliery's whole work-force in something more than moral support, exploded suddenly, like a mighty head of steam. Practically every downstairs window in the village was smashed; doors were bludgeoned in an effort to break them in; a cat belonging to Pete Stavely was seized by its tail and flung across the road, to survive miraculously and vanish, shrieking, up a tree. Any blackleg unfortunate enough to be encountered out of doors was unmercifully beaten in the lust for revenge.

Arthur Barlow, seeing that the situation was now beyond his control, threw his scruples to the wind, and allowed himself to become one of the hot, sweating, noisy mob as it roared along the village street with only one objective in mind: Laurel Cottage, where each man had a score to settle with Hugh Stafford.

Margaret had already heard the shouting as she moved between dining-room and kitchen, carrying and stacking the dirty dishes. Hugh jerked his head towards the window as she returned to the dining-room, tying the strings of her apron.

'Some horseplay going on somewhere,' he said. 'A few of the lads playing football, I shouldn't wonder.'

The words were scarcely out of his mouth when William burst in. He had lost his hat and his hair was plastered to his forehead with sweat.

'Trouble,' he gasped. 'The strikers have beaten up some of the men trying to cross the picket lines, and now they're rampaging through the village like madmen. They're breaking every window in sight.' He supported himself against the table, catching his breath. 'They're making for here, and they're in a very ugly mood. I'll take the trap and go for the police.' He looked at his father. 'Get Margaret and the children somewhere safe as soon as possible.' As Margaret, trying not to show the fear which suddenly gripped her, went into the garden to fetch Lilian and Ralph, William spoke again to Hugh. 'I'm off now. I'll leave by the back way, and drive through the lanes. Fasten all the doors and windows. I'll be back as quickly as I can.'

Thirteen

Margaret had barely gained the safety of the house, pushing the protesting children in front of her, when a stone crashed through the dining-room window. Ralph jumped and Lilian screamed. Both clung to her.

'Get down. On the floor. As flat as you can. Under the table,' Margaret added, as another, larger rock crashed in, to lie beside the first.

The pickets were all over the front garden by now, trampling the flower beds, churning up the grass with their heavy boots. One of them was hammering on the front door, which Margaret had had the presence of mind to shut and bolt behind her. Normally, during the day, it stood wide open: only the glass-panelled inner door was closed.

'We're coming in, Stafford! We know you're in there! We'll find a way in if we have to tunnel under the walls!'

Margaret thought the voice belonged to Arthur Barlow. Lilian began to whimper and she held her tightly. Hugh came into the dining-room. Margaret could just see his feet.

'Stay still,' she ordered the children, and lifted the edge of the brown chenille tablecloth, with its tasselled border. 'Hugh, we're down here.'

'Where? . . . Ah! I've locked the back door. That'll hold them for a bit. I hope until William gets back with the police. I've told him to go for the miners' agent, as well. Perhaps Plumstead can knock some sense into the stupid buggers.'

'Are you sure they won't be able to get in?' she asked anxiously. 'Surely they can break down the doors?'

'It will take them time. The real danger is if they manage to open a window by getting a hand through a broken pane of glass.' Hugh reached down to Margaret and the children. 'Out of here, quickly!' he ordered. 'Get Ralph and Lilian into the cupboard under the stairs. It sounds as if they're growing more violent.'

The volume of noise had increased during the past few minutes. The boys and young men – the youngest carting-boy was fourteen, the eldest twenty-two – were now yelling mindlessly, caught up in the runaway excitement of the mob. Many of them were to claim, later, that they could remember nothing with any clarity after the first stone was tossed through the window of Laurel Cottage.

As she scrambled in Hugh's wake, dragging the terrified children with her, Margaret could see one of the pickets trying to scale the drain-pipe beside the broken window. He called to someone below: 'I can get this bastard open!' As he spoke, he inserted his arm cautiously through the gap in the pane and began to grope around for the latch.

Margaret did not wait to see whether or not he found it. She picked up Ralph, grabbed Lilian by the hand and dashed into the hall. Hugh was already holding open the door of the stair-cupboard.

It was dark and musty inside, adding to the children's terror. Margaret remembered just in time to stop Hugh from shutting them in.

'For heaven's sake! There's no air in here. We shall suffocate. And you can only open the door from outside.' Hugh grunted. 'Where are you going?' she asked him.

'The less you know, the better,' he snapped. She could sense the fear underlying his terseness. 'Stay there with Ralph and Lilian, and don't come out until I tell you.'

She had no time to question him further. The children were demanding her attention, Lilian in tears and positive that she could hear rats scuffling about in the darkness.

'Nonsense!' Margaret declared stoutly. 'I had everything out of this cupboard last week to sweep it, and there weren't any rat-holes then.' She could not honestly recall whether she had seen one or not, but it seemed the most sensible thing to say.

Muffled by the velvety blackness, the clamour outside the house was now barely audible. Margaret felt about, amidst the clutter of years, and, eventually, as her eyes became accustomed to the gloom, located an old trunk containing some of the first Mrs Stafford's clothes, which Hugh had stubbornly refused to part with. She sat down on the lid and drew Ralph and Lilian, still trembling with fright, to sit one on either side of her.

'We shall be safe here,' she said with a confidence she was far from feeling. What was Hugh up to? What did he think he could do against two dozen or so half-crazed miners? 'The men will soon go away.'

'Why bad men smashing my house?' moaned Ralph, and Margaret could feel the uncontrollable shaking of his little body.

She pressed him close to her, trying to imbue him with some of her own spurious optimism.

'It'll be all right, honey,' she reassured him. 'They're just angry because Mr Devereaux won't pay them more money. They have a certain amount of right on their side,' she added, more to salve her own conscience than in the hope that a child, not yet three, would understand.

'Bad men!' Ralph said. 'Ralph hate them!'

Margaret was taken aback by her son's vehemence. She could just make out the forward thrust of his lower jaw, the pugnacious set of his features, which were so like Hugh's.

'Sing a song, Mummy,' Lilian begged, snuggling closer.

Her brother nodded. 'Sing "Gory, gory, halejoodah",' he commanded.

Correctly interpreting this as a request for the 'Battle Hymn of the Republic', Margaret began:

'Mine eyes have seen the glory of the coming of the Lord,
He is trampling out the vintage where the grapes of wrath
   are stored,
He hath loosed the faithful lightning of His terrible, swift
   sword,
Our God is—'

But the words 'marching on' died on her lips as the comparative silence which had descended on the house for the past few minutes was shattered by the unmistakable report of a gun.

Lilian shivered and Ralph began to grizzle. 'What was that, Mama?' the little girl asked.

'I think I'd better find out. Both of you are to stay here, do you understand me? You are not to follow me. I shall be very, very cross if you disobey. I'll be back as soon as I can.'

'Don't go. Don't leave Ralph.' Her son clutched fearfully at Margaret's skirt. Gently she freed herself and he began to sob.

Lilian looked up at her mother, and Margaret could see the whites of her eyes gleaming fearfully in the darkness, but she made no sound. Margaret hesitated, but the noise of a second shot reinforced her decision.

She said: 'Lilian will look after you, Ralph. Be a brave boy.' And she pushed open the cupboard door.

As she straightened up in the hallway, her heart beating ridiculously fast, she was aware that the front door was open, Hugh framed against the evening sunlight which was pouring in from outside. He was holding his shot-gun.

'And next time, I'll shoot to wound,' he was shouting. 'So get out of my garden and back to your picket lines. Better still, get back to work. And don't think you've heard the last of this! I know every one of your faces, and I shall inform the police of your identity as soon as they arrive. You'll be bloody lucky if you don't all end up in prison.'

A voice yelled: 'Fucking bastard!' and Hugh swung to his left and took aim.

'No, Hugh! Don't!' Margaret came up behind him, seizing his right arm and trying to force it down.

With a furious imprecation, he shook her off. There was another report, a scream, and one of the men toppled over, his blood staining the flower-bordered path. Hugh reloaded his gun from the box of shot which he had placed on a window-ledge, near the door.

Arthur Barlow had dropped to his knees beside the injured man, turning him carefully on to his back and feeling for a pulse. The man was moaning and half-unconscious, bleeding copiously from a superficial wound in the shoulder. Arthur slowly stood up again and addressed his comrades.

'You all saw that,' he shouted. 'A cold-blooded and deliberate intent to kill.'

'Rubbish!' yelled Hugh. 'If you think I can't aim any better

144

than that. . . .' But the rest of his words were lost in the resultant confusion.

Someone hollered: 'Let's get the murdering bugger!' and there was a concerted rush towards the door. The collective sanity which had been partially restored by the sight of Hugh's shot-gun degenerated once more into mindless anarchy. Hugh backed away, aware of forces he could no longer control.

Margaret flung herself at the first man across the doorstep, hammering with her fists against his chest.

'Keep out of my house, you goddam lunatic!' she cried. 'This is my home! Keep out! Do you hear me!'

It occurred to her, fleetingly that a quarter of an hour ago she had been arguing the cause of the carting-boys with Hugh, yet now was prepared to offer them violence. She was filled with rage at the sight of them trampling into her hallway. An aspidistra in a blue-and-white bowl that Jessie had given her crashed to the floor as its pedestal was roughly overturned. Earth and fragments of china were everywhere. The hallstand was toppled in a flurry of hats and coats, its mirror splintering into a dozen pieces. Two men emerged from the dining-room door, having climbed into the house through one of the shattered windows. Others followed.

'Here. Hold this bloody spitfire while we deal with Stafford,' said Arthur Barlow, and Margaret realized whom she had been attacking. He shoved her aside as easily as if she had been a featherweight, with a strength belying his delicate appearance. 'He killed my brother with his criminal negligence. Stay out of it, lady, and you won't get hurt.'

'That's right, missus.' One of the younger boys gave her a push which sent Margaret staggering back to strike her head against the wall. Another of them elbowed her in the stomach, winding her. Dazedly, she saw Hugh retreat to the foot of the stairs and begin, slowly, to mount backwards, keeping his eyes fixed on the angry mob in front of him.

One of the men picked up a shard of the broken china bowl and threw it. It caught Hugh on the face, gashing him over one eye. A trickle of blood ran down his left cheek.

The sudden, sharp pain seemed to infuriate him. He levelled his gun and shouted: 'Stay where you are, all of you!

145

The police will be here soon.' He glanced desperately towards the open door, searching for some sign of William and the forces of law and order.

'Take no notice!' yelled Arthur Barlow. 'He's wounded one of your ackers! Get his fuckin' gun!'

His words galvanized the pickets once more into action. Two of the carting-boys at the foot of the stairs made a sudden dart at Hugh. One of them got hold of the gun by the barrel; the other tried to pinion Hugh's arms to his sides. The other boys pushed forward and Hugh fell on his back, disappearing under the press of bodies.

Margaret, shouting incoherently, dragged ineffectually at the nearest pair of legs.

'Do something!' she called to Arthur Barlow, who was taking no part in the mêlée. 'For God's sake! They'll suffocate him!'

There was a muffled report as the gun exploded. Ralph and Lilian were screaming again. They had opened the cupboard door, but were too terrified to come out. Everyone else had fallen silent.

Slowly the men picked themselves up and backed away. Only Hugh remained where he was, motionless, slumped against the staircase. His head lolled to one side, and a red stain was spreading across the front of his shirt. Margaret pushed her way between the now unresisting men and knelt beside him, shaking him by the shoulders and calling his name.

'It's no use, missus,' one of the boys said hoarsely. 'He can't hear you. He's dead.'

Margaret took no notice. She continued, stupidly, crazily, trying to rouse her husband. She was still there five minutes later, when William arrived with the police.

She had not seen Paul since the day of Beatrice's death. Now, wearing her widow's black, it was strange to meet again in the impersonal surroundings of Taunton Assize Court.

Margaret thought that his face looked thinner, the features more sharply defined, the nostrils pinched. But that might simply be on account of the freezing weather, the whole country locked in winter's icy grip. In London, there had been moonlight tobogganing on Parliament Hill; but such frivolities, read of in the newspapers, seemed as remote to Margaret as did the approach of Christmas, enclosed as she was in her self-made prison of remorse and guilt.

'You must forget it, Maggie,' Jessie had remonstrated with her. 'I know it was an awful thing to happen, but you have to put it behind you. Start living again, for the children's sake, as well as your own.'

'You don't understand, Jess,' she had answered, clutching her sister's hand. 'I was glad when I realized Hugh was dead. All I could think of was that, at last, I was free.'

'Shush.' Jessie had indicated Ralph and Lilian, who had been playing nearby with Mark. 'You don't mean it. It's just the shock talking.'

They had been sitting on a seat in Sydney Gardens, while the three children played hide-and-seek amongst the trees. Recalling the incident now, Margaret remembered that Lilian had been close at hand. Could she possibly have overheard?

Jessie and Daniel had been wonderful, arriving at Long-reach on the night of Hugh's death, insisting on staying with her. Mark had been left in the care of a neighbour.

The following day, Jessie had said: 'You can't remain here. If the police are agreeable, you're coming back with us. We'll manage somehow. This place isn't safe. There's more trouble to come, you mark my words.'

She had been proved right that same afternoon, when the whole colliery came out on strike in protest against the arrest of Arthur Barlow and ten of the carting-boys. There had been rioting. Houses were stoned, and two constables injured. There had been ugly scenes as the Black Maria arrived to take away the accused men. The bad feeling had continued throughout the month of August and the whole of September, only being resolved with the dismissal of William Stafford from the post of colliery surveyor, and Paul Devereaux's promise to give the carting-boys' grievances serious attention. A new manager had been appointed, and moved, with his family, into Laurel Cottage. Daniel and Jessie had made all the funeral arrangements and seen about putting Hugh's furniture into store. William had left the district; vanished without a word.

147

Hugh's will had come as a further shock. He had left everything – the contents of Laurel Cottage and the several hundred pounds which were his life's savings – solely to William. The will had been drawn up just after his first wife's death and never altered.

'I take back all the excuses I ever made for that man,' Jessie had fumed.

Margaret smiled, but the feeling of self-blame persisted. She could not forgive herself for the brief moment of elation when she first realized Hugh had been killed.

Daniel, as well as Jessie, began to lose patience with her.

'A Methodist conscience is all very well in moderation,' he had told her sharply, the evening before she and Jessie left for Taunton, where she was to be a witness for the prosecution at Arthur Barlow and the other men's trial. 'But you're punishing all of us, not only yourself. I don't intend having my Christmas ruined while you play the spectre at the feast. You are a sensible woman, my dear. An intelligent woman. Too many regrets only atrophy the soul. They're a form of self-indulgence. So pull yourself together, Maggie, please.'

Jessie was inclined to think her husband had been too severe.

'It's not that I don't agree with you, Daniel, but Maggie has been through a bad time and the wounds will take a while to heal. It's not like you to be so unsympathetic.'

'I know,' Daniel had replied miserably. 'I hated saying it. But it's for everyone's good. If justice is to be done at the trial, Margaret must give her evidence clearly and rationally, untormented by guilt and self-doubt. Her attitude is bound to influence the jury, and that means a lot to the men on trial. And she'll have to meet Paul Devereaux again. I managed to keep him away from Hugh's funeral.'

The point of this last remark had been lost on Jessie, who had never had the slightest suspicion of there being anything more between Margaret and Paul than the relationship between employer and employed. It came, therefore, as a shock when she saw the expression on Paul's face, the tenderness, the naked affection, as he walked towards them across the entrance hall of the Assize Court, after the trial. He had eyes only for Margaret as he took her hand. Jessie might have ceased to exist.

'I've tried to make amends,' he said. 'I know that, in part, you blame me. But I think my evidence, as well as yours, was instrumental in getting the men lighter sentences than might have been expected. You see, some of the things you accused me of, that evening at Longreach, struck home. My one regret is that Arthur Barlow didn't receive a longer sentence.'

Margaret freed her hand immediately. 'I think six months' hard labour is quite sufficient for inciting a riot in a just cause,' she answered tartly.

Animosity sparked between them. Where, a moment before, they had looked as though they could drown in one another's eyes, there was now nothing but open aggression. Yet even their enmity, Jessie recognized, was more fraught with passion, with more uncompromisingly sexual overtones, than anything she had ever experienced with Daniel. She tightened her lips in outraged disapproval. How long had this been going on? And Beatrice only six months dead. It occurred to Jessie that Daniel knew all about it. She would have something to say to him when she returned home tomorrow.

Paul said quietly: 'Don't let's quarrel,' and Margaret shook her head, the tears blinding her eyes.

'No,' she said. 'No, I'm sorry.'

Paul sat beside her on the hard public bench, and again took her hand. 'You were right about Hugh. There were many things wrong at Longreach; things I should have made it my business to know. From now on, I shall take a keener interest in the running of the colliery.'

She smiled sadly. 'It's nothing to do with me any more. But I'm glad, for the sake of the men.' She noticed a policeman regarding them curiously from the other side of the hall, and once more withdrew her hand, but this time gently.

'What are you going to do now?' he asked. 'Have you made any plans?'

Jessie drew on a pair of serviceable black leather gloves and remarked briskly: 'We are going back to our lodgings, Mr Devereaux, for a quiet evening meal and an early night, as befits two respectable women who are still in mourning.

149

Tomorrow we are returning, by courtesy of Great Western Railways, to Bath.'

Paul blinked, as though suddenly aware of Jessie's presence for the first time.

Margaret gave a little laugh, which caught in her throat, and said: 'Oh, do be quiet, Jess. I think Mr Devereaux is asking about my plans for the future.'

'I should not have thought it his concern,' was the huffy reply. 'You have a family, perfectly capable of looking after you.'

Margaret said nothing. Her sister knew quite well that it was impossible for her and Daniel to provide a home for three extra for very much longer. The living space above the shop was too cramped for six people, especially when three of them were noisy and vigorous young children. And Margaret had no money. Hugh's failure to provide for her had left her almost destitute, except for a few carefully hoarded savings of her own.

Paul said: 'Will you permit me to take you both to tea? There's a tea-shop in Mary Street, which I think would be suitable. I'm sure you're both Anglicized enough by now to feel the need of a cup after your ordeal.'

Outside, it was nearly dark, and a thin rain was falling, slanting in bright arrows across the face of the gas-lamps. People were hurrying home, heads bent against a nipping wind. The tea-shop in Mary Street was an oasis of comfort and warmth after the bleak, impersonal atmosphere of the law-courts and the cold dreary streets outside. Even Jessie's manner thawed slightly. They settled at a corner table, and Paul caught a waitress's eye.

'Tea and . . . uh . . . and—'

'Tea and toast and cakes, if you please,' ordered Jessie, competently taking charge. Paul Devereaux was plainly unused to these sorts of places. He looked acutely uncomfortable, and when the tea-things arrived sipped the cup of tea which Jessie poured for him, refusing all offers of anything to eat.

He looked at Margaret across the table. 'I want you to come back as Mareth's and India's governess,' he said.

She raised her eyes briefly to his, but his face gave nothing away. Nevertheless, she knew precisely the offer he was making, and her heart sang. It was all she could do to prevent herself from laughing out loud. All the guilt she had been harbouring, all the self-recriminations concerning Hugh's death, slunk back into the shadowed corners of her mind. Her only regret was in distressing Jessie, whose expression was ominous. Having once had her eyes opened to the situation between Margaret and Paul Devereaux, she had not mistaken the true nature of his proposal, either.

'He won't marry you, you fool!' she exclaimed harshly. 'In this country, his sort doesn't marry the governess. *Jane Eyre* is just a story, not real life.'

Margaret smiled. 'Jess, dear, I'm aware of that. But it doesn't matter. We love each other, and now we're both free. There are no more obligations. No one to get hurt. If English society won't countenance our marriage, that doesn't worry me. Things will change one day. They always do. You can't halt progress, even though it might take longer than you'd like. So, until that day comes, I'll live in private as Paul's mistress, and in public as his daughters' governess. If needs be, for the rest of my life.'

Part Three 1911

To take a wyf withoute avysement

Fourteen

The sea, far below, was sapphire-blue, shot through with turquoise. On the opposite side of the inlet, a spur of rock thrust out like a cloven hoof into the placid depths. Clumps of rusty sorrel and pink sea-thrift made patchwork of the grass. Sunlight drenched the ruins of Tintagel Castle and all that remained of the ancient Celtic monastery, which had been old before St Patrick went to Ireland. A yacht, white sails spread, floated like a swan on the drowsing waters.

India sat gracefully on the folded rug, amid the debris of their picnic, very conscious that, at sixteen – although only just sixteen; today, the tenth of August, was her birthday – she was leaving childhood behind her. She had refused to join in the noisy games of the others, preferring to sigh romantically over Tennyson's *Idylls of the King*; although Margaret suspected that her choice was prompted by a desire to keep her dress clean and to sit still in the sweltering heat.

'It must be eighty in the shade,' Margaret observed languidly, fanning herself with a folded copy of *The Times*. 'I honestly don't know how those children find the energy to run about. Mareth! Put your hat on! At once! You'll get sunstroke. And Ralph, you and George sit down quietly for a moment. You're both far too heated. Lilian! Come here a minute, honey. I'll pour us all a drink.'

'I'll get them, Mrs Stafford.' Polly Ching, the latest in a long line of nursery-maids, who came and went with increasing frequency as Nanny Watkins's temper became ever more uncertain, scrambled to her feet. She was a round-faced, rosy-cheeked Cornish girl, taking life as it came, as did all her kind, and totally unruffled by the irregularities of the

155

Latchetts nursery. It was a matter of indifference to her that its two youngest members, Henry and Antonia Dunham, were the illegitimate children of Mrs Stafford and her master.

When Henry was born in October 1908, he had been registered, at Margaret's insistence, under the name of Dunham. She had not wished him to be called Stafford; it seemed unfair to Hugh. Nor was she willing for Paul to compromise himself by giving Henry the Devereaux name. And when Antonia had arrived at the end of the following year, she also had been called Dunham.

The birth of the children had proved to be the final straw as far as Jessie was concerned. The break between the sisters, to Margaret's great distress, was now complete. Jessie adamantly refused to answer any of Margaret's letters or to acknowledge the existence of her new nephew and niece. She wrote pointedly to Lilian and Ralph on their birthdays and at Christmas, and had them to stay in Green Street as often as they wished. But all the arrangements attendant upon such visits were conducted either through Daniel or with Lilian direct.

Lilian, herself, had become extremely withdrawn. Never a demonstrative child, she had grown even more reserved, treating Paul with an aloof politeness which he found far more hurtful than overt hostility He had tried by all the means in his power to win Lilian's affection, but had never managed to disarm her. For her eighth birthday, in May, he had presented her with a charming necklet of jade and ivory beads, the jade just matching the colour of her eyes. Lilian had thanked him with her meaningless little smile, and put it away with all the other unworn, or unused, trinkets which he had given her over the past four years.

Ralph, on the other hand, was in his element, ready to take everything that was offered him. He was, Margaret reluctantly admitted, a greedy, self-centred child, whose horizons were bounded by his own wants and needs. His loyalty to people, even to his mother, was governed by what they could give him, and whether or not, and how often, they would let him have his own way. The one exception to this rule, the one genuine love in his otherwise self-absorbed little world, was George Devereaux, now four years of age. For some reason best known to himself, Ralph adored young George; would give him his last sweet, let him ride on his sturdy back, read him stories, and always allow George to win all their games.

It was an affection which Margaret found hard to understand, for George Devereaux, unlike his parents or his sisters, was completely lacking in charm. He could be stubborn and sullen, or boisterously rowdy. His fierce blue eyes looked out at the world from under a pair of bushy eyebrows and a thatch of straight brown hair which he had inherited from his maternal grandfather. Margaret saw Coleman Smith live again in his grandson; the looks, the drive, the determination always to win. Margaret could only hope that, as George grew older, he would also display his grandfather's saving grace of humour; the honesty to admit that he could sometimes be wrong.

She leaned back against the moss-and-grass-covered stones, all that was left of the Celtic monastery, and closed her eyes, letting the heat of the sun seep into her bones. These past four years had been the happiest of her life, and, with the exception of two small clouds, in the shape of Lilian and Jessie, she had no regrets for the decision she had made. She had known a love with Paul, a union of flesh and spirit, which had transcended anything she had ever dreamed of. It did not worry her that, nowadays, she rarely left the confines of north Cornwall, never went to Bath or London, rarely even to Plymouth. Beyond the countryside immediately surrounding Latchetts was another world; a world which Paul inhabited, and, occasionally, India and Mareth, but from which she had chosen voluntary exile. Now and then, in odd moments, this incarceration worried her; old loyalties and memories stirred; old commitments beckoned. But for the most part she was happy in her ivory tower, enclosed by her enchanted forest, shut up with her lover and her children, indifferent to the life outside.

What really surprised her was the ease with which India and Mareth had accepted the relationship between herself and Paul. Even the arrival of a half-brother and sister had not upset them, although they were both at an age when most girls would have found the fact at least an embarrassment. But they had already been very fond of her, had been delighted at her reappearance in their lives and, more important, they were Devereauxs. From the cradle onwards, they had been taught a splendid disregard for the morals, manners and attitudes of lesser people.

There were others who felt the same. As long as Paul did not flaunt her openly, as long as she remained discreetly in the background, maintaining the fiction of being merely his children's governess, a widow with four children of her own, Margaret's presence at Latchetts was widely accepted. However, there were some who disapproved and made their feelings known; one or two families, like the Bastardos and that of the local vicar, who no longer called at Latchetts, but they were few and far between. It was difficult to forget that Paul was first cousin to a duke, particularly when the Duke and Duchess of Leamington continued to visit him on the same terms of friendship as before.

To Olga, the situation seemed perfectly natural, and the Dunham woman – she either could not or would not remember Margaret's married name – was a model of discretion. She kept to her own rooms whenever they were at Latchetts and did not eat with the family. The Duchess might have been less complacent had she guessed that Margaret's reason for doing so was a rooted dislike of the Duke. Olga, however, had forgotten that unfortunate incident between Margaret and her husband, all those years ago. But if she had, Francis had not.

It had been Francis's one consolation, whenever he recalled that unflattering episode in his amatory career, that he had misjudged his quarry. Such a reflection had been humiliating enough in one who congratulated himself on being able to distinguish at a glance a respectable woman from a 'muslin skirt'. But then to be confronted by the fact – or what he thought to be the fact – that he had not been mistaken, merely rejected, had lacerated his most vulnerable spot, his pride. He hated Margaret quite as cordially as she detested him, but had sufficient sense to accept the present situation with outward grace. Once, when speaking of her to Paul, he had referred, with a little, self-deprecatory gesture, to the incident in the gatehouse-room, and admitted magnanimously that he had been at fault.

'The best man "won fair lady" after all, dear boy,' he had

said, clapping his cousin affectionately on the back. 'Of course, had I known the true state of affairs, I should never have chanced my arm.'

It was useless for Paul to protest that, at the time, there had been no 'state of affairs'. The Duke remained unconvinced. Although he was now more than fifty years of age, Francis pursued women as single-mindedly as ever. At present, he was supporting two mistresses in separate establishments, one of them a well-known actress on the West End stage. Margaret was his only defeat, and he would never forgive her for that.

'Dunny.' India uncurled herself from the rug and looked about her. 'Do you believe that King Arthur was really born at Tintagel?'

Margaret glanced up from the letter she had started to read when the younger children's noisy resumption of their game had sent sleep flying. The letter was from an old friend of hers, Daisy Larkin, in New York, with whom she maintained a fitful correspondence. New York was changing, Daisy wrote sadly; Margaret would barely recognize it. Longacre Square was now Times Square; the Methodist chapel on Willett Street had become a synagogue; even Gramercy Park was no longer sacrosanct, with new buildings being added to its hallowed precincts. The letter depressed Margaret, making her homesick for the past, and she was glad to lay it aside.

'I don't know,' she answered. 'Your father says not. He says it's a medieval fiction. The castle, according to him, is twelfth century. But the monastery, these stones we're leaning against, belong to the fourth.' She smiled. 'After all these years, I can never get used to the age of things in this country. In the States, anything over eighty years is old.'

India pouted. 'I think Papa ought to have been here for my birthday. He's never missed it before. All for some old Parliament Bill! Why did he have to go to London? He's not a member of the House of Commons.'

'His Grace asked him to go. The voting is in the House of Lords. The Duke wanted his moral support, or some such thing. Honey, it's no use asking me to explain, because British politics are a closed book as far as I'm concerned. But your papa will be back tomorrow. He promised. And he'll probably bring you an extra-special present from London to make up.'

India's eyes brightened at the thought. The other children, worn out at last by the heat and the prospect of the downward climb, were lying on the grass in a variety of postures. Ralph was flat on his back, arms and legs spread-eagled. Mareth, her hair like an untidy halo in the afternoon sun, was seated on a rock, searching for daisies to make a chain. George nestled in Polly Ching's lap, one thumb in his mouth, his eyelids drooping. And Lilian was lying on her stomach, as far away from them all as possible, watching a seagull wheeling overhead.

Margaret got up and went across to her daughter. 'Lilian, honey, are you all right?'

The face, so like her own, with the same promise of beauty which had been Margaret's at a similar age, did not turn towards her. The slender shoulders were hunched. After a moment's silence, however, Lilian said: 'I had a letter from Auntie Jess this morning.'

'I know. I saw it on the table in the hall, before we left.' Margaret sat on the grass beside her daughter, linking her hands around her knees. Lilian often received letters from Jessie, but never discussed them with her mother. The fact that she so obviously wished to do so now filled Margaret with foreboding. Nervously she picked a leaf from a samphire bush and crushed it between her fingers. Its soft, aromatic fragrance filled the air. 'Do you know how samphire got its name?' she asked, talking for the sake of talking. 'It's a corruption of Saint Pierre. *L'herbe de Saint Pierre*, the Normans called it. Look how delicate the colour of the flowers is, a sort of greenish white.'

'Don't you want to know what Auntie Jess said?' Lilian enquired.

'Yes. . . . Yes, of course I do. Is she well? And Uncle Daniel? Mark? It's such an age since I saw them all. I really must—'

'Auntie Jessie and Uncle Daniel want me to live with them. They want Ralph, too, but he won't go. I asked him. They want me permanently. Auntie Jess says that Latchetts is no place to bring up children.'

The silken shadows of late afternoon were stealing across the grass and what remained of the ancient castle, built on its two promontories of rock, the wild Atlantic ocean washing in between. Far out, above the sun-fretted water, seagulls called to one another with their sharp, staccato cries. At any other moment, Margaret would have been entranced by the beauty of the scene. Now, however, she saw none of it.

'What nonsense!' she exclaimed furiously. 'I think it's time I wrote to Jess! How dare she make such a suggestion behind my back! Words fail me. Who does she think she is?'

'I want to go, Mama.' Lilian rolled over and sat up, staring out to sea.

'The audacity of it! The nerve! To suborn my own children without my knowledge. . . . What? What did you say?'

'I said I want to go, Mama.' Lilian spoke in a small, hard voice, her eyes fixed on the horizon. Her face was set in the mulish lines Margaret knew only too well. 'I don't want to live at Latchetts with you and Mr Devereaux. I want to go home.'

'But, honey, Latchetts is your home.' Margaret was frightened now. She knew her eldest child too well to suppose that Lilian was showing off or being awkward. Young as she was, Lilian never did or said anything merely for effect. There were a hundred wiles in India's and Mareth's armouries for manipulating their elders and getting their own way. But Lilian's approach was always direct. 'Paul and I love you. Besides, you're only eight years old. As if I should allow you to live with your Auntie Jessie!'

'Latchetts isn't my home.' Lilian's eyes filled with sudden tears, which she defiantly wiped away, resisting her mother's attempts to take her in her arms. 'I hate it. I hate Mr Devereaux. He's a wicked man, and I wish I were dead, like my father.'

'Lilian!' Margaret's voice was stern. 'I will not have you say such things. Paul loves you. He would do as much for you as for his own daughters, if only you would let him.'

'Would he?' Lilian, now, was scornful. 'Well, I shan't let him!' She jumped to her feet, her thin body shaking with unhappiness and rage. 'Nanny Watkins says you're a loose woman. She says that Henry and Tonia are illeg . . . illeg . . . oh, illeg-something, and one of the stable-boys called them bastards.' She obviously had no idea what the words really meant, only that they were derogatory in some way. 'And

Auntie Jessie told me that you're the talk of three counties.'

Margaret could just hear Jessie saying that. It was the sort of sweeping, grandiose phrase which would appeal to her sister. And the idea was so ridiculous that instead of growing angrier, Margaret began to laugh. Once started, she found it difficult to stop.

'Oh dear, oh dear!' she gasped at last, mopping her streaming eyes. 'I'm sorry, honey, but the notion that no one between here and Bath has anything better to do than talk about me is too stupid!' She saw that the other children were looking curiously in their direction, and got to her feet. 'Come along,' she said, holding out her hand, 'it's time to go home. Let's forget all this nonsense, shall we? I'll write to Auntie Jess tonight and try to put her mind at ease. I suppose, in a way, I can't blame her. She's only concerned about you and Ralph. Now, let's be friends again, honey, please.'

For answer, Lilian pushed past her, running down the grassy slope to the path. She made no effort to help the others repack the picnic-basket, and was silent throughout the steep cliff descent to the beach and Merlin's cave. And all the way back to Latchetts, as the trap bowled smoothly along the leafy Cornish lanes, she refused even to glance at her mother.

A lamp was still burning in a window of the house in Mount Street when a cab drew up outside, allowing the Duke of Leamington and his cousin to alight.

'Come in for a nightcap,' Francis offered, yawning. 'It must be nearly midnight.'

'It is,' Paul grinned. 'I never knew that the Lords could be so eloquent.'

'We have our moments,' murmured the Duke, paying off the cab and unlocking his front door. 'I told poor old Harvey to go to bed. I had an idea it was going to prove a marathon session.'

He led the way into the library, on the ground floor, where a tray with decanter, siphon and glasses had been set out on a side-table. Francis turned up the lamp and waved his cousin to one of the two leather armchairs.

'Whisky?' he enquired.

'Please. Just a splash of soda.' Paul rubbed his aching neck.

'Well, you've done it. You've beaten the Halsburyites, but, like Waterloo, it was a damn close-run thing. A majority of seventeen.' He grinned slyly as the Duke handed him his drink and sat down in the opposite armchair. 'I must say I never thought to see the day when you voted with the Liberals.'

Francis shrugged. 'Needs must, when the devil drives. One couldn't put HM in the invidious position of having to create two hundred and fifty new peers.'

'Would that have happened?'

'God, yes! Asquith was determined not to have his precious Parliament Bill thrown out again. I have it on the best authority – Winston's, if you really want to know – that the PM had drawn up a list of potential nominees. And if the Peers had been flooded with two hundred and fifty of Asquith's creatures, we'd have been finished.'

Paul sipped his whisky thoughtfully. The almost tropical heat of the day – the temperature in the capital had stood, at one point, at over one hundred degrees fahrenheit – had cooled a little with the coming of night, but it was still sultry. No breeze from the open window stirred the curtains.

'It seems to me you're finished, anyway,' he observed. 'You've agreed, by passing this bill, to veto your own veto. Self-castration, I should call it.'

'Dear boy, as the blessed St Martin, or someone equally dreary, once remarked, half a loaf is better than no bread at all.' Francis swallowed his drink in two gulps and rose to pour himself another. 'This way, at least, the Lords has survived. But if we'd been swamped by two hundred and fifty new Liberal peers, we'd have been sunk without trace.' He returned to his seat, holding his tumbler up to the lamplight and watching the tawny liquid slop gently up the sides of the glass. 'HM'll be pleased. Poor George! These first fourteen months of his reign have been burdened with one constitutional crisis after another. Two elections last year. . . . Ah, me! We're living in perilous times, dear boy. Our houses are all built on shifting sand. Thank you for coming to give me your moral support. Olga's no earthly use when it comes to politics.'

'I hope you appreciate that I've missed India's sixteenth

birthday for you. It's going to cost me that gold and pearl bracelet we saw in Bond Street to worm my way back into favour.'

The Duke laughed shortly. 'If you're expecting sympathy, forget it. What do you want me to say? That my heart bleeds for you and all those lovely American dollars that Beatrice left you? Dear boy, I have problems of my own. Just when we were beginning to see some return from our speculation in the Lena goldfields, my sister-in-law wants to pull out.'

'Anna?'

'I've no other sister-in-law, Allah be praised!'

'But why does she want to pull out now?' Paul stifled a yawn and glanced at the silver-case clock on the mantelpiece, a beautiful example of the work of Edward Webbe, which he had always secretly coveted. The hands stood at twenty minutes past twelve. His present country habits were making him sleepy.

'God knows! And I mean that, literally. Or Anna does. She has some bee in her bonnet that it's wrong to speculate. When I asked why God hadn't told her that four years ago, she flounced out of the room in a pet, and I got a wigging from Olga.'

Paul finished his drink and refused the offer of a second. 'I'll buy her out, if you really feel you can't afford it. Or we'll split, fifty-fifty.'

The Duke made no answer for a moment or two. One of the new motorized taxi-cabs rumbled past the window and turned into Berkeley Square.

'Well?' Paul asked impatiently. It had been a tiring, if exciting, day, and all he wanted now was to sleep. In less than five minutes, he could be in Hill Street and safely tucked up in bed. This time tomorrow, he would be at Latchetts, where Margaret would be waiting. He no longer 'did' the Season. The grouse-moors of Scotland had not seen him for the past four years.

'I was just thinking, dear boy.' The Duke looked at his cousin from beneath drooping lids, at his most suave and persuasive. 'Olga and I were saying only the other day that you ought to think of marrying again. You need a hostess for Hill Street and Latchetts. You shouldn't become a recluse,

164

you know, if only for the sake of the girls. Someone has to bring them out, when the time comes, and it's not an easy thing for a man to do alone. Of course, I quite see that in your – er – peculiar circumstances, you wouldn't want a wife who would make demands on you, or fancy herself romantically attached. So all things considered . . . one way and another . . . Olga and I both agree how very suitable dear Anna would be.'

Fifteen

'You've been very silent since you returned from London,' Margaret said. 'Silent and preoccupied.'

'What? . . . have I? I'm sorry. I'm just tired.' Paul put his arm around her waist and squeezed it gently.

They were walking in the woods above Latchetts. Paul had been home a week, but from the first he had been absent-minded. Their love-making had been as good as ever. The night of his return, Margaret had experienced that same thrill which she had known in the gatehouse-room, all those years ago. He seemed hers even more completely than before he went away. Yet, in the morning, he had been morose, barely answering her questions, handing her the flat, velvet-lined box containing a diamond brooch with as much indifference as if he had been giving her a stick of seaside rock. Previously, he had always taken great pleasure in the presents he had given her, insisting that she try on any piece of jewellery at once, and boyishly pleased at her delighted exclamations.

'I enjoy giving you things like that,' he had once said, when she had protested against the extravagance of a pair of ruby earrings. 'You've never had them. Giving jewellery to Beatrice was like taking coals to Newcastle. Her father anticipated her every whim.'

There were other differences between Margaret and Beatrice which he had not mentioned. He had loved his wife, but he could appreciate now how dignified and reticent that love had been. It was not that Beatrice had disliked making love; on the contrary, there were many times when she had positively seemed to enjoy it. But there had always been an element of maternal indulgence, and, afterwards, he had felt

166

appropriately grateful. With Margaret, there was no need, or wish, for gratitude. With her there was only a deep, abiding happiness.

He could not marry her, they both knew that. He would be ostracized immediately by society if he did so. A man in his position did not marry his children's governess without a good deal of scandal and unpleasantness. Neither had it been Paul's intention, when Margaret first became his mistress, to cut himself off from his former friends and acquaintances. He had not envisaged any drastic alteration in the way he lived. Yet, inevitably, it had happened. He had gradually withdrawn from any kind of public life, spending more and more of his time at Latchetts, going only occasionally to Bath, and even less frequently to London. The reason for this seclusion had been his reluctance to be very long away from Margaret; a sense that any time spent out of her company was wasted. He still felt that, even today, although not quite so intensely as he had once done. And this recent trip to London had awakened one, at least, of his old enthusiasms. He had always enjoyed the cut and thrust of political life, even as a mere spectator. He realized that he had begun to vegetate, and the thought irked him.

'You always said you'd stand for Parliament one day,' Francis had reminded him. 'Now's your chance. We're about due for a Conservative revival.'

The old ambitions had begun to stir. The excitement engendered over the passing of the Parliament Bill had remained with him, even after he reached home. The affairs of Latchetts, the demands of his growing family, no longer seemed as all-absorbing as they had done. He had tasted blood and he was ready for the hunt.

But, as the Duke had reminded him, he needed a wife. Apart from anything else, people expected him to marry again. Four years as a widower was quite long enough for any man. And in the not-too-distant future, India and Mareth would be presented at court. There would be coming-out balls, parties, soirées, and they would need a chaperon. It was something which he had begun to consider even before this last trip to London, but which he had tried to put out of his mind. The idea of any other woman after Margaret was unbearable. And he had no illusions that she would regard his remarriage as anything but the grossest betrayal. Besides, how could he possibly court a woman with a mistress and her children in the background? A mistress, moreover, whom he had absolutely no intention of leaving.

And then Francis had suggested Anna; Anna, who might be happy to exchange her life of social dependence on sister and brother-in-law for marriage. She knew of Margaret's existence, of course, but she was Russian, and believed in the right of men to do exactly as they pleased. Furthermore, she had no great liking for the country. She could queen it in London, while Margaret and her children remained at Latchetts. Her religion was the one stumbling block. She was unlikely to abandon Russian Orthodoxy as Olga had so obligingly done when she married Francis; but it was probable that she and Paul could come to terms.

'Dear boy,' Francis had assured his cousin, 'it's the ideal marriage for you. Everything will work like a dream.'

In London, Paul had deluded himself that Francis could be right. The closer he got to Latchetts, however, the less feasible he thought it. It was never easy, even in her absence, to picture Margaret as the compliant, docile little woman; Paul had only to be in her company for twenty-four hours to recognize the strong-minded, independent spirit which characterized women from across the Atlantic, even more than their British counterparts. Margaret lived with him as his mistress because it was what she wanted to do, because she loved him and because she accepted that he was unable to marry her without doing himself and his children irreparable harm. She had given up a great deal for his sake – family, reputation – and in return she had a right to expect his loyalty. Even his own conscience jibbed at what he was about to propose.

Nevertheless, he needed a wife, one of equal birth and social standing as himself, if he were to enter the political arena, and Margaret would never be accepted by the Conservative party in that role. But was there really any need to mention it yet? He had not even put his proposal to Anna. Surely he could afford to let the matter drift for a while.

The woods were beautiful today, the trees standing like

ghosts in the quivering heat. A bank frothed with rose campions, and little clumps of scarlet pimpernel gleamed like blood among the grasses. He turned to smile at Margaret. Each time he came back to her, her beauty struck Paul afresh. She was even lovelier at thirty-one than when she had first come to England ten years earlier.

'You're a miracle,' he said, pausing to kiss her. He began pulling the pins from the heavy coils of auburn hair.

She did not resist. Her total lack of inhibition was one of the many things about her which fascinated him. Margaret had no scruples, as Beatrice would have had, about making love in broad daylight under the trees. She knew that at this time of the morning John Penfold would be at home, in the gamekeeper's cottage, having his dinner. The younger children were in the nursery with Nanny Watkins, while Mareth and India had been invited to Kynance for the day. This gesture of the Bastardos was plainly intended to convey that, although they strongly disapproved of Paul, they exonerated the girls as innocent bystanders. Moreover, India and Mareth were both dotingly fond of little Raymond Bastardo, a bright, chubby, dark-haired child of five. Paul had been in two minds whether or not to allow the visit; but Margaret's amusement, coupled with his own desire that his two elder daughters should not suffer by any action of his, had eventually decided him in its favour.

They lay on the ground, on a bed of last year's leaves and twigs, tinder-dry now in the fierce summer heat, and made love. Later, Margaret lay contentedly, looking up at the starred sunlight glimpsed between the interlacing branches of the trees, her arms linked behind her head. She grinned lazily at Paul, who was still buttoning his jacket.

'London must have been unbearable this summer,' she murmured. 'Henry has been running around the nursery stark naked.'

Paul laughed. 'I'm sure Nanny Watkins didn't approve of that.'

'Oh. . . . She doesn't have much to do with Henry and Antonia. I thought it best for her just to be responsible for George. Polly Ching and I manage the other two between us. And Lilian can be useful . . . when she wants to be.'

'What has Nanny been saying?' Paul's voice was grim.

Margaret sat up and hugged her knees. 'Honey, don't make a fuss, please. Nanny is entitled to her opinions. It says something for her loyalty that she stays with you at all, considering how much she dislikes and disapproves of me.'

'She has no cause to dislike you. You go out of your way to be polite.'

'That's just my good New England upbringing. Nanny's attitude is the same as most other women's, in this country and in the States. My own sister has disowned me. . . . No! No, Paul! I don't want to hear again how grateful you are! I have pleased myself. I love you. . . . Talking of Jessie, I found out while you were away that she has been trying to persuade Lilian and Ralph to go and live with her. She wrote a letter to Lilian.'

'That's preposterous!' Paul broke out angrily. 'How dare she! I know you don't read your children's letters, so I'm happy that Lilian had the good sense to tell you about it.'

'Lilian told me about it because she wants to live with Dan and Jessie,' Margaret said drily. 'Of course, I informed her that in no circumstances would I permit it. She had already put the proposition to Ralph, on her own initiative, which he turned down flat.' Margaret stared at the patch of sun-bleached grass in front of her. It was odd how little she respected her elder son for that decision.

'Sensible chap, young Ralph. Got his head screwed on the right way, like poor Hugh.' Paul's reaction was simple and predictable. He was not plagued by doubts about people's motives. 'But Lilian must be made to forget this nonsense.' There was a moment's silence before he added plaintively: 'I can't understand why she isn't happy here.'

Margaret sighed. 'Honey, that's because you've never been an eight-year-old girl. No matter how badly other people behave, girls of that age expect their mothers to conduct themselves with propriety. The only time I feel really guilty about what I've done, the only occasion on which my "good Methodist conscience", as Daniel calls it, troubles me, is when I consider the effect my actions are having on Lilian.' Paul looked at her, and she saw again the uneasiness in his eyes, but for once she misread his expression. 'Honey, don't let it bother you. It's my problem, not yours. It's something I shall just have to live with.'

'If you ever feel you . . . you want to leave me. . . .'

Margaret laughed and got up, reaching down to help him to his feet.

'I love you,' she repeated.

Paul put his arms around her. 'And I love you,' he whispered. 'Whatever happens, remember that.'

She leaned away from him a little. There was something in his manner which worried her.

'Now, what does that mean?' she asked with suspicion.

He muttered evasively, but before she could probe further she heard Polly Ching's voice, anxiously calling her name. She stepped up out of the sheltering hollow to the top of the bank.

'I'm here, Polly. What's the matter?'

'Oh, Mrs Stafford, mum! Oh dear! I don't know how to tell you.' The girl's cap was awry and her face was tear-stained. 'Oh, mum, we can't find Miss Lilian anywhere. We've all been looking for an hour or more, even Nanny.' Polly started to cry again, while Margaret stood petrified, too frightened to speak.

Paul said sharply: 'Pull yourself together, girl, and tell Mrs Stafford exactly what's happened.' He gave her his handkerchief, as she continued to sniff.

Polly made a desperate effort to be calm. 'She – Miss Lilian – was in the little nursery, with me and Master Henry. Miss Antonia was asleep. Then Miss Lilian said she was going along to the schoolroom to see her brother. He was playing Snap there, with Master George.'

'And?' prompted Paul, as Polly threatened to subside once more into tears.

'She never went there, sir. Oh, mum! I'm sorry, but I didn't check on her for almost an hour. I didn't think there was any need. But she's disappeared, mum. We've looked everywhere we can possibly think of, and she's nowhere to be seen.'

'We came as soon as we got your message,' Margaret said.

The flat over the shop seemed unusually oppressive in the continuing August heat-wave. She was glad now of Paul's

171

decision to accompany her to Bath, although, at first, she had tried to dissuade him. She had felt that she would prefer to deal with Daniel and Jessie alone.

The sight of Lilian, however, clinging to her Uncle Daniel and begging not to be sent back to Latchetts, had upset her so much that it was comforting to feel Paul's hand on her shoulder. For fully a minute, she had not trusted herself to speak.

'How did she get here?' Paul asked.

It was Daniel who answered. 'Apparently she hid in the back of a hay-cart which was going to Bodmin Road station. When she got there, she told a railway porter that she was waiting to see an aunt who was passing through on her way from Truro to Bristol. The porter told her what time the next up-train was due, and when it arrived she managed to scramble into an empty compartment and hide under one of the seats.'

'But did no one discover her?' Through her anger and hurt, Margaret could not help feeling proud of her young daughter's resourcefulness. It demonstrated remarkably quick thinking for a child of eight.

'Not until they were well past Taunton. The gentleman who eventually found her informed the guard. Lilian gave him our address, and a policeman brought her here yesterday morning.'

'And now that she is here,' Jessie put in, grim-faced, 'I hope you'll have the decency to let the child stay.'

'Lilian's place is with her mother,' Paul said coldly.

'Not,' retorted Jessie, 'when that mother is dead to all sense of shame. Not when that mother flaunts herself in the eyes of the world as a scarlet woman! Not when that mother is so careless of what she owes to her family that she can bear two children out of wedlock, with the constant threat of more to come.'

'Be quiet, Jess,' begged Daniel. He looked acutely miserable, as Margaret had no doubt he was. Her brother-in-law's inclination to avoid any sort of unpleasantness must, on this occasion, be bitterly at war with his sense of duty.

'I shall not be quiet. It's high time Maggie knew exactly how I feel.'

'I've always known that, Jess,' Margaret said, with a tired

smile. 'You've always made your feelings perfectly plain.' She suddenly wanted to be done with the whole business and get back to Latchetts. She addressed her daughter. 'Lilian, honey, come here a minute.' She held out her hands. 'It's all right. I'm not going to force you to do anything you don't want to do.' The child went to her reluctantly, returning her mother's gaze with hostile eyes. 'Do you truly want to stay here, with Aunt Jess?'

'Margaret, don't be foolish—' Paul was beginning, but she frowned him into silence.

'It's all right,' she reassured him with an effort. 'Lilian, I'm waiting for your answer.'

'Yes,' Lilian replied sullenly. 'I want to stay here, with Uncle Dan and Mark.'

Margaret hesitated, appreciating, as did no one else in the emotion-charged room, the subtle difference between what she had asked and Lilian's answer.

'There you are!' Jessie exclaimed triumphantly. 'And she can have her own room. I shall clear out the little store-room at the back of the shop.'

Margaret turned once more to her daughter. 'Honey, are you certain, absolutely positive, that you don't want to come home to Latchetts?'

'It's not home,' Lilian said hotly. 'It's not my home. It's his!' She indicated Paul scornfully. 'And Henry's and Tonia's.' She began to cry. 'I hate them! They took you away from me. Why couldn't we have stayed as we were, after Papa was killed? Just you and me and Ralph!'

Margaret struggled to keep her voice steady. 'Oh, honey. Honey! I didn't realize you felt as badly as this.'

'How did you expect her to feel?' Jessie interrupted. 'Pleased that you'd foisted a bastard half-brother and sister on her?' Daniel made a protesting noise, and she rounded on him. 'Oh, don't be such a pea-goose! Do you think the child has lived in an immoral household for more than three years without understanding what the word "bastard" means?'

Margaret ignored her. She had eyes and thoughts only for her daugher. 'Lilian, why didn't you tell me?'

'Would it have made any difference if she had?' Jessie was determined not to be silenced.

'You wouldn't have cared if I had told you,' Lilian declared. 'You don't love me. You don't love Ralph. You didn't love Papa. I heard you tell Auntie Jessie once that you were glad he was dead.'

There was a sudden stillness in the little room. A horse clopped by outside; a motor-car wheezed down Milsom Street. No one seemed able to move. Daniel, looking at the scene with less than his customary detachment, was nevertheless reminded of the court of Polydectes, turned to stone after gazing on the Medusa's head.

Margaret heard someone say: ' "Out of the mouths of babes. . . .",' and realized that it was herself.

The bell jangled in the shop below. Daniel rose to his feet with alacrity and Jessie sniffed. She could not recall the last time she had seen her husband so eager to attend to a customer. As he passed Margaret's chair, however, Daniel paused.

'She'll get over it, Maggie,' he said in a low voice, so that Lilian should not overhear. 'Give her time. But until she does, Jess and I will be very happy to have her living here with us.'

He left the room and his footsteps receded down the lino-covered stairs. A moment later, they heard his voice raised cheerfully to greet whoever was in the shop.

Margaret got up and smoothed down her dress, a fashionable expensive pale-green silk, the soft folds draped to a narrow hem. Her hat was a matching straw, its wide brim upswept to one side, the crown almost covered with plumes of green-shaded feathers. Jessie noted sourly that her sister's earrings and brooch were set with real emeralds. She fingered the narrow gold chain round her neck and remembered mockingly how proud she had been of it when Daniel had presented it to her for her birthday.

Margaret made one last appeal to Lilian. 'Honey, are you quite, quite sure that you want to be left here?'

Lilian turned away, staring out of the window without speaking. Her face had momentarily lost its prettiness, and was dark and surly. Margaret looked at her sister.

'I shall send you an allowance every month, Jess.'

Jessie would dearly have loved to disclaim all need for the money, but she knew it was impossible. She inclined her head stiffly.

174

'Very well. But I won't accept charity. You are to send no more than is strictly necessary for Lilian's upkeep. And every penny you send will be spent on her alone. Is that understood?'

Margaret nodded mutely as she picked up her parasol of green twilled silk. Her eyes were fixed on Lilian's rigid back.

'Honey . . . Paul and I are going now. Won't you at least say goodbye?'

Lilian shook her head without turning round.

Margaret took a step towards her, but noted the unconscious tensing of Lilian's muscles. She glanced helplessly at Paul.

He tucked her hand into the crook of his arm and pressed it. 'Let's go,' he said quietly. 'There's nothing to be gained by staying here. We've done everything we possibly can.'

Margaret nodded. Tears were very near, stinging her eyelids. She mastered her overwhelming desire to seize Lilian in her arms and promise her anything she wanted in return for just one smile, one little token of forgiveness. But it was too late for promises, and the only one Lilian wanted, Margaret was no longer free to make. If there had been no Henry, no Antonia, she would have sacrificed her personal happiness, and Paul's; not gladly, perhaps, nor willingly, but sacrificed it all the same, for the sake of her eldest child.

Daniel had come upstairs again and was standing in the doorway, watching her. It bothered Margaret that she had lost her brother-in-law's good opinion; but the suspicion that it was because she had supplanted Beatrice in Paul's affections, rather than because she was 'living in sin', as Jessie had once told her sternly, assuaged the feeling of guilt which his disapproval aroused. She smiled as best she could, and held out her hand.

'We're leaving now, Daniel. Look after Lilian for me.' Her voice broke and she was unable to say any more.

'Of course,' he answered, swallowing hard. He, also, was feeling the strain. He took her proffered hand and shook it. Paul he ignored.

Margaret looked over her shoulder at Lilian, but the child had not moved from her position by the window. Jessie, too, remained where she was, in her favourite armchair by the empty fireplace. She nodded curtly in response to her sister's tentative: 'Goodbye, Jess. I'll have all Lilian's things sent on.'

'Goodbye, Maggie.' There was something horribly final in the way she spoke. Margaret knew that unless, until, she left Paul, Jessie and Lilian were lost to her.

'If we don't go now, we shall miss our connection at Bristol,' Paul reminded her gently. It had been agreed between them, before they left for Bath that morning, that they would not stop overnight at Bladud House. Margaret had not been inside it since Beatrice died, and, today of all days, she could not face the prospect of raising ghosts.

She gave one last, imploring glance at Lilian, then preceded Paul out of the room, down the stairs and through the empty shop, into the sun-drenched alleyway of Green Street.

Sixteen

'Dear boy, it was good of you to come,' beamed the Duke, as he ushered Paul on to the terrace at Hawksworth. 'Particularly as I know how worried and busy you must be at the moment, with all this agitation amongst the miners. Demanding a minimum wage, indeed! I don't know what this country's coming to! Getting just like France. Bloody revolutionaries everywhere.' He waved Paul to one of the wicker chairs set around a small table where a tray of coffee-things had been placed. It was one of the Duke's few rules never to drink alcohol before eleven thirty in the morning. 'Mind you, it's not just this country,' he went on, 'the whole damn world's in a mess. You've heard, of course, that Stolypin's been assassinated? On the first, at the Kiev Opera House? Bad business. Naturally, the girls' – he referred indulgently and a little sarcastically to his wife and sister-in-law – 'can't talk of anything else. They're convinced that this priest fellow, Rasputin, is behind it, but I told them that's nonsense.' Francis poured two cups of coffee and pushed one towards his cousin. 'According to *The Times*, the assassin was some police informer called Bogrov. But that doesn't satisfy Olga and the Countess. They're so incensed against this *strannik*, or *starets*, or whatever they call him, that they'd hold him personally responsible for stealing the Mona Lisa, if they could. Incidentally, that's another bad business. Security at the Louvre must be getting damn lax, that's all I have to say.'

Having delivered himself of this diatribe, the Duke leaned back in his chair and surveyed his rolling park and pasture-land with all the complacency of a man untouched by the world's misfortunes. The sky was a lake of deepest blue, with,

177

swimming in it, one small cloud, shaped, appropriately, like a fish. Sunlight edged across the well-trimmed lawns, and in the distance the gilded trees were emerging gradually from the early morning mist. But on this September day there was a hint of autumn in the air; the smell of wood-smoke, ripe apples and the evocative scent of new-mown hay.

Paul sipped his coffee. 'I was surprised to get your letter,' he said. 'I thought this was your time for visiting Marienbad, or one of the other European spas.'

'Used to be, dear boy, used to be. When good old Teddy was alive, we all went to Marienbad, every September, to keep him company. But nowadays' – the Duke shrugged – 'the court is much quieter, less mobile. HM doesn't care for "abroad". Been invited to Balmoral, though, for a country week-end. Not my cup of tea, really, but Olga's pleased, and that's all that matters. Makes life so much simpler if she's happy.' He glanced at his cousin. 'One thing that would make her happy – very happy – is to see Anna satisfactorily married. She's thirty-six. Ain't getting any younger.'

'Ah,' Paul said, keeping his eyes fixed on the pleasant prospect in front of him.

'Thought you seemed rather taken with the idea, when I put it to you last month in London. I wondered if you'd thought any more about it?'

Paul understood now why Olga, who, in spite of her lazy ways, was a punctilious hostess, had not greeted him on his arrival and had so far remained unseen.

As if he knew what was passing through his cousin's mind, Francis said blandly: 'Olga has taken Anna to visit some friends near Chippenham. Long-standing engagement. She asked me to give you her apologies.'

The Duke's letter, inviting Paul to Hawksworth for the week-end, had arrived at Latchetts two days earlier.

'Why don't you go?' Margaret had urged him. 'It will do you good. I haven't been much company for the past few weeks.'

Paul had not contested her statement, but he understood the reason for her recent rather churlish behaviour. She was still worried about Lilian, fretting over whether or not she had done the right thing in letting her stay with Jessie. He had tried to persuade her to talk about it, but she had refused, turning in on herself and making him feel like a stranger. He thought that perhaps she was right, and that a short separation might be beneficial for both of them.

So he had come to Hawksworth when really he should have been at Bath, consulting with his manager about possible trouble at Longreach, now that miners all over the country were agitating for a minimum wage. There had been a lot of unrest throughout the long hot summer, not just among pit-workers, but also among the armed services, firemen and dockers. Nationally, there had been a damaging miners' strike, but there had been comparatively little bother at Longreach. The disaster of four years earlier seemed to have quenched their desire for confrontation.

Instead, Paul reflected with a wry grin, he had let himself in for another sort of confrontation; out of the frying pan and into the fire. In the trouble over Lilian, he had almost forgotten his cousin's proposition, pushing it to the back of his mind.

'It really isn't a propitious moment,' he said to Francis, refusing a second cup of coffee and, for once, deploring his cousin's stringent rule of nothing stronger until after mid-morning.

The Duke raised his eyebrows, but was too well-bred to ask for details.

'A pity,' he remarked, after a moment's silence. 'I expect you know that old Brimley, the Member for Hawksworth and Clarendon, is seriously ill. Can't last much longer I hear, so there's sure to be a by-election sometime soon. I was thinking you might want to put up. Brimley's agent assures me that the party has no one particular in mind. But you'd have to regularize your marital position, dear boy. A wife would be an incalculable asset.'

'And Margaret?'

Again the Duke shrugged. 'Keep her and the – er – children quietly down at Latchetts, and there should be no insuperable problem. There are more MPs than our virtuous middle classes would like to think with a mistress tucked away in some discreet corner. Lloyd George's private life wouldn't bear looking into, for a start. I'm not saying it wouldn't be better for you if you could manage to disentangle yourself

179

from your enchantress's clutches. . . . No? . . . All right, all right. I was afraid you would find that a bit too much to swallow.'

'It would be impossible,' Paul snapped.

'Very well. Impossible, if you insist. But whatever your feelings for the beautiful Mrs Stafford, if you want to go into politics, dear boy, you need a wife. And not merely a smoke-screen. You need her as a hostess, as a proper step-mother for the girls, above all, for respectability.'

'And Anna would provide all these things.'

'Exactly. With the added advantage that she wouldn't forever be hanging around your neck, demanding that you love her. But I said all this in town. A sensible arrangement, that's how Anna will see it. A barter. A home for her, a wife for you.' The Duke leaned across the table and shook his cousin's arm. 'You have all week-end to think about it, dear boy. I'm sure you'll come to the right decision.'

'There's a person to see you,' Nanny Watkins said, poking her head around the door of the schoolroom, where Mareth, India and Ralph were doing their Monday-morning lessons.

Margaret, who had been unsuccessfully trying to inspire her pupils with an interest in the Peasants' Revolt, was grateful for the diversion.

'What sort of person?' she asked.

Nanny Watkins sniffed. 'I didn't enquire. I'm not employed as a messenger. I'm just telling you what Mrs Hinkley told me, that's all.'

'Where is this person?' Margaret was resigned by now to Nanny's hostility.

'Outside the back door. Mrs Hinkley wouldn't let him in the house. In fact, she would have sent him packing at once, she said, except that he was so insistent he knew you. Turned very nasty, apparently, when she told him to scarper.'

Feeling that she had already imparted more information than she had intended, Nanny withdrew. Her parting sniff implied that she had always known that Margaret had low connections. A shame, Nanny muttered to herself, as she hurried along to the nursery, a crying shame that Mr Devereaux had ever clapped eyes on that woman.

180

Intrigued, and finding that it was almost noon, Margaret dismissed her little class and went downstairs. Mrs Hinkley was rolling out pastry on the marble slab in the kitchen.

'Nanny says that someone wants to see me.'

Mrs Hinkley raised her head. She did not approve of the 'goings-on' which had taken place since the mistress's death, and had more than once considered handing in her notice. But in spite of her disapproval, she could not help liking Margaret, and had fallen an unwilling victim to Henry's and Antonia's charms. So she tolerated the situation and made sure that Hinkley did, too. As she constantly reminded him, they were unlikely to find such comfortable and well-paid positions elsewhere.

'He's out the back,' she said, jerking her head. 'He's an unpleasant customer. I should say he's been on the road for weeks. Smells like it, anyway. I was going to get a couple of the lads to see him off, but I think he's telling the truth when he says he knows you.'

'He gave no name?'

'No. But just you shout for help right away if he gets nasty. I've sent one of the scullery maids to fetch two of the lads in from the gardens.'

The man was seated on the bench outside the back door, scuffing the gravel of the yard with his boots. These, like everything else he had on, were deplorable, the upper of the left one parting company with the sole and showing a dirty and blistered foot. His trousers were darned and patched, and the lower halves of the legs were white with dust. His coat was out at elbows, his flannel shirt collarless. His hands were badly calloused, and Margaret's first impression was that he was old; an impression borne out by the stout ash-stick leaning against the bench at his side. But the eyes, when she encountered them, peering at her from the tangle of matted hair and beard which, together, almost covered his face, were those of a young man. There was something familiar about them, with their hazel-flecked irises and dark crescent lashes. Even so, it was not until he spoke that she recognized him.

' 'Morning, Mrs Stafford.' The harsh, grating accent of north Somerset, which she had once heard every day, now fell strangely on her ears after years of listening to the soft Cornish burr.

'Arthur Barlow! What are you doing here?'

He grinned, but it was an effort. His head lolled on his shoulders from exhaustion.

'That's not much of a greeting when I've walked all this way to see you.'

'Walked all the way?' She was horrified. 'Sleeping in the open?'

'Why not? It's been hot and dry. And when you've been in prison, you appreciate the great outdoors.'

'Prison?' Then she remembered that he had been sentenced to six months' hard labour for his part in the riot which led to Hugh's death. 'But that was more than three years ago.'

'It stays with you. Especially when you can't get a job because of it. My mother's in the workhouse, did you know? We lost our cottage, of course. It belongs to the mine. I've survived by doing labouring jobs, when I could get them, but people don't like employing you once they discover you've been in prison. No Somerset mine owner will touch me with a barge-pole.'

'What about Wales or the north?'

He shook his head and coughed. 'I'm a west-countryman. I should die in those alien places. Besides, I want to be near my mother.' He swayed suddenly. 'Do you . . . do you have any food? I haven't eaten for the past two days.'

'I'm sorry! I should have thought. . . . Wait here.'

Margaret went back into the kitchen, where Mrs Hinkley was trimming a steak and kidney pie. She had been joined by the scullery-maid and two big, red-faced Cornish boys, who helped out each day in the gardens.

'Everything all right?' she asked, as Margaret appeared.

'Yes. He must have something to eat.'

'He's not setting foot in my kitchen until he's had a bath and those clothes have been burnt,' the housekeeper replied grimly. 'But there are some pasties just out of the oven, if you want to take him one of those.'

Margaret seized one of the pasties and went out again to Arthur Barlow. He fell on the food ravenously, cramming it into his mouth, quite oblivious of the fact that it was burning his tongue. When he had finished, he wiped his mouth with the back of one hand.

'That was good,' he said thickly. 'Any cider?'

Margaret went to the barrel which always stood on the stone-flagged floor of the dairy passage. A wooden cup hung on a chain from the wall. She unhooked and filled it, and carried the mugful of golden liquid outside. Arthur Barlow drank it straight down.

'I'll suffer for that presently,' he said. 'Prison food ruined my digestion. But it's worth it. I've never tasted a pasty like that before.'

Margaret sat on the bench beside him, trying to ignore the smell. 'What are you doing here?' she asked again.

'I'm here because I'm desperate. So desperate that I'm even willing to come crawling to you, to ask you to get me a job in the Longreach mine.'

'Me? But what on earth can I do for you?'

Arthur Barlow looked at her scornfully. 'You're his fancy-piece, aren't you? Mr Paul bloody Devereaux's fancy-piece. Everyone in Longreach says so.'

Margaret flushed, but answered defiantly: 'I'm his mistress, if that's what you mean.'

He glanced at her again, but this time with more respect. At least she hadn't tried to deny it.

'Well then, if anyone could persuade him to give me a job, you could. I'm too old now for carting-boy, but I'll do anything else he likes to offer.'

'You have a nerve. . . . What makes you think I'd be willing to speak to Mr Devereaux on your behalf? I'm sure just the mention of your name would make him extremely angry, so why should I risk his displeasure?'

'Because you have guts. Or you did once, before you went soft. You used to be on our side.'

'I was never on anyone's side. I simply wanted to see justice done, that's all.'

'You won't see it done consorting with the bosses,' he answered bitterly. He looked about him, suddenly furious. 'You really sold your soul.'

'To the devil?' Margaret, too, was growing angry. 'If that's

how you regard Paul Devereaux, why do you want to work for
him again?'

'It's how I see all bosses,' he retorted. 'But I have to live,
and mining is what I know. And the only way an ex-convict
can get a job is by what Counsel would call special pleading. I
don't know anyone else who could exert the sort of pressure
you can. That's why I've walked all these miles to see you.'

Margaret sighed, her anger evaporating. 'I think you over-
rate my influence with Mr Devereaux, Arthur, but I'll do my
best. He's been away these past few days, visiting his cousin,
but he'll be back tonight or tomorrow. What will you do in the
meantime?'

'I was rather hoping—' He hesitated, then went on: 'I was
hoping you might be able to help me.'

She regarded him critically. 'I can probably get you a razor
and a suit of clothes. Maybe even a bath. And if you don't
mind roughing it for another night, you could sleep in the
stables. I think Mrs Hinkley might be persuaded to feed you.'

He smiled and held out his hand. He looked almost dead
from exhaustion.

'Done,' he said. 'I always knew you were a spunky little
Yankee-doodle-dandy.'

'No, Margaret,' Paul said roundly, 'that's enough. I've told
you that I am not prepared to re-employ Arthur Barlow. The
man's a trouble-maker. I am exceedingly angry that he should
have bothered you. Whatever has happened to him is his own
fault. He may keep the suit of clothes you found for him, but
that is as far as my charity goes. He must be off my property by
tomorrow morning. Now, that is an end of the matter.'

Margaret bit her lip. She disliked failure, but she had spent
the last hour pleading Arthur Barlow's cause, all to no avail.
She had no intention of spoiling Paul's first evening home with
fruitless bickering. She smiled as they rose from the dinner-
table and went into the drawing-room.

'It's lovely to have you back again,' she said.

His response was to hold her so tightly that she could feel
the thumping of his heart beneath his jacket.

'I love you,' he told her fiercely.

'Paul! Paul!' she protested, laughing. 'We shall be seen.'

But what did it matter if they were? Everyone at Latchetts accepted their relationship, and, with one or two exceptions, like Nanny Watkins, was beginning, unconsciously, to treat her as the lady of the house.

In the drawing-room the lamps were already lit. The Worcester coffee service had been laid out on a low circular table inlaid with Cornish minerals set in serpentine, a marble found in the Lizard peninsula. Both items were two of the many gifts showered on Beatrice by her father. Although she saw them every day, tonight, for some reason, they impinged on Margaret's consciousness, shocking her out of her sense of well-being. She crossed to the table and began pouring the coffee.

'Leave that!' Paul spoke so abruptly that she started. Some of the hot liquid splashed on her dress. She looked at him questioningly, suddenly irritated.

'Really, Paul! Look what you've made me do. Coffee stains are difficult to get out.'

'Margaret.' He was standing near one of the windows, partly in shadow, so that she could barely make out the contours of his face. 'Margaret,' he said again, with a kind of quiet desperation, 'Countess Anna Rastorguyeva and I are going to be married. I asked her yesterday, before I left Hawksworth, and she has done me the honour of accepting.'

A stillness settled over the room like a pall. Margaret continued dabbing futilely at the mark on her dress, but without any idea of what she was doing. After a while, she said mechanically, in a voice totally unlike her own: 'Congratulations. When would you like me to leave?'

He moved forward then, into the golden circle of lamplight. His face was haggard. 'For God's sake, Maggie! Don't talk that way.'

She looked up from her seat by the table. Her face was as white as his own.

'But you just told me—' Had he really told her, or was it part of a nightmare? 'You told me you were going to be married.'

'I am. But that's no reason why things should be different between us. Listen, Margaret, darling, let me explain.'

She could hear him; she could hear all the arguments in

favour of his marriage to Anna which he was so cogently urging. Part of her mind could even understand the reasoning behind them. But it was as if she were listening to someone in another room, far off and muffled.

'So you see,' he finished lamely, 'there's no reason why things should change between us.'

He really believes that, she thought, still looking at him from her bubble of detachment. She felt very high and light, floating somewhere near the ceiling, watching him a long way down below. He genuinely believed that a wife, a career in politics, a return to the social round, would not affect them; or, at any rate, would not affect her. She would be there, as always, when she was wanted. . . .

A hot, bright anger began to burn inside her. The bubble melted and she was facing him across the coffee cups and the inlaid table. She had a sudden urge to pick everything up and throw it at the nearest wall.

Instead, she stood up slowly and said: 'I'll leave first thing tomorrow morning. Ralph can come with me. I'll send for Henry and Antonia as soon as I'm settled.'

'And where will you settle?' he asked, attempting to keep his voice as level as her own.

She answered coldly: 'I'll find somewhere. I presume that even with your dubious sense of honour you won't permit your children to starve.'

'I may elect to keep them.'

'Then I shall drag you through every court in the land. I'll create such a fuss that your political career will be finished before it's begun.'

'That's blackmail.'

'If you like. But no more than you deserve.'

Why, in heaven's name, couldn't she scream and yell like a fishwife? Why did her damn pride always stand in her way?

'You bitch,' Paul said deliberately, trying to break through that barrier of icy calm.

He succeeded. She lashed out, hitting him across the cheek. He caught one wrist, pulling her against him, struggling with her, kissing her neck and face.

'Let me go!' she panted. 'I hate you. I never want to see you again.'

Behind the trite words lay an agony of bewilderment and betrayal. Yet, behind that again, was the knowledge which she had carried within her for the past four years, that one day their relationship would have to progress; that she could not keep him stagnating forever at Latchetts, while the rest of the world moved on, without him. In some ways, it was a relief that the moment she had so dreaded had come at last.

She stopped struggling, leaning passively against him, while he pleaded with her.

'Don't leave me, Margaret. Please. I love you. I need you. I can't imagine life without you.'

She started to cry softly, a prey to her own emotions. She hated him for what he was doing to her; for the feeling so many women knew, of being used. But she loved him. She could not in the space of half an hour tear her life up by its roots. Yet she had done it once, when Paul had asked her to be his mistress. Years of loving, of soft living, had weakened her. She was not as resolute as she had been four years ago. Had she, as Arthur Barlow had said, sold her soul?

If so, she was too tired to care. She sat beside Paul on the couch, his arm around her waist, her head on his shoulder, and, despising herself, allowed herself to be lulled by his promises that everything would remain – almost – the same.

'You will stay?' he whispered against her hair. 'Promise me.'

Yes, she would stay. In her own mind, she had already capitulated. But there was one small sop she could throw to her conscience.

'I'll stay,' she replied wearily. 'But, in return, you must do something for me. Find a job for Arthur Barlow at Longreach. I don't think that's too much payment to ask.'

Part Four 1914

If love be good, from whennes cometh my woo?

Seventeen

'Must you go?' she asked. 'Is it absolutely necessary that you attend?'

Paul kissed her tenderly, then got out of bed. Margaret watched him go to the washstand, where he poured water from the jug into an ornate china bowl patterned with cupids.

'Of course I must go,' he said, splashing cold water over his face and body. 'A visit of the British Navy to St Petersburg is an event, my love. Anna and I have been invited, and an Imperial invitation is as good as a command.'

'But you and the Countess lunched at Kronstadt yesterday, aboard the *Lion*. You paid your respects to Admiral Beatty then.'

'And today, he and his officers visit Tsarskoe Selo. Their Imperial Majesties would be deeply offended if their invitation were not honoured. Anna and I would be ostracized.'

Margaret made no reply, leaning back against the pillows and linking her hands behind her head.

Beyond the tall, curtained windows ran the Russian capital's main thoroughfare, the Nevsky Prospect, and the river Neva, on its sluggish way to the Gulf of Finland. Since her arrival the preceding month, Margaret had been assured that she was seeing St Petersburg at its best in the glorious summer weather. She had been told that in the winter it could be cold and damp and foggy, with wind and snow that froze the bones, blowing across the Gulf from the northern arctic wastes. But at its best or not, Margaret was glad that they were not staying long. She disliked St Petersburg.

Why had she let herself be persuaded to come? Paul's

decision to bring George with him on this trip to visit Anna's few remaining relatives had been, she was sure, nothing more than a ruse to ensure her presence as the child's governess.

'He needs a firm hand,' Paul had pleaded. 'He doesn't like Anna and won't mind her.'

'Why take him, then?'

'He is my heir. It would be polite to introduce him to Anna's cousins. And travel will be good for him. It will broaden his outlook.'

'He's only seven,' Margaret had reminded him. She had made no further objections, however, because no more than Paul could she endure the thought of three months' separation.

She despised herself for it. She despised her whole way of life, but she was unable to break free. She loved Paul as passionately as ever.

Paul and Anna had been married in the April of 1912, the month which had witnessed the sinking of the *Titanic*, the introduction of the Minimum Wages Act for miners, and, in Russia, a strike in the Lena goldfields, during which two hundred workers had been killed. Paul had been horrified by the latter incident, resulting in so many deaths because a drunken police officer had ordered his men to open fire. Even the Duke had talked of selling his shares, but Anna and the Duchess had merely remarked that if the *canaille* got out of hand shooting was the only effective way to deal with them.

'Like dogs,' Anna had declared.

The Russian government had taken a more serious view of the affair, and the Duma had ordered a Commission of Enquiry, headed by Alexander Kerensky, whose findings had forced the resignation of the Minister of the Interior.

'Kerensky is a revolutionary. He should never have been appointed,' the Duchess had fumed. 'What do we want with the Duma? The Tsar is *Batiushka*. Little Father. He alone is our ruler. A Duma is a sign of the changing times in Russia.'

If that were so, Margaret had seen little sign of any other changes. Even while reproaching herself for the American habit of snap judgements and instant opinions, she was more aware than Paul or Anna, or any member of the glittering, hedonistic society in which they moved, of two Russias, neither of which had advanced very far beyond the medieval concept of lord and peasant. The present Tsar's grandfather, Alexander II, might have emancipated the serfs in theory, but in practice it was difficult to throw off the customs of a thousand years. In the countryside workers were still knouted, often with fatal results, and in the cities the Cossacks and secret police were everywhere.

In St Petersburg, Margaret had glimpsed the filthy alleys and courtyards lurking behind the palatial façades of the Nevsky Prospect and Million Street. Across the river from the grey-green frontage of the Winter Palace was the grim old fortress of Saints Peter and Paul, where the son of Peter the Great, on his father's orders, had been tortured to death, as had been hundreds of other hapless prisoners. . . .

Paul came back to the bed, pulling on his dressing-gown.

'I must return to my own room,' he said. 'The servants will soon be stirring.'

It was very early morning, but already it was daylight. In this northern city, the summer days were as long as the winter nights. Dawn came soon after midnight.

Margaret nodded. 'And Anna will be up and about, or rather on her knees, praying to one of those hideous icons. And you wouldn't want to upset her, would you, in her condition?'

Paul looked unhappy. He knew how much the fact of Anna's pregnancy disturbed Margaret, particularly as she herself seemed unable to have more children, but he also felt angry at being made to feel guilty. Had she really believed that he would never sleep with Anna? Wasn't it sufficient for her that he did not love his wife? That she was still, as she had been for the past seven years, everything to him? That he could not be separated from her for as little as three months? Why would she not understand that it was his duty to have another son if he could? If anything should happen to George, Latchetts would pass into the hands of some Australian cousin whom he had never seen.

'I love you,' he said. 'I spend nearly all my nights with you. Isn't that enough?'

She wanted to say: 'Of course it's not enough!' But he looked so miserable, so like George or Henry when one of them was in need of reassurance, that she smiled instead.

'I guess I'm missing the children, and I'm afraid they might be missing me.'

He squeezed one of her hands. 'My love, India and Mareth are grown up now. And Henry, Ralph and Tonia are perfectly happy at Latchetts. Particularly as your absence means an extended holiday from the schoolroom.'

She laughed outright at that. 'Oh, go away,' she said, 'before you completely undermine my confidence.'

He grinned down at her. 'What will you and George do today?'

'George is taken care of. That cousin of the Countess who lives near the Moika Canal has invited him to spend the day with her and her children. I shall take him there at ten o'clock, and then the rest of the day is my own.'

'Enjoy it. Go to the shops. Fabergé's. Buy yourself something pretty.'

She did not answer. He went out of the room, closing the door softly behind him.

'Buy yourself something pretty.' That was what she had become: the kept woman, the secret mistress. Or, in her case, the not-so-secret mistress. She was sure that Anna must know of her relationship with Paul. The Countess was no fool. Even if she were, the Duchess must surely have enlightened her. What Margaret doubted was Paul's confident assertion that, if Anna knew, she certainly did not care.

'It was a business transaction. A marriage of convenience. Such arrangements are common in Britain and on the Continent, however rare they might be in America. Anna is no fonder of me than I am of her.'

But Margaret had seen the way the Countess looked at Paul whenever his attention was elsewhere; a look compounded of desperate longing and frustration. Margaret had first noticed it during the brief visit Anna had paid to Latchetts shortly after her marriage; but she had refused to draw the obvious and disturbing conclusion. It had been easy, at first, to resist the notion that the Countess was in love with Paul, because she remained for the most part in London, and spent two months of every winter at Hawksworth. It had not been possible, however, for the two women to be kept completely apart. Inevitably, and with increasing frequency, their paths had crossed; and each time they met, Margaret became more convinced that Anna secretly adored her husband.

The corollary to that idea, of course, was that Anna hated her husband's mistress. It would explain many of the Countess's actions with regard to her step-children: her insistence, last year, that India's coming-out ball at Hill Street be the most brilliant of the Season; her constant showering of Mareth with expensive gifts; her indulgent attitude towards George's rudeness.

'She is trying to make them fonder of her than they are of me,' Margaret had once said to Paul, keeping her tone light and matter of fact.

'Nonsense!' he had retorted. 'In any case, she won't succeed. They don't even like her.'

But while this was true of George, India and Mareth had grown closer to their step-mother during the past twelve months.

Their initial reaction to their father's proposed marriage had been one of outrage and horror.

'That old fuddy-duddy! Papa, you can't be serious!' Margaret could remember India's exclamation of disgust.

'She's such a bore,' had been Mareth's reaction. 'I hope she doesn't think we're going to leave *you*, dear Dunny.'

But in the end, Margaret reflected wryly, getting out of bed and crossing, in her turn, to the washstand, they had left her of their own volition. What Paul had said three years ago was true; they needed someone of their own world to chaperon them into society, to play hostess at all those receptions and parties and balls which followed a young girl's presentation at court. Next year, it would be Mareth's turn, and Margaret would be as useless to her as she had been to India.

At least Paul's political ambitions had not yet been realized. The Member for the Hawksworth and Clarendon constituency still lingered on, against all the odds, and there had been no by-election. It was, however, bound to happen sometime, and Paul had been promised the Conservative candidacy. If he won – and Hawksworth and Clarendon had returned a Tory Member of Parliament since 1802 – Anna would then become as necessary to her husband as she had become to both his daughters.

Margaret did not want to think about it. She washed and dressed quickly in her coolest summer frock. Then, as it was still only a quarter to six, she drew back the curtains and seated herself in a chair near the open window. She would read until it was time to fetch George down to breakfast.

Tsarskoe Selo – the Tsar's village – stood some fifteen miles south of the Russian capital, at the edge of the great St Petersburg plain. It was an enchanted fairyland, created over centuries by the country's rulers as a refuge from Peter the Great's artificial and uncomfortable granite city, built on marshland and spread across nineteen islands. At Tsarskoe Selo, two palaces – the Catherine Palace and the Alexander Palace – a lake, a red-and-gold Chinese pagoda, a pink Turkish bath, acres of velvety lawns, winding paths, grottoes, groves of trees, monuments, obelisks and triumphal arches all made it, in the words of one overawed British midshipman, 'a bloody miracle!'

The young man spoke without thinking, and glanced nervously in the direction of his commanding officer. But Admiral Sir David Beatty, walking ahead with the Tsar and Tsarina, his youthful, clean-shaven face alight with eagerness as he answered Nicholas's questions about the Royal Navy's First Battle Cruiser Squadron, had not heard him. The four young Grand Duchesses, following in the wake of their parents, exchanged shy smiles with the British officers who had escorted them around the flagship *Lion* the previous day.

Paul and Anna were at some distance, amongst the crowd of guests, court officials, ambassadors and members of the diplomatic corps. Anna, four months pregnant and feeling the heat, was looking, Paul thought, a little queasy. Perhaps he had been unwise to give in to her over this Russian trip.

Her sudden demand to pay a belated 'bride-visit' to her relatives in St Petersburg had taken Paul by surprise. In all the nineteen years she and Olga had lived in England, neither of them had expressed the smallest desire to return home, or mentioned any family with whom they were on cordial terms. Now, it appeared that various cousins, an aunt and her own

196

old nurse were all deeply offended at not having received a visit from their 'dearest Anna'. It did not occur to Paul that his wife had invited these protestations; that she, plain, uninteresting Anna Rastorguyeva, almost forty, wished to parade her handsome husband before her astonished and admiring relations. He had finally succumbed to her insistence that the visit was necessary for her peace of mind – and that in her condition, at her age, she should not be thwarted – partly because he could see that she had set her heart on it, and partly because he was feeling restless and in need of a change.

He had been disappointed over the Hawksworth and Clarendon parliamentary seat. The present Member, Joseph Brimley, had made a partial recovery from the heart attack which had felled him, and obstinately refused to resign. True, he had promised not to seek re-election, but in the meantime Paul was growing restive. Hugh Stafford's successor at Longreach had so far proved himself an excellent manager, inspiring confidence in the men and increasing productivity. Indeed, had it not been for the reinstatement of Arthur Barlow, Longreach might have been totally unaffected by the miners' strike which had dragged on throughout 1911 and the early months of 1912.

Paul had frequently regretted his promise to Margaret. At the time, giving Arthur Barlow a job had seemed such a small price to pay for keeping her that it would have been madness to refuse. Now, however, he was not so sure. Instead of being grateful for a second chance – a thing few ex-prisoners ever received – Arthur Barlow had immediately begun to stir up trouble. He had done his best to bring the whole Longreach work-force out on strike in support of miners in the rest of the country; and, since the end of the strike in April 1912, had been, so Paul was reliably informed, in contact with 'Big' Bill Heywood, John Reed and other American dissidents. When the Paterson strikers had marched up Fifth Avenue on 5 June the preceding year, Arthur Barlow had sent them a cable of congratulation. His colliery manager had urged Paul most strongly to rid himself of this thorn in his side, and was amazed by his employer's reluctance to do so. But Paul had given Margaret his word, and, whatever the cost to himself, refused to go back on it until she gave him the necessary permission. Nevertheless, deep down, a grudge had formed of which he was, as yet, barely conscious.

He bent towards Anna and whispered: 'Are you all right? Shall I find Count Vladimir and ask him to make our apologies to Their Imperial Majesties? They will make every allowance for your present condition.'

Anna shook her head. 'Of course not. It is only slight indigestion from something I ate at lunch. I will not have my condition made a topic of conversation with Their Majesties. It would be most improper.'

Paul smiled. 'My dear, the Tsarina is a granddaughter of Queen Victoria. She was practically raised by her. And, contrary to popular opinion, Victoria was not a prude. She was too much of a Hanoverian for that.'

Anna frowned. 'Then I will not be made a topic of conversation with that old Finn Count Vladimir Fredericks.'

Paul sighed, but merely said: 'Very well, my dear. But if you feel at all unwell, please tell me. I realize that you are not a young woman. Having a first baby at the age of thirty-nine—'

'You think me old,' she interrupted him, with heightened colour. 'I am well aware of that.'

'Nonsense.' Paul tried to retrieve his position. 'You are the same age as myself. Would I be so foolish as to call you old? I was simply pointing out that it is not young to be having a child.'

'I am six years older than . . . than her. *She* is only thirty-three.'

'To whom are you referring?' Paul knew perfectly well to whom his wife alluded, but he needed a moment to collect his wits. Surely Anna was not choosing this of all moments to make a scene? Pregnant women were known to be at the mercy of peculiar whims.

He glanced at Anna and reflected that pregnancy did not become her. Although she had not yet lost her figure, her complexion was pasty and there were dark circles beneath her eyes. She suffered continuously from indigestion, which, in its turn, made her feel ravenously hungry, so that she ate all the foods most likely to cause her even greater distress. Her taste in clothes had not improved, either, in spite of his encouraging her to visit the best London fashion houses. Since their arrival in St Petersburg, he had urged her to consult the Tsarina's own *couturière*, Madame Brissac, who was patronized by every lady of distinction in the city. Anna had refused.

'I prefer my own clothes,' she had said. 'I do not wish to be a peacock like Lili Dehn and that silly fat friend of the Tsarina, Anna Vyrubova.'

Paul could only hope that she was not so devastatingly frank within the hearing of either of those ladies. The odd thing was, he had grown fond of her since their marriage. He would never be in love with her, but he pitied her most sincerely. Her religion, he suspected, was a substitute for that affection which she craved, but never inspired.

He squeezed her hand, which lay in the crook of his arm, as they returned to the state apartments of the Alexander Palace for a cold buffet of caviar, radishes, cheeses, pickled herrings and all the other dishes so dear to Russian hearts, which Anna loved and which Paul found so unappetizing. He was relieved that she had chosen not to answer his question and appeared willing to let the matter drop.

'I shouldn't eat too much, my dear, if I were you,' he advised her. 'Especially as you still seem to be suffering from the effects of luncheon.'

Anna shrugged. 'I shall eat what I choose,' she responded coldly. 'After all, apart from food, what is there?'

Margaret had duly delivered George into the care of Countess Anna's cousin and returned to the house on the Nevsky Prospect, which had been hired by Paul, complete with servants, for their three months' stay. As she spoke no Russian and the servants spoke no English, communication was difficult; but one of the maids brought her food in her room at half past one, and bobbed and curtseyed in obvious pleasure when Margaret said: '*Spasibo*,' a word she knew to be the equivalent of 'thanks'.

When she had finished her meal and the tray had been removed by the same pleasantly smiling girl, Margaret considered what to do with herself until six o'clock when she had arranged to collect George. She felt low in spirits. She did not like St Petersburg with its winding canals and dozens of arching bridges. Perhaps, in other circumstances, she might have thought it beautiful; if she and Paul had visited it together, without George, without Anna, in the winter when the huge baroque palaces of red and yellow, green and blue, were floodlit throughout the long dark evenings; when the strange fires of the Aurora Borealis flickered in the black night skies; when the *troika*s sped along the icy streets to the opera or the ballet at the Maryinsky Theatre. Yes, she might have thought it beautiful then.

But not now; not in the heat; not when the days stretched endlessly, emptily, ahead, while Paul disappeared for hours at a time with Anna. Margaret had never been more conscious of being the 'other woman', of having to take second place. At Latchetts she could forget her invidious position for ten months out of the twelve. Even when Anna was present, there was always a feeling that she, not Margaret, was the intruder. The Countess had an unhappy knack of antagonizing servants, with the result that the Latchetts staff resented her and were pleased when she had gone. After seven years, they regarded Margaret as mistress of the house, and looked on Anna as an interloper. Even Nanny Watkins's attitude had mellowed; although she would never like Margaret, she loathed Anna, the Countess's acid tongue and high-handed ways having been the cause of Nanny's humiliation on more than one occasion. Anna had also made it plain that she considered it a waste of money to keep a nanny at all, now that George was out of the nursery. Henry and Antonia she did not mention.

Margaret sighed and got to her feet, searching for her hat. She could not remain cooped up all day, moping. It was her own fault; she should not have agreed to come. Common sense had warned her that it would be disastrous for her peace of mind, but she had ignored that still, small voice within her because she could not endure being separated from Paul for so long. She had not realized then that Anna was pregnant.

She wandered aimlessly along the wide, dusty streets, recalling the Duke of Wellington's remark that if St Petersburg were the finest city in Europe, it was nevertheless the dullest. Margaret doubted if any Russian alive would agree with that stricture, but for her it lacked the vitality and excitement of New York, or the bustle and sense of purpose which were to be found in London. St Petersburg seemed to be a city built for one purpose only: selfish, heedless pleasure.

Margaret passed the Fabergé showroom, with its heavy granite pillars and air of Byzantine opulence. It was crowded, as always, with hordes of fashionable women, choosing from an Aladdin's cave of treasure some jewelled trifle which would set their escorts back many thousands of roubles. She continued walking, crossing bridge after bridge, constantly retracing her steps, taking no notice of where she was going; simply killing time.

She found herself at last in Senate Square, a vast rectangle of which the Neva river formed one side and the Palace of the Senate, the Admiralty Gardens and Buildings, and the Cathedral of St Isaac the other three. In the middle, dominating the whole, was the huge equestrian statue of Peter the Great, known as the Bronze Horseman. It had been in this square, on 14 December 1825, that the young revolutionaries, known afterwards as the Decembrists, had made their stand.

Margaret stared up at the bronze statue behind its railings. She did not hear her name called with breathless excitement until a hand was laid on her shoulder, making her turn.

'It *is* you,' said Hilda, beaming at her friend in astonishment and delight. 'I told Sergei it was you. Maggie Stafford! Whatever are you doing in St Petersburg?'

Eighteen

Hilda and Sergei Zhirov had an apartment, three small, insanitary rooms, in a narrow alley near Pergevalsky Street, where Raskolnikov had lived in *Crime and Punishment*. Margaret followed her friends under a low archway from which the plaster was crumbling in dusty flakes, and picked her way amongst the rubbish and debris which littered the courtyard beyond. Lines of washing, hanging limply in the heat, were strung between the apartment blocks on either side. Along one wall, someone had chalked a slogan. Sergei said it read 'Bei Zhidov' – Beat the Jews. All the windows were dirty, many of them broken.

Sergei pushed open a door which had once been green, but now showed patches of splintered wood beneath the peeling paint. Inside was a flight of worn stone steps, guarded by an iron handrail, vanishing upwards into the gloom.

'We're on the fourth floor,' Hilda said with an apologetic little laugh. 'I hope you can stand the strain.'

'Of course,' Margaret assured her; but she had already walked a long way that afternoon, and by the time the top landing was reached she felt dizzy with the effort.

Sergei unlocked one of the two doors at the head of the stairs, and Hilda ushered her friend inside. The little room was like an oven, even though most of the sunlight was blocked by the buildings on the other three sides of the court-yard.

'Sit down,' said Hilda, 'and I'll make some tea. Proper English tea, with milk, not that horrible black stuff with lemon.'

Margaret laughed as she seated herself on a hard wooden

chair near the table, and thankfully took the weight off her feet.

'The English are amazing,' she said. 'They go to the four corners of the earth, and carry on as though nothing had happened.'

Sergei nodded. 'That is what I tell her when she walks for miles and spends money we do not have on English tea from the expensive shops.'

'How can I spend what we don't have?' Hilda demanded irritably, taking a pan and filling it with water from a tap on the landing. She came back and set it on top of the little tin stove in the corner, which was adding to the heat of the room. 'Maggie, for heaven's sake, don't sit there. Sergei, what are you thinking of? That chair's not safe. Give her the armchair by the window.'

'That has a broken spring,' Sergei said, pointing to the coil of metal which protruded through the worn material. 'I have spoken to the landlady, but—'

'It's no use speaking to that old harridan,' Hilda snapped at him. 'What you need is a proper job, then we can buy our own furniture.'

'I'm perfectly all right here,' Margaret said quickly. 'Tell me again what you're doing in St Petersburg. I couldn't concentrate properly while we were walking.'

'Sergei lost his job at the brewery six months ago, and instead of looking for something else in Southwark, he decided to come home. And you know how keen I was to see Russia. So here we are. But if I'd realized it was going to be quite like this—' Hilda broke off and stared around her before continuing: 'It is good to see you again, Maggie. Why ever did we lose touch?'

'You expressed yourself rather forcefully after I went to live at Latchetts,' Margaret responded drily, and Hilda blushed.

'Oh God, that awful letter . . . I remember it now. All the same . . . I'm still not quite sure why you did it.'

'I love Paul Devereaux.'

'A man like that?'

'A man like what?'

'Well . . . you know.' Hilda glanced at Sergei for support. 'One of the bosses.'

Margaret laughed. 'You sound like Arthur Barlow.'

'Who's he?'

'It doesn't matter. Just a young man who told me I'd sold my soul to the devil.'

Sergei nodded. 'We thought you were one of us.'

'I'm not one of anybody,' Margaret replied with suppressed violence. 'For pity's sake, I'm me!'

'I'll make the tea,' Hilda interrupted swiftly, going to a cupboard and pulling out a brown teapot which Margaret recognized from her stay in Tabard Street. 'You see, I managed to bring a few things with me.'

'How's Betty?' Margaret asked, following Hilda's lead and steering the conversation away from her own concerns.

'Married now. Married to a porter on the railways. Got two kids. Got Ma living with her, too, since Pa died. The others have all grown up and left home. Girls have gone into service, and my brother's working on the docks.' Hilda spooned tea from a small orange packet into the pot and poured on the boiling water. She leaned out of the window and brought in a jug from the outside sill. 'I'm afraid it's only goat's milk,' she said.

The goat's milk was slightly rancid and gave the tea a peculiar taste. Margaret would rather have had Russian tea with lemon. She tried to drink without grimacing.

Hilda perched on the edge of the broken armchair, avoiding the offending spring.

'So the Countess has come on a visit to her relations, has she? She'd probably remember Sergei. One of her cousins might be prepared to give him a job.'

'No!' her husband exclaimed angrily. 'I shall never again be beholden to any member of the *pridvorny*!'

'Lower your voice, for goodness' sake,' Hilda begged him. 'You said yourself that you never know who might be listening.'

'One day,' Sergei said, looking fiercely at her, 'it will all be different.'

'So you keep telling me, but I can't see it myself. Lenin's in Galicia, Trotsky's in Paris and the rest are scattered. You're not going to achieve anything on your own.'

'I'm not on my own,' he replied scornfully. 'There are

hundreds of us. Thousands. More each day. There are more than seventy thousand workers in this country on strike at the present moment. The Government is crumbling, only Bloody Nicholas hasn't the wit to see it.'

'Why do you call him that?' Margaret asked. 'He looks a mild enough man to me. He's almost the double of King George.'

'They're first cousins,' Hilda said. 'Their mothers are sisters.'

'You should read the history of my country to know why I call him Bloody Nicholas,' Sergei spat at Margaret. 'He is the Tsar, that is enough. All the Tsars are tyrants. And *Nemka* – the German woman – what is she but the whore of the *starets*, Grigor Rasputin?'

'Will you shut up?' Hilda implored him for the second time. 'You're not in England now. And no one knows for certain that Alexandra is Rasputin's mistress.'

Margaret, from all she had ever heard of Queen Victoria's favourite granddaughter, thought it extremely unlikely, the Tsarina's adoration of her husband being well known. However, she had no desire to be a party to the argument, and asked instead: 'What's wrong with the little Tsarevich? He is, by all accounts, a sickly child.'

'Nobody knows. Whatever it is, his parents keep his illness a secret.'

The conversation flagged, and Margaret suddenly wanted to be gone. The dark, stuffy, little room seemed to be closing in on her. She needed sun and air and space to breathe. She consulted her watch and found to her relief that it was almost five o'clock.

'I must go,' she said. 'I promised to fetch George at six. It's been lovely seeing you both again, after all these years.'

'You'll come often,' Hilda urged, and Margaret recognized a note of desperation in her friend's voice. 'Now you know where we live. You'll visit us again before you go home?'

'Yes . . . yes, of course I will. We don't return to England until the end of July.'

Hilda followed her out on to the landing.

'Maggie—' She seemed awkward and a little frightened. 'Maggie, you won't— What I mean is . . . Sergei talks wildly sometimes. I shouldn't want ... Mr Devereaux or the Countess to know.'

Margaret kissed her cheek. 'I shall repeat nothing I've heard him say to anyone. I promise. I'm only sorry you felt you had to ask.'

She went down the stairs and across the courtyard, where a boy and girl were now playing. The girl was cradling a billet of wood in her arms like a doll, and the boy was adding to the chalk marks on the wall. He formed the Russian characters slowly, giggling all the while. Margaret passed beneath the echoing archway and turned into Pergevalsky Street. She quickened her pace, anxious to be back in the wide, pleasant boulevards which belonged to the rich and their guests.

She stopped suddenly, oblivious of the people hurrying past. What was happening to her? Was this poor creature, unable to face up to the realities of life, really Herbie Dunham's daughter? Had she become such a snob that she despised her less fortunate friends? Perhaps there was some truth, stripped of its theatrical language, in Arthur Barlow's accusation. She had abandoned many of her principles, along with her self-respect, after Paul's marriage to Anna. The girl who had been born and brought up in the Bowery, who had played on Lafayette Street and in Shinbone Alley, who had thought the De Vinne Press Building one of the wonders of the modern world, was now critical of any surroundings which fell short of the perfection of Latchetts.

She put up a hand and found that her cheeks were wet. She had not been aware that she was crying. What a ridiculous spectacle she must be making of herself! She noticed two men regarding her covertly, eyeing the expensive yellow dress with its elegant, hand-embroidered lace. She took a firmer grip on the beaded handbag which Paul had given her last St Valentine's Day, and went in the direction of the Moika Canal to collect her charge.

It was just over a week later that St Petersburg was shocked by the news of the murder of Archduke Franz Ferdinand, nephew and heir of the Austrian Emperor, in the Bosnian capital of Sarajevo. His wife had also been killed, both of them shot by a young Serb named Gabriel Princip.

206

Disturbing as the news was, however, no one considered it momentous. The Tsar and Tsarina were aboard the royal yacht *Standart*, on their annual summer voyage along the Baltic coast, but there was no suggestion that Nicholas should return to his capital. Indeed, the news of an attempt on Rasputin's life, the day before the events at Sarajevo, was considered much more likely to curtail the royal cruise, if anything could.

The information that the *starets* had been severely wounded delighted Anna, as it did so many others.

'I could kiss the feet of this Khina Gusseva,' she announced that evening while dressing for the ballet. Her eyes shone fanatically in her small white face. 'They say she stabbed him in the stomach and that he will not live.'

'I shouldn't bank on his death, my dear,' Paul advised her, as he sat watching her maid comb and braid her hair. 'I hear that the Tsar's own surgeon has been ordered to Tyumen, to perform whatever operation is necessary to save Rasputin's life. I had it on very good authority this morning at the English Club. And now, my dear, if we don't hurry, we are going to be late. Are you certain you feel well enough to go?'

'Of course.' Anna nodded dismissal to her maid and picked up her blue velvet evening cloak, whose sole concession to frivolity was a ruched collar of matching satin. It was too hot to wear it, and she folded it over her arm, glancing sideways at Paul as she did so, suddenly malicious. 'If you are thinking of taking Mrs Stafford in my place, you may put the idea out of your mind.'

'Why should I want to do that?' he asked levelly, refusing to let her see that she had shaken him.

'Because she is your mistress. Because you love her. Because I know you only married me for convenience. Because sometimes you wish that I were dead.'

Paul frowned. It was the first time she had ever referred openly to his relationship with Margaret. He said curtly: 'I have never wished that you were dead.'

'Haven't you?' she whispered, and raised her face to his.

For a fleeting second, Paul thought he glimpsed a softened expression in those dark eyes regarding him so steadily, and he winced. Marriage to Anna was bearable as long as she remained unemotionally involved. Any attempt on her part to claim his affection would be unendurable. He could be fond of her just as long as he thought her as uncommitted as himself.

Anna turned towards the door, her back poker-straight, her head held high.

'You need not answer,' she said. 'The question is of no importance. I apologize if I have made a scene. I know how the English dislike them.' She smiled. 'Shall we go? As you say, we don't want to be late.'

The sumptuous blue-and-gold auditorium of the Maryinsky Theatre was full, as always, even on a summer evening at the end of the Season, when many people had already left for the country. The ballet was *Swan Lake*, which Paul had seen before, and did not care for. He found the music cloying and over-romantic, the story feeble. The fashionable audience – the women, in true Russian style, laden with jewels – began to irritate him. For the first time in his life, he questioned a society which would have penalized him for marrying a woman like Margaret because she had neither wealth nor birth to recommend her. Yet she was beautiful, intelligent, cultured, a match for any woman he had ever met.

By the time the final curtain was lowered, he was more than ready to leave. He felt tired and depressed. Things would look better in the morning. He and Anna made their way through groups of people still animatedly discussing the night's performance, and looked for their carriage. Anna's cousin, who had rented them his house, had also provided them with transport.

'Over there,' Paul said, offering Anna his arm. The big, bearded Russian coachman raised his whip to attract their attention.

Paul did not notice the young man pushing his way through the crowd until he was almost upon them. Then, suddenly, he found a pistol pointed at his chest, while he was abused in a torrent of Russian. It all happened so quickly that he did not even feel Anna push him aside. There was an explosion, people screamed, and Anna lay huddled on the ground.

'How is she?' Margaret asked in a low voice, as Paul entered the library. 'Here. Sit down. You look all in. Let me pour you a whisky.'

Paul sank into a chair and closed his eyes. In the early morning light his face was grey.

'The doctor says she's going to be all right. He's given her a sleeping draught. By a miracle, she hasn't lost the baby, and the bullet didn't touch any of the vital organs. But naturally, she's very shocked. The doctor recommends peace and quiet for at least six weeks. We may have to postpone our return to England.'

'The bullet is out of her shoulder?'

'It has been taken out. A clean wound. Dr Veliaminov is sending round a nurse tomorrow. I mean this morning.'

Margaret gave Paul his drink and sat down on a stool by his chair.

'Why, Paul? Why would any Russian want to kill you? It must have been a mistake.'

'No, apparently not. The police have taken statements from witnesses who say that the man was shouting something about the Lena goldfields. The man himself escaped in the confusion, but they think his father was one of those killed in the strike two years ago.'

'But that was nothing to do with you.'

'The Lena Gold-Mining Company is partly British owned. Both Francis and I have shares in it. Anna used to own some, but she gave them to me as a wedding present. This young man must have learned about my involvement.'

'It still doesn't make sense. You're not responsible for his father's death. It was the police who fired on the strikers.'

Paul smiled wanly. 'Hate makes people irrational. You should know that. It's why Hugh died.'

Margaret took his empty glass and refilled it, resuming her seat by his chair.

'The young man this evening, he meant to kill you, didn't he?'

'Yes. If it hadn't been for Anna, he would have done.'

Margaret shuddered. The idea was too awful to contemplate. She had been in bed when Anna was brought home, and was still in her nightdress and dressing-gown. One of the servants had roused her and she had taken charge, summoning the nearest doctor, soothing the frightened maids, persuading George, who had been wakened by the fuss, to go back to sleep. While Dr Veliaminov had removed the bullet from Anna's shoulder, she had bullied the servants into relighting the samovar and serving tea to the police.

'Anna loves you, doesn't she?' Margaret asked now. 'She didn't marry you just to get away from Hawksworth; to have a home of her own. She loves you.'

There was a long silence, then Paul said heavily: 'I'm afraid so.'

'It makes a difference.'

He leaned forward, forcing her round on the stool to face him. 'What difference?' he demanded harshly. 'Anna knew I wasn't in love with her when I married her. It can't make any difference to us.'

'But it does,' Margaret insisted, her eyes filling with tears. 'We're robbing her of something she wants, something which is rightfully hers.'

'You were mine long before I married Anna.' Paul was frightened. His hands gripped Margaret's shoulders painfully.

'But you married her!'

'It was a marriage of convenience, for both of us!'

'No, not for her.' Margaret shook off his hands and got up, pacing about the room which was already flooded with daylight after the few short hours of summer night. 'A woman doesn't risk her life for someone for whom she feels nothing. We daren't delude ourselves any longer.'

Paul drained his glass and set it down on the table beside him. 'What, precisely, are you saying?'

Through the open window came the first early morning sounds: a peal of church bells; the rasp of a barge, carrying in all probability a load of green wood, as one of its sides scraped against the granite embankment of the Neva; a street vendor calling his wares.

'I'm saying,' Margaret replied steadily, 'that you – that we both owe the Countess a debt impossible to repay. Your life.' Margaret twisted her fingers together, avoiding Paul's eyes. 'I'm saying that you made a serious mistake when you assumed that she did not love you.'

'A mistake for which I must now pay, is that it?' he asked grimly.

'For which we must both pay.'

'You mean you've grown tired of me. You don't want me any more.' In his panic at the thought of losing her, Paul was prepared to use any tactics in order to keep her.

'No!' The cry was agonized. Margaret clasped her arms across her breast, like someone crouching inward upon a wound.

He got up and went to her, putting his arms about her, enfolding her as he would have done an injured child.

'I'm sorry,' he said huskily. 'I didn't mean it. Forgive me. But I can't give you up. You must know that I can't. Why should I?'

'Because our love is hurting your wife.'

'Oh God!' He released her, angry now, two fine white lines running from his nostrils to the corners of his mouth. 'You bloody Nonconformists are all the same. You have this Old Testament obsession with atonement. Nothing's changed from this time yesterday. Presumably Anna loved me as much then as she loves me now.'

'But we didn't know for certain.'

Paul threw out his arms in despair, the anger draining out of him. 'I love you,' he whispered. 'I can't lose you. You're mine.'

'No,' Margaret answered quietly, 'I belong to myself.'

And she turned and left the room, closing the door behind her.

Hilda had been dreaming. She slept badly on the hard narrow bed which she shared with Sergei; and the coarse Russian bread and goat's-milk cheese which were the staple ingredients of their diet gave her indigestion.

She had dreamed she was back in Southwark, wandering along Borough High Street, looking for the Frenshams' butcher's shop. She had been unable to find it, and for some reason this frightened her. She began hammering on the nearest door. . . .

Suddenly she was wide awake, but the sound of knocking persisted. She sat up in bed, then shook Sergei, who lay on his back, open-mouthed and snoring.

211

'Wake up!' she whispered. 'Sergei! Wake up. There's someone at the outer door.'

'What?' Sergei opened one eye and stared blearily at her. 'What's the matter? What time is it?'

'Four in the morning, and there's someone knocking at the door.'

Sleep went flying. Sergei was out of bed and cautiously peering from the window.

'I can't see anyone in the courtyard. The police usually work in pairs.'

'Police?' Hilda was really frightened now. 'Sergei, what have you been up to?'

'Nothing.' He tiptoed out of the bedroom and across the living-room to the outer door. 'Who is it?' he whispered in Russian.

A voice answered from the other side. 'Nickolai Brodkin. The son of Pavel Brodkin. Let me in. I need your help.'

Sergei withdrew the bolts. He had tried to find his former cell-leader after his return to St Petersburg, but the older man had vanished. Someone thought he had been sent to Siberia.

Nickolai Brodkin stumbled into the apartment, half-dead from fatigue and fear. Hilda, a sheet draped over her nightdress, stood in the bedroom doorway, listening mistrustfully to the sharp Russian exchange between the two men.

'What's he saying?' she demanded. 'More to the point, what's he done? Is he running away from the police?'

Sergei pushed the boy on to the rickety chair and poured him a measure of vodka. Nickolai gulped it down.

'What's going on, Sergei?' Hilda asked again. 'I have a right to be told!'

'He's shot someone,' her husband answered slowly. A crease appeared between his brows. 'He says he tried to shoot some Englishman, but wounded the lady who was with him instead.'

Nineteen

'How long is he going to stay here?' Hilda dumped her basket
of shopping on the table and stared accusingly at Nickolai
Brodkin, who glowered back at her from his corner. 'He's
been here over three weeks. You do realize, Sergei, what it's
costing to keep him? If I hadn't found the job at the Restaurant Cuba there wouldn't be food for us, let alone him.
Besides, having him here is so bloody dangerous.'

Before Sergei could answer, the youth in the corner burst
forth in Russian, the only word distinguishable to Hilda
being *Okhrana*, which she knew to mean the secret police. Her
heart began to beat unsteadily and her mouth went dry.
Before going into the bedroom, she said fiercely to Sergei: 'Get
rid of him!'

Sergei had changed since his return to St Petersburg. He
had made no effort to search for work, and spent his days
looking up old friends, revolutionaries like himself, whose one
aim in life was to overthrow the Tsar. Hilda had not previously realized how dangerous it was in Russia to speak one's
mind. Used to hearing all kinds of inflammatory talk at
Speakers' Corner, while the London bobbies looked benevo-
lently on, she had been unable to visualize a society where any
word against the government was regarded as sedition, and
where people went in fear of their lives. Sergei had tried to
warn her but she had thought he exaggerated. Once she
grasped, however, that he had been speaking no more than
the truth, she had begged him either to return to London or to
accept that he would never change things and settle down as a
law-abiding citizen.

'I'm not the stuff heroines are made of,' she had told him

bluntly. 'Nor martyrs, either. I don't mind being a member of the Labour Party in England, but I'm damned if I'm going to risk my neck for a country that isn't even my own.'

It was the first time she and Sergei had really quarrelled in all the years they had known one another. He had called her an 'insular, petty-minded bourgeoise' and struck her across the face. She had retaliated by kicking him hard on the shins and shouting that he was a 'lazy, useless bastard' who could not even give her a child. That had been the day before she met Margaret in Senate Square; and the day after, she had tramped all over St Petersburg, determined to find work herself as Sergei would not. It had taken her a week to be taken on in the kitchens of the Restaurant Cuba; a twelve-hour day, standing at a sink washing up the endless flow of dirty dishes, regarded with hostility and suspicion by her fellow workers because she was able to converse with the head chef and the waiters in her school-book French. By that time, Nickolai Brodkin had become their lodger.

That first day, when she and Sergei had finally unravelled Nickolai's story and realized who had been the object of his murderous attack, and why, Hilda's initial reaction had been one of sympathy. She had disliked Paul Devereaux ever since Margaret had gone to live with him as his mistress. Hilda was genuinely fond of Margaret, and had been reluctant to saddle her with all the blame for what she saw as a kind of betrayal; so she had transferred much of her resentment to Paul. She had known about the Lena goldfields massacre, and, after hearing from Nickolai Brodkin that Paul was a shareholder in the Anglo-Russian Gold-Mining Company, her dislike of him had grown. She had felt sorry for Nickolai Brodkin and told Sergei that he could stay for the coming night.

'But mind,' she had said, 'he leaves first thing tomorrow morning.'

Nickolai had not gone, however, nor had Sergei insisted on his departure.

'He is the son of my friend,' he had pointed out angrily when Hilda had returned from work at night, only to find the young man still in the apartment. 'He will remain here as our guest until it is safe for him to leave.'

'Or until the police arrest all three of us.' Hilda had been frightened. 'You're a fool, Sergei. Get him out of here!'

Three weeks later, Nickolai Brodkin was still with them, eating their food, sleeping on the floor in the living-room, going out only at night, in those two brief hours of darkness which separated sunset and sunrise.

Hilda sat down on the edge of the bed, rubbing her aching legs. She had been on her feet since she left the apartment at five o'clock that morning. She had walked all the way to and from the Restaurant Cuba, stopping to shop on the way home, and had had very little to eat all day. She had hoped, at least, to find the supper laid and the samovar bubbling; but the two men were heatedly discussing politics, an empty vodka bottle standing on the table between them.

Hilda swung her legs on to the bed and lay back against the pillows. If those two lazy good-for-nothings could not be bothered to get a meal, then neither could she, hungry as she was.

The bedroom door opened and Sergei came in. 'What about food?' he asked. 'Why aren't you preparing supper?'

Hilda opened her eyes and glared at him. 'Get your own supper! I've been working all day. And when you've eaten, throw that madman out!'

'It's the woman's place to cook,' Sergei answered hotly. 'That's the way we do things in Russia.'

'I wish to God we'd never come to Russia!' Hilda screamed at him. 'You were never like this in England! You worked hard. You were kind and considerate.'

'In England there was nothing better to do. Here, there are more important things than work.'

'Like talking and drinking, you mean. Go away, Sergei, and leave me alone.'

Her husband came towards her with such a ferocious look on his face that Hilda was suddenly afraid. She rolled off the bed. 'Don't you dare lay a finger on me!' she cried.

'Get the supper then. Now. This instant.'

But Hilda was still angry in spite of her fear. 'No!' she panted. 'I've told you. You can get your own.'

Sergei made a rush at her, but she slipped past him, through the open bedroom door and across the outer room. She wrenched open the door to the landing – and fell straight

into the arms of two men who had just reached the top of the
stairs.

Margaret knocked on the library door and went in. Paul was
standing by one of the windows, staring out into the street, but
he turned his head as she entered.

They had seen very little of each other during the past three
weeks. Margaret had remained as much as possible with
George, either in the schoolroom or accompanying him on
tours of the city, and Paul had devoted himself to his wife
throughout her convalescence. This had been shorter than
either Paul or Dr Veliaminov would have wished, but Anna
was determined to miss nothing of the celebrations attendant
upon the visit of President Raymond Poincaré of France.

Three days earlier, against all advice and looking paler
than ever, she had accompanied Paul in one of the hundreds of
pleasure barges to watch the arrival of the *France*, bearing the
President and his entourage. The same night, she had insisted
on attending the banquet at the Peterhof to which she and
Paul had been invited; a small, joyless figure in black velvet
and amethysts, amid the dazzle of brocades and satins, the
blaze of diamonds, sapphires, rubies and pearls. Yesterday
she had made Paul drive her to Krasnoe Selo for the military
parade, and sat for hours under the blazing sun watching sixty
thousand Imperial troops perform for the French President,
the royal family and all the élite of St Petersburg. Tonight she
had every intention of dining aboard the *France*, when President Poincaré entertained the Tsar and Tsarina. Paul, noting
how ill she looked, had tried to reason with her, but Anna had
turned on him angrily.

'I have been asked as the representative of the Rastorguyev
family. No matter how ill I feel, I shall do my duty and
go.'

'But it is only by chance, my dear,' Paul had argued, 'that
you are in St Petersburg at present. Suppose we had not come.
And who has represented the Rastorguyev family for the past
twenty years?' But he failed to understand the effect returning
to her native country had had upon Anna; how very Russian
she had suddenly become. Recently, there had been other
matters to occupy his time and attention.

He motioned Margaret to a chair. She sat down, eyes raised anxiously to his face.

He said slowly: 'I have managed to obtain the release of Mrs Zhirova from the fortress of Saints Peter and Paul, on the strict condition that she returns to England without delay.' He suppressed Margaret's exclamation of relief and gratitude with a gesture of his hand. 'Her husband and the man who tried to kill me I can do nothing for, even if I wanted to. They are Russian citizens, and both known dissidents. It was only by enlisting the help of the British Ambassador, Sir George Buchanan, by his personal representations to the Tsar himself, that I was able to do anything for your friend.'

'Thank you,' Margaret said, wanting to say so much more, but realizing that it would merely embarrass him. 'I'll make certain that Hilda returns to England.'

'I should be grateful if you would.' His tone was formal. 'I have no wish, for Anna's sake, to be embroiled a second time in Russian internal affairs.'

'It's good of you to have done so much,' Margaret answered with difficulty. It was disconcerting to be grateful and angry at one and the same time. 'I am aware that I could have achieved nothing on my own.'

He inclined his head; then suddenly made her jump by slamming his right fist hard into the palm of his left hand.

'How long are we going to keep up this charade?'

'We . . . I . . . we agreed the other night,' she answered unsteadily, 'that things have changed between us. Anna loves you. She saved your life.'

'And that is to keep us apart forever?'

'You chose to marry her. It was your decision to jeopardize what we had.'

'I see.' His voice was harsh. 'You are still determined to punish me.'

'No!' She got up and went to him, standing breast to breast. 'I love you, God help me. I don't always like you, and I'm certain you don't always like me. But I love you and I need you. Take me if you want to.'

He stared at her, desire, anger, frustration, all registered in his face. He half-lifted his hands, then dropped them again to his sides.

'No,' he said heavily, 'of course you're right. I shouldn't have married her. But I honestly didn't believe that she had any affection for me. Francis assured me that she didn't.'

Margaret grimaced. 'He would, naturally. He must have known that you wouldn't marry her if you had suspected the truth, and he wanted to injure me. He hates me because I refused him all those years ago.'

Paul looked shocked. 'I can't believe that.' But even as he spoke, he knew that it was really a question of not wanting to believe it; of refusing to accept that his cousin might have manipulated him for his own petty ends. 'I won't believe it,' he added, rejecting his suspicions.

Margaret said nothing. It was useless trying to persuade Paul against his will. She felt tired, drained by the worry of the last few days. When she had gone to visit Hilda and learned of her arrest and imprisonment from the landlady of the apartment, who wanted her arrears of rent, Margaret had known that she must do something. Hilda was her friend. She could not leave her to her fate; and the only thing she could think of was to enlist Paul's aid. He had not failed her.

She hoped Sergei Zhirov was suitably grateful for his wife's release, but she doubted it. It was doubtful if he would have been grateful for his own freedom. Like so many revolutionaries, he seemed to Margaret to be bent on martyrdom. Why else had he returned to Russia? Yet, as a United States citizen, as someone born into and brought up in a republic, she could not help but sympathize. She had read enough about Russia, seen enough during her months in St Petersburg, to realize how repressive was the Tsarist regime. Something her father had once said, however, made her uneasy.

'It's not wise to destroy a system,' Herbert Dunham had told his younger daughter, 'unless you are sure you can replace it with something better. If you can only substitute evil for evil, leave well alone.'

She became aware that Paul was watching her intently. He smiled faintly and said: 'A penny for them.'

She returned his smile with an effort. 'It's time for George's morning walk. We're visiting the Cathedral of Our Lady of Kazan today. I believe the basilica is a replica of St Peter's in

Rome. You see, I'm trying to educate him as Beatrice would have wished.'

He nodded mutely, unable to speak.

'Thank you again for all you've done for Hilda,' she said, and left the room.

Someone was shaking her awake. Margaret rolled on to her back and muttered: 'Go away, George. You're big enough to get your own drink of water.'

Paul's voice said: 'It's not George. Wake up, Margaret, please! It's Anna. She's collapsed.'

Margaret struggled up in bed and glanced at the clock on the opposite wall. It was three in the morning and Paul was still wearing his evening clothes.

He went on: 'We returned from dining aboard the *France* half an hour ago, and just as we got indoors Anna fainted. Her maid has undressed her and put her to bed, but she seems very ill. I've telephoned for Veliaminov and I should like you to be there when he comes.'

'But why? What will he think . . . ?'

'It doesn't matter what he thinks. I should just like you to hear what he has to say. Please.'

She got out of bed at once, alarmed by the urgency of his tone. 'Of course, if you really need me. I didn't mean to sound unfeeling. I'll get dressed immediately.'

Ten minutes later she joined him in Anna's room. The Countess, lying in the huge double bed, looked like a little wax doll. There were shadows beneath her closed eyes, and the dark hair, released from its severe chignon, spilled across the pillows, emphasizing by stark contrast the bloodlessness of her skin. There was a blue tinge about Anna's mouth which made Margaret reach for her pulse. The Countess's personal maid, Maud Jenner, who had accompanied them from England, was regarding her mistress grimly, while the young Russian girl, Katya, who had been summoned from her bed to assist Maud, was standing in front of an icon of the Virgin and Child, her lips moving in silent prayer.

'The pulse is weak,' Margaret said, after a moment or two, 'but steady enough. Probably all she needs is rest.' She was conscious of Maud Jenner's glance of disdain, but she was inured to the dislike of Anna's personal servants. After three years, it no longer upset her.

Dr Veliaminov, when he arrived, confirmed in his excellent French that the Countess did indeed need rest; at least two months in bed if she were not to lose the baby and imperil her own life.

'She has over-taxed her strength, Monsieur Devereaux, as we knew she would. All the gadding about of the past few weeks has been the height of folly. Oh, you need not tell me, my dear sir, that you were unable to prevent her. I have known Countess Anna and her sister since they were children, and they both have the Rastorguyev obstinacy in full measure. But this time she will have to do as she is told, or I cannot be answerable for the consequences.' And he nodded his fine old leonine head at Paul.

Margaret, whose French had improved sufficiently during her stay in the Russian capital to understand most of what Dr Veliaminov said, also understood his remark as he moved with Paul towards the bedroom door.

'Is it true, Monsieur, do you think, this rumour which is flying around the city? I refer, in case you have not heard, to the story that Austria has presented Serbia with an ultimatum because of the Archduke's death last month. Some people are concerned that such a move might lead eventually to war.'

'But. . . . You will come back as soon as possible?' Margaret asked, her head still in a whirl over Paul's sudden decision to return to England.

'Of course. I shall only be gone for a matter of weeks.'

'But if there should be a war—'

'There won't be. I've just come from lunching with the Buchanans, and Sir George thinks it highly improbable, even if Austria goes to war with Serbia, that either Great Britain or Russia will become involved. "A little flare-up in the Balkans" is how he described what's happened.'

Margaret sat down. The late July heat was intense, and she was feeling slightly sick. She hated this library, the whole house, St Petersburg, Russia. She longed to get back to her children.

'Must you go? Cannot you wait until the Countess is fit enough to travel?'

'George must be settled into his prep. school by the end of August. As you are aware, we should all have been on our way home by now.'

'But why do you wish me to stay behind? My role as George's governess is finished, and I have no useful purpose here. Besides, there are matters to be settled when I get to England.'

'I see.' There was silence for a moment, then he asked: 'May I enquire what your intentions are?'

'I'm not sure. As I said . . . there are . . . things to be arranged between us.'

'And do those "things" include our children?'

She shut her ears to the bitterness in his voice. 'The future of Henry and Antonia will have to be discussed, of course.'

There was another silence, which seemed never-ending. Then Paul said: 'You may be sure that whatever you choose to do I shall provide amply for the three of you. But, before that happens, I am asking you to do me one last favour.'

Margaret stared down at her hands, tightly clasped together in her lap. Perversely, now that Paul had all but agreed to let her go, now that he accepted the responsibility towards Anna which she had urged on him, she was engulfed by self-pity. Why had she not let well alone? Why had she allowed her conscience to destroy everything which made her life worthwhile? Anna was nothing to her. There were many women who loved but were not loved in return. There was no reason why she should feel responsible for the Countess's unhappiness. . . .

Margaret raised her head and tried to smile. 'Of course, if it's within my power to do so.'

'Then please stay here, with Anna, until I return.'

'But why? She doesn't even like me. And Maud Jenner and the nurse supplied by Dr Veliaminov do all that is necessary in the sick-room. Without George, I shall have nothing to do.'

'Nevertheless, just in case . . . I should be grateful.'

'What do you mean, "just in case"? You do think there might be a war.'

'No.' He was angry. 'I shouldn't leave you if I did. I was

thinking that your will is every bit as strong as Anna's.' He gave a little snort of laughter. 'I should know, believe me. I'm afraid Maud Jenner is too devoted; she allows herself to be overborne. With the best will in the world, if Anna decides to ignore Dr Veliaminov's orders Jenner is not the woman to prevent her.'

'And you think I am? You think that the Countess will listen to a word I say?'

'Perhaps not. But I can rely on you to send at once for the doctor, or, if all else fails, to lock Anna in her room. I am sure you would manage if she tried to do something foolish. There is the child's life to be thought of, as well as her own.'

'Very well,' Margaret conceded quietly, ignoring a stab of jealousy and self-pity; the sense of having been badly used and deeply wronged. Blaming others for her own mistakes was an attitude to life she deeply deplored. 'If it will make you easier in your mind, I will stay. It won't be for very long, after all.'

He said huskily: 'You're a remarkable woman. I don't know if I've ever told you.'

'I'd better start packing George's clothes. When are you leaving?'

'Tomorrow. We shall travel via Warsaw and Vienna, then straight through to Paris, where we shall spend a couple of days. After that, Calais, Dover, London. . . .' His voice tailed away. He wanted to tell her something, but was uncertain what it was that he wanted to say.

Margaret said: 'If you go to Latchetts, give the children my love. Tell them I shall be seeing them very soon.'

They were both conscious of the fact that she had ceased to call Latchetts 'home'. Well, she thought, as she opened the library door, she would at least be able to visit Jessie and Daniel again. She would be able to see Lilian. She might even persuade her daughter to live with her once more.

'Margaret!' Paul had crossed the room and was standing close to her, both hands outstretched. 'Won't you even say goodbye?'

She hesitated, but only for a second. Then she was in his arms, clinging to him as though she could never let him go. But after a few minutes, she released herself, kissed his cheek and went upstairs to her room.

Part Five 1917–1918

Thise floures white and rede

Twenty

Margaret lay in bed, staring at the ceiling, trying to forget how hungry she was. Her feet ached. The previous day, Saturday, she had queued for six hours in the freezing cold outside the bakery on Liteiny Prospect in the hope of getting a loaf of bread. It had been the same the day before, and the day before that. The terrible Russian winter had dealt the country's railway system, already in chaos after two and a half years of war, its death-blow. Deep drifts of snow blocked long sections of the tracks, nearly sixty thousand railway-cars were unable to move, over twelve hundred engine boilers had burst, leaving the capital without supplies. There was no coal, no bread, no meat, no grain, except what had been hoarded by the speculators and which could be bought only by those with enough money to pay their extortionate prices.

Margaret supposed that she and Anna were more fortunate than most. They were kept from starvation by odd gifts of food from the British and American embassies, and because Anna had had the foresight to sell her jewels six months ago, when there had still been a market for such things. Now, in the beleaguered city, a bag of sugar or candles was of more value on the open market than sapphires or diamonds.

Shivering with cold, Margaret got out of bed and began to dress. She heard little Natasha wail fretfully and guessed that Anna would be needing her help. The Countess found the child too much to cope with on her own. She had never fully recovered her health.

Margaret pulled back the curtains and looked out on the Nevsky Prospect as she had done each morning for the past two years and eight months; ever since, in fact, Paul had left

225

for England, and Europe had been plunged into war. She and Anna had been trapped in St Petersburg, except that the city was not called by that name any more. One of the Tsar's first acts after the Russian declaration of hostilities had been to change the German-sounding St Petersburg to the more patriotic Petrograd.

At first, it had not occurred to Margaret that they would be stranded for more than a couple of months, until such time as Anna was fit to travel. The idea of a war involving almost the whole of Europe was alien to her, as it was to so many others. She had been unable to conceive of country after country being turned into one vast battleground. Besides, everyone had said that the war would be over by Christmas. Germany and her allies stood no chance against the British and French in the west and the Russians in the east. The Kaiser would be suing for peace by autumn.

Margaret sighed, glancing up and down the broad street, unusually quiet after the riots of the past few days. There was a hint of spring in the air on this Sunday morning, the gilded onion-domes of the churches glimmering in the sunlight, ice melting and running from the roofs and gutters of the houses. The sky was a soft opalescent blue above the grey waters of the Neva. Margaret felt a corresponding lift of the spirits. Then she remembered, as she always did in the silence of early day, Paul and her children, so far away, cut off from her without any means of communication. It was now that the panic began to rise; the feeling of hopelessness that made her want to hammer her fists against the nearest wall. She had come to Russia for three months, and been forced to stay for nearly three years. It was like a nightmare, one of those awful dreams where she was shut inside a room and could not find the way out.

Perhaps there had been a time, in the very early months of the war, when Russia was winning, defeating the Germans at Tannenburg, the Austrians at Lemberg, and pushing deep into Galicia, when she and Anna might have made it home. But Anna had been too ill for almost a year even to leave her bed. Natasha had been born in November 1914, a difficult breech birth which had impeded her mother's recovery, and by May of the following year the Russian armies had begun to retreat. A more recent offensive under General Brusilov, last summer, had been checked, and the Imperial army driven back once again.

It was then that the rot had set in. Demoralized by conditions at the front, and knowing that their families were suffering equal hardships at home, the soldiers had mutinied. The murder of Rasputin by Prince Felix Yussoupov and Grand Duke Dmitry Pavlovich, at the end of 1916, had done nothing to stem the tide of anti-royalist feeling which was sweeping the cities. As the church bells had ushered in 1917, strikes and riots grew along with the queues for food and a sense of imminent disaster. The Tsar had returned to his headquarters after being with his family at Tsarskoe Selo for Christmas, ignoring warnings from Sir George Buchanan and the French Ambassador Maurice Paléologue that revolution was being spoken about openly in the capital's streets. Nor did he seem aware of the disaffection among his own Imperial Regiment of Cossacks. His one aim was to return to the front to plan the spring offensive. He was advised in vain that the government was on the verge of collapse. . . .

There was a tap on Margaret's door and Anna came in, carrying the two-year-old Natasha in her arms. The child had been crying and was struggling peevishly to be freed. She said in her clear, oddly accented English: 'Put me down.'

It had been Anna's choice that her daughter should be brought up speaking her father's language.

'After all,' Anna had said, 'when this war is over, England will be her home.'

There had been more than a hint of bravado in the decision. Sometimes, far oftener than either woman would admit, they wondered if the war would ever finish, or whether they would ever leave Russia alive.

So Natasha spoke English with a quaint mixture of Russian and American accents. Now, as her mother lowered her to the floor, she toddled towards Margaret, embracing her about the knees.

'Hello, Ma'gwet, honey.'

Anna dropped wearily on to the bed, rubbing her shoulders and neck.

'That child,' she said. 'I don't think she's slept more than three hours all night.'

'You should have called me or wakened Maud. I expect, though, she's hungry.'

'I know.' Anna leaned her forehead wearily against the bedpost and sighed. 'But there's nothing we can do. All the food Sir George sent us last week has gone.'

'I'll go out again presently,' Margaret offered. 'There might be a shop open somewhere with something to sell.'

Anna shook her head and began to cough. 'No,' she said as soon as she could speak, 'it's my turn. You and Jenner have done enough already.'

'You're in no fit state to go anywhere,' Margaret answered briskly. 'You will return to bed and get some rest. I'll make you a drink before I go. If, that is, we have any tea or coffee left.'

If anyone had told her, three years earlier, that she and Anna would one day become good friends, even grow fond of one another, she would have said it was impossible. But the fears and, more recently, the hardships they had endured together had forged a bond. To start with it had been no more than a sense of mutual sympathy; a feeling that they had been caught in the same trap and that continued enmity could only exacerbate the situation. A truce had been declared; but Margaret's devoted nursing of Anna throughout her long illness and subsequent convalescence had turned wary acceptance into liking.

Paul was the one subject they avoided as far as they were able. Neither woman ever spoke of her fears for his safety. They knew, from the half-dozen letters which had reached them during the first twelve months of the war, that he had been given a commission in the British army and that he had been hoping to be sent to France; but the last communication Anna had received from him had been sent from Aldershot and dated 12 July 1916. Since then there had been nothing, and the loss of Allied troops on the western front had been heavy. Sometimes, when news of a British reverse was received, they would look at one another in terror, but still said nothing. And in the past weeks, with conditions inside Petrograd rapidly worsening, they had been almost exclu-

228

sively concerned with themselves and their survival. Nothing and no one else any longer seemed of importance.

Margaret went out just before noon, accompanied by the faithful Maud Jenner. Anna and Natasha were curled up together in Anna's big bed, sound asleep. Margaret had found a wedge of stale cheese and two eggs, which had somehow been overlooked yesterday, and had made an omelette which the four of them had shared. There were no other servants now except Maud, not even little Katya, who had remained loyal right up until a month ago, coming in each day to clean. In the end, however, Margaret had been forced to dispense with her services, as they could no longer afford to share with her what few provisions they had.

There were a lot of people in the streets, but the majority were moving quietly about on business or in search of food. One or two went into the churches to pray. Even the pro-testers were marching in an orderly fashion, in contrast to the riots of the past few days. There was no transport of any kind. Trams, taxis and trains had come to a halt, and practically all the factories in the capital were closed because of strikes. The essential services, gas, water and electricity, were still operat-ing, although no one was quite sure why. On all the news pillars there were notices signed by General Khabalov, Commander of the Petrograd garrison, ordering the strikers back to work, but most of them had been defaced. Someone had urinated over the one in Znamenskaya Square.

Maud Jenner was unusually quiet. Normally she had a great deal to say about 'foreigners' and 'foreign ways', but today the general feeling of depression and foreboding which hung over the city seemed to have affected her spirits.

'What do you reckon's going to happen, Mrs Stafford?' she asked, breaking a protracted silence, as the two women turned once more towards Nevsky Prospect just before two o'clock. The broad street was crowded and there appeared to be a demonstration going on in the square.

'I don't know. I wish I did,' Margaret admitted, quickening her pace.

Anna would probably be awake by now, and Margaret knew how nervous she became if left alone for too long. But at least their tiring journey had not been wasted. They had

229

managed to buy some meat – horsemeat, Margaret guessed – from a greasy little man with a sack near the Nicholas station.

Maud Jenner huddled deeper inside her thin coat, over which she had wrapped one of Anna's big shawls.

'I don't like it,' she said. 'I don't like the smell of things, Mrs Stafford, and that's God's truth.' She jerked her head at a group of demonstrators, who had linked hands across the road and were singing at the tops of their voices. 'Listen to 'em! Heathenish lingo! It's like being on a desert island, surrounded by hostile natives. I wouldn't mind so much if I could understand the things that they jabber. Do you think we'll ever get back to England?'

'Of course we will.' Margaret tried to speak with confidence. She thought enviously of Hilda, safely in London, as she glanced at the sea of faces all around her. Again, she had the nightmarish vision of a society on the verge of disintegration. She and Maud resolutely pushed their way through the crowds, trying to reach the safety of their own front door. A big, bearded face was thrust close to hers, and a blast of garlic-laden breath demanded something in the 'heathenish lingo'. She tried to push the man aside, while his sweeping gesture of rage knocked off Maud Jenner's hat. Several women immediately made a dive for it, fiercely disputing its ownership.

Suddenly, the quality of the shouting and singing changed from aggression to alarm. The man towering over Margaret abruptly withdrew his face and turned to stare in the opposite direction. Margaret's glance followed his, and she saw, to her horror, a dozen or more soldiers deploying across the street. They were armed with rifles, and were preparing to use them. Margaret looked for Maud Jenner, who was too busy trying to reclaim her hat to notice what was happening. The officer in charge of the soldiers barked an order.

'Maud! Get down!' Margaret yelled, throwing herself flat on the ground as she did so.

The next moment, a volley of bullets peppered the crowd. There were screams and groans. People staggered around, blood running down their faces and bodies. Margaret, raising her head slightly to look for Maud, saw a boy of about sixteen stop in his tracks, twist slowly in a semi-circle, then crash to his knees, his blue eyes wide with astonishment, blood gushing from his nose and mouth.

The remainder of the crowd was stampeding now in panic as the soldiers prepared to fire a second time. Margaret felt unable to think clearly. It was only blind instinct which made her roll over the man lying next to her and huddle against the wall of the house. Even so, she was kicked several times by heavily booted feet as their owners fled, leaving the dead and dying behind them.

The noise, after a while, receded into the distance, to be succeeded by a terrible silence. The officer barked out another order and the soldiers marched away; but it was not until even the echo of their footsteps had diminished that Margaret moved from her position by the wall.

Trembling violently, her hands splayed against the granite behind her for support, she stood upright, then retched as the world began to spin. There was blood everywhere, spattered over her coat and over the walls of the houses. It seeped from the dead and wounded to form great puddles in the road. Margaret drew in her breath, taking gulps of air to calm her heaving stomach. After a few minutes her vision cleared and the nausea subsided.

'Maud!' she called weakly. 'Maud Jenner, where are you?' There was a faint moan somewhere to her left, just audible above the groans and curses. 'Maud!' she shouted again, her voice strengthened by fear. 'Answer me! Where are you?'

Then she saw her, lying face down in the road, the hat, triumphantly wrested from one of the Russian women, still clutched in her hand. But even from where she stood Margaret could see the blood streaking Maud's temple. Her heart pounded wildly. She stepped across the intervening bodies and knelt by Maud's side. The eye she could see was open, and seemed to show a flicker of life.

'Where are you hurt?' she asked, but as she spoke she noticed the blood-matted hair. Reason told her that Maud was already dead, but in rising hysteria she went on shaking the other woman's arm. . . .

Sir George Buchanan, in the midst of all his worries, made time to visit them the next day, and offered to make the necessary arrangements for Maud Jenner's funeral. He was deeply shocked by what had happened, his aristocratic face beneath the silver hair thin and worn after his seven years in Russia. He peered earnestly through his monocle and said: 'A dreadful thing! A terrible thing, Countess, when we are unable to protect the lives of British citizens.'

The ambassador did not stay long, recognizing that the two women were too much distressed for conversation. He did tell them, however, that more than forty people had been killed yesterday in Znamenskaya Square; that there were rumours this morning that the men of the Volkonsky Regiment had mutinied, killing a couple of officers; and that the crew of the battle-cruiser *Aurora*, in dock at Petrograd for her winter overhaul, was reported confined to ship by Captain Nikolsky after demonstrating its support for the strikers.

'Let me urge you to remain indoors, Countess,' Sir George begged, on parting. 'Both you and Mrs Stafford.' He smiled at Margaret, plainly smitten by her beauty. 'I shall see to it that you receive a supply of food.'

Neither woman needed a second bidding. They were still too shaken to venture out of doors. By midday, the Nevsky Prospect was full of people marching up and down, chanting the 'Marseillaise'. When a servant from the British Embassy arrived later that afternoon, bringing, under cover of darkness, a hamper of food, he told them that the crowds had sacked the arsenal on Liteiny Prospect, taking more than seven thousand rifles and revolvers.

As Margaret let him out of the back door, the young man paused.

'I didn't like to say too much in front of the Countess, Mrs Stafford. She seems nervous enough already. But they do say that all the prisoners in the Litovsky Castle and the house of detention have been freed. And from the Kresty Prison. Also, the police station at Kirpochny has been attacked. For God's sake, lock all your doors and windows, ma'am, before you go to sleep.'

Sergei Zhirov followed like a sleep-walker in the wake of the crowds who had released him. Two and a half years in prison had left him, like his fellow convicts, weak and dazed. He was finding it difficult to come to terms with his sudden freedom.

'Don't question it,' he told himself. 'Just keep walking. Just get accustomed to light and air and the sense of space.'

'Where are we going?' he asked the man next to him. His speech was slurred, like a drunkard's.

His neighbour and the other men all around him really were drunk. Bottles of vodka were being passed from hand to hand. Someone shouted that the District Court building on Liteiny Prospect had been set on fire, and that the Romanov eagles were burning. Fire engines appeared round the corner of the street, as if to verify the statement. The crowds raced to head them off, dragging the firemen from their seats, battering them with rifle-butts and clubs. Sergei looked at the red, pulpy mess which had been a man's head and promptly threw up.

His neighbour said: 'Here! Have a swig of this!' and forced some vodka down Sergei's throat.

He choked, but felt better. The narrow cell, with its spy-hole and bare boards, which had been his world since the late summer of 1914, began to recede. He swallowed more vodka and started to cheer with the rest. The neat spirit in his empty stomach made him light-headed. After a few moments, his feet no longer seemed to touch the ground. When the mob entered a police station and began killing and wrecking, he seized someone's rifle and beat a policeman over the head. He went on and on in a senseless, blinding fury, until somebody laughed and told him: 'You're making sure that poor bugger's well and truly dead.'

He glanced down at the blood and brains at his feet and experienced a glow of satisfaction. The murdered policeman meant nothing to him; it had been another whom he had been obliterating: someone who had obtained Hilda's release from prison and spirited her back to England. It had been Paul Devereaux.

As Sergei stood there, swaying on his feet, drunk with power and vodka, faces from the past, half-forgotten under layers of hopelessness, swam up to meet him: Hilda, Pavel and Nickolai Brodkin; and, further back in time, his mother, Olga and Anna Rastorguyeva, the English Duke. And Paul

Devereaux, who, according to Nickolai, held shares in the Lena goldfields. . . .

'Come on, mate!' Somebody jogged his arm. 'We've finished here. We're going to the Tauride Palace to kill the government.'

But when they surged into the palace courtyard, thronging its corridors and overflowing into its halls, Alexander Kerensky came rushing out to greet them, shaking their hands, agreeing to their demands that 'Bloody Nicholas' must abdicate, and greeting them in the name of the People's Revolution. Other members of the Duma followed suit.

'But it must come gently, slowly,' Kerensky told the crowds, who had now fallen silent, hanging on his every word. 'Go to your homes. Your grievances are safe in the hands of your government.'

Reluctantly, people began to disperse, leaving the Provisional Executive of the Petrograd Soviet to convene in room thirteen of the palace. Outside, however, groups began to re-form. A man with an eye-patch and a scar down his left cheek flung one arm across Sergei's back, supporting him under the armpit.

'Come on, my friend,' he encouraged him. 'The night isn't over yet.'

Sergei hardly knew what he was doing. He had eaten no food since the sparse prison meal of the previous evening, and his wits were fuddled by drink. He tried to concentrate on what was happening to him, but could only think of Paul Devereaux. Fucking bastard Englishman! Aristocrat! Exploiter of the poor! Hadn't Hilda once told him that there had been trouble at one of the Devereaux mines? Shooting . . . killing . . . somebody dead . . . Paul Brodkin was dead. Had he been shot by Paul Devereaux? Betty, his sister-in-law, had been dismissed. He was fond of Betty. . . . Everything was running together in his mind, which refused to obey him. All his thoughts were blurred. He wanted to sleep. Everything would become clear to him in the morning. . . .

People were cheering. The man with the eye-patch was embracing Sergei.

'The navy's with us,' he was shouting. 'The Baltic fleet has joined the revolution. Come on, my friends! We're going to the shipyard to inform Captain bloody Nikolsky of the *Aurora*!'

But Sergei was not interested. It was doubtful if he even heard. He sank down by the side of the road, while the crowd surged past him, and was violently sick. Afterwards he felt a little better, but still bewildered. It was happening. The revolution which he and his fellow dissidents had talked about, schemed for, hoped for, planned for, but never really believed would happen, was actually taking place. But where were Lenin, Stalin, Trotsky and the rest? Why weren't they here? Why weren't they snatching the leadership from that old woman Kerensky, with his prattle about self-restraint and democratic government?

The problem was too much for Sergei. He dragged himself into a doorway, his prison clothes fouled and muddy, his teeth chattering from the cold, until he was rescued by one of the city's prostitutes who helped him through the doorway and upstairs to her room. He collapsed on the bed and was asleep in two minutes. Late the following afternoon, his benefactress woke him to the smell of hot cabbage soup and the news that the *Aurora*'s crew had broken out of detention and murdered Captain Nikolsky.

Twenty-One

'What's happening? Have you heard anything while you were out?'

'Give me a moment, Anna, for pity's sake.' Margaret sat down at the kitchen table, one hand pressed to her side. There had been an ugly mob in Znamenskaya Square, and she had been forced to run. Any kind of exertion tired her nowadays. The unvarying diet of soup and bread was beginning to tell on all three of them.

Margaret and Anna lived in the kitchen during the daytime. They had agreed, after Maud's death, to shut up the rest of the ground- and first-floor rooms. They had also closed all the bedrooms except Anna's, which they shared. Natasha's little cot-bed had been set up in one corner. Anna's cousin, who had so generously allowed them to continue living in his house after the outbreak of war, no longer wrote from his *dacha* near Moscow to enquire after their well-being. Anna had received no word from him for over six months, and had no idea what had happened to him.

The last eight months had passed like a dream. The Tsar had abdicated and been sent with his family to Tobolsk in Siberia by Kerensky and the Provisional Government. On the eve of the United States' entry into the war, President Woodrow Wilson had acclaimed the event.

'Does not every American feel that assurance has been added to our hope for the future peace of the world by the wonderful and heartening things that have been happening within the last few weeks in Russia?'

The British government had been less ecstatic, but a move by Kerensky to obtain asylum for the Imperial family in

England had been blocked by the Labour and Liberal parties.

During the summer the Provisional Government had renewed the offensive against Germany in Galicia. It had failed, mainly because the Russian army was being decimated, not by the enemy, but by its own deserters. Conditions on all fronts deteriorated week by week. Russia had turned in upon herself and was no longer interested in the outside world.

A new force had slowly been making itself felt in Petrograd with the return of Lenin and Trotsky. The Bolsheviks were everywhere, in spite of the fact that Lenin had been forced at one point to escape in disguise to Finland, and Trotsky had been imprisoned. For days now there had been talk that the Provisional Government was on the point of collapse. Refugees, streaming into the cities from the countryside, reported that many landlords were being murdered, crops burned in the fields, animals slaughtered, houses razed to the ground.

In the cities themselves, conditions went from bad to worse. Law and order had ceased to exist. People were robbed at gun-point in the streets and empty houses looted. The railway stations were full of vagrants and deserters from the front, all of them hungry, most of them drunk. Vodka seemed the only commodity in limitless supply. Horses were rarely seen on the streets any more: most of them had been eaten.

In the late summer there had been local elections. The Bolsheviks gained thirty-three per cent of the vote for the Petrograd City Duma, and later won a majority in the Petrograd and Moscow soviets. Sir George Buchanan warned Kerensky that Bolshevism was the root of 'all the evils from which Russia is suffering'. He added that if Kerensky could smash the Bolsheviks he would go down in history as the saviour of his country. Kerensky had merely shrugged. In common with other members of the Provisional Government, he had the feeling that time was running out. The current of events had proved too strong for him ever since he had been forced to call on the Bolsheviks for aid in halting General Kornilov's march on Petrograd at the head of his loyalist troops.

'Well,' Anna repeated impatiently, after Margaret had

been silent for a full minute, 'have you heard anything today?'

Margaret kicked off her shoes and arched her back wearily. 'Kerensky's gone,' she said.

'Gone?' Anna's voice was shrill. 'Gone where?'

'The rumour is that he left Petrograd this morning in a car belonging to the United States Embassy, flying the American flag. It's reported that he's gone to rally what's left of the army, but God knows whether or not it's true. The rest of the government is holed up in the Winter Palace. Lenin and the Bolsheviks have taken over the Smolny Institute, whatever and wherever that is.'

'It is – was – a girls' school,' Anna replied absently. 'You must have seen it and passed it dozens of times. A long grey building, with a blue-and-gold cupola, at the eastern end of the Shpalernaya. . . . What do you think is going to happen?'

Margaret shrugged. 'Your guess would be as good as mine. I'm starving. Is there anything to eat?'

'What . . . ? Oh, yes. I've saved you some onion stew, and there's a hunk of bread.'

The bread was mouldy and the stew greasy, but Margaret swallowed both with as much relish as if they were caviare and oysters. It was amazing how unfussy hunger had made her. 'Where's Natasha?' she asked presently.

'Asleep. She complained of being tired. Now she'll be awake all night.' Anna shivered. 'I feel so cold.'

'That's not surprising, considering how little wood we have to burn. That reminds me. Here.' Margaret reached into the basket at her feet and brought out the legs of an old wooden chair. 'I found these among the pile of rubbish near the cathedral. I managed to grab them before anyone else had noticed.'

Anna put a hand to her forehead. 'I don't know how you can,' she said. 'Grub about in those piles of rubbish, I mean.'

'It's a good thing I'm willing to sink my pride then, isn't it? A good job my blood isn't too blue to "grub about" as you call it.' Margaret's sudden spurt of anger faded and died. She stretched out her hand to Anna. 'I'm sorry, honey. It's just that I'm not quite myself these days.'

Anna gave her a quick, nervous smile and took the proffered

hand. 'I'm sorry, too. It was a silly thing to say. Of course I'm grateful.' She burst into tears.

Margaret got up and went round the table to comfort her, kneeling beside Anna's chair. They clung to one another.

'It's all right,' Margaret whispered. 'For goodness' sake, don't let's quarrel. What would we do without one another to talk to?'

The older woman gave a watery sniff and began hunting for her handkerchief. 'You've been so good to me and Natasha. I know I'm selfish and useless. I was never brought up to look after myself, you see.'

'I know that. You've coped very well. This war is bound to be over soon, now that America's come in, and then we shall be able to go home, to England.'

Anna nodded, trying to put a brave face on things. But both women knew, though neither spoke her thoughts aloud, that the war in Europe was no longer important. It was what was going on inside Russia that mattered.

Sergei Zhirov was one of the many hundreds of people thronging the Smolny Institute that grey winter's morning. The news that Kerensky had left Petrograd had been greeted earlier by cheers; but subsequent information that the rest of the Provisional Government was still entrenched in the Malachite Chamber of the Winter Palace had provoked anger and dismay.

Shortly after ten o'clock, Sergei emerged from the Institute's basement, which had been turned into a canteen, where he had just breakfasted on cabbage soup, black bread and a mug of tea. He had managed to conceal part of the bread in one of his pockets. His little prostitute would be glad of it, because although hers was the city's one thriving profession, an increasing number of clients refused to pay. Only two nights ago she had returned home with a black eye and a split lip after a satisfied customer had told her to 'fuck off' when she demanded her fee. Her strident insistence on payment had resulted in a beating. Sergei shook his head sadly. The silly bitch just would not learn.

As he reached the top of the stairs, a man came out of the room where Lenin and other members of the Military

Revolutionary Committee had been closeted for the past two hours. The man, whom Sergei did not know, was clutching a sheaf of papers.

'Hey, you!' he called to Sergei. 'Round up some others and take one of the trucks. Lenin wants this proclamation put up all over the city as soon as possible.' He pushed the pile of notices into Sergei's arms and went back into the room. As the door opened and closed, Sergei heard a babel of excited voices.

An hour later, the proclamation was everywhere, nailed on doors, trees, news pillars and the walls of houses.

To all Russian citizens!
  The Provisional Government has been overthrown. Power is now in the hands of the Petrograd Soviet of Workers and Soldier Deputies.
  The causes for which you have fought – the abolition of the landowners, workers' control and the establishment of soviet power – are now secure.
  Long live the revolution!

It was not quite true that the Provisional Government had been deposed, but it was a justifiable anticipation of what must surely be only a matter of hours.

Sergei nailed up his last copy of the proclamation near the Astoria Hotel, and was on his way back to the waiting truck when he heard his name called. Looking round, he saw Nickolai Brodkin. The two men embraced, tears pouring down their cheeks.

'I thought you were dead,' Sergei moaned, rocking the younger man to and fro. 'My God, I was sure you must be dead. I've searched for you everywhere these past months. When were you released?'

'When they raided the Peter and Paul prison. Where are you living? What are you doing? What's happened to your wife?'

Sergei shouted to his comrades in the truck that he would return to the Smolny Institute later. He and Nickolai found that, between them, they had the price of a bottle of vodka and went in search of one. In the end, they did not need their money. They simply walked into the Astoria Hotel and were given two the moment they asked. So they sat in the dining-room until mid-afternoon, drinking and catching up on one another's news.

'So your wife was sent back to England, eh?' Nickolai looked regretfully at his empty glass, but did not dare reach out his hand to refill it. The table tended to do queer things if he moved any part of himself too suddenly. 'What happened to that bastard I tried to kill?'

'I've made enquiries,' Sergei answered. He had drunk far less than Nickolai and was a great deal more sober. 'He went back to England, as well, just before the outbreak of war.'

'Pity,' muttered the other, measuring the distance between his glass and the bottle of vodka with an appraising eye. If only the damn thing would stop moving, he might grab hold of it.

'But his wife and that friend of Hilda's are still here,' Sergei went on. 'The Countess was ill and couldn't leave with her husband. She and Mrs Stafford were trapped here by the fighting.'

Nickolai was not interested in the friend of Hilda Zhirova, only in the Countess. 'How do you know all this? Are you sure of your facts?' he asked.

Sergei grinned. 'As sure as I can be. The girl I lodge with used to work for them. She was one of old Count Denisov's servants, and went with the house when he let it. She stayed on after the war started, with the Countess and Margaret Stafford. All the servants, except the men called up for the army, stayed on for a while. But gradually they left, one by one, until just Katya and the Countess's maid remained. Earlier this year Katya was turned out because they said they couldn't feed her. She was destitute and had to take to the streets. I've been living with her ever since I was released from prison. She picked me up out of the gutter the first night, when I had nowhere to go.'

Nickolai Brodkin spat on the expensive red-and-grey carpet of the Astoria Hotel. Some people at the next table turned to stare at him, then looked hurriedly away again. In the general day-to-day uncertainty, it was impossible to say who would be in power by tomorrow.

'The *pridvorny*,' he said, 'I hate them.' His words were slurred and his hands shook as he at last managed to pour himself more vodka. 'Well, the Englishman's out of reach now, but I could still get her. His wife. She once had shares in the goldfields too.'

Sergei moved the second vodka bottle beyond his friend's grasp and asked: 'How did you find out about Devereaux?'

Nickolai struggled to clear the fumes from his fuddled brain. He had had nothing to eat since early morning and the vodka was making him feel sick. He furrowed his brow in an effort of concentration, trying to recall a name which Sergei had mentioned a few moments ago, recognizing that it had some relevance.

'What was the name?' he asked carefully.

'What name?' Sergei was beginning to get impatient. There would be important work to be done later in the day. It was foolish to be sitting here while Nickolai drank himself stupid.

'Name of your wife's friend. Said she was living with the Countess.'

'Mrs Stafford? What are you burbling about? Pull yourself together, man!'

'Same name.' Nickolai wagged a finger in self-justification. 'Don't always recognize these foreign names. Recognize that one. 'Bout four years ago, summer of thirteen, went to visit my cousins in Poland.'

'What's all this garbage leading to?' Sergei interrupted rudely. 'Drunk as a wheelbarrow, that's you.'

'Asked me a question. Giving you the answer. Friend of one of my cousins was an Englishman, working in one of the Polish coalmines. His father had been killed in similar circ . . . circ . . . circ'stances to mine. M' cousin told me all about him. Name of Stafford. Father had worked for this Devereaux.'

Sergei recalled that Margaret Stafford had a step-son, with whom she had lost touch. Nickolai's Englishman could well be the same man. It had not been unusual, before the war, for Englishmen with mining experience to take jobs abroad, particularly in eastern Europe where their expertise was highly prized and paid for.

He nodded and motioned the younger man to silence. He could work out for himself what had happened. Nickolai had been interested in William Stafford because of the similarity of their fathers' deaths. Through his cousin, he had learned of Paul Devereaux's involvement with the Lena goldfields. Nickolai had stored the name away in his memory, and when, the following year, fate had obligingly brought Paul Devereaux to Russia Nickolai, hardly crediting his luck, had made his attempt on the Englishman's life. When it failed, he had fled to his father's old friend, not dreaming that he too had a tenuous connection with his enemy.

Like all Russians, Sergei believed strongly in destiny and the workings of fate. He did not accept the idea of coincidence or chance. The complicated tangle of relationships which had led to the attempt on Paul Devereaux's life, and his own subsequent involvement, had been for a purpose, which must be followed through to the end. If Paul Devereaux himself had escaped retribution, then it was obvious that Countess Anna was the person pre-ordained to atone for Pavel Brodkin's death.

For the moment, however, it could wait. First he must return to the Smolny Institute to check on the morning's developments. He put an arm round Nickolai and heaved him to his feet. Nickolai was immediately sick. The manager rushed over and started to protest, but then he too thought better of it. It was known that the cruiser *Aurora* was anchored in the Neva opposite the Winter Palace, and she was flying the red flag of the Bolsheviks. Her guns were trained on the city. God alone knew what the situation might be by tonight. He watched the two men wend their way out of the hotel, then snapped at a waiter to clear up the mess.

A cold wind had been blowing all day, bringing squalls of sleet trailing in its skirts. The streets had been very quiet, people going about such business as they had in an orderly fashion, as though trying, after all the civil disobedience and disorders of the past eight months, to pretend that nothing was really wrong.

Anna, sitting at the bedroom window looking out into the wet and windy street, found it quite easy to imagine that the Tsar and Tsarina were still in residence at the Winter Palace. She recalled, with a nostalgia she had never experienced until

243

recently, the balls which she and Olga had attended in their youth.

It was ironic that she should remember them now with such affection, when she had detested every moment at the time. She had always been so thin and awkward; always such a wallflower, while her sister had been one of the belles of every ball. It was not that Olga was, or had been, beautiful; she had been round and plump and jolly, but with an easy camaraderie which men thought attractive. Anna had been stiff and withdrawn, hiding her shyness behind a cold formality. She had hidden behind Olga, too, knowing that she could rely on her sister's protection. When their father died, and Olga had made up her mind to marry her English Duke, Anna had known full well that Francis did not really want her living with them at Hawksworth. If she had had one spark of self-reliance she would have stayed in Russia, but she had been unable to face life on her own. So she had left St Petersburg for London and the English countryside in the company of Olga and that odd boy of old Katia Nicolaievna's, Sergei Zhirov, whom her sister had insisted on taking with them.

Margaret came into the bedroom, closing the door very quietly behind her so as not to wake Natasha, who was asleep in her cot.

'I've locked up the kitchen,' she said, 'and I've been round as usual, bolting all the doors and windows.' She sat on the bed, pulling the quilt around her. 'I'm sure no one can get in.' She spoke cheerfully, knowing how nervous Anna was. It would do no good to point out that anyone determined enough could easily break in. 'Aren't you cold over there?' She patted the bed beside her. 'Come and get under the quilt.'

Anna did so, kicking off her shoes, and they lay side by side, fully clothed, the coverings right up to their chins.

By tacit consent, they had stopped talking about 'after the war'. It was an unnecessary form of torture. They had ceased to believe in tomorrow: it was sufficient to live from day to day.

After a while, Anna said: 'I was thinking about the balls Olga and I used to go to when we were young; when the present Tsar's father was on the throne.' She did not even notice the slip, did not remember that there was no 'present

Tsar' and probably never would be again. She went on: 'The great Imperial balls always began at half past eight in the evening. Their Imperial Majesties would arrive from their private apartments in the Winter Palace and dance the first dance alone. Tsar Alexander was a huge man, over six feet tall, and the Tsarina Marie was lovely – she still is, if it comes to that – unusually dark-eyed for a Dane. She wore the most beautiful gowns and jewels. It's odd that I remember that, because clothes have never interested me. I've always thought choosing them a dreadful bore.

'Then everyone would dance. After the dancing, there would be supper. It was normally served in one of the rooms overlooking the Neva. In the depths of winter, you could look through the windows and watch the flurries of snow blowing along the frozen river. . . .'

Anna's voice drifted into silence. Natasha moved restlessly in her cot, whimpered a little, but did not wake.

Margaret chuckled. 'How unlike the home life of the Bowery,' she said. 'I don't think I've ever been to a ball in my life.'

'What's it like, New York?' Anna asked curiously.

So Margaret told her about Lafayette Street and Broadway and walking miles on a Sunday morning to John Street Methodist chapel, just because her father thought the preaching there was better than anywhere else. She told her about the Jubilee Singers, and how Herbert Dunham had seen the soldiers marching off to fight in the Civil War. And she told her about a day, long forgotten even by herself but suddenly recalled, when she and Jessie and Beatrice had been taken in the Smith carriage high up into the hills, and had looked back across a score or more of towns to see New York; the bay, the Narrows and the sound, lying like an enchanted fairyland, far away, below them.

There was silence for a long time after she had finished speaking. Then Anna asked abruptly: 'You love him, don't you?'

For a moment, Margaret was nonplussed. She had been so wrapped up in those childhood memories that she had forgotten everything else. She turned her head enquiringly towards Anna, whose face was a pale oval blur in the gloom.

245

'You love him. You love Paul,' Anna insisted, and this time it was no longer a question. 'What is more to the point, he loves you.'

Margaret was unprepared for this sudden attack after years of avoiding the subject. She was not quite sure how to answer.

'We've loved each other for a very long time,' she said finally, suppressing the little catch in her throat.

'Before Beatrice died?'

'Yes. Before then. Before my husband was killed. Before I was even married.'

Anna nodded as though she perfectly understood. 'He couldn't marry you, of course.'

'Not in England. Not anywhere in Europe, I suppose. Not without the scandal that a misalliance brings.'

Anna said quietly: 'Things like that won't matter so much after this war. It's going to change a great deal.'

Margaret again glanced at the face beside her, now turned to her in profile.

'It won't make any difference to Paul and me,' she said. 'I shall take my children and go right away. Perhaps I shall go home, to New York.'

'Why? Why should you do this for me?'

'Because I've grown fond of you and Natasha. Because you love Paul, too. Once we'd realized that, we agreed that everything must be over between us. He knew when he left here three years ago that once I returned to England I should leave him.'

'But it's you he wants, not me.'

'You mustn't say that. I'm sure—' Margaret hesitated, unable to finish the glib lie which she had started.

Anna completed the sentence for her. 'That he loves me in his own way? But even if you're right, it isn't good enough for me.'

Margaret cast about desperately for something to say, but there was no satisfactory answer. Damn Paul! Damn all men and the trouble they caused between women!

'You must—' she was beginning, but got no further. The peace of the night was shattered by a deafening explosion.

Twenty-Two

It was a little after half past ten on the night of 7 November by the European calendar – 25 October by the Russian calendar – that the cruiser *Aurora* fired a blank shell from one of her six-inch guns and signalled the start of the Bolshevik revolution. By two o'clock the following morning, what remained of the Provisional Government had surrendered, and its members were under arrest.

It had been a peculiar day altogether, Sergei thought, as, earlier in the evening, he had lounged around the corridors of the Smolny Institute, or descended into the basement for one of those endless tin mugs of tea. In the afternoon Lenin had made a speech, but other than that nothing much had happened. Comrades coming in from the street reported that everything was quiet, even normal. Some of the trams had started running again; shops, even though they had nothing much to sell, were open; the ballet was going forward at the Maryinsky Theatre. Sir George Buchanan had been seen strolling on the quay near the Winter Palace, in company with the American Ambassador David R. Francis, a former Governor of Missouri, who had arrived in Petrograd the previous year bringing with him, as an indispensable item of ambassadorial luggage, a portable spitoon.

Nickolai Brodkin had sobered up after being pumped full of tea and allowed to sleep off his hangover in one of the upstairs rooms. He reappeared shortly after six o'clock, red-eyed and white-faced, but otherwise ready for anything which the evening might bring.

'What's happening?' he asked Sergei, who shrugged despondently.

247

'Nothing at the moment.'

Nickolai grinned weakly. 'There's a hell of a lot of activity going on for nothing.'

Soldiers with rifles, women with important-looking files and bundles of papers, men arguing, talking, gesticulating, all seemed to be hurrying somewhere, doing something. A few, like Sergei and Nickolai, sat on benches lining the corridors and watched them.

'When are we going to take over?' Nickolai asked peevishly. 'When is the *starik* going to give the signal?'

'Old man' had been Lenin's nickname ever since he had become prematurely bald in his early twenties, and had been used for as long as anyone could remember. Now, however, it seemed sacrilegious, and Sergei frowned in disapproval.

'Lenin will make the right move at the right time,' he said, with more conviction than he actually felt. It had always been his private opinion that Lenin was a better orator than man of action. Action was the province of men like Trotsky and Stalin. The *starik* was more of a dreamer, who had forced himself into a position of power within the Party because of his way with words. And Lenin had that magic ingredient, personality; a fact which Margaret Stafford had long ago recognized.

Thinking of Margaret brought back to Sergei memories of that night in London, when she had been staying with them in Tabard Street, and had accompanied him and Hilda to the meeting in Whitechapel and, later, to the Anarchist Club. Lenin had told him afterwards that he thought Margaret Stafford one of the most beautiful women he had ever seen, and Stalin had given a little grunt, a sort of outward echo of internal mirth.

Sergei had liked Margaret himself in those days, before she had betrayed her class and her principles by going to live with Paul Devereaux as his mistress. Sergei was sure that she had been behind Hilda's release from prison and repatriation to England. He had felt no gratitude for that act of clemency on the part of the authorities. He had loved Hilda, and she had been persuaded to abandon him. Once freed, she should have gone to earth somewhere and awaited his own release.

Deep down, he knew that he was being unreasonable; that

Hilda, with only a few words of Russian at her command and a text-book knowledge of French – the language spoken by the nobility and well-to-do – could not have survived on her own in the city; that, in the normal course of events, it would have been many more years before his sentence was finished. Yet he continued to feel aggrieved and angry, as though he had been robbed. He persisted in blaming Margaret for what he saw as Hilda's disaffection. He and Nickolai both had a score to settle with those two women in the house on Nevsky Prospect, and the time was rapidly approaching when they would be able to take their revenge.

There was a sudden burst of significant activity. A door further along the corridor was thrown open and a dozen or more soldiers appeared, rounding everyone up and urging them towards the main hall, where Lenin would address them. Half an hour later, looking tired and unkempt, Lenin climbed on to the rostrum and told them that the Revolutionary Committee had decided on a plan of action. The members of the Provisional Government holed up in the Malachite Chamber of the Winter Palace would be asked to surrender. If they refused, a red lantern would be hoisted on the fortress of Saints Peter and Paul, and the *Aurora* would fire a blank shell as a signal for a general assault.

Sergei and Nickolai cheered with the rest and streamed out of the Smolny Institute to walk along the banks of the Neva and stare at the grim old fortress across the river. Lenin and Trotsky withdrew to get some rest, sharing a blanket on the bare floor of a cupboard-like room. Any minute now, things would start to happen. The revolution, so long dreamed of, would become a reality. . . .

After an hour, the groups of huddled men were beginning to stamp their feet and blow on their fingers, murmuring anxiously to one another about the delay. They had no means of knowing that in the fortress confusion reigned because no one could find a red lantern; nor that the fortress guns were unfit for use after being neglected for more than a year. The most important moment in Russia's long history was threatening to degenerate into farce.

'What time is it?' Nickolai muttered.

Sergei turned to ask the man behind him, so missing the

hoisting of a lantern which had been hurriedly covered in red crêpe paper.

'Just after half past ten,' he told Nickolai.

There was a sudden violent explosion as the *Aurora*'s crew fired the blank shell, the noise echoing and reverberating across the water to lose itself among the quayside palaces.

'Come on!' yelled Nickolai. 'This is it!' and he and Sergei surged forward, borne along by the press of bodies all around them. The excitement flowed with them like a tidal wave, bearing them up so that their feet seemed divorced from the ground.

Outside the palace, some armoured cars and small guns were drawn up. They opened fire just as Sergei and Nickolai reached the square, seconds ahead of the rest.

Someone shouted: 'Halt!' The front ranks pulled up short, and everyone started cannoning into everyone else. Sergei and Nickolai, finding themselves in danger of either being trampled underfoot or blown to bits, ran for their lives across the square and dodged into the nearest doorway.

The firing lasted about thirty minutes, and, as the guns fell silent, a procession could be seen approaching. This turned out to be two hundred members of the Duma, demanding admittance to the Winter Palace so that they might die with the ministers who were still inside.

'Let us pass!' a voice shouted out of the darkness. 'We wish to be allowed to sacrifice ourselves.'

'Die and welcome!' bawled Sergei, and the cry was immediately taken up by those around him.

A group of sailors who had been patrolling the other side of the square barred the way of the procession.

'Go and kill yourselves at home!' one of them cried. 'Take poison, anything you like. But you're not committing suicide here. We have orders to prevent it.'

One or two of the more intrepid Duma members were inclined to argue, but in the end the rifles and bayonets of the sailors carried the day. The procession broke up and dispersed, followed by a detachment of Cossacks who until then had been half-heartedly guarding the palace. Their departure was greeted with prolonged cheering, which was ended abruptly by the roar of gunfire from the fortress of Saints Peter and Paul. Two of its guns had at last been sufficiently cleaned and oiled to go into action; while everyone raced for cover, thirty or forty shells whistled across the river, aimed at the Winter Palace. Little damage was done, however. Only some masonry was cracked.

It was now past midnight. Sergei and Nickolai returned to the comparative comfort of their doorway. They did not speak to one another, each afraid of expressing doubts about the outcome of the night's proceedings. The action seemed to be fizzling out in the wind and rain which squalled along the Nevsky Prospect. More soldiers arrived in a truck, and stationed themselves close enough for Sergei and Nickolai to overhear their conversation. They were discussing trouble of some sort at the Smolny Institute. It appeared that several of the non-Bolsheviks had accused Lenin of trying to seize power for himself, and had deplored the shelling of the palace. Lenin had made no answer, but Trotsky had fired up and told his friend's detractors that they were 'so much rubbish, only fit for the refuse-tip of history'.

'That's telling 'em, eh?' Nickolai whispered in Sergei's ear, and Sergei nodded.

Suddenly, one of the soldiers, who had been reconnoitring nearer to the palace than the others, came back to say that nearly all the defenders had gone.

'Come on!' he shouted. 'Forward!' and started waving his arms.

There was a concerted movement as people crossed the square and began entering the side doors of the palace, swarming in their hundreds up the great staircases, filling the vast ballrooms and salons and reception-halls; staring first in awe, then with the sharp gleam of greed in their eyes, at the exquisite porcelain and paintings and jewelled statuettes.

Sergei looked about him in disbelief. In his wildest imaginings, he had never pictured extravagance and luxury on such a scale. There was gold everywhere; on walls, on floors, on ceilings. It surrounded mirrors, decorated screens, veined marble pillars. Doors sported golden fluting; there were gilded frescoes and Gobelin tapestries; baroque boudoirs and the lavish crimson and gold of the throne-room. His mind simply could not take it all in. A man, he thought dazedly, could wander around the palace for a week, and still not see all that there was to see.

The Malachite Chamber, which the last members of the Provisional Government had been using as their head-quarters, was equally breathtaking, with its columns and fireplaces of green Urals stone, its malachite tables and vases. The walls were decorated with angels, and the doors with elaborate traceries of gold-leaf. The ministers themselves had decided to bow to the inevitable, and at ten past two in the morning they were led away under guard to the fortress of Saints Peter and Paul.

It was all over, with only six casualties between the two sides. Sergei felt a terrible sense of anti-climax. All his thirty-five years he had been planning for the revolution, never really believing, in his heart of hearts, that it would come. When the country had celebrated the tercentenary of the Romanov dynasty in 1913, there had been no assurance that it would not continue for another three hundred years. Now, suddenly, in a matter of months, everything had been swept away. The great new era of the Communist State was beginning. . . .

He had been separated from Nickolai in the crush, and now went in search of him, wandering from room to room, pushing his way through the milling crowds of men and women. Looting was in progress. Around the walls of each room were steadily growing piles of glass, china, bedspreads, rugs, vases, clocks, jewelled boxes and mirrors. Anything that could be moved was being crammed into packing-cases and pockets, or carried away in armfuls. People were searching for the back stairs and side entrances, anywhere where they might not encounter the soldiers. Sergei was conscious of disgust; an ache of disappointment that the revolution had not changed anything.

He told himself not to be stupid. It was too early yet: he was too impatient. The great era of equality had scarcely begun. When there were no more rich and poor, people's natural cupidity would have no scope. He ran down a flight of marble stairs, trying to ignore the nagging doubt which that last thought had raised in his mind. He spotted Nickolai emerging from a doorway on the left, a gold clock with a diamond and ruby face clasped in his hands. Sergei took the last three stairs in one bound and grasped Nickolai's arm.

'Get rid of that, you idiot! Don't you know that the Military Revolutionary Committee has forbidden all looting? You could get yourself shot.'

Nickolai, who had jumped guiltily when Sergei first touched him, put down the clock and began emptying his pockets; a long string of milky-white pearls, a golden chicken with sapphire eyes, a small diamond-framed icon and an exquisite little hardstone carving of a Russian peasant woman by Fabergé, were all tossed on to a nearby heap.

'Let someone else have them,' he mumbled.

'And take the blame,' agreed Sergei. He gripped Nickolai's arm even harder and piloted him out of the nearest door before temptation could once more overwhelm him.

Outside in the square, they were stopped and searched by a group of soldiers. Sergei hoped grimly that Nickolai had held nothing back, and heaved a sigh of relief as they were allowed to pass.

It was almost three o'clock in the morning. A ring of bonfires gave the soldiers some much-needed warmth, and one of the men offered Sergei and Nickolai tea. As they stood sipping the bitter black brew from the hot tin mugs, Sergei noticed how quiet it was everywhere. There were no more crowds, no shouting or cheering. Behind him, the lights still blazed in the Winter Palace, but the moment of elation, the sense of history in the making, had passed. He remembered Hilda once quoting some British poet who had said that it was better to travel hopefully than to arrive. That was how he felt now. He had reached his destination, and suddenly the view from the window was flat and unexciting.

He and Nickolai handed back their mugs and walked back to the deserted Nevsky Prospect, the long line of baroque houses and palaces seeming insubstantial in the cold night air.

'Come on,' he said brusquely to Nickolai, 'we have our own vendetta to pursue.'

The younger man's eyes brightened hopefully. 'You mean we're going to kill the Countess now?'

'Don't be a fool! And don't call her the Countess any more. There aren't any titles after tonight. No, we're going to do our duty as citizens. We're going to report the woman Devereaux to the Military Soviet.'

By the middle of December there were five other families living in the house on Nevsky Prospect, and Anna, Margaret and Natasha were confined to the bedroom. A little tin stove had been placed in one corner and was used for cooking what food they managed to obtain. The two women fetched water from the kitchen, but the bathroom was out of bounds. It had been appropriated by a railway worker and his family. Three of them slept in the bath.

The sharing of accommodation had been only one of the many decrees issued by the new Revolutionary Government. The sale and purchasing of houses was forbidden. Anyone possessing more than one fur coat was ordered to give the others to the army. The duties of education and the powers of marriage and divorce were taken away from the Church and put in the hands of the civil authorities. All assets were frozen, and no one could withdraw more than a hundred and twenty-five roubles from the bank in any one week. Revolutionary courts were set up to preside over criminal and civil cases alike. Margaret felt as though she were living in prison.

Anna had been ill again with a cold, which in the past few days had turned to fever. Margaret had tried opening a window to let air into the fetid bedroom, but she had been forced to close it again. The snow lay thick outside and the temperature was below freezing.

Natasha, oddly enough, seemed to thrive on the changed circumstances. She liked always having her mother and Margaret close at hand. She adored being the centre of attention. She would toddle around the bedroom on her surprisingly sturdy young legs, laughing and chattering, turning somersaults or holding endless pretend tea-parties on the carpet. The lack of fresh air did not seem to bother her.

'Oh, you Anglo-Saxons and your fresh air!' Anna said, trying to laugh, but coughing instead. 'It's a wonder to me that all the British and Americans don't die of an inflammation of the lungs.' She was lying in bed, too weak to get up, while Margaret sat by the window, staring into the street. 'Is there anything interesting happening out there?'

254

Margaret shook her head, thinking that she would almost rather have the riots and alarms of the past ten months than the dreariness which had settled over the city. She had never liked Petrograd, not even when it had been St Petersburg, but at least in the old days it had shown a certain gaiety and sparkle.

'Well, as Pollyanna would have said, there's something to be glad about,' she remarked, getting up from her seat and pouring out some water for Anna from the jug on the bedside table. 'Now that all religious festivals have temporarily been banned, we shan't have to decide when to celebrate Christmas. It would be nice if Russia could adopt the Gregorian calendar like everyone else.'

She watched Anna sip the water. It was unnerving, she reflected, how she no longer talked of going back to England; how Russia, and everything about it, now seemed to her of paramount importance. Refusing to calculate months by the Julian calendar, and working out the date as it would be at home, was her last gesture of defiance against the three-and-a-half-year nightmare, which she could have avoided had she been willing to abandon Anna and her child. At the beginning of the war, as a citizen of a neutral country, she could probably have reached England. But Anna, being by birth and marriage a member of two of the combatant nations, would have been interned had she been caught. She might even have been arrested as a spy, such was the anti-Allied fervour which the Kaiser had whipped up amongst the Germans. Now, of course, it was too late anyway. The United States had been in the war for over six months. Moreover, she and Anna had very little money and nothing left to sell, since all jewellery and gold had been confiscated from bank vaults and houses, along with any hoards of foreign currency.

Margaret vividly recalled the day, four weeks ago, when the police had come to search the premises, taking away with them Anna's jewel-case. They had been rough and unnecessarily rude, ordering the two women to stand facing the wall while the room was ransacked. Drawers had been emptied on to the floor, the bed stripped, pictures torn from their hooks and a chair back slashed, in spite of Anna's repeated assurances that all her jewellery was in the blue leather case beside

255

the bed. Margaret had thought that they were both going to be raped, and her terror had brought back echoes of that long-ago night in the gatehouse-room at Latchetts. She was sure that it had only been the presence of Natasha which had saved them. The child, unconscious of danger, and convinced that it was all a game, ran about prattling gaily to the police who, like all Russians, adored children and fell easy victims to their wiles.

By the time the men finally left the room to search the rest of the house – even though they had little hope of finding anything worth seizing from the other families – Margaret was uneasy on another score. She had noticed two of the policemen whispering to one another, looking at Anna as they did so, while the third had raised his eyebrows and muttered what was plainly a question. When they had gone, Margaret asked Anna if she had overheard any of their private conversation.

'No, nothing,' Anna had said, and Margaret saw that she was trembling violently from shock.

She had remade the bed, forced the older woman into it, and tidied the rest of the room by herself. The next day Anna had started her cold, and two days after that had developed a raging fever.

She was over the worst of it now, but she was still very gaunt and pale. She was forty-three, but seemed much older. The dark hair was salted with grey and her skin was unhealthily white. She looked far too elderly, Margaret thought, to be the mother of Natasha. She had gained very little from her marriage to Paul, and Margaret felt an unexpected surge of anger against him.

Neither woman had mentioned her feelings, or discussed him again in anything but the most general terms, since the night the Winter Palace was taken. Odds and ends of news had filtered through from the western front, but no one knew enough to distinguish rumour from fact. There were stories of fighting around Cambrai; rumours that the British had attacked, but had been repulsed by the Germans. The real preoccupation of the food queues, however, was how much longer Russia could continue in the war. Lenin, it was said, wanted to make peace with the Germans. . . .

Anna, who had been lying against the pillows with her eyes

closed, suddenly reached out and tapped Margaret's wrist. Margaret, who had been almost asleep, jerked upright, blinking.

'I'm sorry if I startled you,' Anna said, 'but there's something I want you to know, just in case anything should – well – happen.' She saw the question in Margaret's eyes and went on: 'To me, I mean. It's no good saying it won't because anything is possible. No, don't interrupt. What I want to say is this. The police . . . they didn't get everything.' She nodded towards the commode which stood on the opposite side of the room.

'But they looked in there,' Margaret protested.

'They didn't remove the chamber-pot because it was full. Underneath it is the diamond bracelet Paul gave me when we were married. I hid it in there when I guessed the police would be coming. I didn't tell you because I thought you would act naturally if you didn't know. If we have a chance to escape, the bracelet will provide us with the necessary money. There must be people, surely, who would still buy it.'

Margaret nodded slowly. It would be very dangerous to sell it, but it could be done. No wonder Anna had been so frightened when the police were searching the room. She looked at the older woman in admiration, then stretched out her hand and held Anna's.

'We'll get out of here together,' she promised.

Twenty-Three

Sergei Zhirov was now a member of the Red Guard, a reward for his years of loyal support for the Bolshevik movement both in England and in Russia. Furthermore, unlike some of Lenin's former comrades, he fully approved of force as a means of strengthening the Party's hold on the capital. He remembered that years ago, in London, Lenin had said that if the Paris commune of 1871 had been prepared to consider the use of coercion against its enemies it would not have been suppressed by Thiers.

'But if murder and violence and secret police are wrong for the Tsar, why is it all right for us to use them?' Nickolai Brodkin wanted to know. He, too, was a member of the Red Guard.

'Because we don't intend using them forever,' Sergei snapped back. 'They're just temporary measures until the new order is created.'

He and Nickolai still shared the same apartment near Pergevalsky Street, but now they paid no rent. The landlady and her hoard of money had been taken away one night, and neither had reappeared.

The rooms were filthy, the bed unmade, dirty crockery piled high in the tiny sink. Occasionally, in unwary moments, Sergei recalled how it used to be when Hilda was there; clean and tidy with the pervasive smell of cooking. Then he would shrug. Hilda was gone and he doubted if he would ever see her again; and he knew whom he had to thank for that. As he buttoned on his uniform, he wondered impatiently why his information about Anna Devereaux, lodged eight weeks ago, had produced no response from the authorities. She and her

English husband had been shareholders in the Lena goldfields, where men had been killed. Surely that made her an enemy of the state?

'The complaint's probably been filed away somewhere and overlooked,' he said to Nickolai. 'I think it's time we jogged a memory or two. Everything's such a shambles at headquarters.'

'It's a shambles everywhere,' Nickolai answered gloomily, and Sergei glanced sharply at him. He was beginning to have doubts about his old cell-leader's son. There was a lack of backbone about Nickolai that made him unhappy.

Nevertheless, there was some justification for what Nickolai had said. Law and order had broken down. There were dozens of burglaries, murders, lynchings, every day. Anyone could denounce anyone else and get him executed without trial. Russia was falling apart at the seams; and every now and then he was afraid that no one, not even Lenin, could cobble it together again. There was, of course, always Josef Stalin. . . .

'Are you coming?' he asked irritably. Nickolai was still sitting on the edge of the bed, pulling on his boots.

They walked quickly in the grey morning light, the snow crunching beneath their feet. They said little. Sergei remarked that there was talk of the capital being moved temporarily to Moscow, as Lenin thought Petrograd too vulnerable to attack, and Nickolai grunted. But apart from that there was no conversation until they had almost reached the Smolny Institute, where they saw a group of sailors attacking two youths and a man.

'What's up here?' Sergei demanded.

The younger of the two boys was, he judged, already dead. He lay face down in the snow, which was slowly turning crimson. The man was screaming, blood streaming from his left eye. The second youth's face was also covered in blood. He was too petrified even to whimper.

'They're speculators,' one of the sailors replied, and another one shouted: 'Bastards!'

A third one said: 'They've been hoarding food in the basement of their house.'

'We haven't!' screamed the man. 'It's all lies! They've never been near my house. They don't even know where it is.'

259

Sergei hesitated. There was something·about the man which compelled belief, but at the same time he did not want to think he was telling the truth. He nodded curtly at the sailors.

'Finish them off,' he ordered. 'Toss 'em in the Neva, then follow me. I've more important work for you to do.'

An idea had come to him. As Nickolai had pointed out, this sort of citizen's arrest and summary execution was commonplace nowadays. Why wait for Anna Devereaux to be officially apprehended and tried? He could settle things himself within the hour.

Ignoring the old man's shrieks and pleas for mercy, he touched Nickolai on the arm and strode ahead, leaving the sailors to follow when they had finished their grisly work.

'Where are we going?' asked Nickolai, puzzled.

'To complete the job you bungled three and a half years ago,' answered Sergei, quickening his pace. 'The Englishman's gone, but at least we can still settle our score with his wife.'

Margaret had been out since first light, ostensibly trying to buy food.

The situation was even worse since the Bolsheviks had seized power, but if anything at all was to be found in the shops early morning was the time to find it. She had managed to get half a loaf of black bread, a few ends of bacon and one very stale cabbage.

The temperature was below freezing, but she had nevertheless taken Natasha with her. The man who now lived with his family in what had been the library of the house on Nevsky Prospect was a carpenter by trade, and had rigged up a box-on-wheels as a kind of push-chair. It had cost Anna her sealskin coat.

'What's the use of keeping it?' she had asked with a shrug. 'The army will only requisition it if I don't give it away, and I might as well get something for it.'

Margaret had agreed, even though her thrifty New England soul had winced at the unequal exchange. The coat had hardly been worn, the two women having been forced to buy new clothing during the winter of 1914. They had only brought summer dresses with them from England.

Natasha had taken joyfully to her box-on-wheels, and was particularly pleased by the sensation she caused wherever she went. The sight of the little girl seated in such an odd-looking contraption, jabbering away in a foreign tongue, attracted the attention of men and women alike. Margaret had long ago given up trying to explain in her few, inadequate words of Russian that Natasha was not her child. Now, when women pointed first at Natasha and then at herself, she simply nodded and smiled.

Margaret's feet began to drag as she passed the Nickolaevsky Bridge. The wooden box was difficult to push through snow, and she had walked a long way that morning. She had carried out an extremely dangerous transaction, and her heart still thumped against her ribs when she contemplated the risk she had taken.

The previous evening, when Natasha was at last asleep, Anna had said: 'Do you know anyone, anywhere, to whom you could sell that bracelet?' She had added desperately: 'I must get away! I can't go on.'

Looking at her white, tense face, at the shape of the skull beneath the paper-thin texture of the skin, at the staring, red-rimmed eyes, at the hands which shook uncontrollably, Margaret could well believe her. Anna would lose her sanity if they did not manage to escape from Petrograd soon. There were a few trains running again. If they had the money, they could simply walk to the station and board the first train to arrive. It would not matter where it was going as long as it took them to some part of Russia where the Bolsheviks were not yet in power. At the moment that power, although growing fast, was confined mainly to the areas around Petrograd and Moscow.

But where could she sell the bracelet? Her lack of Russian meant that Margaret had no contacts. She had never been able to follow the half-whispered conversations in the food queues between her neighbours and the shifty-eyed characters who suddenly materialized from alleys and doorways, then melted away again into the shadows.

She had woken abruptly in the middle of the night, from a confused dream in which Hugh and Latchetts and Nanny Watkins were all mixed up, to the recollection of an incident she had witnessed a few weeks back near the old Franco-Russian Shipbuilding Works. She remembered seeing two men obviously bargaining over something, but as soon as the shorter of the two had seen her watching he had muttered a few words to his companion and they had moved off, the tall man with the grey spade-shaped beard leading the way down some steps to a basement shop. If she took the bracelet to Greybeard, he might, even if he were not in the market for it himself, know where she could dispose of it.

She had sat up in bed, being careful not to disturb Anna, and stared into the darkness, her heart beating raggedly. She would be taking a terrible risk. The man could be a police informer, or simply denounce her for the sake of his own skin. Worse still – and perhaps more likely – he might attack and rob her of the bracelet. But everything was a risk nowadays. It was a risk to stay put and do nothing, with Anna so over-wrought and frightened. It was a risk just being alive, with the Red Guards patrolling the streets; with murder, rape and arson everyday occurrences. And she had not liked the way the police had looked at Anna when they had searched the room. . . .

She had told Anna her plan this morning, as she dressed to go out just before daybreak.

'I realize it's probably futile, but it's the best I can do.'

Anna had climbed out of bed, her wasted body shivering under the thin covering of her nightdress. The shortage of all types of fuel made it impossible for them to light the stove before midday. Margaret thought that Anna was going to beg her not to do anything so foolhardy, but all she said was: 'You must take Natasha with you. I'll get her up and dressed.' She had swept aside Margaret's horrified protests. 'Don't you see? Natasha will be a sort of protection. A woman with a child is viewed with less suspicion. She commands respect. And the man in the shop, he will be less likely to consider violence in the presence of a little girl. All Russians love children.'

After a lot of argument, Margaret had given way, acknowledging that Anna was right. She would be less vulnerable, protected by Natasha's innocence. The little girl had been roused from her cot, bad-tempered and still half asleep, bundled into her warmest garments, given a crust of bread to gnaw and carried downstairs to her box, which was kept in the once-beautiful but now derelict entrance-hall.

'I shall pray for you before my icon of the Virgin and Child all the time you are gone,' Anna said. 'Be careful, and if there is the least hint of danger, if you feel at all suspicious, do not approach that man. Promise me.'

Margaret promised fervently. 'I have no intention of doing anything foolish. More foolish,' she amended, aware that the whole project was riddled with more holes than a sieve. She wished Anna could have gone with her to do the talking, but the Countess was in such a state of nerves that she would only prove an encumbrance. Margaret left the house wondering if she would ever see it again, or whether, by tonight, she would be inside the fortress of Saints Peter and Paul.

In the event, it all proved ridiculously easy. Margaret had done her shopping first, working her way as naturally as possible towards the old Franco-Russian Shipbuilding Works by buying the three different items at three different shops. One or two people, in spite of their own concerns, had stopped to admire Natasha, undeterred by the child's furious and tearful demands that they 'go away! I'se hungwy!' No one knew what she was saying in any case, and fretful children were commonplace nowadays.

At the steps leading down to the shop, Margaret paused. The premises looked shuttered and deserted, and she suddenly felt that the bracelet was burning a hole in the inner pocket of her coat. Then she noticed a chink of light under the door. Taking her courage in both hands, she descended the steps, bumping the box-on-wheels in front of her to the accompaniment of vociferous protests from Natasha. The frozen snow was very slippery, and she was thankful to reach the bottom.

Greybeard answered her knock with a kind of surreptitious anxiety, his face peering at her round the edge of the door. He was obviously suffering from a hangover and his breath smelled powerfully of stale vodka. Margaret wasted no time trying to make herself understood. She simply unbuttoned her coat and withdrew one end of the bracelet from her inner pocket. Immediately, the man ushered her and Natasha inside.

263

The shop, no more than a small room with a table in one corner, was dark and musty-smelling. All Margaret's fears returned, and even Natasha was silenced, her eyes round and scared in the gloom. With her heart thumping, Margaret produced the bracelet. Greybeard's hand shot out and snatched it before she could stop him.

'This is it,' she thought miserably. 'Now he'll order me out of the shop and swear the bracelet is his. He knows I won't dare call the police.'

Greybeard, however, muttered something which Margaret recognized as meaning: 'Wait here!' and disappeared through a door at the back of the shop. Before she had time to feel more frightened than she already was, he returned carrying an old tin box. It was then that Margaret realized she was in no position to haggle over the price. Her Russian was totally inadequate. She would simply have to accept what she was given.

'Dear God,' she prayed silently, 'don't let it all have been for nothing.'

A moment later, the man was pressing a heavy canvas bag on her, which chinked alarmingly. Even as Margaret weighed it in her hands, Greybeard urged her towards the door, snapping it shut as soon as she and Natasha were safely outside.

There was no question of counting the money, and, until she reached home, no means of knowing whether or not she had been cheated. Oddly enough, she was convinced that the man had played fair by her. She was unable to explain the conviction. Undoubtedly he would sell the bracelet for more than he had paid her. Nevertheless, she was sure that she was not holding a bag of worthless stones. For one thing, the chink was too metallic.

She peered up the flight of steps. It was lighter now; almost nine o'clock. There were people about. She felt in her basket for the loaf of black bread, tore it apart as best she could with her numb fingers, and wedged the canvas bag between the two pieces. She piled the bacon and the cabbage on top and shook the basket gingerly. The tell-tale sound was faint and muffled. Satisfied, she mounted the steps, pulling Natasha in the box-on-wheels behind her. It had begun to snow again, and no one was watching as she hurried away from the shop. By the time she reached the Nickolaevsky Bridge, reaction had set in. She suddenly felt desperately tired and faint. She quickened her pace all the same. She wanted to get indoors, out of the icy wind, to reassure Anna and count the money. She wanted most of all to make certain that Greybeard had not robbed her.

She was a hundred yards from the house when she noticed the two sailors on guard outside. There were little knots of spectators, too, huddled together, watching with that expression of shocked avidity which Margaret had noticed all too often on the faces of people expecting to witness violence. Someone inside the house was screaming, and more sailors erupted through the open doorway on to the street. Behind them came two members of the Red Guard, dragging a woman in her nightdress. With a sick feeling in the pit of her stomach, Margaret recognized Anna. In the same split second she also recognized one of the guards as Sergei Zhirov. She dropped the handle of the box-on-wheels and started to run towards them.

She knew, as soon as she saw Sergei twist the terrified Anna's arms behind her back and the other guard raise his revolver, that she would never reach them in time to prevent what was happening, even if she could. She heard the report, saw Anna's head jerk back and the red stain begin to spread across the nightdress. She heard the laughter and ribald voices of the sailors, saw Sergei lift the limp body as though it were a bale of straw and toss it into the freezing waters of the Neva. . . .

Margaret had no idea how she came to be in Million Street, leaning against the wall of a house. She only knew that she was retching violently. It had all happened with such horrifying speed that her mind was still reeling from the shock. It was just a bad dream, and she would wake up in a minute if she gave herself time. . . .

She started to tremble. Anna was dead! Anna was dead! She and Natasha were all alone. Natasha! Oh God, Natasha! Where was she? Filled with shame, Margaret pushed herself away from the wall and began to run towards Nevsky Prospect. Her legs felt like rubber and her feet were hampered by the snow. Dear God! How could she have forgotten the child and left her to the mercy of those brutes?

Natasha was sitting in her box-on-wheels where Margaret had left her; not crying, not peevish as she had been all morning, but happily watching the commotion in the street. She beamed when she recognized Margaret, but gave no other sign of having missed her.

Margaret dropped to her knees in the snow and put her arms around the little girl, holding her close.

'Tasha too tight. Can't breave,' Natasha protested.

Margaret glanced up the street. The crowds outside the house had grown, but the doorway was still visible. Sergei Zhirov came out and shouted at one of the sailors who was staring idly at the river. She thought: 'They're waiting for someone.'

She stood up quickly, her fingers closing over the handle of the box-on-wheels. Of course: Sergei was waiting for her. He would know that she had been living with Anna.

The money! Her basket with the money concealed in the bread! What had she done with it? Where had she dropped it? Margaret stared frantically about her, and it was only when something grazed against the wall of an adjacent house that she realized it was still on her arm. Instinctively, she had held on to it throughout everything, without being conscious of doing so.

'Home,' said Natasha, smiling up at her. 'Tasha hungry.'

'We're not going home yet, honey,' Margaret said. She saw the child's smile fade and the little face crumple. As Natasha prepared to make her disappointment vocal, Margaret went on swiftly: 'How would you like to go on a train, sweetheart? You know, like the boy and girl in your picture-book. You've never even seen a train, not a real one, have you? Don't you think that would be an exciting adventure?'

The station was cold and dirty, packed with people, some of whom were waiting patiently for trains to take them wherever it was they wanted to go; others going nowhere, sleeping on platform benches or camped out in waiting-rooms; yet others who had long since given up all hope of ever reaching their destinations and sat staring into space like zombies. Margaret recalled arriving here with Paul and Anna almost four years ago, but it seemed impossible now that it was the same place, the same country.

She lifted Natasha out of the box, settling the child on her hip in the time-honoured fashion. Natasha had stopped grizzling now, intrigued by all the movement about her. Gripping her basket tightly in her other hand, Margaret pushed her way through the crowds to what she hoped was the ladies' cloakroom.

It was, but she half-expected it to have been taken over as living accommodation, like the waiting-rooms. There did, indeed, appear to be a family living at the far end, and several of the cubicles had the doors hanging off their hinges. The wash-basins were filthy, and the once beautifully polished taps were covered in verdigris; but there were one or two lavatories left intact, offering privacy. Margaret went into one of them and locked the door, putting Natasha down before she did so. Then she took the canvas bag from between the two pieces of loaf and, heart in mouth, peered inside.

She breathed a sigh of relief. Greybeard had not cheated her. There was enough money there to get her and Natasha away from Petrograd and support them for at least a few months; perhaps longer. She extracted as much money as she would need immediately and put it into the inside pocket of her coat, letting her coat swing loose so that she could reach it without fuss. The remainder she left in the canvas bag, pulling the leather drawstring tight about the neck. But where could she keep it safely? She could not put it back in the basket; she and Natasha would need the food on the journey. Margaret had never eaten raw bacon and cabbage, but if they were not to starve she knew that they must try.

She looked down at the child, who returned her look with interest. Was it possible to hide the money anywhere on Natasha, amongst her layers of clothing? No, that was no good. She was too young to keep the secret. It would have to be on herself. Margaret lifted her skirt and petticoats and tied the bag to the laces of her corsets, flattening out the coins as best she could. When she had rearranged her clothes, she buttoned the flannel waistcoat of her suit as tightly as possible and then, to Natasha's intense delight, spun round and gave a little jump. There was no betraying noise. She took Natasha's hand and grinned.

After another few minutes, they emerged from the cubicle and went back to the platform. There were long queues in the booking-hall, and people were being turned away all the time. No, there was no train to Moscow, no train to Kiev or Sebastopol or Murmansk. As she moved slowly along one of the lines, Margaret strained her ears, trying to understand what was being said.

Half an hour later, the queues came to a halt. Natasha was growing tearful and Margaret gave her a crust of bread to keep her quiet. She herself had eaten nothing since the previous night, and was beginning to feel faint.

A railway official appeared and started shouting. People left their places in the queues and crowded round the ticket-office, brandishing money. A train must be leaving, going somewhere, and Margaret did not care where. She picked up Natasha and pushed her way forward with the rest, ruthlessly using her elbows. Just as she reached the ticket-office, someone yelled that the train was leaving. Margaret, her senses sharpened by panic, was able to understand that much.

She pushed some money – she had no idea how much – under the grille, grabbing her ticket as she did so. She saw the booking-clerk's startled face, heard him call after her, but she did not stop. Clutching Natasha and her basket, she ran along the platform, up some stairs, along the bridge and down the other side. Her lungs felt as though they were bursting. The train was already moving, belching out great clouds of steam. Desperately, tears streaming down her face, Margaret staggered towards it. Just as it began to gather speed, someone opened a door and hauled her and Natasha inside.

Twenty-Four

She felt as though she had been travelling forever; that she had never known any life outside the swaying, rumbling train and the hard wooden seat. But at least she had a seat, for which the presence of Natasha was responsible. A young man, a student, with tired, kind eyes and a greasy beard, had insisted that she took his place. And at every stop, when it was necessary to leave the train for a while both for Natasha's comfort and her own, he would zealously guard it until her return.

The train was packed from end to end, with people sitting in one another's laps and standing so close together they could barely breathe. No one asked anyone else where he or she was going, or why; but everyone sang and joked and shared food or water with neighbours. The discovery that Margaret was a foreigner made her the object of particular courtesy and attention, and the young student, who was able to speak a little English as well as French, was glad of the opportunity to improve his conversation.

He also lent her a copy of *Nicholas Nickleby*, which he was reading in English.

By deciphering the Russian lettering on her ticket, Margaret found that she was headed for Rostov-on-Don. No thought of leaving the train earlier, at one of the stops along the way, occurred to her. Her one idea was to put as much distance as possible between herself and Sergei Zhirov.

In spite of the hardships and length of the journey, Natasha was extraordinarily well behaved. Her love of company and of showing off made her a model traveller. She did become restive now and again, but there was always a pair of willing arms to relieve Margaret of her burden. Natasha learned a whole string of Russian words with surprising rapidity, and was soon able to form complete sentences.

'She's sharp,' Margaret thought. 'Sharp and clever. She doesn't really remind me of either Paul or Anna.'

Now, at last, she had time to think of Anna's death, to mourn a woman she had once regarded as her enemy but come to look on as a friend. The unshed tears burned inside her lids, and she was consumed by the slow, burning anger which violence of any kind aroused in her. She remembered her father telling her of the atrocities committed by both North and South during the Civil War.

'War's an evil, Maggie,' he had said. 'It brutalizes innocent men; turns bank-clerks into killers. I don't believe there's such a thing as a holy crusade.'

It was true, Margaret thought. Lenin, Trotsky, Stalin; when she had met them in London they had been crusaders against oppression. And yet, within months of seizing power, they had resorted to the very methods used by the Tsars.

The young student left the train somewhere along the line. Margaret was dozing and did not see him go. He just disappeared one evening and did not come back. He left her his copy of *Nicholas Nickleby*, but Margaret found it difficult to read. Dickens's London held no more reality for her than the memories she conjured up of Latchetts, Bath or New York. It was like watching the shadow-play of puppets behind a Chinese screen. Even Paul's and her children's features had grown blurred in her mind.

And then, flicking through the pages one morning, while Natasha sat on the floor between the seats jabbering away to a little Ukrainian boy in her mixture of English and Russian, Margaret came across two quotations pencilled on the fly-leaf, both in English, and both from *Richard the Second*.

The first was *The pale-faced moon looks bloody on the earth, And lean-look'd prophets whisper fearful change, Rich men look sad and ruffians dance and leap.* The second: *Oh call back yesterday, bid time return.* She read and re-read them several times. It was as though the words unlocked a store of emotion which had lain dormant inside her for a very long time. Suddenly she was sobbing uncontrollably, her shoulders heaving, her whole body hunched in grief. She could not stop crying, and was only vaguely aware that Natasha was crying too; a frightened, high-pitched wail as she clasped Margaret about the knees.

People crowded round. She was engulfed by a torrent of Russian sympathy, offers of assistance, murmurs of endearment, only a few of which she was able to understand. Finally, a big peasant woman dressed in the traditional rusty black, a scarf tied over her head, ousted Margaret's neighbour from his place and sat down, cradling the younger woman against her breast.

It was a long time before Margaret regained control of her emotions, but at last she lay quietly in the woman's arms, feeling washed out, lifeless, drained of the will to do anything but sleep. Someone passed her a leather and silver hip-flask which had obviously seen better days, and which contained not the inevitable vodka, but brandy. She took a sip and the liquid coursed hot and fiery through her veins. She began to feel pleasantly drowsy. For the first time, the lurching of the train was soothing, and her eyelids drooped.

When she regained consciousness, it was daylight. She was still folded in the arms of the Russian peasant woman, who was beaming down at her, nodding and smiling in encouragement. Margaret sat up, smiling in return. She was still filthy, her clothes smelled and she had not washed for days; but somehow this morning it no longer seemed to matter. She felt a renewal of spirits. She was able to cope once more.

Natasha climbed into her lap and patted her cheek.

'Better now, honey?' she asked, her head tilted enquiringly to one side.

'Yes, better now,' Margaret answered, hugging the thin little body to her.

She was suddenly confident that from now on, everything was going to be all right. One day the war would be over and they would be able to go home again.

In the early spring of 1918, Lenin made peace with the Germans at Brest-Litovsk. After nearly four years of some of the bloodiest fighting anyone could ever remember, Russia was out of the war. The rest of the Allies fought on.

271

Margaret had been living in Rostov-on-Don for almost ten weeks, first with the peasant woman who had befriended her on the train, and then in a tiny apartment with two English spinsters, the Misses Barraclough; unflappable sisters from Yorkshire who had lived in Russia for the past twelve years. They had met Margaret in the street a week after her arrival, heard her speak English to Natasha and made themselves known. When she had told them where she was living, they were frankly appalled.

'My dear child, you can't possibly remain there,' the elder Miss Barraclough had protested. She was tall and thin, with a *pince-nez* which perched on the end of her aquiline nose. 'You and the child must stay with us, mustn't they, Lizzie?'

Miss Elizabeth Barraclough, a softer, rounder version of her sister, had agreed.

'My dear, those peasant cottages smell! They're unspeakably dirty, as you must have realized by now, and children, poultry and dogs all crawl about on the floor together. So unhygienic. We'll come with you and get your things.'

They had been as good as their word. Margaret packed her basket with the few necessities she had bought for herself and Natasha since coming to Rostov, pressed three roubles into the peasant woman's hand, said goodbye to her husband and children and departed, showered with the good wishes of the entire family. That night she had slept in a bed for the first time since leaving Petrograd.

Natasha thought it a poor exchange. Sleeping, rolled in a blanket, on the floor with the ducks and chickens had been her idea of heaven. She disliked having to behave, wear clean clothes and sit at a table for her meals.

'She has been turning into a little savage,' Margaret said that first evening in the Miss Barracloughs' apartment, when Natasha had reluctantly gone to bed. 'Months living in one room with her mother and myself, days on the train and then that—'

'Hovel,' said the elder Miss Barraclough starkly. 'Oh, it was very kind of the woman to take you in, no doubt, but difficult all round, I should have thought, particularly as you don't speak much Russian.'

'My dear, what terrible experiences you have had in St

272

Petersburg,' Miss Elizabeth Barraclough murmured, her china-blue eyes large with concern. 'Things have not been good here lately, but there has been nothing of the violence you have described. There was an attack on the Post Office last November by the local Bolshevik Red Guard, but the Cossacks drove them off, didn't they, Amy?'

'With guns and whips,' Amy Barraclough answered with deep satisfaction. 'Of course, it's Cossack country round here, you know. Their ancestors were serfs who had run away from their villages. They came to this part of the world to make a new life for themselves. Very desolate country about here, as you may have noticed. It must have been a wilderness a century or more ago. The Cossacks hate the Bolsheviks, who want all land divided up equally under government control. Such nonsense! If that happens we shall go back to England, even though Lloyd George is Prime Minister.'

'Mind you, there was more trouble a week or so ago,' her sister added. 'There was fighting near the centre of the town. Almost three days of it. Then the Bolsheviks gave in. We didn't see anything ourselves, although we heard the guns firing. The old gentleman in the apartment below told us there were quite a number killed. But things go on pretty much as usual. All the theatres and picture-palaces are open. I do so love Charlie Chaplin, don't you?'

Margaret admitted that she did; but she was unable to share her hostesses' optimistic view that everything would shortly return to normal; that the Allies would send troops to reconquer Russia for the Tsar. She was worried, too, because she did not know how long her present situation would last, and how much money she would need. She felt obliged to pay the Miss Barracloughs a weekly rent for the room which she and Natasha shared, and had been forced to spend a considerable amount on clothes for the two of them. Each day brought more refugees pouring into the higgledy-piggledy little town with its jumble of vividly-coloured, oddly-shaped houses and domed churches, all bringing stories of some new act of terror by the Bolshevik army, which was hot on their heels.

'You really ought to withdraw all your money from the bank and hide it in the house,' Margaret said one evening, as

273

she and the two ladies were having supper. 'If the Bolsheviks get here, one of the first things they'll do will be to close the banks.'

'But my dear, they won't get here,' argued Elizabeth Barraclough. 'The Cossacks won't let them.'

A few days later, however, the first Bolshevik shells landed in the outskirts of the town, followed by the booming of the guns.

Margaret and Elizabeth Barraclough were returning from a matinée at the theatre. Amy had nobly offered to sit with Natasha while they went; nobly because the little girl did not care for the elder Miss Barraclough, and had no hesitation in making her dislike plain. The two women paused to listen, glancing nervously at one another.

'What . . . what's happening?' Elizabeth Barraclough quavered after a moment.

'I think the Bolsheviks have arrived,' Margaret answered. 'Let's pray that the Cossacks can hold them.'

'They will. Of course they will.' But Elizabeth Barraclough spoke without her former conviction. The previous skirmishing had been with the local Bolsheviks; raw youths most of them, who had escaped conscription because of lack of fitness. But Lenin and his soviets now commanded what remained of the army; men trained to fight and kill; men who had proper guns and weapons. 'What shall we do?' she went on piteously, laying a trembling hand on Margaret's arm.

'We must get home,' Margaret said. 'If there is going to be street fighting, the best place to be is indoors.' There was another burst of gunfire. 'Hurry,' she ordered.

All around them, people were running for shelter. Everyone seemed to be on foot. Trams and taxis had come to a halt and were disgorging their passengers on to the pavements as drivers refused to carry on. A feeling of panic was spreading like wildfire through the streets.

Without warning, Margaret and Elizabeth found themselves surrounded by a crowd of running people, borne inexorably along on a tide of fear. Everyone was shouting and pushing and jostling. A shell whined overhead and crashed to earth two streets away. Several women screamed and tried to claw their way out of the press. Other people attempted to go back the way they had come. Within seconds, the flight had become a dangerous stampede.

Elizabeth Barraclough had had hold of Margaret's arm, but now they were forced apart by two men and a woman pushing between them. Margaret saw her companion, her hat gone, her eyes wide with horror, carried away in the opposite direction. At the same moment, she was conscious of difficulty in breathing. Bodies were pressed against her like a human wall. She opened her mouth, gasping for air, but there was no space in which to inflate her lungs. The blood was pounding in her ears and there were black spots dancing in front of her eyes. She knew that in another minute or two she would lose consciousness.

She was vaguely aware that the man next to her was turning blue in the face and making strange gurgling noises in his throat. The head of the woman in front of her was already lolling grotesquely on its neck, as though it had been broken. She thought: 'I'm going to die. What will become of Natasha?' The last word vibrated senselessly inside her head, like an echo in an underground cavern. The black spots began to merge together, and her bruised ribs felt as though they were being ground to powder.

Then, just before she slipped over the edge of consciousness, she was suddenly able to breathe again. She saw a shop doorway and felt a hand drag her inside. She remembered trying to say 'thank you' to her unknown rescuer, but she could make no sound. The ground came up to meet her as she fell.

Miss Barraclough came back into the living-room and sat down at the table opposite Margaret. Natasha had been given a pile of *Ladies' Journal*s to keep her quiet.

Margaret stretched out her hand, and after a moment's hesitation the older woman held it, ashamed of even this slight indication of weakness. If she had been crying, there was no indication now of any tears, although her eyes looked suspiciously red-rimmed.

'I've laid her out,' she said. 'She looks very peaceful. Do you . . . do you think they'll let us bury the dead?'

'Yes, of course. I mean, they must. They'll want life to continue as normally as possible.'

Amy Barraclough snorted and jerked her head towards the window. 'You call what's been going on out there for the past few days normal?'

Margaret made no reply, both women recalling the sights and sounds they had witnessed all too frequently of late; old men and young boys, who had helped resist the Bolsheviks, being bayoneted in the streets until the gutters were congested with blood; others being shot outside their own front doors, their families forced to look on. Servants had denounced masters, masters had indicted servants, each with the sole aim of saving his or her own skin.

Before that, before Margaret and Amy Barraclough had been able to search for the missing Elizabeth, who had never returned home, there had been hours of street fighting after the Bolsheviks had finally ceased their bombardment and entered the town. Later the same night, the dead Cossacks had been stripped and piled into carts. Margaret thought that she would remember those piles of degraded bodies for the rest of her life.

They found Elizabeth's body, one of many, crushed against a wall. With the help of a passing stranger, they had carried her the short distance back to the apartment. There Amy had taken over, insisting on doing everything for her sister by herself. She had gently, but firmly, refused all Margaret's offers of help.

'I can manage, and I'd like to be alone with her for a while.'

Margaret had understood and not intruded. She had sat with Natasha on her lap, trying to keep the child amused by leafing through the pile of old and yellowing magazines, brought long ago from England.

'You were right about the banks,' Amy Barraclough continued now. 'I saw the old gentleman from down below earlier this morning, and he tells me that the Bolsheviks have taken them over. And the town has been ordered to pay twelve million roubles for its resistance.'

Margaret smiled faintly. 'What in?' she enquired. 'We have Tsarist money, Kerensky notes, Don Republic money issued by Kaledin, and Don notes printed by the Bolsheviks.' Thank heaven the dealer in Petrograd had paid her in coin!

Two days after Elizabeth's funeral, the position deteriorated still further. A young Bolshevik officer arrived to inform them that the houses and apartments of the bourgeoisie were no longer the owners' property. They belonged henceforth to the state, and rent had to be paid accordingly. Size, he added magnanimously, would be taken into account.

'But this apartment is mine!' Amy Barraclough insisted wrathfully, in her fluent but heavily accented Russian. She looked the officer up and down through her *pince-nez*, a thousand intrepid British matrons at her shoulder as she spoke. 'Now please go, and don't let me see you here again.' The officer, to Margaret's astonishment, went, and Miss Barraclough's eyes gleamed with satisfaction. 'That's the only way to deal with foreigners, you know. It's the only sort of language they really understand. We shan't have any more trouble.'

Margaret disagreed. She had seen the look on the young man's face as he left the apartment, and suspected that he would return.

He came back the next day, bringing with him two more members of the Red Guard and their girl-friends: a couple of Moscow prostitutes who had followed the army south.

'We are requisitioning this apartment,' the officer told Amy. 'You and the woman and child' – he indicated Margaret and Natasha – 'may keep one room. My friends are moving into the rest. You will have to wait your turn for the kitchen and bathroom. These ladies will have priority.'

'Ladies!' spat Miss Barraclough. 'They need whipping at the cart's tail. They're a disgrace to the name of women.'

Fortunately, in her anger, she had resorted to English, and no one except Margaret understood what she was saying. Before she could repeat it in Russian, Margaret intervened.

'We must do as they tell us,' she urged quietly, 'or we shall be in serious trouble. We could find ourselves without a roof over our heads at all. Think of Natasha,' she added, encountering the martial light in Amy's eye.

This final appeal won the day; and so, three months after leaving Petrograd, Margaret was again living in one room, only this time in darker and more cramped accommodation than the bedroom of the house on Nevsky Prospect.

Every day brought a spate of rumours which no one could either confirm or deny. The Germans were approaching; the Poles were near at hand; the White Russian army, all those men still loyal to the imprisoned Tsar, would soon liberate the town. Each time she stood in a food queue Margaret heard a different story. Everyone's nerves, including the Bolsheviks', were stretched to breaking point as day after day passed and nothing happened.

And then one morning, while she was waiting outside the bakery, hoping to be one of the lucky ones who would get a loaf of bread, a lady and gentleman approached her. The man raised his hat to reveal a balding head.

'Excuse me, but aren't you the young lady staying with Miss Barraclough?' he asked in English. 'We were so sorry to hear about Miss Elizabeth. Allow us to introduce ourselves. Arnold and Mary Chivers. We're part of Rostov's English community. Miss Barraclough will know our names.'

His wife, a faded woman with pale, anxious blue eyes, confided: 'We're leaving Rostov. All the foreigners in the town are banding together. Last night some of us went to see the authorities here, and they have agreed that we may charter a train north to Murmansk, where it's possible we might find a ship to take us all home. It will cost money, of course, but we thought that if we pooled our resources— In short, we wondered if you and Miss Barraclough might be interested?'

Margaret could hardly believe her ears. She was afraid she was going to be sick with excitement, something that used to happen when she was a very small child. She managed to keep her wits about her long enough to ask for the couple's address, then ran all the way back to the apartment, quite forgetting the bread. Stumbling upstairs, she burst into the room she now shared with Miss Barraclough and Natasha.

When she had finished pouring out her news, there was silence. Amy Barraclough made no immediate response, but sat staring at her hands. Finally, she raised her head.

'My dear,' she said, 'you and the child must go, of course, but I shall remain where I am. There's nothing for me in England any more. I left there too many years ago and all my family is dead. And this present Russian madness can't last forever. In a few months sanity will return. The Tsar will be restored to his throne and everything will be as it was before the war. This is my home, especially now that Elizabeth is buried here.'

Margaret spent the rest of the day arguing with her, but to no avail. Amy was adamant, and nothing Margaret could say would move her. She went to the station, a week later, to see Margaret and Natasha off, along with many of her acquaintances and friends. She had given Margaret her good leather case, on the grounds that she would not be needing it again.

Margaret would have kissed her goodbye, but she knew how the Englishwoman frowned on any demonstration of affection. But at the last moment, just as Margaret was boarding the train in the wake of the eager Natasha, Amy Barraclough stepped forward and pecked her quickly on the cheek. Then she blew her nose defiantly.

'Goodbye, my dear, and good luck. I hope you get safely back to England. I shall miss you, though. And the child.'

Margaret leaned from the compartment window as the packed train began to draw out of the station. Ahead of her lay a long journey of discomforts and delays, with only a dubious chance at the end of getting home. She waved her hand until the platform and the stiff, upright figure of Miss Barraclough disappeared from view. Then she sat down, wedged between a fat Frenchwoman and a small Welshman who, during the course of their first conversation, revealed that he was from Pontypridd. He had married a Russian wife and had lived in Rostov for the past nine years.

Natasha climbed into Margaret's lap, settling down to sleep, and Margaret too closed her eyes. The swaying of the train soothed her. She had no passport, no papers, nothing but a little money and a very few clothes. But for some inexplicable reason she was filled with optimism; a feeling that amounted almost to certainty that the long nightmare was finally over. Soon she would be back in England; home with Paul and her children.

Part Six 1922–1925

What is this worlde? What asketh men to have?

Twenty-Five

Sometimes, when she was half asleep, her thoughts drifting out of control, Margaret would find herself back on the train, travelling from Rostov-on-Don to Murmansk. She would experience again the lice, the bugs, the hundred and one discomforts, the nerve-racking, interminable delays. She would hear the guns firing and the shells whistling overhead as the carriages lurched and swayed through the fighting zone around Moscow, or took refuge for hours – sometimes days – in railway-sidings. She could smell once more the stench of sickness, hear the fevered cries, as one passenger after another succumbed to the influenza which was decimating half Europe. She would recall her terror that Natasha might contract it; or that she would become ill, leaving the child alone and unprotected. She would relive the crawling hours as two thousand refugees from all over Russia crowded on to a ship provisioned for eight hundred. She would wake, sweating, her heart beating wildly, from the memory of a rolling grey sea and mountainous waves. . . .

Four years had not lessened the potency of that dream. Not even the calm and solitude of her beloved Latchetts could prevent it coming to haunt her in the nights. She would sit up in bed, searching for the light, while images of Anna and Sergei Zhirov jostled at her elbow. And always, Paul's arms would close around her, holding her close, soothing away her phantoms and her fears. They would comfort one another.

Paul's years in the mud and blood of Flanders, although he had sustained no physical injury, had left him mentally scarred. The agony of uncertainty over Anna's and Margaret's fates had made things worse. He had written letter

283

after letter, which had never been answered for the simple reason that they had never been received. The ships carrying them, along with supplies for Britain's ally Russia, had been destroyed by the German navy. From the middle of 1916 until the summer's day four years ago when Margaret and Natasha had arrived, unannounced, at Latchetts, he had been without news and almost without hope.

By the greatest piece of good fortune, he had been on ten days' leave in that early part of May 1918. There were very few pre-war servants left, and most of the house had been turned into a convalescent home for army officers. It had been Mrs Hinkley who had recognized Margaret as she was being questioned at the gatehouse by the sentry on duty, and who had come tottering into the library, screeching that she had seen a ghost.

It had been a strange reunion, the shadow of Anna's death lying between them and muting their joy. The realization, too, that their time together was short, that Paul would have to return to France within the week, that the war could drag on for years, had terrified them both. To be separated almost immediately after finding each other seemed an unnecessarily cruel stroke of fate.

To add to everything else, there had been Natasha, the daughter whom Paul had never seen and whom he had little time to get to know. She had regarded Margaret as her personal possession and had resented her father's intrusion. She had thrown jealous tantrums whenever he had monopolized Margaret's time, and had been delighted when he had gone back to France.

Four years later, now a tall, coltish eight-year-old, she still resented him; just as she resented her half-brother and sister, Henry and Antonia Dunham, and Ralph Stafford. Her other half-brother, George, she actively disliked. The visits of India and Mareth, both now married and living in London, she could tolerate, but not for too long.

Natasha could scarcely remember Anna, and when she did recall her it was as someone who had always been cross or ill. Long before they left Russia, Margaret had been the centre of her life; the one person she wanted to impress. The sudden discovery of all these other people who had claims on

Margaret's time and affection – in some cases, stronger claims than her own – had bewildered and infuriated her. The early lack of discipline and the strange life she had led had made her wild. Margaret was the only person who could control her, and then not all the time. She had flouted Nanny Watkins's attempts to turn her into a young lady, had defied her father in spite of beatings, but had excelled in the schoolroom to please Margaret, and also because she genuinely liked to learn. Although five years younger than Antonia, she could from the beginning run rings around her half-sister, the only other member of the class after Henry left to go to boarding-school.

Margaret had protected Natasha as much as she was able, standing between her and her father's anger and the dislike of the other children. George and Ralph had been away at school for much of the time; but, in this summer of 1922, Ralph was back for good. George, three years younger, was still at Eton, and was destined for Oxford. He had, however, confided to Margaret during the Easter vacation that, if his father could be persuaded, he proposed to skip university and go straight into the business. He wanted to take over the running of the Longreach mine as soon as possible, freeing Paul to pursue the political career he coveted, which, because of the war and its aftermath, still eluded him.

'With your help, Dunny,' George had said, 'I think Father might be persuaded.'

Margaret thought so too, but was perfectly well aware that George was not prompted by any altruistic motives. He was a shrewd, hard-headed young man, with the itch and natural flair to make money inherited from Coleman Smith. The old man, Margaret reflected, would have been proud of his only grandson.

'And I want Ralph to help me,' George had added. 'I want him as my right-hand man.'

The odd friendship which had sprung up between them when they were young had not diminished with the years. They respected one another, Margaret supposed, recognizing kindred spirits. Each saw his own drive and ruthless ambition reflected in the other. Both were realists. Ralph accepted that as Hugh Stafford's son his social standing was not so great as that of George. George recognized that Ralph, older than himself and brought up for the best part of his life almost like a brother, could have been resentful of him, and therefore treated him with a consideration he showed to no one else. The understanding between them went deep, and Margaret was not certain that it was for the general good.

Henry and Antonia, with only a year's difference in age between them, had always been close, and remained so even after Henry went away to school. They wrote to one another regularly and were inseparable in the holidays. Even now that they were fourteen and thirteen respectively, with a burgeoning interest in the opposite sexes, they were still firm friends. All of which isolated Natasha quite as much as the age gap and her own fierce pride and independence.

The August sun was warm against her half-closed lids. Margaret, relaxing in one of the garden chairs, could hear the chorus of birdsong from the nearby trees. Long shadows scythed across the lawns, green once more and well tended, after the depredations of wartime ambulances and lorries. The blue-rimmed distances were hazy with summer heat.

She wondered idly where everyone was. It was pleasant to have the house full again for the summer holidays; George and Henry home from school, India and Mareth and India's husband occupying the girls' old rooms. But it was equally pleasant to be alone for a while, free for the moment even of Paul. The postman from the village waved to her as he cycled up the drive. It was almost too much of an effort to wave back. Her eyes closed without her knowing it, and the book of poems she had been reading slid off her lap to the ground. There were no bad dreams today, just the vacancy of approaching sleep. . . .

'It's come,' Paul's voice said from somewhere above her, and his hand gripped her shoulder. 'Margaret, it's here! It came in the midday post.'

His sense of urgency roused her. She sat upright, pushing back from her forehead a stray tendril of auburn hair – which, in spite of the pleas of Mareth and India, she refused to have cut – and crossing one silk-stockinged leg over the other. Short skirts suited their elegant proportions.

'What's come? Paul? What is it?'

For answer, he handed her a letter typed on official paper. She stared at it stupidly for a moment or two before the jumble of black characters sorted themselves into words.

'It's been confirmed at last,' Paul said. 'Anna's death. The Russians have finally agreed that she died in Petrograd in December 1917. I shall finally be able to obtain a death certificate.' He sat down beside her on the seat and put his arms about her. 'Margaret dearest, I'm free.'

But she was only half-listening. The coldly official jargon, the long-awaited confirmation of what she had known but could not prove, invoked once more the memory of that terrible day on Nevsky Prospect; raised again the spectre of Anna, terrified, helpless, in the brutal hands of Sergei Zhirov. Margaret began to tremble, racked by long, dry sobs.

'Sweetheart, stop it! Margaret! Pull yourself together!' Paul, recognizing the signs of hysteria, shook her hard. 'Listen to me, darling. Be quiet, now. Are you listening?' She nodded and managed to smile. He kissed her approvingly and folded her once more in his arms. 'I want you to marry me, darling. I want you to be my wife.'

Margaret gasped, struggling to lean away from him so that she could see his face.

'We can't,' she protested. 'We mustn't. Your political career! It's only just beginning.'

He grinned and kissed her on the nose. 'Darling, I love you. I'm going to marry you. I had a lot of time to think while I was in the trenches in France. I didn't know then that Anna would be killed; but I did know that I had been terribly at fault to marry her when I was in love with you. If she hadn't died, I should have abided by the agreement we made before I left St Petersburg, but it would have broken my heart. So for God's sake, don't deny me. Promise that you'll be my wife.'

'But what will people say? Honey, you haven't thought.'

'I've done nothing but think for the past four years, ever since you told me that Anna was dead. I made up my mind that when the war was over, as soon as things could be sorted out with the Russian government, I should ask you to marry me. Of course, I didn't know then that there would be all this delay.'

'I don't suppose her death was ever officially recorded,'

Margaret said absently. 'Everything was so chaotic after the Bolsheviks came to power. . . . But, sweetheart, you're still Paul Devereaux, and I'm still the governess and your mistress.'

'Attitudes are different now,' he asserted confidently. 'Four years of carnage have made people realize what is important and what is not.'

'Not everyone was in Flanders or in Russia,' she retorted drily. 'There were plenty living at home, in comfort, whom the war didn't touch. Why should their attitudes have changed? There's going to be an election soon. Lloyd George is being pressed to end the coalition government. You want to stand for Parliament, you know you do. Marrying me would spoil your chances.'

'Nonsense!' He tilted her head back, smiling into her eyes. 'Darling, women are bobbing their hair, shortening their skirts, reading Edith Sitwell and Wilfred Owen. We have strange voices coming to us out of the air, courtesy of the British Broadcasting Corporation. Northern Union Rugby Football is calling itself Rugby League. The modern world is destroying all the old shibboleths. . . . Margaret, will you marry me? Please!'

She laughed and twined her arms about his neck. 'Honey, are you sure? If you have the slightest doubt, I'm quite content as I am.'

'I'm sure. A respectable Conservative Party candidate should be married, not keeping a mistress. Besides which, I love you. Not that that's important, of course.'

'Fool,' she said, returning, at last, his kisses. 'Of course I'll marry you. I only hope that I shall be a good Conservative wife.'

She wondered if he took her last remark as seriously as she did herself, and she tried to stifle the doubts in her mind. But they would not be stifled. Somewhere, deep inside her, she was still Herbie Dunham's daughter.

She freed herself from Paul's embrace and retrieved the book of poems from the grass, brushing its blue-and-gold cover free of earth.

'Is that Daniel's new book?' Paul asked, and when she nodded, went on: 'Somehow, even now, when he's such a

288

success, I can't equate Daniel Cooper and poetry. Though those articles he did on the war – the ones that were printed in *The Times* – were extraordinarily good. They really summed up what a lot of us felt out there.'

'He was always good,' Margaret said. 'He's written poetry for years, although very few people knew about it.' She grinned wickedly. 'Poor Jess! She simply cannot adjust to being the wife of a well-known writer. She hated selling the sweetshop and going to live in that cottage near Mells. She thinks it's immoral to receive money for something she doesn't regard as work. And it genuinely confuses her that his newspaper articles and books of poetry bring in more than they used to make in the shop. When I was staying with them last month, Dan was telling me about the novel he plans to write. You should have seen the look on Jessie's face.'

'She should be very proud, and consider herself very lucky,' Paul grunted, 'that Daniel has made such a success of his writing. After that injury at Ypres he would never have been able to stand the pressures of a business. Nor would he, literally, have been able to stand behind a counter all day. I suppose' – he hesitated – 'I suppose Lilian didn't say anything about coming home?'

Margaret shook her head. 'She doesn't regard this as home. She never has, and she's lived so many years now with Daniel and Jess that she looks on them as her family. She's nineteen, Paul. A grown woman. Besides, I think there's another reason she won't come back.'

'She still hates me,' Paul said bitterly. 'She still, in some obscure way, holds me responsible for poor Hugh's death.'

'She doesn't like you,' Margaret agreed diffidently. She gave a broken laugh. 'But then, she doesn't really like me either. However, that wasn't what I meant. She's in love with Mark.'

'She told you so?'

'She didn't have to. I could see it for myself. Jess knows, too. She doesn't like the idea of first cousins marrying, but, as she said, there's nothing much she can do. Mark was twenty last month.'

'And is he in love with Lilian?'

Margaret leaned her head against Paul's shoulder.

'Perhaps not in love, but he's certainly very fond of her. What's more important, she's more or less his creation. Galatea to his Pygmalion.'

'I don't understand,' Paul said, frowning.

'I mean he's shaped her political views. Mark's very radical. He's a member of the Labour Party and a passionate admirer of that Bristol trades unionist, the one they call the "dockers' KC". Bevin, is that his name? Ernest Bevin. Mark was very active last year during the miners' strike. He wants the pits nationalized, and he's thick as thieves with Arthur Barlow at the Longreach mine.'

'What has this to do with Lilian?'

'I told you. Thanks to his teaching, she's just the same. Worse, perhaps; more militant in the way that women so often are when they espouse a cause, because their reasons for doing so are usually more emotional than men's. In Lilian's case, not only is she deeply in love with Mark, but she also wants to hit out at us. She wouldn't admit it, of course, but I can guess, because I'm a woman too.'

'You don't have to tell me that,' Paul answered, brushing her hair with his lips, at the same time trying to quell a growing sense of uneasiness.

It was virtually certain that he would be accepted as Conservative candidate for the Hawksworth and Clarendon constituency. The present MP, who had succeeded old Brimley, had decided not to stand again. Paul was not quite sure how big a part Francis had played in this decision, and had no wish to know, as anything in the nature of bribery was strictly illegal. He did know, however, that he wanted the seat even more than he had when the idea was first mooted eleven years earlier. And he wanted – God! how he wanted – to marry Margaret. Until a few moments ago, he would have said that in 1922 the two things were no longer incompatible. Now, suddenly, he was a little less sure. How would the selection committee look on a candidate whose step-daughter was an active member of the Labour Party, and who, at an election, would probably be making speeches aimed against everything he stood for?

Hell and damnation! He did not want to have to make a choice. In fact, there would be no choice. However badly he wanted a parliamentary career, his love for Margaret was bound to come first. Nevertheless, he could not help remembering that it was she who blackmailed him into taking Arthur Barlow back at the Longreach mine, and had held him to his promise all these years. Arthur Barlow was a born trouble-maker. During the strike last year, George had demanded why his father did not get rid of him. When Paul had attempted to explain, George had poured scorn on the validity of a promise given so long ago.

'But if that's how you feel, get Dunny to release you from it, Father,' had been his advice.

Margaret, however, when applied to, had gently refused. She could not tell Paul why; that Arthur Barlow was a sop to the social conscience which had, in all other respects, lain dormant within her for so long. Paul had been hurt and angered by her refusal. She had realized that she was taking advantage of the honourable streak in his character which believed, against all evidence to the contrary, that an Englishman's word was his bond. She wished Paul could understand.

He did understand; enough, at any rate, to know that there was a radical bias to her nature. Whatever she believed the reasons to be for Lilian's rebellion, and whatever Lilian believed those reasons to be herself, mother and daughter were far more akin than either thought possible. However much he might reject the idea, however frequently he told himself that Margaret's experience in Russia at the hands of the Bolsheviks must have scarred her for life, Paul could never be quite sure. In spite of everything, he could still see her, if the situation ever arose, waving a red flag and singing the 'Internationale'.

He would not think about it. If there was one thing the holocaust of the trenches had taught him, it was not to worry about tomorrow. It might never come.

'Sufficient unto the day is the evil thereof,' he told himself, and, glancing up, saw his two eldest daughters strolling towards them arm in arm across the lawns.

'Come along, you two,' called India. 'It's lunch-time. Papa, you're not to hide Dunny away like this. We want to see something of her, too.'

291

India had just turned twenty-seven: her sister was two years younger. Both had fulfilled their childhood promise of beauty, although Mareth was too like her father to be as well-favoured as India. India, with Beatrice's blue eyes and blonde hair, had been voted the loveliest debutante of her year, and had married Viscount Rodyate, only son of the Earl of Chelwood. Mareth, with her smiling eyes and tough Devereaux chin, still retained something of the tomboy about her. She wore her fashionable clothes a trifle self-consciously, and was a bruising rider to hounds, taking all her fences with a lack of concern that was the despair of her more cautious friends. Her husband, a rising young barrister fast making a name for himself in the Inns of Court, was enchanted by everything she did, and made no secret of the fact that he adored her. Unfortunately, unlike the Viscount, he had not found the time to accompany his wife to Cornwall.

'Tonia telephoned half an hour ago,' India said. 'She's bringing Raymond Bastardo to lunch. Cook was all set to throw a fit, but I had the presence of mind to promise her those half-dozen pairs of artificial-silk stockings I bought last month at Selfridges. They're all the rage in town at the moment, but I can't stand them. Far too shiny.'

'I bet Raymond's parents don't know he's coming to lunch,' Mareth chipped in. 'They don't approve of Papa's ménage.' She wrinkled her nose. 'Stuffy old hypocrites! I don't know how they came to have such a nice son as Raymond.'

'Well,' Paul said, rising, 'they soon won't have any reason to disapprove. Margaret and I are getting married as soon as possible.' He waved the letter he was holding. 'I received official confirmation today of Anna's death.'

'Papa!' breathed India. 'How wonderful! Oh dear, that sounds such an awful, callous thing to say. And although I didn't want you to marry Anna, I grew quite to like her after a while. But – oh, you both know what I mean. Darling Dunny, I am so pleased.' She threw her arms around Margaret and kissed her.

'So am I. Delighted!' exclaimed Mareth, pushing her sister out of the way so that she too could embrace Margaret. 'Dearest Dunny, it's what I've hoped for for years.'

Half-laughing, half-crying, Margaret returned their kisses.

'I shall be very strict and proper,' she joked. 'The wicked step-mother. You yet may live to regret it.'

'Mmm. I can't see that happening, somehow.' India linked her arm through her father's. 'Papa, you have your daughters' blessing. And I fancy Tonia will be overjoyed. She's very fond of Raymond Bastardo.'

'The child's only thirteen,' her father demurred. 'And young Raymond isn't that much older.'

'Pooh! I'd been in love at least twice by the time I was thirteen,' declared Mareth. 'Girls mature so much more quickly than men.'

'So women are constantly telling us. But there are exceptions. George, I am sure, was born with an old head on his shoulders.'

'Oh, George!' exclaimed both his sisters simultaneously and dismissively, Mareth adding: 'The only thing that will ever make George's pulse beat faster is a rise in the stocks and shares index. But why are we all standing about here? Let's go indoors and give everyone the good news.'

Twenty-Six

Not everyone greeted the news of the engagement with as much pleasure as India and Mareth. Antonia, it was true, was as happy as her half-sister had predicted, and Viscount Rodyate offered his warmest felicitations. Ralph was politely indifferent, while George murmured half-hearted congratulations before resuming a mainly one-sided discussion with his brother-in-law on the irrelevance of a classical education in the twentieth century. The Viscount, who thought George a precocious young puppy, would have preferred to join in the general conversation.

Natasha received the news in stony silence, her thin face settling into its habitual sulky lines. Margaret went over to her where she sat on the window-seat, while the older members of the family sipped their sherry and waited to be summoned to lunch. She put an arm about the bony shoulders.

'Tasha, honey, aren't you pleased? I shall really be your mother now. Your step-mother, anyway. You'll be like my younger daughter.'

'Antonia will still be your real daughter, though, won't she?' Natasha asked. 'Don't you say in England that blood is thicker than water?'

It was one of her defences, when angry or resentful, to lay stress on her Russian blood; to pretend that she was wholly foreign instead of having been brought up to speak nothing but English from the day she was born. At such times, also, she took great exception to any of her half-brothers or sisters referring to, or addressing, Olga as 'aunt'.

'She's not your aunt!' Natasha would argue heatedly. 'She's mine! Mine! Mine! Mine! She's only your cousin by marriage!'

On these occasions, Margaret would lose her temper, knowing full well that Natasha did not even like the Duchess, and had once received a merited spanking from her father for calling Olga an 'overdressed old cow'.

Margaret said firmly: 'There's no point in discussing the matter, Tasha, if you're going to be silly. I thought you'd see my marrying Paul as an advantage, but as you don't there's not much I can do about it. We'll discuss it later, when you're in a better frame of mind.' She got up and rejoined the others.

Throughout lunch Natasha remained subdued, pointedly refusing her father's offer of a glass of champagne.

'I don't think I should, do you?' she asked in a cold, sententious little voice. 'Not when I'm so much under age.'

There was silence, while Paul looked savage and India and Mareth exchanged exasperated glances.

Margaret said hurriedly: 'No, of course she ought not to drink it, Paul. Natasha's quite right. Eight years old is far too young.'

General conversation was resumed. Natasha slumped back furiously in her chair, refusing her favourite dessert of apple pie and thick, rich, clotted Cornish cream. If only she and Margaret had stayed in Russia! If only they had never come home!

She was too immature as yet to realize that she thought of England – Latchetts in particular – as home. It had become second nature to resent her father and the rest of her unwanted family. She failed to understand that her feelings towards Margaret were changing. Somewhere the thought stirred that she was growing up and did not need Margaret, or depend on her, as she had once done. Then Natasha glanced at her father, and the faint flicker of reason died. All the old jealousies flared again, convincing her that she detested him. Perhaps she could find a way of stopping this marriage; then she and Margaret would go away together and set up house on their own.

Childlike, she ignored the improbability of this conclusion, and concentrated instead on the practical problem. Looking at Margaret's radiant face, however, she became aware that if she succeeded she would be destroying not only her father's happiness, but Margaret's as well.

'I'll make it up to her,' Natasha thought. 'I'll make it up to her somehow.'

The difficulty was, how did she set about preventing the wedding? Anything she said would simply be ignored; any tantrums punished. She followed the others into the garden where they drank their coffee, listening with only half an ear to the conversation. She sat on the grass, her long legs curled under her, staring at the ordered lawns and flower beds and, beyond the gatehouse, the rising banks of trees. Unwillingly she reached the conclusion that there was nothing she could do, except make herself thoroughly unpleasant.

She heard India mention 'Aunt Go-go'. How dare her half-sister persist in speaking of Olga as her aunt, especially by that stupid baby name? It only made matters worse that Olga actually liked it, and had once tried to persuade Natasha herself to use it. But then, Natasha reflected scornfully, Aunt Olga was a stupid babyish kind of woman. She was lazy and fat and wore hideous clothes.

A thought occurred to Natasha. The Duchess did not like Margaret, and neither did the Duke. Natasha had realized that years ago, when she was still quite young, and it was one of the reasons for her own dislike of them. Of Aunt Olga, at least: she had never been sure what to make of Uncle Francis. Natasha, from listening to odd scraps of conversation, from subconsciously interpreting looks and things left unsaid, knew that neither the Duke nor the Duchess approved of Margaret's relationship with Paul; that if anyone might wish to prevent this marriage, they would be the ones. She had no idea what they could do, or even if they would be successful if they tried, but they were her only hope.

Muttering that it was too hot, Natasha got up and went indoors. The hall was deserted. She crossed to the old Spanish chest where the telephone stood and unhooked the receiver.

'Number please,' said the clipped, ladylike tones of the village postmistress, who was also the local telephone operator.

Natasha hesitated. There was still time to think again.

'Number please,' enunciated Miss Pascoe, this time with a hint of impatience.

Natasha made up her mind. 'I want the Hawksworth

number, please, Miss Pascoe. This is Latchetts. Natasha Devereaux. I'd like to speak to my uncle, the Duke.'

'That was a lovely day,' Margaret said, standing in her night-dress by the open window and looking out over the park. The night sky was velvet, dusted with stars. The distant trees had turned to rusty black, the first shreds of moonlight netted in their branches. An owl hooted. There was a ghostly quality about the scene, Margaret thought, like something half-remembered from childhood.

Paul, already in bed, smiled and held out his hand. 'I'm glad you enjoyed it. Everyone was delighted with our news, weren't they?'

'We-ell,' she began, turning away from the window and moving towards him. Then: 'Yes, they were,' she said. Why spoil the moment with too much honesty? She climbed into bed beside him, returning his smile.

'I shall go up to town first thing tomorrow morning,' he said. 'Would you like to come with me? I want to buy you a wedding ring and get a special licence. You can go round the fashion houses and choose your trousseau. We'll be married here next week, while the children are all at home. Do you mind if it's a quiet family wedding?'

'Not as long as there's time for Jessie and Daniel to get here. Lilian, too, if she wants to come. I wrote to Jess telling her of our engagement this afternoon. She should receive the letter first post tomorrow.' Paul tried to take her in his arms, but Margaret held him off for a moment, regarding him shrewdly from beneath half-closed lids. 'Why the desperate hurry, sweetheart? To get married, I mean. We've waited this long. A few more months wouldn't make any difference, surely?'

'I thought you wanted to marry me,' Paul blustered. 'Why should we wait? What's the point?'

Margaret absently twisted the diamond and emerald cluster ring, which had belonged to Paul's mother, round and round on her finger. 'You talked of a family wedding,' she said. 'Does that include Olga and Francis?'

'They'll be away,' Paul answered smoothly. 'In Scotland, for the shooting.'

'But wouldn't it be polite to inform them of our engagement? Even if they can't come to the wedding?'

'I – er – I don't know where they're staying. Later on in the year we'll give an "at home" in Hill Street for all our friends. We can invite them to that.'

'Your friends,' Margaret corrected, adding: 'Why don't you want the Duke and Duchess to know?'

He moved away from her to his own side of the bed. He reminded her of a sulky schoolboy, detected in some misdemeanour.

'What is this? A cross-examination? Why should you think I want to keep our marriage a secret from Olga and Francis? Good God! They'll find out soon enough.'

'But by then it will be too late. Short of the scandal of divorce, there will be nothing they can do. That's what you're afraid of, isn't it? That the Duke will do his utmost to stop you marrying me?'

'He couldn't, if he tried,' Paul answered stoutly. 'Oh, all right! I give in. Yes, I think Francis might try to throw a rub in our way. As I've just said, he wouldn't succeed, but he could make things damned unpleasant. Once we're married, he'll accept that there's nothing to be gained by making a fuss. He's a sensible man. He knows when he's licked. Look, darling' – he turned towards her again, drawing her, this time unresisting, into his arms – 'if I could wave a magic wand and make all my relations love you as much as I do, be sure I'd do it. But I can't. Neither of us can, and I don't flatter myself for a minute that Jess will be overjoyed to have me for a brother-in-law. I suspect that if she and Francis could exchange views on the subject they'd find themselves very much in accord with one another.'

Margaret was tempted to say: 'For very different reasons,' but she did not. It had been a lovely day, in spite of the reminder of Anna's death, and it would be a shame to end it on a note of disharmony. Paul was right. It would be better to get married first and inform the Duke and Duchess afterwards. There was no point in courting disaster. She had a lurking suspicion that her father would not have approved. Herbie Dunham had always liked to meet trouble head-on; but Margaret was not sure that it was necessarily the wisest course of action. Discretion was still sometimes the better part of valour.

She smiled and raised her mouth for Paul's kiss. His hands slid down over her body, over the pale, clinging oyster satin of her nightgown. How much more sensuous clothes were nowadays. Women no longer had to hide themselves away under yards of cotton or flannel. The age of the emancipated female had dawned at last. Women were no longer ashamed to show off the natural contours of their bodies.

And yet, just at that moment, she did not feel, perhaps did not want to feel, like an emancipated female. She wanted simply to be secure and loved, a woman with her husband and family around her; no more hiding in corners; no more pretence; no more being ignored by people who did not, or should not, matter. They must get married as soon as possible, before anyone or anything could stop them. Margaret was filled with a sense of urgency which she could not explain. She wished suddenly that the wedding was tomorrow.

'How was London?' asked Mareth, as she welcomed Paul and Margaret back to Latchetts two days later. 'It must have been dreadful in this heat.'

'It was. It was also very noisy and dusty,' Margaret replied, watching Paul and one of the maids unload cases and boxes from the back of the big four-cylinder Austin 20. 'The traffic was appalling. We were caught for an hour yesterday in a traffic jam near Charing Cross. It really is terrible all round Cockspur Street and Trafalgar Square. All those huge double-decker buses and trams made me feel quite nervous. Only the British could have invented such monstrosities.'

'Careful,' laughed Paul, overhearing her last remark. 'You'll be British yourself after next week.'

Margaret picked up one of the cardboard boxes. 'Come up to my room, Mareth. Where's India? I want you both to see the dress I bought at Harrods. My wedding dress,' she added, almost shyly.

Just at that moment India came out of the house, blinking cat-like in the glare of the sun.

'Have you told them?' she asked her sister.

Mareth shook her head. 'Not yet. I was just going to.'

'Told us what?' asked Paul, rescuing the last parcel from the back seat of the car. 'I don't know what on earth you've got here, Margaret. Half of Selfridges, I should think, and most of Harrods.'

Antonia joined India on the steps. 'Ooh! Parcels!' she exclaimed gleefully. 'Did you bring anything for me?'

'We've only been gone two days,' Margaret reminded her daughter. Then, as Antonia's face fell, she gave her a swift hug. 'Yes, of course we've brought you something, but it's in my case. You'll have to contain your soul in patience until I unpack.'

'Uncle Francis and Aunt Go-go are here,' India said with ominous quiet. 'And I should warn you, they know about the wedding and they're not best pleased.'

Paul let out a groan. 'Hell,' he swore. 'What damn bad luck.'

Mareth grimaced. 'I'm afraid it isn't luck exactly. It seems that Natasha phoned them.'

'Natasha!' Paul exclaimed incredulously, then his face darkened. 'Where is she? I'll have her hide!'

'No! Paul!' Margaret laid a hand quickly on his arm. 'She's only a child. She couldn't possibly have known that we didn't . . . that we didn't intend inviting them to the wedding. If she telephoned them, it would be natural for her to mention we were getting married. Why should she think we wished for concealment?'

Paul stared at her for a few seconds, then his face relaxed. 'No. Of course you're right. All the same, I wish she hadn't done it. However' – he tucked Margaret's hand into the crook of his arm – 'it won't make any difference.' He glanced at his eldest daughter. 'When did they arrive?'

'Yesterday morning. They were very put out to find that you weren't here. Mrs Hinkley's put them in their usual room, but somehow I don't think they'll stay longer than they have to.' India kissed her father's cheek. 'Whatever mischief they want to make, Papa, don't take any notice.'

'I don't intend to,' Paul answered cheerfully. 'In fact, before I discuss anything with anyone, I am going to bath and shave and have my dinner. I feel covered in London grime.'

'Quite right,' Mareth approved. 'And India, Tonia and I

are going to help Dunny unpack all her parcels. I telephoned Maurice, by the way, and told him that he has to come down for the wedding, or I'll never speak to him again. Poor darling! It'll probably be the day he's due to defend a really exciting case.'

Dinner was an uncomfortable meal. The presence of the Duke and Duchess cast a gloom over what should otherwise have been a happy gathering.

Natasha was not present. She had pleaded a stomach upset and gone to bed, to be fussed over by the septuagenarian Nanny Watkins. Margaret had been in to see her just before the dinner gong sounded, but could not make up her mind whether the illness was real or faked. She had given Natasha the benefit of the doubt and kissed her affectionately as she said goodnight.

'Sleep tight, honey. I'll give you your present from London in the morning.'

Natasha said nothing, burrowing under the bedclothes in spite of the warmth of the evening. Margaret wondered if she were running a temperature.

'No, I'm all right,' Natasha snapped in response to Margaret's question. 'Go away and leave me alone.'

'Don't worry, I shall,' Margaret snapped back, restraining the urge to slap her. She stood, irresolute, looking at the tousled head on the pillow, remembering all that she and Natasha had gone through together. It was no wonder the child was unlike other girls of her age. She was too old, too devious, too knowing.

Margaret had sighed and gone downstairs to dinner, taking her place naturally – she had done it without a second thought for so long now – at the opposite end of the table from Paul. She saw the Duke and Duchess exchange glances, and Olga frown in disapproval.

Olga had grown fat. What it had once been charitable to describe as plumpness had now become thick rolls of flesh. The skin around her eyes was puffy, her figure shapeless, her chin almost non-existent as it merged into the folds of her neck. She still dressed badly, with a fondness for bows and frills and too much jewellery. Tonight she wore a heavy diamond necklace and matching pendant earrings, an assortment of gold bracelets and a ring on every finger. A ruby and pearl brooch was pinned to the shoulder of her mauve organdie evening gown by Worth. India, slim as a lath and elegant in a black foulard silk with an overskirt of pale grey lace, hissed in Mareth's ear that the House of Worth must wish that Aunt Go-go would patronize someone else. Mareth stifled a giggle.

Margaret did her best to keep the Duke entertained, and was thankful that George was seated on her other side. His self-confidence and precocity were, at such times, a godsend.

Finally, however, the meal was over, and the ladies rose to withdraw. The Duke said: 'Paul! I should be grateful for a word in private. If you could spare me an hour of your time.'

Paul glanced at Margaret and shrugged. 'Now, if you like,' he answered. 'I'm sure these young people can get on perfectly well without us. We'll take coffee in the music-room. I'll give word that we're not to be disturbed.'

Francis inclined his head. 'Mrs Stafford, I should be grateful if you would join us. It would save a lot of time.'

'I see no need—' Paul was beginning, but Margaret interrupted him.

'I prefer to come,' she said. 'I'm interested to hear what His Grace has to say. India, take Her Grace to the drawing-room, please, and ask Mrs Hinkley to send a separate pot of coffee to the music-room. Thank you, my dear.'

The music-room, cool now in the long shadows of evening, was more or less as it had always been; the patterned plaster ceiling, the William Morris chrysanthemum wallpaper, the leather armchairs and brocaded sofa were exactly as they had been twenty years ago, when Margaret had first come to Latchetts. The Broadwood piano still stood in its corner. Only the Kirkman Trichord had been moved, pushed back from its place of honour in the centre of the room to one side of the long French windows. And Sargent's portrait of Beatrice had gone, removed to Hill Street. In its place was a David which Paul had managed to acquire while he was in France.

'I won't beat about the bush,' Francis said, refusing a seat and going to stand with his back to the empty fireplace.

Margaret and Paul sat side by side on the sofa. Paul found Margaret's hand and held it.

There was an interruption as one of the parlour-maids brought in the coffee-things. She set the tray down on a low table in front of Margaret, who murmured: 'Thank you, Ruby,' and started to pour. As soon as the door had shut, behind her, the Duke resumed.

'As I said, I won't beat about the bush. There is almost certainly going to be an election later this year, and the plain fact is, Paul, that if you marry Mrs Stafford you will lose the Conservative nomination for the Hawksworth and Clarendon constituency. Furthermore, I confidently predict that you will not be accepted by any other. No, no coffee, thank you.'

Paul had half-risen from his seat, but sank back again as Margaret handed him a cup and saucer. For the first time in his life, he hated Francis. He was determined, however, not to lose his temper.

'I think you're mistaken,' he told his cousin evenly. 'Attitudes have changed since the war. Plenty of politicians have had mistresses, and married them, too. The people of this country, thank God, have never exhibited a prurient interest in the private lives of their rulers. The newspapers are equally reticent.'

'That may alter,' Francis retorted grimly. 'There's a different kind of newspaper being born in Fleet Street. But, in any case, that's not what I meant. I am referring to Mrs Stafford's personal involvement with the Bolshevik Party.'

Slowly, Paul set down his cup and saucer on the tray. 'What in hell's name are you talking about?' he demanded angrily. 'You know damn well that Margaret was a victim of their persecution. She was trapped in Russia. She stayed to look after Anna!'

'And let her be murdered,' the Duke accused venomously. 'While she' – he stabbed a finger at Margaret – 'escaped! Haven't you ever asked yourself why?'

'Suppose you tell me,' Paul invited quietly, his eyes glittering dangerously in his paper-white face.

'Because she's a personal friend of Lenin and all his henchmen. Before you say anything, ask her if she ever met them when they were in London before the war. Ask her if she went to one of their meetings. Ask her if she went to the Anarchist Club with them.' The Duke rounded on Margaret. 'And if you deny it, I shall call you a liar! My valet saw you go into the club and he saw you come out. He saw you with those men whose faces have become familiar to the whole world.'

'I have no intention of denying it,' Margaret answered through stiff lips. 'I am only sorry for your valet who must have had a very long wait, snooping around Jubilee Street until I and my friends emerged.' She turned to Paul. 'I went to a meeting with Hilda and Sergei when I was staying with them once, in Southwark. The following night we all went to a music-hall. I never met Lenin or any of the others again after those two nights.' She stood up, her coffee untasted and growing cold on the table. 'And if Your Grace repeats the accusation that I connived at your sister-in-law's death, I shall sue for defamation of character. And don't think I don't know why you're doing this.' She laughed scornfully. 'You've never forgiven me, have you, for having the good taste to repulse you that night?'

The Duke sneered. 'My dear woman, if you think I remember every servant I've tried to lay, you're very much mistaken.' Paul came to his feet, the table bearing the coffee-things overturning with a crash, but Francis ignored him. His eyes were fixed on Margaret. 'I warn you,' he said, 'if you insist on marrying Paul, you will ruin his political chances. I shall consider it my bounden duty to warn every Conservative agent in the country that his wife is a political hazard of the most embarrassing sort. And as the Duke of Wellington might have said, my dear: "Sue and be damned!" The publicity will harm Paul far more than it will ever hurt me.'

Twenty-Seven

'I thought I should find you here,' said Jessie, pushing open the door of the gatehouse-room. 'I remember how you always liked it.' Her eyes came to rest on her sister, slumped in one of the wicker chairs near a window. 'For goodness' sake, snap out of it, Maggie! You're getting married tomorrow.' Margaret made no response, did not even glance at her. Jessie, who hated to be ignored and had to put up with it from Daniel, moved purposefully into her sister's line of vision. 'Stir yourself, Maggie Dunham! There's plenty to be done up at the house.'

Margaret raised her eyes slowly, as though just aware of Jessie's presence. She said irritably: 'Please leave me alone.'

Jessie drew up another chair and flicked its dusty cushioned seat with her handkerchief, tut-tutting under her breath. Then she sat down and crossed her legs, regarding her sister severely. Her sandy hair was liberally streaked with grey and had been bobbed, Dutch-doll fashion, with a heavy fringe which almost covered her eyebrows. It was not an attractive style, yet, oddly enough, it suited Jessie's round, plump face, making her look more than ever like an inquisitive sparrow. Modern clothes, especially the shorter skirts, did little for her, but she had never been interested in her appearance.

There was a discontented twist to her mouth, and her general demeanour was that of someone trying to make the best of a disappointing job. She felt that life had cheated her. When she first married Daniel, it had not seemed to matter that he did not love her, nor she him. But the older she grew, the more she needed his affection and the more she resented that it had never been hers.

The realization that he had been deeply, hopelessly, in love with Beatrice had burst upon her suddenly, two years ago, after reading one of his poems. She had only read the thing because she was bored; because the cottage gave her too little to do; because Lilian and Mark had both been absent; and because Daniel was shut up in what he liked to call his study, but which Jessie pointedly referred to as the 'back parlour'. It had broken her heart to leave the shop and the bustle of city life. In spite of the long hours, the hardships, the lack of money and her constant stream of complaints, life had been full and busy. While Daniel was away in France, she had run the shop single-handed and had made a success of it. Takings had gone up by twenty-five per cent. There had been no one to sabotage her efforts with free gifts of sweets for every child with a hard-luck story; no one to bully, to watch, to keep up to scratch. She had felt less tired at the end of each day in spite of the hard work.

Then the war was over and Daniel was home again, with a book of war poems which were not only accepted for publication, but, when printed, became an immediate success. He started writing full time: articles for various newspapers about his experiences in the trenches; more poems, this time not about the war. A book of short stories followed, and more articles. Suddenly there was no need for the shop, no need to stay in Bath, where the noise disturbed Daniel and the flat gave him no privacy.

The business was sold and they bought a cottage near Mells. Daniel became more and more absorbed in his writing, Lilian and Mark in one another, leaving Jessie on her own. She kept the cottage like a new pin, but it was insufficient to occupy her. She did not care for her neighbours and was uninterested in country matters. She cleaned and polished and cleaned again. And then, one day, in a moment of frustration, she picked up a book of Daniel's poems. . . .

There was no doubt in her mind, either at the time or afterwards, that the one called 'White Flower' referred to Beatrice, and was a love poem. Jessie had never discussed it with anyone, never even admitted to having read it, but she knew, and the knowledge hurt her. She had never imagined Daniel capable of a love which could survive undiminished for all those years. Beatrice's death had apparently made no difference to his feelings. After decades of marriage, of sharing his bed, after bearing his son, Jessie realized that she had never really known her husband. And so she felt cheated.

Her defence was to become more down to earth, more matter of fact, renouncing anything in her nature which might be construed as in the least artistic. She stigmatized anything to do with literature, painting or music as 'rubbish'. She took up knitting and dressmaking, bottled her own fruits, made her own pickles, won prizes for her cakes at the chapel bazaar. She put up every possible barrier between herself and Daniel, and was angry that he did not even seem to notice. She grew bossier and more managing, until it became second nature to her. The situation she found at Latchetts on her arrival for Margaret's wedding was irresistible. She could not refrain from meddling.

'You had better decide,' she said, impatiently tapping her foot, 'whether you are going to marry Paul Devereaux or not. You only have twenty-four hours in which to make up your mind.' When Margaret still said nothing, Jessie went on: 'Don't be a fool, Maggie! Don't give up the best offer you're ever likely to have in your life for a scruple. Paul has no doubts. He's told you that his political career doesn't matter.'

Margaret closed her eyes. She looked as though she had not slept for the past few nights.

'He's a gentleman. Of course he'd say that. How do I know he means it?'

'You don't, and it doesn't matter if he does or not. He's said it, that's the important thing. Just take him at his word.' Jessie uncrossed and recrossed her legs, revealing a length of black silk stocking. 'I think you've been clever, showing a decent amount of hesitation. He can't in future accuse you of having held him to his promise against his will. But it's time to stop playing such a dangerous game, and be sensible. Good heavens! It's not every day a woman gets the chance to become mistress of a place like Latchetts.'

Margaret opened her eyes and looked at her sister as though she were a stranger, which, in a sense, she was. Jess had always been practical, but never, until now, hard and cynical.

'You speak as if that's all that matters,' she said. 'Paul and I love one another. Doesn't that count for anything?'

Jessie flushed. 'I don't know what love means,' she said. 'It's just a word which most people find hard to define.'

'Go away, Jess,' Margaret pleaded, 'and leave me alone. I need to think. There's no point in staying, because if you don't go, I shall.'

'Very well,' her sister snapped, 'but you have no one to blame except yourself for this muddle. I always warned you that the dubious company you kept would land you in trouble one day. Of course, I blame our father. He should never have exposed you to his radical ideas.'

Left on her own once more, Margaret lay back in her chair, staring at the view beyond the window. It was drizzling, and mist obscured the tops of the trees. She shivered, wrapping her arms about herself for warmth and comfort.

The last week had been a nightmare. It did not matter how many times Paul reassured her that he understood, that his political ambition meant nothing to him beside the desire to make her his wife; she was still unable to believe him. There was something about the look in his eyes, some doubt which he did his utmost to suppress without ever quite succeeding.

She remembered the long years during which he had waited so patiently for the coveted parliamentary seat. The Hawksworth and Clarendon nomination would assure him of it. Only she stood between him and his dream.

Damn Francis! Damn him, damn him, damn him! She hoped he rotted in hell!

Appalled by such a thought, she jumped up from her chair and began pacing the room. It was still a favourite retreat of the younger generation, and also of Mareth and India when they were at home. A book, Lytton Strachey's biography of Queen Victoria, lay open on one of the chairs, Henry's fishing-nets and jam jars were piled in a corner, and Antonia had been doing some sewing, now thankfully abandoned, at one end of the wicker table. The old Albion paraffin heater with its dimpled red glass dome had given way to a Belling electric convector, and there was electric light overhead, but there were very few other changes. The furniture was the same, and the crockery in the cupboard for tea on wet afternoons was the same plain white kitchenware that Margaret remembered. The room and its contents provided a point of reference, a thread of continuity, in a rapidly changing world. Until these past seven days Margaret had always loved coming here. Now she hated it.

She picked up Antonia's half-finished blouse, then put it down again, without any idea of having done so. She walked to the windows and stared out disconsolately at the ghostly scene. There had been a breeze earlier in the day, but now it had died, and a corpse-like stillness shrouded everything.

She turned and faced into the room again, saying loudly and distinctly: 'I am going to be married tomorrow. This time tomorrow I shall be Mrs Paul Devereaux.' But the words had a hollow ring to them. At that moment she knew that she could not go through with it.

The Duke and Duchess had left Latchetts the day after Francis had made his disclosures. Paul had told him, calmly and quietly, that he withdrew his name as parliamentary Conservative candidate for the Hawksworth and Clarendon constituency.

'I refuse to be blackmailed,' he had told Margaret when she remonstrated with him later in the day. 'There will be other chances, other elections. And if there aren't, we shall be together, and that's all that matters.'

But Margaret could not accept his repeated assurances. She could foresee a time when he might regret having forfeited all his political ambitions in order to marry her; when he might well resent the fact that their viewpoints did not always coincide. She knew that, deep down, he harboured a grudge about Arthur Barlow and her refusal to release him from his promise.

'Listen to me,' Paul had said to her again, only that morning, 'marrying you will be the most important thing that has ever happened to me. Francis will forget his threat eventually. I doubt if he ever really intended to carry it out. In a few years' time, when he realizes how happy we are, how necessary you are to my comfort, he will be thoroughly ashamed of the things he said here the other night.'

Margaret had made no answer, thinking that if Paul had a blind spot it was his misplaced confidence in Francis's better nature. He had never been able to see his cousin clearly; to accept the vindictiveness and gross self-consequence which lay beneath the affable, hail-fellow-well-met exterior. The idea that the Duke still harboured a grudge against Margaret because she had rebuffed and humiliated him all those years ago seemed preposterous to Paul. He saw Francis's interference simply as an attempt to prevent what he considered to be an ill-judged marriage.

'He's old-fashioned,' Paul had laughed, kissing her between the eyes and stroking her hair. 'He just hasn't realized yet what a difference the war has made. My darling, all we have to do is to give him time. I'm only forty-eight, and as Members of Parliament go that's quite young. You'll see. I shall take my seat in the House of Commons before I'm fifty-five.'

Margaret sat down wearily again in the chair. For the past hour or so, since that last conversation with Paul, she had been forcing herself to realize that she had to leave. She had no choice but to go right away somewhere. She could not remain at Latchetts on the old footing: Paul would not allow it. If, on the other hand, she stayed and married him, his political career was over before it had begun. She had no doubt whatsoever that Francis, already furious at Paul's stubbornness, would keep his word. He would see to it that everyone who mattered heard about her association with Lenin and the other Bolshevik leaders. The incident would be distorted and magnified out of all proportion, and the insinuations about Anna's death repeated until they were accepted as facts. The social implications would be as bad as the political ones; a man who had married the virtual murderess of his second wife. . . .

Margaret leaned forward and buried her head in her hands. She could feel the tears prickling against her eyelids at the thought of leaving Henry and Antonia behind. She had missed so many years of their childhood, and now she was going to abandon them again. For a moment she toyed with the notion of taking them with her, but she knew it was impractical. She had nowhere to take them. Latchetts was their home. It would be cruel to uproot them, to take Henry away from a school she would be unable to afford, to inflict unnecessary hardship upon them. They had been happy without her before; they would be so again. They were more necessary to her than she was to them.

The thought steadied her, warding off the threat of hysteria which had been rising inside her. She sat up straight, drawing a deep breath and tidying her hair. It was time she had it cut; time it became a symbol of her emancipation.

She must think carefully what to do. Her departure would have to be secret. She would not be permitted to leave without a fuss if anyone knew. And yet the prospect of leaving entirely alone depressed her. She doubted if she could do it without some kind of moral support. If only Lilian had agreed to come to the wedding, Margaret was certain that she could have counted on her elder daughter. But both Lilian and Mark had pointedly refused their invitations. It would have to be Daniel, then, who had stood her friend so often in the past. She told herself that he would understand her motives; and even if he did not, he would never coerce her into doing something she did not want.

Margaret got up, calmer now that she had come to a decision. She threw a last glance around the gatehouse-room, then resolutely went in search of her brother-in-law.

'Well!' exclaimed Jessie, dumping her cases on the floor of the cottage living-room and glaring at her sister. 'I thought I should find you here! You've really burned your boats this time, my girl! I don't suppose Paul Devereaux will ever speak to you again.' Outside, the taxi-cab which had brought her from Bath station moved off with a grinding and clashing of gears. Jessie turned on her husband. 'As for you, you great fool, I suppose you thought you were doing Maggie a service. And how like you to sneak off like a thief in the night, leaving me alone to face the music!'

'Now, hold on a minute, Mother!' Mark slid off the arm of the sofa and stood between Jessie and Daniel. 'Father did what he thought was right, and Lilian and I support him. You should be glad that Aunt Margaret came to her senses in time.'

'Hear, hear!' said Lilian, who was seated beside her mother on the sofa. 'Paul Devereaux is a capitalist pig.'

'Oh God!' Daniel complained wearily. 'Where have we heard that old chant before? *À bas les aristos!* Haven't we had enough hating and killing? Doesn't any generation learn from its elders? And there's no need to stand there like Saint George about to slay the dragon, Mark. I'm quite capable of dealing with your mother.'

In spite of her unhappiness, Margaret was forced to smile. Four years of war had changed Daniel. He was less inclined to run away from unpleasant situations. He had even tried, the day before yesterday, to persuade her to remain at Latchetts and tell Paul how she felt. It was only when she had at last convinced him it would do no good that he had agreed to help her escape. But he had insisted that she return with him to Mells.

'You can have the spare room,' he had said, 'just until you decide what to do.'

Margaret had demurred, but Daniel had been adamant. He had always felt an inexplicable responsibility for his sister-in-law; far more than for Jess. During the afternoon, while everyone was busy with preparations for the following day, he had left a note on the bedroom table for his wife and brought his old Ford tourer round to the side entrance, where Margaret was waiting for him. He had stowed her one suitcase on the back seat and driven her away. No one had noticed them because of the mist, and they had reached the cottage late the same night. A startled Lilian had been on the point of going to bed, but as soon as she was in possession of all the facts had insisted on making them supper.

'You've come to your senses at last, Mother,' she had approved, embracing Margaret and kissing her cheek. 'I'm proud of you.'

Margaret had been too tired and too miserable to eat, but Daniel had done justice to the bacon and eggs which Lilian placed before them.

'Think yourself honoured,' he had told Margaret. 'She doesn't do this for everyone. She feels that women would be better employed training for the revolution than slaving over a kitchen sink. Jess says she gets more like your father every day.'

Margaret had thought, but not said, that Jess was doing their father an injustice.

Mark, who put in an appearance the following day, was less demonstrative but no less approving than his cousin. He had solemnly shaken his aunt's hand, saying: 'Welcome back, Aunt Margaret.'

Back to what? she had wondered. The fold?

Depressed through worry and lack of sleep, she had found it difficult to respond, and had spent a miserable day on her own. Mark and Lilian were at work, and Daniel, his duty done, withdrew to his study to get on with the novel he was writing. She had been afraid to leave the cottage, half-hoping that Paul might telephone, half-expecting Jess to arrive.

But the hours dragged by and nothing happened. Today, Saturday, Margaret had cooked breakfast for her daughter and nephew before they left for Bath; Lilian to her job as shop assistant in one of the drapery stores in Milsom Street, Mark to his work with an insurance firm. They had both returned at half past six that evening, indifferent to Jessie's non-appearance.

'We're getting on very well without her. You're a good cook, Aunt Margaret,' was Mark's unfilial comment.

Jessie, however, arrived just as they finished their meal. And suddenly, seeing her standing there in the middle of the room, listening to her angry voice, Margaret wished she could have postponed indefinitely this moment of knowing what had happened after her departure from Latchetts.

But her sister's voice went inexorably on, ignoring the interruptions from Mark and Daniel.

'As I said, Maggie, you've really done it this time.'

'Was Paul very angry?' Margaret asked. Surely he must have tried to understand.

'Angry? Of course he was angry! I've never known him more furious in my life. He said you had made a complete and utter fool of him and that his cousin had been right. He should never have asked you to marry him. He hopes he'll never see you again.'

Through her own pain, Margaret could recognize Paul's hurt; the desire to wound because of the unhappiness she had caused him. At the same time, she felt angry that he could not fathom the reasoning behind her action; angry that he persisted in being blind to Francis's faults.

'What about the children?' she asked. 'Did Paul say anything about them?'

'They'll stay with him, naturally. Antonia and Henry were extremely upset.'

Margaret did not want to think about her children until she was alone. 'And what about Ralph?' she queried.

'If my dear brother has an ounce of loyalty towards you,' snapped Lilian, 'he'll leave that house at once and join you here.'

Margaret lost her temper. 'I don't think you're in any position to criticize him, Lilian, do you? Ralph didn't leave me. I left him.'

Lilian blushed and relapsed into angry silence. Mark rushed to her defence.

'I hardly think that's fair comment, Aunt Margaret. Young as she was when she left Latchetts, Lilian was acting out of principle. Ralph, if he remains, is acting through lack of it.'

'Ralph has no principles,' Lilian remarked acidly. 'The only person he ever considers is himself.'

'Then he's no different from quite a number of people I could mention,' Jessie snapped.

Daniel, ignoring this obvious dig, said placatingly: 'Take your hat and coat off, my dear, and have a cup of tea. There's one still left in the pot. And for goodness' sake calm down.'

His wife cast him a look of withering contempt, but she did as he suggested. Margaret got up and poured the tea.

'What about Ralph?' she insisted, as she passed Jessie the cup and saucer.

Jessie shrugged, suddenly very tired after the trauma of the past two days.

'Oh, he'll stay at Latchetts. Paul told him it was his home for as long as he wished. Besides, George would never have tolerated Ralph's being sent away. I'll say that for Paul Devereaux, he's not vindictive.'

'If that's all you can say for him, you're not very percipient, Jess,' Margaret said quietly.

'Then if you feel that way about him, why on earth—' her sister was beginning, but Margaret interrupted her.

'If you don't mind, I'll just go upstairs for a while.'

She fought her way blindly out of the living-room and up the stairs, closing and locking the bedroom door behind her. The low roof under the eaves sloped almost down to the floor. The atmosphere was warm and claustrophobic. Margaret flung herself down on the bed and buried her face in the pillow.

Twenty-Eight

It had turned very warm for early May, and Margaret wished she had worn a summer dress. Her grey flannel suit with its crisp white blouse was all very well for the office, but for her half-day she should have chosen something lighter. She sat down on a seat under a tree and eased off her shoes.

The unexpectedly fine weather, after the rain of the past two days, had brought out the crowds. The British Empire Exhibition in Wembley Park, opened by His Majesty the King the preceding month, was attracting vast numbers of visitors from both home and overseas; and pleasant as it was to see everything at its best in the brilliant sunshine, Margaret could not help wishing she had chosen a cooler day.

Her feet ached dreadfully. She had walked all round the Palace of India and Malaya Building with its domes and twin minarets, visited the new sports stadium, the BBC kiosk and most of the souvenir stalls, and now was in need of a rest. The relief as her feet were released from the confining leather was enormous. She wriggled her toes in their covering of silk, leaned against the back of the seat and closed her eyes. Two minutes later she was almost asleep.

Her head nodded forward and she jerked awake, stupidly trying to remember where she was. A voice from the other end of the bench said: 'You were nearly off there, Mrs Stafford.'

'What . . . ?' She looked round, still confused. A man was sitting a few feet away from her, regarding her with a smile. There was something familiar about his face, although she could not immediately place him. She thought him a little younger than herself, perhaps in his late thirties. He was neatly dressed in a cheap navy pin-striped suit, a blue shirt, and a trilby hat which he had raised politely when she first looked at him. He was lean without being thin, and the eyes were hazel with little flecks of gold in the irises. He spoke with a marked west country accent.

Margaret said: 'Good heavens! It's Arthur Barlow!'

'That's correct.' He grinned at her. 'The last time we saw each other was that day in Cornwall before the war. I have a lot to thank you for, I believe, but I'm no good at writing letters, and our paths haven't crossed again. Until now, that is.'

'What are you doing in London?' she asked. 'Are you on holiday?'

He shook his head. He looked healthier and ruddier than he used to, so it was no surprise to hear he had left the pits.

'I'm working for one of the trades union bosses. And now that we finally have a Labour government I wouldn't mind having a stab at politics.' He gave her a sidelong glance. 'Mr Devereaux's doing well for himself, I see. He wasn't one of those Conservatives who lost his seat in the last election.'

'No. Hawksworth and Clarendon is a very safe Tory constituency,' Margaret answered repressively. She did not want to talk about Paul. 'When did you leave the mine?'

'Two years ago. The late summer of 1922. And I didn't leave exactly. I was dismissed.'

So, she thought, Paul had used what he saw as her desertion to rid himself of Arthur Barlow. He had felt himself to be released from the promise which he had honoured for so many years. And why not? How could she blame him? The only wonder was that he had not done it before.

'I'm sorry,' she said politely. 'It's never pleasant to be sacked.'

Arthur's smile broadened. 'As it happens, he did me a favour. It appeared that various people had been taking notice of my activities at Longreach for quite some time. I was offered my present position within a few days of my dismissal's becoming generally known. It meant a move to London, but as my mother's dead now I had only myself to please. Can I ask what you're doing in London? There was a rumour once that you and Mr Devereaux were going to get married.'

'We were,' Margaret answered smoothly. 'But we didn't. There were reasons.'

'If I said I was sorry you wouldn't believe me. But you still haven't said what you're doing in the wicked metropolis. You used to be a governess, a long time ago.'

Margaret squeezed her feet back into her shoes. 'I gave that up,' she said. 'I learned shorthand and typing at a school in Bath. I work as a secretary at Bloomfield's, the diamond merchants in Hatton Garden. An old friend got me the job. She and I share an apartment in Borough High Street, in Southwark.'

She fell silent, recalling that chance meeting with Hilda – their second chance meeting within ten years: fate seemed determined to throw them together – almost as soon as she had arrived in London eight months ago. She had been standing amidst the grime and gloom of Paddington station on a wet autumnal afternoon, wondering if she had indeed been as stupid as Jess and Daniel told her she was to leave the comparative quiet and serenity of Bath to come to London.

'You have a good job with Beechings,' Jess had chided her. 'A nice apartment in Edgar Buildings. Why for heaven's sake do you want to leave?'

'You're mad,' Daniel had said, more directly. 'I wouldn't live in London for a fortune. A day there visiting my publishers frightens me to death. It's not what it was before the war.'

'Nothing's what it was before the war,' Margaret had answered, and had proceeded to hand in her notice at Beechings, the coal merchants, and return the keys of her rented flat.

She did not know herself why she had felt it so necessary to come to London. Perhaps because it was so large, so safely anonymous. There was far less chance of running into Paul. It was a spectre which had always haunted her in Bath whenever she had known he was at Bladud House. But that first afternoon, with the rain dripping down inside her mackintosh collar from a crack in the station roof, trying to avoid the puddles on the platform, unable to find a porter, she had been tempted to get on the next train back to the west.

Then, suddenly, she had heard her name spoken and there was Hilda, staring at her in disbelief, just as she had done that time in St Petersburg. They had stood in the wet and the cold, laughing and crying, oblivious of the other passengers hurrying past, until an elderly gentleman had asked them somewhat testily to get out of his way.

Hilda, who had been delivering a package for transport by train to Cardiff, insisted that Margaret went back with her to the flat in Borough High Street where she had been living ever since her return from Russia in 1914. They had hardly slept at all that first night, talking until three o'clock in the morning, exchanging their personal histories of the years since they had seen one another.

Hilda had arrived back in London just as war was declared, and resumed her old job with Bloomfield's almost at once. Good clerks were scarce, and most of the younger men had volunteered for the army. Mr Bloomfield had welcomed her with open arms. She had found herself the flat, ignored Betty's hints that she ought to have their mother to live with her, and settled down once more to single life.

She had taken a close interest in the events in Russia, wondering what had happened to Sergei, but was unconcerned by Margaret's revelation that her husband was still alive.

'I shan't marry again, ever. I've had enough of marriage to last me a lifetime. I'm happy as I am.'

She had been horrified, but not altogether surprised, by Sergei's part in Anna's death. His character, she said, had gradually worsened during the years she had known him, partly through discontent and partly, she suspected, because they had no children. He had badly wanted to become a father. The return to Russia had accelerated the process, and his friendship with Nickolai Brodkin had been the final straw.

'But don't you want a divorce? Don't you want to be free of him?' Margaret had asked.

Hilda shook her head. 'No. I've reverted to my maiden name, and I shall stay Hilda Lewisham until I die. Men! You can keep them! I should have thought you would think so too.'

'I love Paul,' Margaret had answered sadly. 'You probably see it as my misfortune, but I shouldn't have left him if I hadn't thought my staying would do him harm.'

'You did yourself a favour,' Hilda had told her friend

briskly; a sentiment which Arthur Barlow, breaking in on her thoughts, was echoing now.

'You and Paul Devereaux would never have suited,' he said, rising at the same time as she did and offering her his arm. 'I never thought you had anything in common. You were always too radical in your thinking for him.'

'So everyone keeps assuring me,' she responded tartly, but taking his arm gratefully, nevertheless. Her feet had swollen with the heat. 'Unfortunately, love between two people doesn't depend on compatibility. There would be fewer unhappy marriages if it did.'

Arthur Barlow laughed. 'Would you let me buy you tea?' he asked. 'There is a restaurant, I believe. I'm not going anywhere special. Saturday's my half-day, so I thought I'd visit the exhibition for lack of something better to do. But it's a bad day to come, especially when it's fine. It always attracts the crowds.'

'We seem to be twin souls,' Margaret replied flippantly. 'I too came for lack of something better to do. And yes, please, I should like a cup of tea. It's the only really drinkable beverage in this country. The coffee's filthy and cold drinks are always tepid through lack of ice.'

He looked down at her. 'You know, I'd forgotten you're American.'

Margaret grimaced. 'There are times, after all these years, when I forget it myself.'

'You've never been back?'

'No. It's twenty-four years since I last saw New York. Nearly a quarter of a century.'

It gave her a little shock, as she said the words, to realize just how long it had been. She had lost touch with her friends at home without even noticing she had done so. Their letters, so precious to her when she first arrived in England, had grown less frequent until they stopped altogether, and she had not even missed them. She read about America in the newspapers, but it no longer seemed to have anything to do with her. The election last year of Calvin Coolidge as President had been of infinitely less interest to her than the death of Lenin, after a series of strokes, in January of this year; Lenin, who had died, in the new Russia he had helped to create, warning his co-workers against the inordinate ambition of Josef Stalin, a man he had grown to distrust.

Arthur Barlow found a table near one of the restaurant windows, so that they could look out at the people scurrying along the paths towards the various stalls and buildings. He ordered tea, buttered toast and fancy cakes, grinning at her provocatively as he said: 'You pour out. You can be mother.'

Margaret reflected how much more confidence he had now than in the old days. He appeared to have lost the chip on his shoulder, the feverish glitter of agitation, but was probably far more dangerous for that. He talked with confidence about the growing power of the trades unions and how, one day, there would be no more bosses.

'Every industry will be nationalized,' he said.

Her instinctive reaction was one of horror. She was still American enough in outlook to believe, if perhaps only superficially, in the concepts of free enterprise and free trade. She answered lightly, biting into her toast: 'That's too radical for me.'

'It'll have to come one day,' he insisted. 'The people of this country won't remain deferential forever. The Scots and Welsh never have been.'

Margaret poured the tea, noting with distaste that the white china teapot was badly cracked and chipped.

'My brother-in-law,' she said, passing Arthur a cup of the dark brown liquid, 'has a theory that class consciousness in England stems from the Norman Conquest, when all the Saxon nobility was wiped out and it really was "them" and "us".' She shuddered. 'Did I say tea was the only drinkable beverage in this country? This tastes like stewed mud.'

Arthur Barlow regarded her over the rim of his cup. He guessed she must be in her early forties, but she did not look it. The auburn hair, cut fashionably short, was as luxuriant as ever. Her green eyes, fringed by thick lashes, were clear and bright, the full lips soft and warm. She had matured; her figure was fuller than it used to be, but it had not lost its shape. Indeed, to Arthur, she was more attractive now than formerly. He had never liked skinny women.

Margaret asked abruptly: 'Do you have a wife?'

He shook his head. 'I always vowed I'd never get married

321

while I was working down the pits. I've seen too many women widowed; left penniless, with young families to bring up. I might consider it now, though,' he added.

Margaret sampled one of the fancy cakes, which was covered in white fondant icing and tasted of sawdust.

'The thing I remember most about you,' she said, 'is your showing me a guss and crook. Do they still use those terrible things?'

'Oh yes. Especially in Somerset, where the coal seams are so narrow. Beat-knee is still prevalent, too.'

'Beat-knee?' She frowned. 'I don't remember anything called that.'

Arthur Barlow laughed. 'I showed you my knees on that famous occasion of our first meeting, but you've obviously forgotten. So much for the impression my wonderful body made upon you.'

'I recollect now,' she answered quickly, suddenly made uncomfortable by his words. 'Your knees were very sore and inflamed. You said it was a condition of carting-boys.'

'Again, especially in Somerset and Gloucestershire, because of the narrowness of the seams. Look,' he went on, 'I shouldn't be talking shop. It's boring for you, and this is your half-day as well as mine. What do you say to giving the rest of the exhibition a miss? We could take a bus back to the West End and go to the pictures. There's a Buster Keaton film showing somewhere. What do you say?'

Margaret hesitated. She had not been out with any man except Paul for so many years that she felt unaccountably shy. She was unsure what would be expected of her, sitting there in the intimate dark of the picture-house. Would he expect to put his arm around her?

Suddenly, the prospect excited her. It might be pleasant to be fussed over again, to have a man buy the tickets and usher her into her seat.

'Thank you,' she said. 'I'd be pleased to come.'

'It's not very much, I'm afraid,' Arthur said, pushing open the door of his rented flat and showing her inside. 'The landlord hasn't got round to electricity yet. We're still on gas.'

He turned up the jet of a wall light which had been left

burning low in the little hallway. The tiny bud of flame blossomed into an incandescent flower, revealing cracked brown linoleum and spotted wallpaper. A fly-blown copy of a Landseer hung on one wall. The living-room was slightly better. A coal fire, slumbering in the grate behind its guard, was soon prodded into life, adding warmth and colour to the drab little room. The place, however, was clean and tidy, smelling of nothing worse than liver and onions which, presumably, had been Arthur's dinner. When he had lit the gas in this room also, Margaret sat down in a chair near the fire and once more eased her feet out of their shoes. Bending forward, she began massaging her cramped toes.

She had enjoyed her evening. She liked Buster Keaton, and she had liked sitting in the musty darkness, sharing a box of chocolates which Arthur had bought for her at Fortnum and Mason's in Piccadilly. He had not put his arm around her, nor even held her hand, although his knee had brushed hers once or twice, whether by accident or design she could not tell. It had made her feel young again; a girl out on her first date, instead of a mature woman with grown-up children. She had felt exhilarated, daring, and when Arthur had said: 'Come back and have supper at my flat,' she had accepted without a moment's hesitation.

The bus ride out to Hackney through the bustling, brightly lit Saturday night streets had kept her from thinking too seriously of what she was doing; of the possible implications of that acceptance. It was only now, with the closing of Arthur's front door and the quiet of the room settling all around them, that Margaret had time to examine her motives for coming, or question Arthur's for asking her in the first place.

She stretched out her hands to the flames. The May night had turned cold after the unexpected warmth of the day. Arthur filled a kettle from the tap in the tiny kitchen and set it on the hob to boil.

'I've only a single gas-ring,' he explained, 'so I keep the fire going at week-ends. It's a bit wasteful on coal, but it helps with the cooking.'

'When did your mother die?' Margaret asked after a little silence.

'Three years ago.' He busied himself inexpertly, like a man

who for most of his life had left domestic matters to the women, setting out cups and saucers, the milk jug and teapot. 'So, when I was sacked, there was nothing to keep me in Somerset. I was offered this post, and I came.'

'A full-time trades unionist?' She had no idea why she spoke so scornfully, except that receiving a wage for the job somehow diminished his integrity in her eyes. Idealism, surely, was not a thing for which one should be paid?

He did not take offence. He sat on the floor beside her chair, warming his feet against the fender. The kettle started to sing.

'Why not? Someone has to organize things for the ignorant masses, and you can't live on air while you're doing it. Six centuries ago, before the Peasants' Revolt, John Ball and Jack Straw relied on people's charity to feed them. The modern equivalent is to ask our fellow workers to support us with their union dues.' Steam began issuing from the spout of the kettle and he got up to warm the pot and spoon in tea from the battered tin caddy. As he poured the boiling water on to the leaves he went on: 'I was in Glasgow five years ago when the strikers and unemployed demonstrated in George Square. January 1919. I was still working at Longreach then, but I said I was sick and went. Robert Smillie – he was President of the Miners' Federation – was asking for a six-hour day, wage increases and nationalization of the mines.' Arthur paused in the act of pouring out the tea, staring back into the past at that exciting and turbulent time. 'The government sent sixty tanks and a hundred army lorries north by rail. The red flag was raised in the middle of George Square. A tram was overturned. . . . There was a deputation to the Lord Provost, headed by Manny Shinwell, David Kirkwood and Bill Gallacher. The police made a baton charge while they were inside, and Kirkwood ran out to see what was happening and got bludgeoned by a truncheon. It was touch and go then, I can tell you. . . . What's the matter? Are you ill? You're shaking.'

He set the teapot down hurriedly and bent over her chair, taking her cold hands in his and rubbing her wrists. He was horrified to see tears glistening on her cheeks.

'I-I'm sorry,' Margaret stammered. 'I'm being silly. But

324

what you were describing just then . . . it reminded me. It took me back. I was in Petrograd, you see, during the Bolshevik revolution.'

'I didn't know.' His eyes blazed with enthusiasm. 'My God! It must have been wonderful to see it all happen.'

She tore her hands free, struggling to her feet and groping on the floor for her handbag. She stood upright, clutching it defensively against her.

'No, it wasn't!' she shouted at him. 'It wasn't wonderful! It was like all violence, nasty, sordid and brutal!' She saw once more in her mind's eye Anna in her nightgown, struggling in Sergei's grip, terrified and screaming. She saw Nickolai Brodkin raise his revolver. 'You don't know! You don't know what mindless slaughter is. You weren't even at the front during the war.'

She thought he was going to strike her, and tensed unconsciously to receive the blow. But instead Arthur seized her by the shoulders, his fingers biting into her flesh as though they were made of steel.

'*I* don't know what mindless violence is?' he shouted, as angry as she was herself. '*I* don't know, when I've worked down a coalmine since the age of twelve? You stupid bitch! I've seen men die slowly, coughing up their lungs. I've seen them and their families starve to death because of the pittance that the owners paid them. My own father choked to death in slime and mud when the cage pulleys broke because your late husband was saving a few pence for the rich Mr Devereaux to get even richer. My brother was killed – murdered! – because the pit-props weren't renewed when they should have been. And you have the gall to accuse me of not knowing about mindless violence! Miners have been killed, maimed and exploited all down the centuries, and not for any ideal or far-flung hope, but for plain, old-fashioned greed!'

They stared at one another, locked in bitter hatred, vaguely aware that someone was banging on the wall from the neighbouring flat. A man's voice called peevishly: 'Shut up in there! I'm trying to get some sleep!'

Margaret was still trembling. She felt curiously light-headed and distanced from herself. In a detached way she realized that the need to do violence was the one emotion most difficult of all to control. It was only by aggression that the species survived. . . .

Arthur's face relaxed suddenly, crumpling up as if he were going to cry. His arms went round her, folding her to his breast, and she clung to him, her cheek pressed against the smooth cloth of his waistcoat, as much in need of human warmth and contact as he. It was nearly two years since a man had shown that he wanted her. What she felt had nothing to do with love or the instinct to procreate. She just needed, for a little while, to be a woman.

They left the tea cooling on the table, forgotten and untasted, and went through to the bedroom with its narrow, squeaky-springed single bed. They undressed like two automatons, not kissing or touching one another again until they lay face to face on the hard, lumpy mattress, the bedclothes pulled decorously up to their chins. For a fleeting second, Margaret wondered what she was doing there, and had to ward off an unbearably vivid memory of Paul. Then Arthur Barlow's arms closed round her and his mouth was groping hungrily at her breast.

Twenty-Nine

'I suppose you realize he's in love with you,' Hilda said. 'You can't just let it go on.'

Margaret dropped the basket of groceries on the kitchen table and looked at her friend, who was standing at the stove with her back towards her. As they left work at the same time each evening, the arrangement was that one should go straight home and prepare the meal while the other did the shopping. This week it was Hilda's turn to do the cooking, which made her peevish, and consequently she took out her annoyance on her friend.

'I assume we're talking about Arthur Barlow,' Margaret said quietly, curbing her temper. 'I've told you, we simply like one another.'

'You "simply like one another"? Is that why you go to bed together?' Hilda gave an affected, incredulous laugh.

'Yes. It's not unknown.' Margaret began putting away the groceries in the rather musty-smelling cupboards.

'Perhaps not. But highly immoral, I should think.'

'For God's sake, Hilda!' Margaret spun round, hands on hips. 'You don't have to be in love with someone before you can go to bed with him! And do we have to go through this ritual of charge and counter-charge every time it's your turn to do the cooking?'

'Is that what you think it is?'

'Why else this concern for Arthur? Look out! The potatoes are boiling over!'

With a curse, Hilda pulled the saucepan clear of the spitting gas-ring and turned her attention back to the two pork chops she was frying. The pungent aroma of burnt fat filled the tiny kitchen.

'I happen to be very fond of Arthur,' she said. 'He's a nice bloke. Too nice to be used as a substitute by you.'

Margaret propped herself against the kitchen table and thoughtfully regarded her friend's back. It was not the first time she had suspected that Hilda, in spite of repeated protestations that she had finished with men, was fond of Arthur Barlow.

During the six months since their affair began he had often visited Margaret at the flat in Borough High Street, and on several occasions had taken both women to a cinema or a theatre. He got on well with Hilda. They shared the same broad, eminently British sense of humour, the same passion for strong tea and fish and chips, and had native indifference to the presentation of food. Arthur, thought Margaret, watching Hilda slap the two burnt chops on to plates and flank them with dollops of mashed potato and over-boiled cabbage, would have found nothing unappetizing in the sight.

'As long as it tastes all right,' he had said to her once, 'why worry? Why waste your time on the way it looks?'

Yes, they had a lot in common, Hilda and Arthur Barlow, including a fanatical devotion to the Labour Party. Margaret found herself drawn more and more towards its hopes and ideals, but her innate Americanism held her aloof from total commitment. She and Arthur had frequent arguments and, on occasions, rows, during which Hilda, if she were present, always sided with Arthur. Yet he continued to treat her as he would another man; with a camaraderie which was almost insulting.

Margaret took off her coat and hung it on a peg behind the kitchen door, then went to her bedroom to wash her hands. The bathroom was along the landing, and communal. By the time she returned to the living-room the meal was on the table, but Hilda, ignoring hers, was deep in the evening paper. Margaret groaned inwardly. The second general election of 1924 was to be held in less than a week, on 29 October. Britain's first Labour government had lasted just ten months. Whether it would be returned for a second term of office was doubtful.

'It's all Ramsay Mac's fault!' Hilda exclaimed, throwing

down the paper in disgust. 'He should never have let himself be stampeded into that vote of confidence.'

'It was a vote of censure by the Opposition,' Margaret corrected her, dubiously eyeing her chop. 'But I agree MacDonald hasn't acted with the coolness that a Prime Minister should, because, quite simply, he hasn't the experience. Neither has his Cabinet. However, that's nothing to be ashamed of in the circumstances. The Party has to learn to walk before it can run.'

Hilda attacked her meal. 'He shouldn't have let himself be linked with the Communists,' she grunted through a mouthful of meat and mashed potato.

The previous month, the Attorney General Sir Patrick Hastings had withdrawn a prosecution against J. R. Campbell, acting editor of the Communist *Workers' Weekly*, and played right into the Opposition's hands. The resulting vote of censure had been carried by three hundred and sixty-four votes to one hundred and ninety-eight. Ramsay MacDonald had had no choice but to go to the country.

During the run-up to the election, the Conservative press had tried its best to equate the Labour Party with Communism. Leader writers warned parents of 'plausible men and women who invite children to join clubs or attend Sunday schools where they are taught to blow up bridges . . .'. Red-spy mania reached hysterical proportions. A Labour government, it was said, was simply a puppet government for the Russians.

There was a ring at the doorbell and, a moment later, Arthur Barlow walked in. He tossed a folded newspaper on to the table.

'Has either of you seen today's *Daily Mail*?' He slumped into an empty chair and poured himself a cup of tea.

Margaret reached for the newspaper and spread it out. Hilda got up and read it over her shoulder. The front page was devoted to a copy of a letter purporting to come from the Third International, and signed 'Zinoviev'. It was directed to the British Communist Party, inciting its members to insurrection. The Foreign Office had apparently protested to the Soviet government, whose *chargé d'affaires* had promptly denied all knowledge of the letter. No one, of course, believed him.

'That's it,' Arthur said dully. 'We might as well not vote. We've lost the election.'

'The bastards!' Hilda fumed. 'The bloody bastards! Of course, it's a forgery. It's too bloody opportune to be anything else.'

'But it's addressed to the Communist Party leaders,' Margaret pointed out. 'Why should that stop people voting for Labour?'

'Oh, for Christ's sake, Maggie!' Arthur said irritably. 'You know how the Tory press has linked the two parties in people's minds. Hilda's right. It must be a forgery. Their other slimy tactics weren't having as big an effect on the voters as they'd hoped, so Baldwin and company have concocted this nasty little intrigue. God! I'd like to break their bloody necks!'

'And I'd like to help you,' Hilda agreed viciously, pushing away her food.

'We don't know it's not genuine,' Margaret pointed out, but their anger was contagious. She found herself spoiling for some action. She recalled seeing that their local Conservative candidate was speaking that evening at the nearby Baptist chapel hall. When she mentioned the fact, Arthur grinned and told them to get their coats.

'Come on,' he said. 'Let's go and do some heckling.'

The room was brightly lit but cold, as no one had bothered to switch on the heating. A table and chairs had been set on the platform at the far end of the hall for the visiting dignitaries, and two blue rosettes had been fixed to the patched and faded stage curtains. The rows of hard wooden chairs in the body of the hall were fast filling up. Pinned around the walls were various idealized and garishly coloured unframed prints depicting scenes from the life of Jesus. The room, Margaret reflected, was probably used as a Sunday school.

They found seats about three rows from the front, but Margaret was already beginning to wish that she had not come. As they entered, she had noticed a couple of big louts seated at the back, sniggering and whispering to each other and obviously bent on trouble. She guessed that they had no political affiliations. They were agitators, and looked on it as some kind of game.

At half past nine the Conservative candidate appeared, followed by his agent, two or three big-wigs from the local Tory party and a guest speaker who, it was explained, had kindly given up precious time from campaigning in his own constituency to lend some much-needed moral support in Southwark.

'You all know him,' the chairman asserted confidently, beaming out across the sea of faces. 'A coming man, tipped for ministerial rank if the Conservatives are returned to power. Mr Paul Devereaux, the Right Honourable Member for Hawksworth and Clarendon in the last two Parliaments.'

Margaret's heart lurched sickeningly as her eyes, along with everyone else's, swivelled to focus on the immaculate figure sitting quietly at the end of the row of speakers. She had not noticed him come in: her attention had been fixed on the others. She was sure, from his composure, that he had not seen either her or her companions. Indeed, he showed no nerves of any kind, acknowledging with a slight inclination of the head the scattered applause which greeted his introduction. She glanced sideways to see how Arthur was taking this unexpected encounter. Their eyes met. His were glittering with a feverish excitement.

The local candidate proceeded to give his address. There was a certain amount of heckling from the crowd, but most of it good-natured. Even the louts at the back of the hall emitted no more than the occasional hiss or boo.

Then it was Paul's turn to speak, the chairman having promised that time would be allotted at the end of the meeting for questions. He took his place at the centre of the table, one hand resting lightly on it, the other thrust into his trouser pocket, his gaze roaming the packed, and mainly friendly, hall. His reputation was good among the general electorate. What rumours there were about the scandal in his past life either endeared him to the voters as one of themselves, or recommended him to the moralists as an example of a man who had put his house in order and temptation behind him. But the vast majority of the public knew nothing about it.

He cleared his throat and began by thanking the chairman for his kind remarks, going on to say how pleased he was to be

in Southwark this evening in support of his good friend. . . .
He got no further. Arthur was already on his feet.

'What's all this crap in the *Daily Mail*?' he demanded
belligerently. Margaret noticed that he had not jumped up in
his usual impetuous fashion but risen slowly, like a snake
uncoiling from its lair.

The effect on Paul was much the same as if he had indeed
seen a snake. He recognized Arthur's voice almost at once and
turned to locate him. The smooth words of praise which he
had been about to utter faltered and died.

'What?' His voice cracked, but he quickly recovered himself. 'Will the gentleman kindly explain what he is talking
about?'

'I'm talking about this forgery your party has concocted in
order to try and prevent Labour winning the election. This
crap here!' And Arthur held up his copy of the newspaper,
stabbing at the headlines with an accusing finger.

'That is a very serious charge you are making, and I
should advise you to sit down and be quiet,' Paul answered
tautly, 'before you say something you might regret. Ladies
and gentlemen, as I was saying—'

'It's a forgery,' Arthur repeated, raising his voice to drown
Paul's. 'And you know it! I only have to look at your face!'

'Shut up!' yelled a woman's voice from the back of the hall.
'Let Mr Devereaux speak. He's a gen'lman which is more'n
can be said fer you!'

Someone else cheered, and Arthur turned about to face the
body of the hall.

'Anyone here who votes Conservative, or even thinks of
voting Conservative, should be ashamed! There is nothing
more pathetic than a working-class Tory!' His scorn poured
over them in waves.

Margaret tugged gently at his sleeve. 'Sit down, Arthur.
You're doing no good.' She saw movements out of the corner
of her eye, and whispered: 'Here come the stewards. They're
going to evict you.'

The wonder was that she made herself heard. Arthur was
now engaged in a slanging match with a man five seats away.
All over the hall people were on their feet either supporting or
condemning him. But as two of the stewards pushed their way

along the row, one from each end, Arthur swung round and punched the nearer one on the jaw. The man reeled backwards, falling across the knees of the other occupants of the row, one of his flailing arms catching the person in front a stinging blow on the back of the head.

Immediately there was pandemonium. The louts from the back of the hall rushed into the thick of the mêlée, fists and boots flying. Arthur was struggling in the grip of the other steward while Margaret and Hilda, both standing up by now, attempted to calm him down. Several chairs were thrown, one aimed deliberately at the platform, and Margaret saw Paul duck to avoid it. Their eyes met briefly, then both looked hurriedly away again. Everywhere there were split lips and bloody noses, and one man was nursing a broken arm, screaming with pain.

The shrill blast of police whistles began to bring people to their senses, and by the time the blue uniforms streamed in through the doors some of the more circumspect members of the audience were already making their way out of the building through the vestries which linked the hall and the chapel.

Margaret and Hilda vainly tried to persuade Arthur to do the same, but instead they only just prevented him from assaulting a policeman. A burly sergeant had now arrived on the scene and was directing operations.

On his orders, the police started making the first arrests.

It was unnerving to be standing in the Hill Street drawing-room again, so familiar and yet so strange. Margaret realized, a little sadly, how very many years it was since she had been there. All her latter years with Paul had been spent in Cornwall.

Through the nostalgia she felt a stab of anger, scarcely acknowledged, barely defined. She was not, however, here to quarrel with Paul, but to thank him. She supposed, with the election campaign in its last few days, she was lucky to find him still here. The butler, new since her time, had informed her that Mr Devereaux could only spare her a moment or two. He was leaving almost at once for Wiltshire.

Margaret glanced around the room. Sargent's portrait of Beatrice, which had once graced the music-room at Latchetts, now hung over the Adam fireplace, its subject gazing serenely out of the canvas with that clear, innocent-eyed expression Margaret remembered so well. For a moment it felt as though Beatrice was in the room with her, instead of having been dead for more than seventeen years. For Daniel, Margaret was sure, she still lived on in all her beauty and serenity and warmth. Margaret had read 'White Flower' and her brother-in-law's other poems about his love for Beatrice. She had been thankful that their meaning would not be intelligible to anyone but her.

The door opened and Paul came in. He seemed much older than he had two years ago. There were deep lines running from mouth to nostrils, and a network of fine wrinkles around his eyes. The eyes themselves were red-rimmed, as though he had slept badly, and his hair was now almost uniformly grey. He was fifty, but had always looked younger than his age. Now, all at once, the years had caught up with him.

Margaret rose awkwardly, gripping her handbag. She had dressed with care for this interview in a pale champagne-coloured coat and skirt, with a matching wide-brimmed hat and a green crêpe de Chine blouse which matched the colour of her eyes.

'I've come to thank you,' she said, 'for bailing me out. And for paying Mrs Zhirova's bail as well. Although Hilda doesn't like being called by that name any more. She's reverted to her maiden name, Lewisham.' She was talking for talking's sake to hide her nervousness. Why in heaven's name didn't he say something? Make some sign that he had at least heard her, instead of just standing there like a graven image? 'It was very kind of you, in the circumstances. All the circumstances,' she finished lamely.

There was a silence, which seemed to last for hours. In fact, Margaret supposed, it was only a second or two before Paul cleared his throat – a nervous trick she had heard for the first time the previous evening – and moved into the centre of the room.

'I left a signed statement with the police,' he said coldly, 'confirming that you and Mrs Zhirova had tried to restrain the man Barlow from making a scene. I think it should clear both your names.' He turned away again. 'And now, if you'll excuse me, I am extremely pressed for time. . . . I trust that what has occurred will not affect your present employment?'

'No. Not at all. Mr Bloomfield has been most understanding.' She watched him cross to the door and open it, politely waiting to show her out. She could not let him go like this; not with just these stupid, stiffly formal phrases.

'How . . . how are the children?' she asked wistfully. 'And Natasha? I saw pictures of India and Mareth and their husbands in the *Tatler* the other day.'

Paul hesitated, and for a moment, Margaret thought he was going to insist on her leaving. But he closed the door and came back into the room.

'They are all well. Growing up, of course. Antonia's fifteen. Quite the young lady.'

'Yes . . . yes, I know. She enclosed a photograph when she wrote and thanked me for her birthday present. Henry writes regularly. He seems to be doing very well at school.'

'Yes. He's a bright boy. . . .' The conversation petered out; but while Margaret was desperately trying to find something to say which would both sound natural and prolong the moment, Paul suddenly remarked: 'You should wear those earrings Beatrice and I gave you with that blouse. The silver filigree ones with the emerald-green brilliants. Do you still have them? They were our present to you your first Christmas at Latchetts.'

'My first Christmas in England. Yes, I still have them.' She gave a little laugh. 'As a matter of fact, they're in my handbag now. I put them on this morning, and then took them off again just before I got here and put the sleepers in.' Self-consciously, she touched the little gold hoops in her ears.

'Why did you leave?' he asked abruptly. 'Why did you desert me?'

She sighed. 'Must we go into all that again? Because Francis would have ruined you politically. Can't you understand that, even now? Do you still believe that he wouldn't have done it?'

. Paul looked stubborn. 'He's too fond of me,' he objected.

'But not fond enough not to hurt you in order to get at me! How can you persist in being so blind?'

'It's you who are blind,' he retorted angrily. 'You played

straight into his hands without even calling his bluff.'

'By the time I'd called his bluff, it would have been too late. You wouldn't have been the Member for Hawksworth and Clarendon these past two years.'

They stared at one another, aware of deadlock.

Margaret said: 'I must go. Mr Bloomfield's very generously given me the morning off, but I've promised to be in by noon.'

'I'll drive you. I can catch the later train.'

Taken aback, she stammered: 'I . . . I . . . thank you, but I'm going home first. Hilda and I are going into work together.'

'I'll take you home then,' he answered. 'Wherever that is.'

She heard herself say: 'Borough High Street, Southwark,' without stopping to think. She was a fool, she told herself in annoyance. She had come to London expressly to avoid Paul, yet here she was, seeking him out at the first opportunity, when a polite letter of thanks would have done just as well; allowing herself to be driven home; agreeing to be shut up with him in the intimacy of a motor car.

The Morris Oxford coupé was new and smelled of leather. Margaret sat stiffly beside Paul, her hands folded on top of her handbag, saying nothing as they made their way along Piccadilly, around Trafalgar Square and into the Strand. But as they negotiated Waterloo Bridge he asked suddenly: 'Why did you remove those earrings before you arrived this morning? Were you afraid that I'd ask for them back?'

She did not pause to reflect that he might be trying to goad her into a reaction; that he might still feel bitter enough to want to inflict some sort of hurt; or, more simply, that the embarrassed silence was getting on his nerves as much as it was getting on hers, so he had said the first words which came into his head. She only knew that all the tensions of the past fourteen hours – the riot, the police station, being charged, the humiliation of the prison cell and, finally, the deep longing for him which the sight of him had provoked – merged suddenly together in an explosion of anger.

'Here!' she exclaimed. She opened her handbag and found the earrings, dropping them disdainfully on the floor of the car. 'Have them back! And stop this automobile at once and let me out. I'll walk the rest of the way.'

'Don't be a fool,' he snapped back. 'Don't be so bloody childish!' They sped along Stamford Street and crossed Black-friars Road. 'I didn't mean it the way it sounded.'

'Why did you say it then? You didn't buy me, you know, for all those years. I wasn't your mistress for what I could get out of it. You can't say anything you like to me just because you've bailed me out of prison.' She *was* being childish: she knew it, but could not stop herself. If she did not keep up this tirade she would burst into tears, and in her present mood that would be a worse humiliation than any she had yet suffered. 'Please stop this car at once. I insist. I want to get out. I won't stay another minute to be insulted.'

His anger now matched her own. He put on the brakes and jerked to a halt in Southwark Street. She jumped out of the coupé and began to run. She heard him call: 'Margaret!' but took no notice. Through a haze of tears, she blundered across Southwark Bridge Road, aware of people turning to look at her, but uncaring. Five minutes later she slammed shut the door of the flat above the hardware shop and stormed into the living-room. Arthur Barlow was there with Hilda. Someone, she supposed vaguely, must have put up his bail, but she was too miserable and too busy sustaining her anger against Paul to enquire who it was. She tossed her hat and handbag on to the table.

'For God's sake, where have you been, Maggie?' Hilda demanded. 'We've promised to be at work in an hour. Mr Bloomfield's not going to like it if we're late on top of every-thing else.'

'I went to see Paul Devereaux, to thank him,' Margaret said, the tears finally spilling unchecked down her face. 'But it's the last time I go near that man! I swear it! I never want to see him again as long as I live!'

Thirty

'You did it, didn't you?' Margaret held out the newspaper to Arthur Barlow and indicated two others tucked under her arm. 'You gave that story to the press!'

Arthur had been anticipating her anger ever since she had telephoned him that morning at Transport House and insisted that he met her in Lincoln's Inn Fields during his lunch hour. To begin with he had considered denying her accusation, but in a way he was proud of what he had done. He saw no need to lie.

'Yes, I did it, and why not? At least it's the truth, not a damnable hoax. And even so it doesn't get much space. Not as much as the Zinoviev letter. Every Tory rag in the country is leading on that.'

'There is also enough about Paul and me in every morning newspaper to damage his chances of re-election.' She thrust the other papers at him. ' "Tory MP bails ex-mistress out of prison." "Ex-mistress of Conservative MP causes riot at lover's election meeting." And of course, they've dug out the bits about the children. Antonia and Henry get more than their fair share of attention.'

'I'm sorry about that,' Arthur said contritely. 'I had no intention of dragging their names through the mud.'

'You admit it's mud, then?' Margaret was trembling so much that the newspaper was shaking in her hand.

'Look!' Arthur tried to put his arm around her but she hit it away. With a shrug of resignation, he continued: 'You hate Paul Devereaux. You said so yesterday morning when you returned from Hill Street. It seemed to me like a good chance to hit back at the Tories in general, and him in particular. I honestly didn't think they'd mention the children. And after all, it hasn't done *you* any harm.'

'Oh, hasn't it?' Margaret's expression was venomous, her eyes like bits of green glass. 'I've just been dismissed, that's all. Mr Bloomfield was prepared to overlook the fact that I had been arrested for causing a breach of the peace because very few people knew about it. But now, thanks to you, it's in all the newspapers as headline news. When Hilda and I left home this morning there were three reporters lying in wait for me. And two more have called at the office during the past three hours. Mr Bloomfield was sorry, but his firm, understandably, won't tolerate that sort of publicity. So I've been fired. I've been given two weeks' wages in lieu of notice.'

'Hell!' Arthur followed her as she began walking away, catching her up and grabbing hold of her arm. 'Maggie! You have to believe me. I didn't imagine for a moment that anything like that would happen.'

'No, of course you didn't!' She rounded on him, her face contorted with rage. 'All you thought about was your rotten politics! People don't matter to you, do they, Arthur? You just manipulate them for your own ends.' She wrenched her arm free and continued walking, breaking every now and then into a run. But he kept pace with her, slipping in front of her and blocking her way.

'Maggie, look! I haven't much time now, but I'll come round and see you tonight at the flat. And don't worry. I'll soon fix you up with another job.'

'I don't want anything from you ever again, Arthur. We're finished. Hugh and Paul Devereaux were right about you. You're nothing but trouble.'

'Don't say that. You'll have cooled down by tonight. You'll feel differently. Expect me about half past eight.'

She pushed past him. 'Don't bother. I shan't let you in.'

She walked on quickly, shivering in spite of the warmth of the October day. She found a seat on the Embankment and sat there, staring out over the river which had brought London its trade for more than a thousand years.

When she had got up that morning it had appeared to be a day like any other, except for the memory of her quarrel with Paul lying like a bruise on her spirits. Now that her anger had evaporated, the tiff seemed wanton and pointless, as though she had been purposely trying to erect a barrier between them. She had attempted to work herself up again, telling herself that Paul's remark had been unnecessarily offensive; and so, in a way, it had. But it was probable that he too had been trying to protect himself against a love which had brought neither of them much tranquillity and more than their fair share of grief. She would write to him, she thought, and apologize. Then Hilda had burst into her bedroom without knocking, waving the morning paper.

Margaret had not needed to read beyond the headlines – the print only a little smaller, a little less black, than those dealing with the Zinoviev letter – to realize that she would never now write that letter to Paul. He would never believe that this was not her retaliation for the thoughtless, snide little remark he had made. And yet, at the same moment, she was saying to Hilda: 'I must telephone him at Hawksworth. I must get in touch with Paul somehow. He must be made to understand that I had nothing to do with this.'

'It's Arthur's doing, of course,' Hilda had said deliberately, watching the idea sink into Margaret's mind and take root. She had seen her chance and taken it. Well, good luck to her, thought Margaret. She was more than welcome to Arthur Barlow.

She had roused the occupants of the second-floor flat and asked to use their telephone, pleading the sudden illness of a relative. After interminable delays, she had at last got through to Hawksworth House, guessing that Paul would stay with the Duke whenever he was in his constituency. In a trembling voice, she had given her name and asked to speak to Mr Devereaux. Within a few minutes, the disembodied voice at the other end of the line had informed her that Mr Devereaux did not wish to speak to her, and requested that she would not bother him in future. Mr Devereaux, the voice added, felt that there was nothing they could usefully say to one another.

The sun had clouded over, but Margaret still sat on, looking out sightlessly across the river to the crowded, bustling quays on the Southwark side. It was not until a few drops of rain began to fall that she suddenly realized she was chilled and had had nothing to eat since breakfast-time. She got up reluctantly, feeling weak, as if she had been suffering from some illness, and walked home across Blackfriars Bridge. She needed food inside her, and then she must decide what to do next.

In the event, however, the decision was taken out of her hands. A telegram awaited her at the flat. It said simply: 'Daniel gravely ill. Come at once. Jess.'

Margaret put an arm about her sister's waist and murmured: 'Come away, Jess. There's nothing more you can do here, my dear.'

The doctor glanced up from the other side of the bed. 'Mrs Stafford's right, Mrs Cooper,' he said. 'Go downstairs and let her make you a nice cup of tea. The nurse will do what's necessary here.' He turned to Mark. 'Perhaps you and Miss Stafford' – he nodded at Lilian – 'would also like to go now. You can come up and see your father again when the body has been laid out.'

Mark inclined his head. He and Lilian opened the bedroom door and went downstairs. Jessie remained where she was, looking at Daniel's face, gentle and peaceful, a half-smile on his lips, as though, she thought resentfully, he were welcoming death. Perhaps he was. Perhaps he was now with *her*. Jessie wondered if anyone else had understood his last word, no more than a faint breath, a mere whisper of sound from his almost paralysed vocal chords. Beatrice: she was certain that was what he had said.

She still felt dazed by the suddenness of Daniel's stroke. One moment he had been sitting at the breakfast table, talking quite normally about his plans for the day; the next he had collapsed, gasping for breath. At first she had merely thought he was choking on a crumb, or had swallowed his tea the wrong way. She had reprimanded him often enough for eating and reading at the same time, his neck twisted awkwardly to look at some book. But as soon as she had knelt beside him and seen his face she had cried out for Mark and Lilian, who were still upstairs dressing for work. Mark had gone immediately for Dr Heydock, while Lilian had remained with her aunt.

Margaret had arrived in the evening in response to her sister's telegram. When told that there was very little hope of

341

Daniel's recovery, she had been deeply shocked and upset; far more upset than Jessie herself appeared to be. Her brother-in-law had been the one stable influence in her life since her arrival in England. In some ways he had taken the place of her father, having many of the attributes of Herbert Dunham. Perhaps, Margaret reflected now, that was why he and Jess had not got along too well together. But for her he had always been a friend in need, even when he had not approved of her actions.

She persuaded the dry-eyed Jessie downstairs at last, and sat her in an armchair in the living-room.

'Close your eyes for five minutes, honey, and try to get some rest. You haven't slept a wink all night.'

'Neither have you. Why don't you sit down, and I'll make the tea? I'll cook some breakfast as well. I don't know about the rest of you, but I'm starving.' Jessie got up and moved towards the door. 'What about you two?' she queried, addressing Mark and Lilian. 'I assume neither of you is going to work today. What do they call it? Compassionate leave?'

Mark nodded his head, adding: 'We shall be going out later, though, to vote. You haven't forgotten that today is polling day?'

'For Pete's sake!' Margaret breathed wrathfully. 'Your father's only just died, and all you can think about is the election?'

Her nephew shrugged. 'It's our future, Aunt. Lilian's and mine. A lot depends on today's outcome as to what we do with the rest of our lives.'

Margaret turned away, following her sister into the kitchen. 'Jess, go and sit down, please. At least let me feel that I'm being useful.'

'I'd rather have something to do.' Jessie banged the frying-pan on to one of the gas-rings, and fetched bacon and eggs from the larder. 'Ask Mark and Lilian if they want fried bread.'

Margaret hesitated, then went back to the living-room where her daughter and nephew were in earnest conclave, sitting close together on the broad-backed sofa. They stopped whispering and looked up guiltily as she came in. Margaret was uneasily aware of a conspiracy, but felt too emotionally drained to ask any questions. Daniel's death, coming as the climax to all the other events of the past few days, had left her feeling that all she wanted to do was sleep. She knew how Timon must have felt when he renounced the world and crawled into his hole in the ground.

She relayed Jessie's message.

'And tomato and sausage, if Mother's up to it,' Mark said, and then smiled. 'Don't look so disapproving, Aunt Maggie. I was very fond of Dad. But to use one of the oldest clichés in the book, life goes on. I'm sorry, but I can't help being hungry.'

Regarding him intently for a moment, Margaret saw the shadows under his eyes, the lines of grief etched deeply about the young mouth, the way he held tightly to Lilian's hand, as if it were a lifeline.

'I'm sorry, too,' she said quietly. 'I didn't mean to imply . . . I had no right—' She broke off, struggling against the urge to break down and cry.

Lilian got up and went to her mother, kissing her with more affection than she had shown since she was a very small child. Margaret clung to her for a few seconds, sensing something valedictory in the embrace. Then, telling herself not to imagine things, she returned to the kitchen to help Jess.

The funeral service, held in the Methodist chapel, was very simple, and afterwards Daniel was buried in the local graveyard, under the elms. He and Jessie had known few people in the village, and apart from the minister and Dr Heydock there was only the family at the funeral breakfast. Later, after the two guests had departed, Mark and Lilian went out; so when they had cleared the table and done the washing-up Margaret and Jessie sat together by the fire, watching the shadows of the early November evening close around them. Margaret got up presently to close the curtains, and would have lit the gas lamps, but Jessie stopped her.

'Let's sit in the firelight,' she said.

Quiet descended on the room once more, as shadows flickered across the walls and drowned in the polished surfaces of the furniture. One of the red-nosed logs fell with a crash into the grate, where fragments sputtered for a while before turning into piles of feather grey ash. Margaret did what she had not done for very many years, and made pictures in the fire; gilded caverns, turreted palaces and molten rivers, all part of that childhood world of faery which she had half-forgotten.

Jess said suddenly: 'He loved Beatrice, you know. Daniel. He was in love with Beatrice. I suppose he always had been, since before I knew him.'

Startled, Margaret asked incautiously: 'How did you find out?' and could have cursed herself for a fool.

Her sister's head turned sharply. 'You knew— You've always known, haven't you? Why didn't you tell me?' Jessie's voice accused her out of the gloom.

'There was no reason to tell you. What good would it have done you to know?'

Jessie repeated Margaret's own question. 'How did you find out? Did Daniel tell you?'

'Yes. A long time ago. He discovered that I was in love with Paul. He thought it might help me to know that . . . that there was someone else in the same boat. But . . . he didn't think . . . I didn't think that you knew.'

'I didn't,' Jess retorted bitterly, 'until recently. I read that poem, "White Flower". That's how I found out.'

Margaret made no reply, recognizing that she constantly underestimated Jessie's powers of understanding. It was largely Jessie's own fault. One of her favourite sayings was: 'I may not have much intelligence, but I've plenty of common sense.' She took a perverse pleasure in blinding people to the truth.

'Did you mind?' Margaret asked after a while. 'Do you mind that Daniel loved Beatrice? Somehow . . . I shouldn't have thought—'

'That I'd care?' Jessie laughed shortly. 'No, I shouldn't have thought so, either. But I did. Strange, isn't it? I felt let down. Betrayed.'

'Were you in love with him, then?'

'Not in the way you were – are – in love with Paul Devereaux. . . . Incidentally, I had a letter from him this morning, saying how very sorry he was to learn of Daniel's death. He wrote very warmly and affectionately of Dan. Said he was proud to have known him. I thought it very kind, considering how he must be feeling.'

Margaret stirred restlessly. 'Our quarrel was equally recriminative. Paul didn't—'

'I meant,' Jessie interrupted impatiently, 'his losing his seat in Parliament. Didn't you know? Oh dear! I'm afraid it's true, though. Lilian told me. She said it was the one bright spot in the Conservative landslide. Apparently Paul Devereaux's constituency, whatever it is, elected a Liberal for the first time in its history. I suppose it was because of the scandal about you and him in the newspaper. Did you notice the minister looking at you today?' Jess could just make out Margaret's face in the glow of the firelight, and added, holding out her hand: 'I'm sorry. I thought you knew, or I wouldn't have sprung it on you like that. For goodness' sake, Maggie, if you still care for him as much as you seem to, go back to him. Here's your chance. He's out of Parliament now. The scandal can't hurt him any more.'

Margaret jumped to her feet and began walking about the room. She felt torn by conflicting emotions: unhappiness for Paul, fury with Arthur Barlow; and yet, at the same time, hope that with Paul out of Parliament for at least four years their life together might somehow be resumed. She remembered their last quarrel; the senseless anger, the stiff-necked pride on both sides; the quickness on her part to take offence; on his, the desire to hurt. If they could only put the past behind them, start afresh. . . . She had said that she never wanted to see Paul again, and Arthur had believed her. If he had known her better, as Hilda did, he would have understood that they were only words.

She went back to her chair and sat down. Jess reached out and took her hand again.

'Write to Paul Devereaux tonight,' she urged. 'Before you go to bed. Don't do what I did. Don't bottle everything up inside. Don't try to pretend to yourself that you don't feel the way you do. Or else, suddenly, you find that it's all too late.'

'Dear Jess.' Margaret leaned towards her sister and their arms went round one another. She could feel Jessie's tears warm on her cheek.

'For heaven's sake, let's have some light,' Jessie protested, freeing herself and searching in her jacket pocket for a box of matches. She got up and lifted the glass shades from the two brackets, one on either side of the mantelpiece, and lit the gas jets beneath. The room was gradually suffused with a warm, incandescent glow. Jess replaced the shades and sat down again.

The door opened.

'We thought you must have gone for a walk as well,' Mark said, entering the room, followed by Lilian. 'We couldn't see any lights.'

Their young faces looked ruddy and healthy, nipped by the cold, above their sombre funeral clothes. They took off their coats and sat down by the fire, holding out hands and feet to the blaze.

'Have you been far?' asked Jessie, glancing affectionately at her son.

But it was Lilian who answered, and Margaret reflected that she and Mark were almost interchangeable personalities, thinking and speaking as one.

'We walked to Mells. There was a light in the church, so we went in. No one was there. I'd never been inside before. Never wanted to. Mark showed me the tombs of Little Jack Horner and his descendants.' There was silence for a moment or two, then Lilian continued: 'Mark and I have been talking. We're going to be married. We're both over twenty-one now. There's nothing to stop us.'

Margaret met her sister's apprehensive glance and said quickly: 'No one wants to stop you. Certainly not Aunt Jessie or myself. I don't suppose we could, even if we tried. But don't you think it's a bit soon after Uncle Dan's death to be discussing wedding plans?' Her voice was not quite steady. She remembered the strange premonition she had had, the other day, when Lilian had kissed her. She was plagued now by the same sense of unease.

'Oh, we don't want a church wedding,' Mark explained hastily. 'It'll be Bath Register Office for us, and a couple of witnesses. And we want to get married as soon as possible, before we go to Russia.'

There was a protracted silence, during which the only sound was the crackling of the logs in the grate. After what seemed an age, Jessie asked: 'What do you mean? Go to Russia?'

Lilian leaned back in her chair, her hands pushed deep in her cardigan pockets. She was quite unconcerned that Mark had just dropped a bombshell.

'We've been talking about it for ages,' she said. 'And this Conservative landslide, after only ten months of Labour government, has convinced us that there's nothing here for us any longer. We want to go somewhere where we can see the benefits of a socialist state first-hand. We want to feel a part of the revolution.'

'But . . . but how long are you going for?' demanded Jessie.

'We don't know,' Mark answered. 'As long as they'll let us stay. We may never come back. I'm sorry, Mother, but it's better to be honest.'

'You may call it honesty!' Margaret exclaimed furiously. 'I call it arrant insensibility! Your father was only buried this morning, and here you are, glibly talking about running off and leaving your mother.'

Lilian spoke, always quick in Mark's defence. 'If we're to talk about running away from our responsibilities, Mother, I don't think you have a leg to stand on.'

Jessie held up her hand. 'Please. No quarrelling. I can't put up with it. Not tonight. And Mark's right, Maggie. It's better I should know the worst than fill up my head with false hopes.' She drew a deep breath and looked again at her son. 'When are you planning to get married? More important, when are you leaving England?'

'Mark's getting a special licence, so we thought the wedding could be some time next week,' Lilian said. 'We shan't give notice at work until we get the final go-ahead from the Russian government. Until then, we intend to go on living here. I can move my stuff into Mark's room.'

'It won't be what you think,' Margaret remarked suddenly. 'Russia, I mean. I was there. I saw what happened. All the old abuses which the revolutionaries had fought against for so long were embodied in their own régime; the beatings, the knoutings, the summary executions, the secret police. Nothing changed. And with Lenin dead and Josef Stalin in power, I imagine it never will. Lenin never trusted Stalin, and, from all I've read, grew to dislike him as well. It isn't going to be at all what you imagine.'

'We'll risk that,' Lilian told her briskly. 'There are bound to be teething problems after any great social upheaval. It's impossible to drag a country straight from the Middle Ages into the twentieth century without resorting to one or two of the old methods at first. At present, it's the only kind of government the people understand. Change will have to come slowly. You must be prepared to give the Bolsheviks time.'

'As they gave Anna?'

'I'm not going to argue with you, Mother.' Lilian spoke as though to a recalcitrant child. 'Well, it's been a long day. I'm going to my room to read for a bit, then I'm going to bed. Mark, are you coming?'

Mark nodded and uncoiled himself from the sofa where he had been sitting. 'I'll read in your room for a while, if I may,' he said. 'Then I might have a bath before I turn in. Good night, Mother. Good night, Aunt Maggie. Don't worry about us. We shall be fine.'

'Selfish young brutes!' Margaret burst out as the door closed behind them. 'Of course they'll be fine. But what about you?'

Jessie heaved herself to her feet. 'I don't know,' she said. 'I can't think about it tonight. I know it's very early, Maggie, but would you mind very much if I went to bed as well? Too much is happening too fast. I need to think; to be on my own.' She bent and kissed Margaret's forehead. 'Stay up as long as you want, my dear, only remember to put the fireguard in place before you come upstairs. And remember, too, to write that letter to Paul Devereaux. That's more important than all the rest.'

Thirty-One

Natasha was always downstairs early, before the rest of the family were about. She liked the empty, echoing rooms, with only the servants for company. And now that her father had moved back to Latchetts after losing the Hawksworth and Clarendon seat, these early morning forays were more important to her than ever. She still would not permit herself to like him, although she acknowledged that it would be logical to do so, now that Margaret had earned her undying hatred.

This almost adult awareness of her own feelings – which made the latest in a procession of governesses complain that she was precociously forward for her age – was coupled with a total lack of understanding of other people's. It was as though she deliberately closed her mind against any motivations except her own. Since Margaret had left without saying good-bye, without even dropping a hint of what she intended to do, Natasha's love had turned to enmity. When she had tried to prevent Margaret from marrying her father – and succeeded beyond her wildest dreams – she had naïvely assumed that Margaret's future plans would include herself. Margaret belonged to her. She stood firmly at the centre of all Natasha's earliest memories. It had seemed impossible that Margaret should abandon her.

But the impossible had happened: Margaret had disappeared without a word, without a sign. And, when she had finally broken her silence, it was to Antonia and to Henry that she had written.

'Only to be expected, miss,' Nanny Watkins had remarked spitefully, just before she retired from Latchetts altogether to live with her widowed sister in Bournemouth. 'They're her real children. You're not even her step-daughter now.'

Natasha had shrugged, pretending not to care. 'It doesn't matter,' she had said. 'I hate her anyway. I wouldn't have her as a mother if you paid me.'

Margaret's desertion could have paved the way for a better understanding between Natasha and her father, but, three months later, in the general election of November 1922, Paul had been returned to Parliament; and from then until his recent defeat he had been at Latchetts for only short periods. With all restraining influence removed, Natasha had been allowed to run wild.

Governesses came and went with monotonous regularity, and both India and Mareth had advised their father to send Natasha to boarding-school as soon as possible. But both women were now mothers themselves, and had little time to spare for their young half-sister. George, in his final year at Eton, was only home during the school holidays, and then he usually went to stay at Bladud House to be near the Long-reach mine, where Ralph Stafford, like his father before him, was working in the management office.

George had carried his point with his father that he should not go to Oxford, but start at Longreach as early as possible. It had amused Paul that his son should think it necessary to 'learn the business' as he put it.

'That's what you pay a manager for,' he had pointed out, but George had been undeterred.

'And that's why so many coalmines are inefficient,' he had retorted, 'because the owners know nothing about them. I don't want to spend three years up at Oxford, polishing my social graces and making all the right friends. Even less do I want to become a country squire at Latchetts. I need to do something positive with my life.'

Paul had bowed to the inevitable, recognizing that it was as unwise to thwart Coleman Smith's grandson as it had been to cross the old man himself.

So for two years Latchetts had belonged almost exclusively to Antonia and Natasha, with the addition of Henry in the school holidays. The two girls had never been close, and were driven even further apart by Natasha's altered attitude towards Margaret. Antonia, quite as bewildered by her mother's sudden departure as her half-sister – particularly when the future had looked so bright – nevertheless defended Margaret against all criticism. She was now fifteen, with her mother's red hair and green eyes, and the promise of becoming equally beautiful. She was also very level-headed, unusually so for one of her colouring. All her life she had watched and listened, refusing to make hasty judgements; and with a maturity beyond her years she had decided that her mother would not have done what she did without very good reasons. She had also defended Margaret through the latest crisis, maintaining stoutly that her mother would never have given such information to the newspapers.

'She would never hurt Henry or me like that,' Antonia had said angrily to Natasha the previous evening. 'And Daddy knows it. He realizes perfectly well that it must have been somebody else, and I'm sure he has his suspicions who it is. He's just being bloody-minded, that's all. In a week or two, when he's stopped feeling sorry for himself and listening to Uncle Francis, he'll admit the truth. And Mummy's sure to write to him to explain what really happened.'

The two girls had been alone together in the drawing-room after dinner, Natasha having been allowed to stay up late for the meal as a special treat, to celebrate Paul's return to Latchetts. It had not needed that concession, however, to warn her that her father's return on this occasion had a permanence which his flying visits of the past two years had lacked. His constant presence would ensure an increase of discipline; and that too, she thought resentfully, could be laid at Margaret's door. As Margaret had chosen to go away, why could she not stop intruding on their lives?

Natasha glanced quickly around to see if she were being observed, then hitched one leg over the banister and slid the rest of the way to the hall. She crossed, as she did each morning, to the old Spanish chest in the corner, where the telephone stood, and where the first-post letters were laid out ready for distribution at the breakfast table.

She recognized Margaret's handwriting at once; a pale blue envelope, addressed to Paul. The letter of explanation, without doubt. Antonia had been right. Natasha's hand reached out almost instinctively to take and conceal it. As good a way of punishing Margaret as any.

'What are you doing?'

Antonia's voice made Natasha jump guiltily. She swung round to face her half-sister.

'Only looking to see if there are any letters for me. You're up early.'

It was Antonia's turn to look guilty. She was dressed in jodhpurs and hacking-jacket.

'I fancied a canter before breakfast, that's all,' she answered.

Natasha smiled. 'I bet you're going to meet Raymond Bastardo. Daddy said you weren't to see him as long as his parents objected.'

'Have you been spying on me? And Daddy said you weren't to use vulgar expressions like "I bet".' Antonia descended the last three stairs, switching her crop menacingly against her boots.

Natasha watched her half-sister carefully, but did not retreat. 'He'd be far angrier about your disobedience than mine. But I shan't say anything if you don't. I don't see why you should take any notice of a horrible stuffy old couple like Raymond's parents. They're a pair of toads.'

It was on the tip of Antonia's tongue to point out that Natasha had also been forbidden to use the expression 'toad' in connection with people, but she refrained. It was better to have Natasha as an ally than an enemy, now that she seemed to know all about the meeting with Raymond. She nodded curtly.

'Very well. But if you do say something—' She did not complete the sentence, but switched her crop again, suggestively.

'I shan't. Why don't Mr and Mrs Bastardo want you and Raymond to be friends?'

'Because Mummy and Daddy aren't married. Everything would have been all right if the wedding had gone ahead as planned.' Antonia glanced towards the letters on top of the chest. 'I suppose there isn't . . . ?'

'No, nothing,' Natasha answered quickly. 'Nothing for you, either. Only some bills and a letter for Daddy from Mareth.'

352

'Oh. I just wondered. Well, I must be going. See you at breakfast. Mind, not a word! If anyone asks, I've gone for a ride by myself.'

Natasha waited until the front door had closed behind her half-sister, then turned back to the letters. A moment later, the blue envelope was safely concealed in the pocket of her skirt.

'Well, that's that. They've gone.' Jessie pitched her hat and handbag on to the nearest chair and took off her coat. She cast a glance around the cottage living-room, with its Christmas tree and decorations. 'I feel like taking this lot down at once, not waiting until the day after tomorrow.'

'Then let's do it.' Margaret also divested herself of her outdoor clothing. 'It'll give us something to do. Keep us occupied. Keep us from brooding.' She began stripping the tree of its ornaments, then paused. 'Isn't it supposed to be unlucky to take down the decorations before Twelfth Night?'

Jessie shook her head. 'Only if you leave them up after, I think.' She laughed mirthlessly. 'Anyway, our luck can't get any worse, can it? Mark and Lilian gone, and God knows if we'll ever see them again. Daniel. . . . And Paul Devereaux never answered your letter.'

'No.' Margaret looked at the trailing pieces of tinsel in her hand as though they were some strange objects from another world. 'I wish Mark and Lilian had let us go with them to London.'

Jessie stood on a chair, reaching for the spray of desiccated holly festooning the mirror.

'What would have been the point? A few more hours, another night, wouldn't have made that much difference. It was better to say our farewells in Bath and get them over. The past couple of days have been bad enough, without prolonging the agony. It was nice to see Ralph at the station, though. Lilian must have let him know, I suppose.'

'No, it was me.' Margaret added three more frosted glass balls to the fast-growing heap on the table. 'I had no idea he was at Longreach until he came into Beechings the other day. I guess that's one piece of luck on the credit side; getting my old job back. Perhaps 1925 is going to be our year, after all.'

353

Jessie snorted. 'I shouldn't count on it. Ralph doesn't know anything, I suppose? He didn't give you any news about Paul?'

'No.' The monosyllable was flat and uncompromising, and Jessie wisely decided to say no more on the subject.

'Oh, let's leave this!' she exclaimed after another few moments. 'We can finish it in the morning. I'll get the card-board boxes from under the stairs and we can pack away what we've already taken down.'

Margaret followed her sister into the narrow hallway. 'I had a letter from Hilda this morning,' she said. 'She's going to apply for a divorce from Sergei after all. Apparently she's been seeing a lot of Arthur.'

'He's stopped pestering you, then?' Jessie went down on her knees and groped around on the floor of the stair-cupboard. 'I thought I hadn't seen any letters from him lately.'

'He sent me a Christmas card.' Margaret took the two cardboard boxes which her sister handed up to her. 'I think the last letter I wrote him, just before Christmas, must have done the trick. He must finally have realized that I meant what I said, at least where he was concerned. Hilda will be more than adequate consolation. They think alike about so many things.'

Jessie stood up, brushing the dust from her skirt. 'That's certainly a help, if she intends to marry him,' she commented drily. 'Not the usual, but desirable, none the less. If you'll start packing away the decorations, I'll make a cup of tea. I've been gasping for one ever since we came in.'

She bustled off to the kitchen, and Margaret was relieved to see her keeping busy. It gave Jessie less time to dwell on all she had lost. Daniel, Mark, Lilian; her whole family had suddenly vanished within a space of less than three months.

That evening, however, as they sat by the fire, both pretending to read, Jessie began to cry. Margaret jumped up and went to her.

'Oh God, Jessie, don't! Don't!' She put her arms around her sister and held her tightly. 'Mark and Lilian will come back, you'll see. They won't like Russia. It isn't how they imagine.'

Jessie fumbled for her handkerchief and blew her nose. 'It's all right for you,' she said. 'You have other children. And

Lilian's been more like my daughter than yours. I'm sorry, Maggie! I didn't mean to be unkind. It's just that I feel so down.'

'I know, I know. And it's no more than the truth. Lilian never really got over my living with Paul. You know, she and Mark have turned out far more like Papa than I ever was.'

Jessie sniffed. 'Yes. And from what Ralph was telling us today, young George Devereaux is another Coleman Smith. Perhaps family characteristics skip a generation.'

'Jess,' Margaret said, after a pause, 'I've been thinking. There's nothing to keep either of us here any more. Why don't we go home, to New York?'

Jessie stopped crying abruptly and turned to stare, open-mouthed, at her sister.

'What . . . ? What on earth are you saying?'

'Don't look so astonished. We *are* Americans, Jess. New York is our home.'

'But . . . but we don't know anybody there any more. Besides, what about Paul and your children?'

'Paul's silence has made it perfectly plain that he's no longer interested. I addressed the letter to Latchetts, but it's had plenty of time to catch up with him at Hill Street or Bladud House or even Hawksworth if he's there.'

'He might have gone abroad,' Jessie suggested feebly, her mind still reeling from the total unexpectedness of her sister's proposition.

'He hasn't. Hilda said in her letter that she saw him driving along Piccadilly just before Christmas. As for the children, none of them truly needs me. Ralph and Lilian haven't done so since they were babies. Tonia and Harry have twice proved that they can survive without me. Judging by their letters, they're both perfectly happy.'

'But what should we do in New York?' Jess wanted to know. 'What should we live on?'

'You can sell the cottage, and there are royalties from Dan's books, and the rest of the money that he left you. I have a bit of money saved. Enough to pay my fare.'

'And where should we live? Oh, I don't know, Maggie. It sounds a cock-eyed idea to me.'

'It sounds a bit one-sided, I'll grant you that, as you'd be doing most of the paying. But I'm sure I could get a job as a secretary. Thank God I learned shorthand and typing.'

Jessie shook her head. 'I don't know, Maggie. I just don't know. I've lived in England for twenty-five years. More than half my life. I feel English sometimes. Going home would be like starting all over again in another country.'

' "But that was in another country," ' Margaret quoted softly, ' "and, besides, the wench is dead." '

'What are you talking about?' Jessie was irritable. 'I suppose Daniel would have understood.'

'It's Marlowe,' Margaret admitted apologetically. '*The Jew of Malta*. And not an apt quotation at that. But, Jessie, a lot of things are dead – well, lost, at any rate – to us in *this* country. So many people who mattered to us have gone out of our lives. America is young, and it's ours!' Was she talking to convince herself or Jessie? She pressed on, without allowing herself to consider the question. 'We hardly know it any more. Isn't it time that we did?'

Jessie regarded her unhappily. 'I suppose so,' she conceded. 'But I'll have to sleep on the idea. You'll have to give me time.'

Margaret hugged her sister. 'That's fair enough,' she said. 'Let me know when – and what – you decide.'

Leaving the chauffeur to put away the coupé in its garage at the back of Great Pulteney Street, Paul was admitted to Bladud House not by his butler, as he had every right to expect, but by his elder son.

'Thank God you've come,' said George. 'According to Ralph, things are pretty serious.' He eyed his father's overnight bag with some misgivings. 'I hoped you'd come to stay.'

'I gathered from our telephone conversation that you considered my presence imperative, otherwise, in this heat, I shouldn't have come at all. I was going to the Island with Olga and Francis for Cowes Week.' Paul permitted his son to usher him into the ground-floor study where Ralph Stafford was waiting for them, but, when George would have plunged immediately into business, Paul held up his hand in protest and rang the bell. 'You'll allow me, at least, to have a cup of tea.' He gave his order to the butler, who arrived with profuse apologies for not having been on hand when Mr Devereaux arrived, and then cast a jaundiced eye over the two empty whisky glasses on the study table. 'Three o'clock in the afternoon is a bit early to be toping, isn't it?'

Ralph Stafford looked uncomfortable, but George ignored his father's stricture.

'What's happening in London?' he wanted to know. 'The miners are refusing point-blank to accept the wage cuts, and they're absolutely mutinous over the termination of the National Wages Agreement. They're all out at Longreach. Incidentally, the union bosses have sent down an old enemy of yours to advise and guide the local stewards. Arthur Barlow.'

'Arthur Barlow!' Paul's head jerked up from his contemplation of the whisky glasses, and he glared furiously at his son. He clenched his hands to stop them shaking. Fortunately, a diversion was created by the entrance of one of the parlour-maids bringing in the tea-tray, and by the time Paul had thanked her and drawn up a chair to the table he had himself in hand once more. 'Herbert Smith and A. J. Cook saw the Prime Minister last Friday,' he said. 'July the thirty-first. Baldwin presented them with all the facts: that the Wages Agreement had been drawn up last year, when the French occupation of the Ruhr had eliminated German competition in coal; that the return to the gold standard at pre-war parity had made it impossible to go on paying the new rates; that cuts in wages are inevitable.'

'And what was their reaction to that?'

'Smith and Cook dug their heels in. Refused to discuss terms. I think the PM had hoped to confuse them with his oratorical brilliance, but Arthur Cook is a former Baptist preacher, and I'm told it was Baldwin who had difficulty getting a word in edgeways. In the end, the Prime Minister granted a subsidy to May of next year, to allow time for a Court of Inquiry to be set up and to report on its findings.'

'Well, thank God for that,' breathed George devoutly. 'At least we can get the men back to work, if only for the time being. Although what happens when next May comes is anyone's guess, unless the Court of Inquiry finds against the owners.'

'I don't think there's any possibility of that.' Paul sipped his tea and glanced at Ralph Stafford. 'Work has come to a complete standstill, I take it?'

As he spoke, he had an odd sense of *déjà vu*. Ralph was so extraordinarily like his father; the same close-cropped curly hair, the same very light greyish-blue eyes. The body, also, was sturdy and compact, like Hugh's, and Ralph had a similar air of truculence.

'Everyone's out,' he confirmed bluntly. 'The pickets aren't letting anyone through.'

'You must visit the mine with me tomorrow, Father, and speak to the men. Tell them everything you know.' George's tone, Paul thought with wry amusement, brooked no opposition.

'They won't just take my word for it,' he protested. 'They'll want confirmation from the union.'

'Well, that shouldn't be long in coming, surely? Meantime, you can calm the men down. Prepare their minds for a return to work.'

'I ought to be getting back.' Ralph picked up his cap from the desk where he had dropped it. He consulted his watch. 'There's a train at five to four. I'll catch that. I'll see you tomorrow then, sir.' He held out his hand.

'You can still call me "Paul" in private, you know,' Paul said, smiling. 'We did share a roof for fifteen years.' He rose and took Ralph's hand. 'How . . . how is your mother?' he asked, not without difficulty.

'She and Aunt Jess are very busy packing up, now that the cottage has been sold. Some of their stuff has already been sent in advance, but there still seems a lot to do and dispose of.' He saw Paul's blank stare and hastened to explain. 'They're going back to America. They're sailing next month, from Southampton.'

'Going to America?' Paul repeated, like a man in a dream.

'Yes. Back to New York. They decided some time last winter. At least, Mother did. It took Aunt Jessie longer to make up her mind. Well . . . I really must go now or I shall miss that train.'

Paul dazedly watched him go. 'Callous young brute,' he thought stupidly. 'He doesn't care whether his mother goes or stays.'

'Not ill, are you, Father?' George returned to the study, having escorted Ralph to the door. 'You're looking a bit white. Perhaps it's a touch of the sun.'

'What . . . ? No, no. I'm all right. Did you know that Margaret . . . Mrs Stafford was planning to go back to New York?'

'Dunny?' George looked vague. 'I think Ralph might have mentioned it. I'm not sure. Now, about tomorrow—'

'Damn tomorrow!' Paul exclaimed violently, to his son's astonishment. 'Antonia and Henry, do they know?'

'I haven't the slightest idea,' George retorted truthfully. 'If it's that important to you, why don't you telephone Latchetts and ask them? I'll speak to you about tomorrow at dinner. It's vital that you plan in advance what you're going to say. According to Ralph, the men are in a very dangerous mood.'

'Pompous young ass!' Paul muttered angrily to himself as George gathered up some papers from the desk and departed. 'I should have insisted that he went up to Oxford. That would have knocked the pretentiousness out of him.'

But he had no time to spare worrying about his son. Indeed, he was perfectly certain that George would run the Longreach mine far better than he had ever done. He lifted the ear-piece of the telephone and asked the operator for the Latchetts number.

It was Mrs Hinkley who answered.

'Miss Antonia?' she repeated, when he had put his question. 'No, sir, she's out. And Mr Henry. Making the most of his holidays, I expect. Miss Natasha's in, though, if you'd like to speak to her. I'll fetch her, if you'll just hold on.'

Two minutes later, Natasha's clear young voice sounded on the line.

'Hello, Daddy. Did you want me?'

Her tone was the one she always used to him, cool and off-hand. It made Paul itch to slap her. Carefully he swallowed his temper.

'Has Antonia – or Henry – said anything to you lately about their mother?'

'What sort of thing? They don't confide in me, you know. They don't like me.'

Paul sympathized with them. 'Has either Henry or

359

Antonia' – he spoke deliberately and distinctly, so that there was no possibility of her misunderstanding, or pretending to misunderstand, him – 'mentioned to you that Margaret . . . that Mrs Stafford is returning to America?'

There was silence at the other end of the telephone. Then Natasha's voice quavered: 'Maggie's going to America? For good?'

'It seems so,' Paul answered grimly.

'She mustn't! Daddy, you mustn't let her!'

'I fail to see how I can stop her. It's her decision, and she evidently feels that there's nothing to keep her here any longer. . . . Natasha? Natasha, are you still there?'

'Yes, I'm still here,' his daughter answered slowly. 'Daddy . . . I think the reason she's going is my fault. . . . There's something I have to tell you that you ought to know.'

Thirty-Two

He knew, as soon as he saw Arthur Barlow on the picket line, the men massed behind him, reinforced by wives and daughters, that he would never be able to make his carefully prepared speech. He would never be allowed to. The miners were already shouting as he emerged from the car. Paul looked unhappily over his shoulder at George and Ralph Stafford.

Ralph, who now lodged in the house where he had lived as a child with his parents, had met them at the other end of the village.

'They're out in force,' he had warned. 'Arthur Barlow's been at them since he arrived this morning.'

George nodded curtly, glancing anxiously at his father, as Ralph climbed into his little Austin Seven and drove in their wake along the almost deserted main street.

'You know what you're going to say, Father, don't you? You're going to tell them about the subsidy and the Court of Inquiry. And leave the car close to the main gate, so that we can get away quickly if we have to.'

Paul made no answer. His heart was no longer in it. All he could think of was that somehow he must see Margaret; tell her that he had never received her letter; that Natasha had destroyed it. And he could imagine only too well what she would have to say about his present mission.

'How would you like to have your wages cut? You and your kind have never known what it is to be poor.'

And she was right. All last night, unable to sleep, he had been blessed – if that was the appropriate word – with a sudden and unnerving ability to see things from the miners' point of view.

361

'That's Bolshevik claptrap,' George had said angrily, when Paul had voiced his doubts over breakfast. 'That's betraying your own class and interests. You have to look out for yourself, Father, or you don't get anywhere. The union leaders are doing all right, don't you worry. The Arthur Barlows of this world will climb to power on the backs of the people and screw them into the ground in the process.'

Paul, half-inclined to agree, was thoroughly confused, and felt too tired to argue. He had driven out to the cottage near Mells the previous evening, only to discover that Jessie and Margaret were not at home. Their nearest neighbour had told him she thought they were in London, but that they would definitely be back the following morning. He had left a message, and asked the woman to say that he would be motoring over later in the day from Longreach.

It had been his decision to drive the coupé himself, in spite of George's protest.

'There is no point,' Paul had said, 'in putting up the men's backs more than we have to. Rolling up at the mine chauffeur-driven would, in my opinion, be asking for trouble.'

But they were in for trouble anyway, he thought, as he berthed the car opposite the main gate, in the lee of a hedge starred with the red and white flowers of the campion. He got out, followed by George, just as Ralph parked the Austin behind them.

His quick glance at Ralph's face shocked Paul, unprepared as he was for such an expression of vindictiveness and loathing. He remembered the riot which had killed Hugh when Ralph was small. Was it possible that anyone could nurse a grudge for so many years?

The men, alerted by some bush-telegraph system of their own to Paul's arrival, were packed solidly across the main gate; not just the pickets, but everyone; row upon row, stretching to the railway track on one side and to the foot of Longreach Hill on the other. Little knots of women stood sullenly ranged along the hedge, waving the same placards as their men. Most of these bore the same slogan: *Not a Penny off the Pay, Not a Minute on the Day*. Arthur Barlow, in his navy pinstriped suit and trilby hat, stood several paces ahead of the

362

rest. The medieval king, Paul thought with a flash of amusement, leading his troops into battle.

'There he is!' Arthur shouted, as Paul crossed the road towards him. 'There's one of the men who want to cut your wages. There's the owner of this mine! Take a good look! You don't often get the chance to see him.'

There was a jeering laugh from the crowd and someone cried: 'Cut the bugger's balls off! That'll learn 'im!'

Ralph Stafford's face turned a dark turkey-red. 'I know that voice!' he shouted back. 'Billy Collins, you're fired!'

A moment's shocked silence succeeded this rash pronouncement; then a low, animal growl rose from the miners' ranks. Paul hurriedly intervened.

'For God's sake, Ralph, don't be a bloody fool! I want to get out of this alive, even if you don't.' He raised his voice and addressed the men. 'The government has agreed—'

Immediately, his words were drowned in a flood of execration. Billy Collins's voice, carrying clearly above the rest, summarized the general feelings. 'Sod the bloody government!'

Twice more Paul tried to speak, but with no more success than the first time. He walked up to Arthur Barlow and said furiously: 'Quieten them down. They must listen to me. The Prime Minister has agreed to a Court of Inquiry, and in the meantime the men's wages will be subsidized at their present level by the government.'

Arthur Barlow lifted his lip. 'I know that,' he spat. 'D'you think I'm a fool? Do you think I haven't been in touch with my headquarters?'

'Well then—'

'Well then, nothing! I just haven't seen fit to tell anyone yet, that's all.'

'It's your duty—'

'Sod my duty! Give me one good reason why I should do anything to benefit you. I'll tell the men to go back to work in my own good time, when the offer is officially confirmed, and not before. Meanwhile, the pit remains closed.'

'I shall report you,' Paul snapped, with no very clear idea who it was he should tell, 'for dereliction of duty.'

Arthur laughed. 'You're not in the bloody trenches now.'

They glared at one another, vaguely aware that the anger which sparked between them had nothing to do with the strike. Margaret's image – hair, eyes, mouth – was uppermost in the mind of each. Paul realized that his analogy, comparing Arthur Barlow to a medieval king, had not been inapt. Now they were two knights, ready and eager to break lances over a woman. It was Arthur who flung down the gauntlet.

'What do you know about mining?' he demanded scornfully. 'Except how to get rich on the profits. What do you know about these men's hardships? About their sufferings? All you and your class do is to slash the pittance you already give them when the going gets rough. The country goes back on the gold standard and the poor bloody miners are the first casualties of war. Do you know what it costs in blood and sweat to bring even a hundredweight of coal out of the ground? Of course you don't! Have you ever been underground in your life? Of course you haven't! You'd be too damn scared. The nearest you've ever got to the pit-head is the manager's office.'

Paul could have retaliated with the horrors he had seen during the war – Mons, Ypres, the Somme – but he knew that to do so would reduce the exchange to the level of schoolboys trying to out-boast each other. He made an effort to take some of the heat out of his tone.

'Are you suggesting that I should go down the mine to see conditions for myself? If so, I'm willing to do so. Better late than never, as they say.'

Arthur Barlow was disconcerted. He had not anticipated that his challenge would be taken up at all, let alone so readily. After a momentary hesitation, however, he said: 'Why not?' He turned to the miners and raised his hand for silence. 'Mr Devereaux is going underground. He wants to see conditions for himself.'

George was beside Paul in an instant. 'Are you mad, Father?' he demanded furiously. 'The pit has been closed for weeks. God knows what deterioration has taken place in the meantime.'

'He's right, sir.' Ralph was looking worried. 'You can't possibly risk it.'

'Did you hear that?' Arthur Barlow called to the men nearest him. 'You can risk your necks every bloody day and no

364

one cares!' He returned fiercely to Paul. 'But *you* ought to care! *You* ought to feel responsible for their safety.'

'If someone will lend me a helmet,' Paul said quietly, 'and if you, Mr Barlow, and some of the other men will come with me, I'll have a look at the conditions you work in.'

'It's insanity,' hissed George. 'In any case, conditions are not, at the moment, an issue. Wages and a return to work are what we came here to discuss.'

He looked at Ralph for support, but Ralph was too shocked to be of much use. Like George, like most of the miners present, he found Paul's sudden decision to go underground an irrelevance. He was equally puzzled by the fact that it was at Arthur Barlow's suggestion. He began to suspect that there was a dimension to the quarrel between the two men of which the rest of them were ignorant. But there was nothing he could do to prevent Paul going down. However frequently George might try on his father's crown for size, Paul was still the owner.

The miners, intrigued by this completely unforeseen development, opened the gates and surged in after Paul and Arthur Barlow. Much of their anger had evaporated at the prospect of a pit-owner actually descending his own mine in order to see for himself the darkness, the cramped conditions, the seeping water and the all-pervading, choking black dust which were an integral part of their daily lives.

Ralph watched miserably as someone produced helmets. He wished to God that the colliery manager had not chosen yesterday and today to slip off on a visit to his mother in Cheltenham, unaware that George, whom he stigmatized as a 'pesky nuisance', had sent for his father. There was one good thing, Ralph thought, as he walked with the others towards the winding-engine shed and the three-deck cage: if anything did go wrong, it could be blamed on the results of the strike and not on any economies that he and old Durnford had practised.

Paul followed Arthur and the three miners who had volunteered to accompany them into the top deck of the cage, and fear punched him in the stomach. For a moment, he was terrified that he was going to disgrace himself and vomit. The helmet with its lamp seemed to press down on his head like a leaden weight. He gripped the bar at the side of the cage to stop his hands shaking, and looked across at Arthur Barlow. There was a slight smile on the other man's face. Paul drew a deep breath and tightened his stomach muscles as the cage gave a sudden lurch and began to move. The rattle of the pulleys and ropes screeched in his ears. The palms of his hands were damp with sweat and slipped on the bar, nearly upsetting his balance.

The darkness rushed up to meet them and the square of daylight above gradually dwindled, then vanished. The lamps on their helmets were now the sole source of illumination, ringing them with dilating and contracting shadows. The descent seemed never-ending. Why, in heaven's name, had he let Arthur Barlow goad him into this ridiculous escapade? What did he think he was proving, either to Margaret or himself?

There was a sudden, sickening crack and the cage battered against the walls of the shaft. He saw, momentarily, the pale ovals of the other men's faces; expressions frozen in disbelief or fear. He heard Arthur Barlow whisper: 'My God! One of the pins has broken.' He knew a second's abject, cringing terror before he was engulfed by a merciful blackness.

'How is he?' asked Jessie, laying down her pen and swivelling round from the desk where she was writing. She looked at her sister's face and got swiftly to her feet. 'Sit down. I'll ring for some coffee.'

The hot August sun flooded the little room at the back of Bladud House which Paul used as a study. The narrow garden beyond the window was dappled with patterns of light and shade, and a faint breeze sent grey and silver shadows racing across the grass. A crimson rose against one wall scattered a shower of petals, like drops of blood.

Margaret sank into the leather armchair and closed her eyes. 'Jess, you've been an absolute brick. I don't know what we would have done without you. The girls are in too much of a state to be of any use, and even George has temporarily lost his powers of organization.'

Jess snorted. 'And a good thing, too. If Master George had been a little less busy, none of this would have happened. But you haven't answered my question.' She pressed the electric buzzer on the wall. 'How's Paul?'

'The same. He still hasn't recovered consciousness. The doctor's coming again this afternoon. . . . You know he says Paul will never walk again?'

Jess nodded and ordered coffee from the white-faced maid who answered her ring.

'Of course I know. It's why I got on to the shipping office first thing this morning and told them to cancel our passages to New York and to unload any luggage that had already been taken on board. Since then, I've been trying to answer some of these letters of enquiry and condolence which keep arriving by every post. As you say, no one else seems capable of dealing with them. Understandably. Don't think I'm complaining.'

Margaret opened eyes swimming with tears. 'Oh, Jess, I'm so sorry. What a mess I've made of things for you. Persuading you to sell the cottage. . . . If you want to go ahead to New York and wait for me there, you have only to say so.'

'And what would I do in New York all by myself?' Jess demanded indignantly. 'Besides, it's time we faced facts. You're never going to leave Paul and the family now. They all need you.'

'That's up to Paul to decide,' Margaret answered in a subdued voice. 'When – if – he regains consciousness, he may not want me.'

'Rubbish!' snapped Jessie. 'Tell him he has to have you anyway, for the sake of the children. And by children, I mean India and Mareth and their husbands as well. They're all behaving like a bunch of frightened five-year-olds. They need you to put a bit of backbone into them.'

'And I need you, Jess. Whatever my future is, I want you with me.'

'Try getting rid of me,' Jessie replied cheerfully. 'I've always had a fancy to live like a lady. And although I never cared for Latchetts very much I daresay I could get used to it with one or two modernizations.'

The maid brought the coffee and they sat drinking it in silence for a moment or two. Then Margaret said abruptly: 'I had a letter from Hilda this morning.'

'Oh? How has she taken the news of Arthur's death?'

'It's hard to tell. She didn't write much. She did say she was pressing ahead anyhow with her efforts to divorce Sergei. . . . Arthur's father died the same way, you know; a broken pin in the winding engine. He suffocated in the mud and slurry at the bottom of the shaft.'

'Arthur's death must have been quicker than that. Don't think about it,' Jess advised. 'At least, not yet. You have enough tragedy of your own to cope with. What's happened about the strike?'

'The men have returned to work. Ralph telephoned George this morning. Everyone was shaken by what happened. Four men dead, and Paul . . . and Paul—'

She set down her cup and burst into tears. Jess knelt beside her, murmuring endearments.

The past days had had a nightmarish quality which neither woman had any desire to live through again. From the moment three mornings ago when Ralph had burst into the cottage, where they were in the final throes of packing, until this instant, real life had been suspended. They were existing in some ghastly miasma of fog and cloud, where it was impossible to see more than one step in front of them; a breathless suspension of life; a time for the end of the world. . . .

Jess rose to her feet. 'Pull yourself together, Maggie,' she chivvied, more like her normal self. 'Paul might regain consciousness at any moment, and you don't want him to see you like this.'

There was a tap at the study door. When Jess opened it, she found Natasha outside.

'I must speak to Maggie,' Natasha said. 'Please. I have to speak to her alone.'

Jessie held the door wide. She glanced back at her sister.

'I'll go up to the sick-room and relieve whoever is sitting with Paul at present. It's time for the nurse's coffee break.' She eyed Natasha's tear-stained face with a compassion laced with disapproval. 'Don't go upsetting Mrs Stafford,' she ordered primly. She could never get used to this child's calling Margaret by her christian name.

When Jessie had gone, Margaret held out her hand, and Natasha ran to sit on her lap, winding her arms suffocatingly

368

about Margaret's neck and bursting into noisy, heart-rending sobs.

'Oh, Maggie! It's all my fault! If I hadn't destroyed your letter, this wouldn't have happened.'

Gently Margaret rocked her. 'What letter? What are you talking about, Tasha? Stop crying, honey, and tell me all about it.'

Natasha sat up straighter and wiped her nose with the back of her hand. For once, Margaret did not scold her. Haltingly, the story came out: how Natasha had taken Margaret's letter to Paul; how upset Paul had been when he discovered what had happened.

'It was the day before the accident, when he heard you were going back to New York. He phoned me at Latchetts to see if I knew anything about it. That was when I told him what I'd done. He was in an awful state. It'll be all my fault if he dies.'

Margaret did not know whether she was appalled by Natasha's confession or elated. She was horrified that her own actions, which she had persuaded herself were in everybody's interests, had hurt Natasha so badly that the child had grown to hate her. She was conscience-stricken by how little she had considered the feelings of Natasha – or Henry or Antonia – in her anxiety not to hinder Paul and his political ambitions. Her self-sacrifice, she thought accusingly, had not really been unselfishness, merely self-indulgence. Was she being too hard? But she was certainly in no position to blame or criticize Natasha.

And happiness flowed from the knowledge that Paul had not ignored her letter; that he still wanted her; that he had always needed her. She held Natasha's thin young body close against her.

'Tasha! Tasha, honey, nothing you did caused what happened. It had nothing to do with your father visiting the mine. He would have done that anyway. Don't start blaming yourself. It's bad enough having George playing the penitent. Not that that will last. . . . Tasha, people, especially adult people, are responsible for their own decisions. Their mistakes are their own, no one else's.'

Natasha blinked tearfully, but looked less unhappy than when she had come in.

'You won't go away again, Maggie, will you? Not without me?'

'I can't make promises. It wouldn't be fair.'

'It would be nice if you could marry Daddy, after all. I didn't want you to, not at first. But I do now. And it would make everything right for Antonia. Mr and Mrs Bastardo would let her and Raymond be friends.'

'Yes,' Margaret said. 'Yes, I expect they would.' Why had she persuaded herself that her children did not need her? They always had done, for one reason or another, which she would have known if only she had paused to reflect.

There was a sudden rush of feet along the passage leading to the study. The door was flung open and India came in, Mareth hot on her heels.

'Dunny! Dunny! Papa's conscious. He opened his eyes a minute ago, and he's asking for you.'

Margaret slid Natasha off her lap and stood up shakily. She stared at India and Mareth whilst trying to command her legs; then she was gone, running for the stairs. Natasha would have followed, but India held her back.

'No,' she said. 'Give them some time alone together.'

Paul was lying staring up at the ceiling when Margaret entered the bedroom. Jessie rose from her chair.

'I am going to telephone the doctor,' she announced, 'and give him the glorious news.' She added in a lower voice: 'Don't tire Paul too much. He's very frail.' She went out, shutting the door quietly behind her.

Margaret sank into the chair vacated by her sister, holding one of Paul's hands in both of hers.

'You've come back to me,' she murmured at last, her eyes brilliant with unshed tears.

He smiled feebly in response. 'Did you doubt that I should?' His voice was barely a whisper. Then the smile faded and he moved his head restlessly on the pillow. 'What happened?' he mumbled. 'The cage . . . I was in the cage and it fell . . . Arthur Barlow was there. I remember now.'

She got up quickly and kissed his forehead. The skin was hot and dry against her lips. Her touch, however, appeared to soothe him and he fell silent, still clutching her hand. He seemed to be drifting into unconsciousness again, but suddenly his eyelids flickered.

'The other men . . . Arthur Barlow . . . are they . . . ? What happened?' He saw Margaret's hesitation. 'They're dead, aren't they? All dead. All of them.'

She nodded. 'Don't think about it now,' she told him, echoing Jessie's advice to herself.

'My legs . . . I can't feel my legs.'

'Don't worry. I'm here now. Everything's going to be all right.' What was she saying, when she knew he would probably never walk again?

Yet, somehow, she felt convinced that everything would be all right, just as she had when she got on the train at Rostov-on-Don. Just so long as they were together.

Paul must have caught the tenor of her thoughts, because he said in a much stronger voice: 'You mustn't leave me. Not ever again.'

She shook her head. 'Not ever again. I promise.'

'We'll be married.' The voice had faded once more and she had to strain her ears to catch what he was saying. 'You won't run away this time.' It was not a question, just a simple statement of fact. She did not answer because there was no need. She pressed his hand and felt him weakly return the pressure. After a pause, he went on: 'No more politics. Finished with all that. Just us . . . and the children.'

Margaret felt a surge of relief and happiness that he had made the decision before he knew about his legs. She stayed quietly, holding his hand, while he drifted into a drug-filled sleep, as yet unaware of his pain. There was a touch of colour in his face for the first time since he had been carried into Bladud House three days before. George had flatly refused his permission for his father to be taken into hospital.

'We'll nurse him at home,' he had argued fiercely with the doctor, and Margaret had backed him up. They had a day-and a night-nurse, and when the nurses went off duty for an hour or two there was always someone to take their place. Mareth and India had arrived from London; Antonia and Natasha from Latchetts.

Jessie came back into the room. 'Nurse has just finished her coffee and she'll be up directly. She wanted to come right away when I told her the news, but I managed to restrain her. And I've telephoned the doctor.' She folded her hands in front of her and looked down at her sister. 'Well?' she enquired. 'I'm waiting to hear what you have to tell me.'

'He's going to have a long, painful fight back to health, Jess. It won't be easy for either of us. But we'll be together, and that's all that matters.' Margaret repeated what she had said to Paul. 'Everything's going to be all right.'

'Of course it is,' Jess agreed, blinking away her tears. 'I haven't doubted it for a moment these past three days. Fate didn't spare Paul for no reason. Ah, here's Nurse, so come downstairs and have lunch with the rest of us. Join the celebration.'

Margaret rose and put an arm around her sister's waist. 'Just for half an hour, then. Paul might wake again and need me.'

And the two women looked at each other, and smiled.

Fiction

Fiction

HORROR/OCCULT/NASTY

☐ Death Walkers	Gary Brandner	£1.75
☐ Hellborn	Gary Brandner	£1.75
☐ The Howling	Gary Brandner	£1.75
☐ Return of the Howling	Gary Brandner	£1.75
☐ Tribe of the Dead	Gary Brandner	£1.75
☐ The Sanctuary	Glenn Chandler	£1.50
☐ The Tribe	Glenn Chandler	£1.10
☐ The Black Castle	Leslie Daniels	£1.25
☐ The Big Goodnight	Judy Gardiner	£1.25
☐ Rattlers	Joseph L. Gilmore	£1.60
☐ The Nestling	Charles L. Grant	£1.95
☐ Night Songs	Charles L. Grant	£1.95
☐ Slime	John Halkin	£1.75
☐ Slither	John Halkin	£1.60
☐ The Unholy	John Halkin	£1.25
☐ The Skull	Shaun Hutson	£1.25
☐ Pestilence	Edward Jarvis	£1.60
☐ The Beast Within	Edward Levy	£1.25
☐ Night Killers	Richard Lewis	£1.25
☐ Spiders	Richard Lewis	£1.75
☐ The Web	Richard Lewis	£1.75
☐ Nightmare	Lewis Mallory	£1.75
☐ Bloodthirst	Mark Ronson	£1.60
☐ Ghoul	Mark Ronson	£1.75
☐ Ogre	Mark Ronson	£1.75
☐ Deathbell	Guy N. Smith	£1.75
☐ Doomflight	Guy N. Smith	£1.25
☐ Manitou Doll	Guy N. Smith	£1.25
☐ Satan's Snowdrop	Guy N. Smith	£1.00
☐ The Understudy	Margaret Tabor	£1.95
☐ The Beast of Kane	Cliff Twemlow	£1.50
☐ The Pike	Cliff Twemlow	£1.25

Fiction

SCIENCE FICTION

☐ More Things in Heaven	John Brunner	£1.50
☐ Chessboard Planet	Henry Kuttner	£1.75
☐ The Proud Robot	Henry Kuttner	£1.50
☐ Death's Master	Tanith Lee	£1.50
☐ The Dancers of Arun	Elizabeth A. Lynn	£1.50
☐ The Northern Girl	Elizabeth A. Lynn	£1.50
☐ Balance of Power	Brian M. Stableford	£1.75

ADVENTURE/SUSPENSE

☐ The Corner Men	John Gardner	£1.75
☐ Death of a Friend	Richard Harris	£1.95
☐ The Flowers of the Forest	Joseph Hone	£1.75
☐ Styx	Christopher Hyde	£1.50
☐ Temple Kent	D. G. Devon	£1.95
☐ Confess, Fletch	Gregory Mcdonald	£1.50
☐ Fletch	Gregory Mcdonald	£1.50
☐ Fletch and the Widow Bradley	Gregory Mcdonald	£1.50
☐ Flynn	Gregory Mcdonald	£1.75
☐ The Buck Passes Flynn	Gregory Mcdonald	£1.60
☐ The Specialist	Jasper Smith	£1.75

WESTERNS

Blade Series – Matt Chisholm

☐ No. 5 The Colorado Virgins	85p
☐ No. 6 The Mexican Proposition	85p
☐ No. 11 The Navaho Trail	95p

McAllister Series – Matt Chisholm

☐ No. 3 McAllister Never Surrenders	95p
☐ No. 4 McAllister and the Cheyenne Death	95p
☐ No. 8 McAllister – Fire Brand	£1.25

Fiction

CRIME

☐ The Cool Cottontail	John Ball	£1.00
☐ Five Pieces of Jade	John Ball	£1.50
☐ Johnny Get Your Gun	John Ball	£1.00
☐ Then Came Violence	John Ball	£1.50
☐ The Widow's Cruise	Nicholas Blake	£1.25
☐ The Worm of Death	Nicholas Blake	95p
☐ The Long Divorce	Edmund Crispin	£1.50
☐ Love Lies Bleeding	Edmund Crispin	£1.75
☐ The Case of the Sliding Pool	E. V. Cunningham	£1.75
☐ Hindsight	Peter Dickinson	£1.75
☐ King and Joker	Peter Dickinson	£1.25
☐ The Last House Party	Peter Dickinson	£1.75
☐ A Pride of Heroes	Peter Dickinson	£1.50
☐ The Seals	Peter Dickinson	£1.50
☐ Gondola Scam	Jonathan Gash	£1.75
☐ The Sleepers of Erin	Jonathan Gash	£1.75
☐ The Black Seraphim	Michael Gilbert	£1.75
☐ Blood and Judgment	Michael Gilbert	£1.10
☐ Close Quarters	Michael Gilbert	£1.10
☐ The Etruscan Net	Michael Gilbert	£1.25
☐ The Final Throw	Michael Gilbert	£1.75
☐ The Night of the Twelfth	Michael Gilbert	£1.25
☐ The Blunderer	Patricia Highsmith	£1.50
☐ A Game for the Living	Patricia Highsmith	£1.50
☐ Those Who Walk Away	Patricia Highsmith	£1.50
☐ The Tremor of Forgery	Patricia Highsmith	£1.50
☐ The Two Faces of January	Patricia Highsmith	£1.50
☐ Silence Observed	Michael Innes	£1.00
☐ Go West, Inspector Ghote	H. R. F. Keating	£1.50
☐ Inspector Ghote Draws a Line	H. R. F. Keating	£1.50
☐ Inspector Ghote Plays a Joker	H. R. F. Keating	£1.50
☐ The Murder of the Maharajah	H. R. F. Keating	£1.50
☐ The Perfect Murder	H. R. F. Keating	£1.50
☐ The Dutch Shoe Mystery	Ellery Queen	£1.60
☐ The French Powder Mystery	Ellery Queen	£1.25
☐ The Siamese Twin Mystery	Ellery Queen	95p
☐ The Spanish Cape Mystery	Ellery Queen	£1.10
☐ Copper, Gold and Treasure	David Williams	£1.75
☐ Treasure By Degrees	David Williams	£1.75
☐ Unholy Writ	David Williams	£1.60

Fiction

HISTORICAL ROMANCE/ROMANCE/SAGA

☐ A Dark Moon Raging	Aileen Armitage	£1.50
☐ Hawksmoor	Aileen Armitage	£1.75
☐ Hunter's Moon	Aileen Armitage	£1.95
☐ Blaze of Passion	Stephanie Blake	£1.75
☐ Callie Knight	Stephanie Blake	£1.95
☐ Daughter of Destiny	Stephanie Blake	£1.75
☐ Fires of the Heart	Stephanie Blake	£1.50
☐ Scarlet Kisses	Stephanie Blake	£1.50
☐ So Wicked My Desire	Stephanie Blake	£1.75
☐ Unholy Desires	Stephanie Blake	£1.50
☐ Broken Promises	Drusilla Campbell	£1.75
☐ Silent Dreams	Drusilla Campbell	£1.95
☐ Stolen Passions	Drusilla Campbell	£2.25
☐ Tomorrow's Journey	Drusilla Campbell	£2.25
☐ Raven	Shana Carrol	£2.50
☐ Paxton Pride	Shana Carrol	£2.25
☐ The Far Morning	Brenda Clarke	£1.50
☐ The Fifth Jade of Heaven	Marilyn Granbeck	£2.25
☐ The Ravensley Touch	Constance Heaven	£1.75
☐ Sutton Place	Dinah Lampitt	£2.25
☐ Captive Bride	Johanna Lindsey	£1.50
☐ Fires of Winter	Johanna Lindsey	£1.50
☐ Paradise Wild	Johanna Lindsey	£1.50
☐ A Pirate's Love	Johanna Lindsey	£1.25
☐ Wild Flowers	Pamela Redford Russell	£2.25
☐ Curtain Call	Rona Randall	£2.25
☐ Dragonmede	Rona Randall	£2.25
☐ The Eagle at the Gate	Rona Randall	£2.25
☐ The Ladies of Hanover Square	Rona Randall	£2.25
☐ Glenrannoch	Rona Randall	£1.75
☐ Full Circle	Judith Saxton	£2.25
☐ The Glory	Judith Saxton	£1.95
☐ The Pride	Judith Saxton	£1.95
☐ The Splendour	Judith Saxton	£1.75
☐ The Fields of Yesterday	Robert Tyler Stevens	£1.50
☐ Shadows in the Afternoon	Robert Tyler Stevens	£1.50

Zenith

☐ The Voices of the Dead	Autran Dourado	£2.50
☐ My Double Life	Sarah Bernhardt	£3.25
☐ Pages from Cold Point	Paul Bowles	£1.95
☐ A Walk Around London's Parks	Hunter Davies	£3.50
☐ Behind God's Back	Negley Farson	£2.95
☐ The Way of a Transgressor	Negley Farson	£2.95
☐ A Small Yes and a Big No	George Grosz	£2.50
☐ A Child Possessed	R. C. Hutchinson	£2.50
☐ Johanna at Daybreak	R. C. Hutchinson	£2.95
☐ March the Ninth	R. C. Hutchinson	£2.95
☐ Shining Scabbard	R. C. Hutchinson	£3.50
☐ Recollection of a Journey	R. C. Hutchinson	£2.95
☐ The Stepmother	R. C. Hutchinson	£2.95
☐ 5001 Nights at the Movies	Pauline Kael	£5.95
☐ Days of Greatness	Walter Kempowski	£2.95
☐ The Hill of Kronos	Peter Levi	£2.95
☐ The Confessions of Lady Nijö	Lady Nijö	£2.95
☐ The Brendan Voyage	Tim Severin	£3.50
☐ Tracking Marco Polo	Tim Severin	£2.75
☐ The Dark Lantern	Henry Williamson	£3.50
☐ Donkey Boy	Henry Williamson	£3.50
☐ The Dream of Fair Women	Henry Williamson	£2.50
☐ The Pathway	Henry Williamson	£2.95

Non-Fiction

GENERAL

☐ English Country Cottage	R. J. Brown	£3.50
☐ English Farmhouses	R. J. Brown	£3.75
☐ Here Comes Everybody	Anthony Burgess	£1.75
☐ The Rich	William Davis	£1.95
☐ Henry Cooper's Book of Boxing	Henry Cooper	£1.75
☐ Murderous Women	John Dunning	£1.50
☐ Strange Deaths	John Dunning	£1.50
☐ Truly Murderous	John Dunning	£1.50
☐ Alanbrooke	David Fraser	£4.95
☐ Ielfstan's Place	Richard Girling	£1.95
☐ The Lore of Steam	C. Hamilton Ellis	£2.95
☐ The Lore of Sail	C. Hamilton Ellis	£2.95

BIOGRAPHY/AUTOBIOGAPHY

☐ Charles Darwin	Peter Brent	£4.95
☐ Go-Boy!	Roger Caron	£1.95
☐ William Wordsworth	Hunter Davies	£2.50
☐ Erin Pizzey Collects . . .	Erin Pizzey	£1.50
☐ Maria Callas	Arianna Stassinopoulos	£1.75

WAR

☐ The Battle of Malta	Joseph Attard	£1.50
☐ The Black Angels	Rupert Butler	£1.75
☐ Gestapo	Rupert Butler	£2.25
☐ Legions of Death	Rupert Butler	£1.75
☐ The Air Battle for Malta	Lord James Douglas-Hamilton M.P.	£1.50
☐ Death in Captivity	Michael Gilbert	£1.75
☐ The Rommel Papers	B. H. Liddell Hart	£3.75
☐ Sigh for a Merlin	Alex Henshaw	£1.95
☐ Hitler's Secret Life	Glen B. Infield	£1.50
☐ Special Boat Services 1: Fireball	John Kerrigan	£1.60
☐ Anvil	Peter Leslie	£1.95
☐ The Hanged Man	Douglas Scott	£1.95
☐ Spitfire into Battle	Group Captain Duncan Smith	£1.75
☐ Women Beyond the Wire	Lavinia Warner & John Sandilands	£1.95

Non-Fiction

POCKET HEALTH GUIDES

☐ Migraine	Dr Finlay Campbell	65p
☐ Pre-menstrual Tension	June Clark	65p
☐ Back Pain	Dr Paul Dudley	65p
☐ Allergies	Robert Eagle	65p
☐ Asthma	Robert Eagle	85p
☐ Cystitis	Diane Fernyhough	85p
☐ Circulation Problems	J. A. Gillespie	85p
☐ Depression and Anxiety	Dr Arthur Graham	85p
☐ Anaemia	Dr Alexander D. G. Gunn	85p
☐ Diabetes	Dr Alexander D. G. Gunn	85p
☐ Heart Trouble	Dr Simon Joseph	85p
☐ High Blood Pressure	Dr James Knapton	85p
☐ Peptic Ulcers	Dr Finbar Martin and Dr Daniel Stiel	85p
☐ Hysterectomy	Wendy Savage	85p
☐ The Menopause	John W. W. Studd and Dr Margaret Thom	85p
☐ Skin Troubles	Deanna Wilson	65p
☐ Children's Illnesses	Dr Luke Zander	85p

HEALTH/SELF-HELP

☐ Girl!	Barbara Brandenburger and Jennifer Curry	£1.25
☐ The Good Health Guide for Women	Cynthia W. Cooke and Susan Dworkin	£2.95
☐ Pulling Your Own Strings	Dr Wayne W. Dyer	£1.75
☐ Clever Children	Dr Joan Freeman	£1.50
☐ Cystitis: A Complete Self-help Guide	Angela Kilmartin	£1.00
☐ *Mother* Book of Baby and Child Care	*Mother* Magazine	£1.75
☐ Fat is a Feminist Issue	Susie Orbach	£1.75
☐ Fat is a Feminist Issue II	Susie Orbach	£1.75
☐ Overcoming Childlessness	Elliot Philipp	£1.95
☐ Health on Your Plate	Janet Pleshette	£2.50
☐ A-Z of Family Medicines	Rosalind Spencer	£1.75
☐ Overcoming Depression	Dr Andrew Stanway	£1.75

Non-Fiction

TRAVEL

☐ Camping in Comfort	Dymphna Byrne	£1.75
☐ A Walk Along the Tracks	Hunter Davies	£1.75
☐ A Walk Around the Lakes	Hunter Davies	£2.50
☐ Weekend Cycling	Christa Gausden	£1.95
☐ Britain by Train	Patrick Goldring	£1.75
☐ Elizabeth Gundrey's Lakeland	Elizabeth Gundrey	£2.75
☐ The Observer Staying Off the Beaten Track	Elizabeth Gundrey	£2.95
☐ Walking in France	Rob Hunter	£1.75

HUMOUR

☐ Pun Fun	Compiled by Paul Jennings	95p
☐ How to Make Love to a Cat	Philip Lief	£2.25
☐ Patient's Revenge	Mark Marek	£1.95
☐ A Dog's Life	Ted Martin	£1.95
☐ Bogart	Ted Martin	£1.50

REFERENCE

☐ The Sunday Times Guide to Movies on Television	Angela and Elkan Allan	£1.50
☐ The Illustrated Dictionary of Musical Terms	Christopher Headington	£2.95
☐ How to Cut Your Fuel Bills	Lali Makkar & Mary Ince	£1.25
☐ Hamlyn Book of Horror and S.F. Movie Lists	Roy Pickard	£1.95
☐ The Oscar Movies from A-Z	Roy Pickard	£1.75
☐ Islam	D. S. Roberts	£1.50
☐ Questions of Law	Bill Thomas	£1.50

COOKERY

☐ Vegetarian Cookbook	Dave Dutton	£1.50
☐ Jewish Cookbook	Florence Greenberg	£1.50

NAME..

ADDRESS...

....

Write to Hamlyn Paperbacks Cash Sales, PO Box 11, Falmouth, Cornwall TR10 9EN.

Please indicate order and enclose remittance to the value of cover price plus:

U.K. CUSTOMERS: Please allow 55p for the first book, 22p for the second book and 14p for each additional book ordered to a maximum charge of £1.75.

B.F.P.O. & EIRE: Please allow 55p for the first book, 22p for the second book plus 14p per copy for the next seven books, thereafter 8p per book.

OVERSEAS CUSTOMERS: Please allow £1.00 for the first book plus 25p per copy for each additional book.

Whilst every effort is made to keep prices low it is sometimes necessary to increase cover prices and also postage and packing rates at short notice. Hamlyn Paperbacks reserve the right to show new retail prices on covers which may differ from those previously advertised in the text or elsewhere.